A Far Horizon

MEIRA CHAND

faber and faber

This edition first published in 2012
by Faber and Faber Ltd
Bloomsbury House, 74–77 Great Russell Street
London WC1B 3DA

Printed and bound by CPI Group (UK) Ltd, Croydon, CR0 4YY

A CIP record for this book is available from the British Library

ISBN 978–0–571–29609–5

CHAPTER ONE

Calcutta, 1756

The evening was already upon Calcutta, light sucked from the sky at an alarming rate. The first bats left their trees and flitted about in a purposeless way. Moths blundered into candles. In the fading wastes above the town, the Pole Star hung, gripped invisibly by God's fingers, incandescent with strange light. A full moon appeared beside it. In the house there was bustle and a heightened sense of expectation not normally to be found.

Sati Edwards twisted the glass bangles on her wrist and sat forward on her chair. Before her a servant, cross-legged on the floor, buffed some bits of silver. A pile of candles was stacked upon a table, before which argued two more servants. The new bearer, a Moslem, refused to touch the candles, saying they were made of pig fat. The chief steward, who had worked for a time in the house, protested that the candles were made from the fat of an enormous fish, and especially imported from France. He rapped the box importantly, with its yellowing picture of a whale.

Sati sensed her stepfather observing her. His grey eyes resembled the monsoon sky and had the effect of a downpour on her. His gaze strayed from her to the table, assessing how many candles would create the right atmosphere for the seance. Too much light would dispel the spectral element. Too little would generate a climate of fear

I

that might drive the curious away. Fabian Demonteguy was normally frugal with the use of the spermaceti since they were not only more expensive than local wax candles, but had to be ordered from France a year in advance of his needs. Tonight he would not spare their use. The candlelight grew steadily stronger as darkness settled outside.

'The Governor's wife will be coming tonight,' Demonteguy reminded his wife.

Rita Demonteguy examined her appearance in a tarnished mirror, her face held close to the glass. The red brass of henna, lit by the candlelight, flamed in her hair. Ignoring Demonteguy's advice, she refused to dress or powder it in White Town fashion. If he ever returned with her to France he knew she would create a stir. At times she caught his eyes upon her, as if scenes already entered his mind that made him shudder with distaste.

'Nobody thinks well of that Mrs Drake,' Rita announced, still observing herself in the mirror. The blemish in the glass disturbed her, moving over her like a disease. However hard she exhorted the servants to polish, the stains remained, untouchable. Behind her reflection floated the image of her daughter, a further blight on her satisfaction. The girl's eyes followed her every move.

'Emily Drake is a lonely woman. Such women seek their own affirmation. But is our Governor regarded with any more respect?' Demonteguy asked, then ordered more candles to be lit. The argument at the table now appeared to be settled. The head steward handled the candles and the bearer carried a taper which he lit from a candle the head steward held, in order to light further candles.

Sati avoided her mother's gaze in the mirror. The sight of her here in the Frenchman's house, and the nature of the glances that passed between them filled her with confusion. She turned her face from Rita's appraisal. A pink ribbon tied up her hair; tight European clothes constricted all movement. Beneath her dress a bodice and skirt, set with bamboo, were hooped about her like a cage. Her pulse seemed to slow, her breath became shallow and her spirit fled deep into hiding. She stared at the room before her and felt only further constriction.

She hated her stepfather's house in White Town, filled with useless objects. Mirrors reflected everywhere, filling the house with inaccessible worlds, throwing her own ghost before her. They deceived through vanity and drew the unwary; they caught and closed away in darkness the secrets of her soul. Danger also lay beneath the chandelier, and its trembling crystal shards. The silk-covered chairs of fashionable design Fabian Demonteguy had brought from France, but the marble-topped console and the inlaid commode had been built to his taste by a cabinet-maker in the local bazaar. The house was a neat one-storeyed affair with a veranda and a small garden. Strange flowers had also been imported from France and grew in a sickly fashion, cajoled from alien soil. Sati gazed out of the window, spurning the vases of ephemeral flowers. Across the fading shapes of White Town she could see the river and Fort William.

The garrison had been built in the days when a fort was worth more than an ambassador. Although it no longer rose threateningly, with the dusk it regained some menace. The town was preparing for the night, but whatever the nature of White Town's preliminaries, it was the bustle of Black Town that came Sati's way. Her stepfather's home, in an unfashionable area of Calcutta, was situated near Black Town's perimeter; the smell of dung fires, frying spices and effluent assailed it. Clanking pans, crying babies, women's voices and the howl of a dog echoed into the sky. Apart from the odours of Black Town, the reek of the Salt Lakes drifted into the room. Newcomers not yet acclimatised to the stench of Calcutta constantly retched. Women sickened politely behind posies of jasmine, their stomachs turned inside out. The open drains and noxious mud flats, mixed with the rot of dead fish tossed up each day on the tide, did not disturb Sati Edwards. Nor did it disturb her stepfather. Fabian Demonteguy was not a man of the East India Company, which was lit from within by its own fierce light. He was an interloper, who had to generate his own illumination as best he could. Calcutta treated his breed with distaste.

Demonteguy turned to assess the room and was forced again to observe his stepdaughter. The girl was from his wife's brief marriage to an English sea captain fifteen years before. He frowned as he stared at Sati. If he could have arranged the evening without her he would have done so, but she was the pivot upon which it would turn.

'You look very pleasing tonight,' Demonteguy said, grudgingly. He wondered as always why the girl could not have inherited her mother's honeyed skin. Instead, perversely, she reflected all of Black Town's intensity.

'You will perform as instructed,' he ordered, suddenly fearing she might yet slip from his grasp. The girl looked up, and he met her amber eyes, disconcerting in their clarity. Those feline eyes and her wild tortoiseshell hair, burnished and streaked as if by the sun, were all she had inherited from her English father.

'Good money has been spent on that dress,' he reminded her, observing the silk he himself had chosen and seen cut by a tailor from France. The ragged *salwar kameez* Sati had arrived in from Black Town he had at once ordered thrown away. Besides Sati's new dress, Rita had also required a suitable outfit. He had purchased a waistcoat for himself as well; the occasion seemed to demand it. Already, a considerable sum had been spent on the evening.

Sati cringed before Demonteguy's scrutiny. The cage of bamboo beneath her dress held her like a vice, squeezing the last of her identity from her. She had seen nothing wrong with her Indian clothes and protested at their disposal. Her grandmother had opened the trunk that stood in a corner of her hut, knowing the importance of the White Town visit. She rarely lifted the lid of the heavy chest filled with the bric-a-brac of her life. From its depths she pulled out an ancient outfit, worn long before in her Murshidabad days. The soft silk and faded embroidery, smelling of damp and incarceration, slipped easily over Sati. For a moment her grandmother's eyes had filled with tears. The dress had been given her by the raja in whose *zenana* she had once lived. Sati knew she did not cry for the raja but for the lost years of her life. The silk flowed like water over Sati, swinging as she walked. She seemed to grow tall with the splendour of it.

Yet on her arrival in White Town, her mother had announced that Mr Demonteguy was disturbed by her appearance. A dress of European design, more suitable to life in the settlement, had already been bought for her. Rita's hands were hard and her breath sour as she ripped the old clothes off her daughter. The soft Murshidabad silk was rolled into a ball and carried away by a servant. Sati cried out and received a smart slap from Rita. She thrashed about in her mother's arms but the clothes were already gone. As she watched, a door was shut firmly upon them. It was as if her own skin were being discarded, like the gauzy moultings of a snake, swept up with the dust and leaves. Except that she was left skinless, unable to make the passage from one body to another. Before her mother she suddenly fell silent and stepped into the strange clothes that were offered, which were then lashed tightly about her. At last she turned to the mirror. It showed her only a distant figure she did not recognise. A crack seemed to have opened within her, parting her soul along a fine line. She belonged to neither Black Town nor White Town. She appeared neither one thing nor the other, but something on her own. Now, sitting on the stool in Fabian Demonteguy's home, she heard her mother speaking.

'The Governor's wife only recently gave birth to a baby. How can we be sure she will come here tonight? I have heard that people avoid Mrs Drake. They only accept official invitations, other times they turn their backs upon her. They say also she is country born. In Surat or Bombay.' Rita Demonteguy stepped away from the mirror, picking up the conversation. She tossed it lightly, like a ball, to shatter Mrs Drake. For a moment she saw no paradox in assuming White Town scorn.

'It is one thing to be country born, another to marry a brother-in-law. *That* is no better than incest.' Demonteguy gave a laugh. 'It is said Mrs Drake's father settled a good sum on each of his daughters. Drake will have got the lot, first from one sister and then from the other. It shows the character of the man. No morals to hinder his greed.'

'Nothing is wrong with being born in India instead of Europe. Who can help where they are born?' Rita's voice was brittle with annoyance as she came up against hard facts. A battle that day with her mother, surrounded by Black Town's pigs, chickens and fruit and vegetable hawkers, had unsettled for a moment the future that seemed so certain in her new husband's home.

She had gone to Black Town with Demonteguy to collect Sati from her mother and found her attired in Jaya's old clothes. Rita's terse comments had angered old Jaya and she had refused to let the girl go. She had clung to Sati, battling desperately for her granddaughter on her Black Town doorstep. Sati was tugged back and forth between the two women. Jaya Kapur screeched abuse at her daughter, Rita Demonteguy let loose unrepeatable words at her mother. Demonteguy waited some distance away, fanning himself with a handkerchief. At intervals, when the odour of Black Town pressed too close around him, he held the square of scented linen firmly to his nose. Sati's cries and the shrill determination of both women had gathered a crowd, who all attempted loud and active intervention. A pig interrupted its rooting to watch, chickens stopped pecking, the vegetable vendor lowered his basket. Demonteguy, in embarrassment, had removed his two palanquins to the seclusion of some coconut palms beside a filthy pond. Women washing clothes in the muddy water raised their heads and stared. The reality of absorbing his new wife's origins caused Demonteguy to sweat profusely. He had never visited his mother-in-law's thatched hut, never heard from his wife the vulgar, guttural notes she now tossed about in abandonment, never entered the labyrinthine depths of Black Town before. The accumulation of all these harsh facts made him feel quite faint. Two mangy pariah dogs started to copulate before him, oblivious to the scene, uttering

6

high cries of ecstasy. He watched them with distracted interest. Languid in his home, wanton in his bed, his wife had blinded him to everything about herself but the ripe willingness of her body.

Eventually, the screeching subsided; some settlement seemed to be made. Accompanied by the curious crowd, Rita and her mother then turned to approach Demonteguy. To his horror, Jaya had climbed into his palanquin, her hand still locked in her granddaughter's. The squash was so great and the odour of his mother-in-law so intense that he was forced to vacate the conveyance and walk behind the runners, leaving the palanquins to the three women. He crossed the Maratha Ditch back into White Town with inexplicable relief.

'And why is to marry a dead sister's husband not a proper thing to do? This I do not understand. Mrs Drake is lucky the Governor married her. It must have been a charitable act. Just look at her; so dried up. No bosom, no backside. No nothing,' Rita announced, turning again to the mirror. 'In India such a marriage is not a bad thing.'

'We are not talking about Black Town customs. Now you are part of White Town,' Demonteguy snapped, watching as the last candles were lit.

Sati listened in surprise. A distant cousin of her grandmother's had married three sisters of the same family one after another as they died, the first in childbirth, the second from cholera. The third and present wife was still alive. But, said her grandmother, should misfortune overtake her also, there was still a fourth and unwed sister who was already nearly twelve. There had been only praise from old Jaya for the dutiful response of this man to the plight of his wife's unmarried sisters. He had demanded less for each new dowry, and most important, said her grandmother, the women were wed and not left, a shameful weight, upon their father's hands. Sati frowned in confusion. *No bosom, no backside. No nothing.* The image of a paper cut-out came into her mind.

Before the glass Rita adjusted the gems at her neck. Her breasts and hips, proportioned like a Hindu statue, were laced into the dress

Demonteguy had ordered from the French tailor. Diamonds circled her in cold fire and flashed on her fingers. In the freckled mirror, her dark eyes, ever mysterious to Demonteguy, were hard when meeting those of her daughter. Sati looked away. Tonight in this room she knew she must climb the steep, slippery slope of approval. The only comfort was that her grandmother had accompanied her into White Town. Old Jaya sat hidden on the back veranda with orders not to intrude. Sati was comforted by the movement of a curtain and a sudden glimpse of her grandmother. The old woman pulled an encouraging face, then let the curtain fall.

Straight-backed chairs had been set in a semicircle about an armchair. To Sati, the waiting seats filled the room with expectation. Perhaps nothing would happen. Perhaps the spirits that came to her would refuse to appear at such a debased summoning. For that was what this seance was, debased. These depressing thoughts were unalleviated by Demonteguy pacing about considering the placement of the chairs and the number of candles to be lit. His profession was opportunity, and this had now spread to include Sati herself.

'Do not be nervous. I have shown you how to do it.' Demonteguy bent and took her hand. She looked down at the bony red knuckles gripping her flesh and immediately drew back.

'The room looks well enough,' Rita said, breasts spilling generously over her dress. She clung to her husband's arm, laughing up into his face, anxious to erase the afternoon's unpleasantness in Black Town. He patted her hand absentmindedly, his attention on the event ahead, but then found a moment to feast his eyes on the succulence trembling so near him. His eyes in the candlelight were bright as a rat's behind his long nose. He exchanged a lecherous glance with his wife; she giggled and looked away. Demonteguy returned to the arrangements.

'Everything is in the details. Word flies around quickly here in Calcutta. Failure with our first enterprise could end a profitable game.' He assessed the room. 'A seance does not demand too much illumination. Perhaps we do not need so many candles.'

'Snuff some out before we start. How will guests enter the house in darkness?' Rita admonished.

'The effect of a sudden darkening of the room will be most dramatic.' Satisfaction spread over Demonteguy's face as he pictured the moment.

A bangle snapped between Sati's fingers, the fragments falling into her lap. She stared at the bits of broken glass and the bead of blood on her wrist. Perhaps this was an omen; perhaps she too would crack in the midst of one of her attacks. This was the word used by Demonteguy to describe the sudden melting of her mind and the entry of personalities who jostled to be heard.

In the beginning these presences had been vague, refusing to clearly reveal themselves. Then Durga had appeared. Now Sati had only to turn her head to see Durga watching from the shadows of foliage or the rafters of a room. She sensed her moving on the edge of time, always drifting near her. When Durga approached, a wildness burned up her spine, pulling her into a darkness from which she remembered nothing. Her stepfather's use of the word *attack* implied some violence, but there was nothing of that in what happened to her. There was only the opening of a door and the entering of immensity. Upon her return to mundane life, her soul seemed to cling to her body by no more than a fragile thread. If it snapped, she would float into a limitless world and never return to reality. Like the strands of a cobweb blown free on the wind.

She returned her attention to the empty chairs with an effort. Their shapely gilt legs resembled Demonteguy's shins of silken hose. Excitement continued to spark between her mother and her stepfather. Their voices were high with tension as they moved about the room in a ballet of anxiety. Yet more candles were lit and then snuffed out, a pillow was placed upon the armchair where Sati was to sit. A small table with three upturned coloured glasses stood before the chair.

On his last visit to France, Fabian Demonteguy had attended a seance in Paris. He wished the performance in his home to correspond to that event. He had produced three tumblers of blue, red and yellow glass, and spent much time instructing Sati. People were to ask her questions, she was to tell what she saw in the glasses. In the blue glass, for example, she might see the sky, a journey upon the sea or a catastrophic event. Blue was easy to remember: sea, sky or the occult clouds of mystery. The red glass could show blood, disease, a fiery accident, but mostly blood. There was no problem with the amount of gore, Demonteguy advised. People liked blood, became riveted to it, and would always come back for more. The yellow glass could represent anything she wished according to the question. A woman in a yellow dress, a golden bird, the festering juices of an ailment . . . She must let her mind play upon the questions, let her imagination soar. If something real entered her mind, so much the better. If not, she must invent it.

Demonteguy had sat himself down before the three glasses to guide her in the matter. They had acted out the seance many times. Under his tutelage her prophecies, in desperation, spiralled to baroque proportions. All the while she had been conscious of Durga beside her, full of sarcastic snarl. Yet in spite of seeing her in the midst of more than one attack, Demonteguy refused to realise her visitor was real and would not be contained in a few coloured glasses. Afterwards, he told her, there would be a collection of money. People would give according to their fear or satisfaction. If they felt neither emotion, nothing would persuade them to open their purse strings.

Already there were sounds of arrival before the house. The night vibrated beyond the door, like a scuffling animal preparing to break in. Strange voices instructed palanquin bearers and made enquiries of the *chowkidar*. Disembodied sounds floated to Sati. Then footsteps and the sudden appearance of a strange face cracking open her world.

Although, in the end, the crowd was not large, the room seemed unbearably full. Breath, voices, heat and candle flames beat their separate wings about her. Sat's head began to hurt. Demonteguy greeted his guests with fawning smiles. His paunch fell forward against his waistcoat buttons each time he affected a bow. Beside her husband Rita went stiffly through the motions of welcome, as instructed by Demonteguy, concentrating on her part. If she failed to maintain the proper White Town demeanour things would be hard for her. In the silence of the night Demonteguy would remember the eyes of other men upon her and demand an unusual selection of conjugal rights.

All this was unknown to Sati. She only saw her mother and Demonteguy make extravagant welcome at the door. Wine was passed around, the glasses shaking on a tray held by an ancient bearer. Candles blazed upon cut glass, wine cradled like blood in the bowls. She drew back in her chair. A play was enacted before her. There was much strutting and nodding and the clear stream of talk. There were the long, colourful tails of parrot-coloured skirts, the matted fuzz of wigs and the loop of powdered curls. The unfamiliar European faces, chiselled as marble, whiskered like cats, raw-skinned or slack as cloth, seemed all to be made of the same floury dough she had once seen a baker kneading. These people were like the almonds her grandmother soaked and divested of their tough brown skins, to lay naked upon a plate.

Gradually the room filled up. The great skirts of the women billowed over stiff hoops. Some rearrangement of chairs was needed to allow them space to sit. The candlelight flickered upon lace ruffles, the silver buttons of a waistcoat, the moist and expectant eyes. It nestled in the hollows of bones, changing shapes, contorting features. People spoke in low voices, as if there had been a death. Women exchanged words behind their fans, eyes resting upon Sati, blowing her backwards down a tunnel to view her from a distance. She touched the gold amulet at her neck threaded upon a black string. Her stepfather had urged her to change it for a string of pearls, but she had refused. For once her mother had supported her, knowing the importance of the object. Within its tiny case, rolled up tight, was an invocation to the Goddess.

One by one the White Town people seated themselves before her. How would she see into their *ferenghi* souls? These people by their absence of colour appeared as disembodied as a company of ghosts. She thought of Pagal, the albino, made freakish in Black Town by his alabaster skin. He hid from the sun, as did these people. His pink rabbity eyes, bleached lashes and hair were also to be found upon the *ferenghi*. Would they claim the albino as their own if he went to live with them? It seemed suddenly confusing. The dark mass of Black Town rose up in her mind then as powerfully embodied, anchored by their colour to the warm, dung-smelling earth.

To calm herself, Sati thought of her grandmother banished by Demonteguy to the back veranda. She imagined her sitting in a soft fleshy heap, the tyre of her midriff bulging out between her breasts and hips like stuffing from a patty. She saw as well her thin plait of hair gleaming in the candlelight, its grey beginnings and hennaed end saturated with musty oil. Each night Sati was required to oil it, each night she slept beside her grandmother, lulled to sleep by the greasy aroma. There was no way to connect old Jaya to this room. Sati wished to run to her, to return to the safety of the thatched hut that until now they had shared. She touched the talisman at her neck again and knew the Goddess would keep her safe. On the veranda, her grandmother must also be turning her prayer beads, imploring the divinity's protection.

Sati was suddenly conscious of a disturbance in the room, like a breeze across a field of wheat. A rustle of comments too low to unravel greeted the arrival of the Governor's wife. Emily Drake nodded to people and received a stiff return. There appeared to be a separateness about her in the crowded room. Her hair, drawn back into untidy loops, was pinned about her crown and had been left unpowdered. The décolletage so favoured by Rita Demonteguy was not for Emily Drake. She wore a modest lace-edged neckerchief, crossed over at the waist. Her thin face had the worn and polished look of stones from the river distressed by strong currents. She settled nervously on a chair beside Lady Russell and stared at Sati, who returned her gaze.

Thoughts tumbled about in Emily Drake's head. Already she knew she should not have come, especially so soon after her confinement. At this time a woman did not cavort about town alone, certainly not at night and for so dubious a reason. Already she was fodder for tomorrow's gossip. It was always a mistake to follow an impulse. There was hardly an occasion she could remember when good had come of such behaviour. And yet a compulsion beyond the normal had driven her to this room. She thought of her child asleep in his cradle and knew she was here for his safety. She had waited until her husband set out on his evening walk. He had announced he would leave the precincts of Fort William to visit Chief Magistrate Holwell. Immediately upon his departure she had summoned the palanquin bearers. As Fort William drew distant behind her, she noticed the swollen moon. She had stared up at the sky and that great bowl of feminine light had given her the strength to follow her impulse, irrational as it seemed. Her heart had been in a flutter. But for what? she wondered now. A half-caste girl from Black Town? She stared in surprise at Sati. The reality of the situation broke suddenly open, like a pod of ripe peas before her.

She had expected somebody older. What could this shrinking, sallow-skinned child impart of importance? It was madness to have come. Perhaps her mind was beginning to shred like worn linen, dissolving before the disparagement of the town. There was not a moment in the day when she was impervious to Calcutta's taunts and disregard. She met Sati's amber eyes and held them for a moment. To her surprise, something stilled within her, as if a secret passed between them. Her breath seemed to die in her throat. Emily Drake turned in agitation to Lady Russell, but she chewed on some aniseed to sweeten her breath. She sought the eye of Mr Dumbleton, but he scratched his head beneath his wig. The candles flickered no more than before; nothing appeared to have changed. Yet something had moved within Emily Drake. She no longer knew why she had come, what urgency had impelled her. If she could, she would have departed. The wing of a passing moth brushed her face, the air stirred strangely about her.

Sati's pulse beat faster, she gripped the frame of the stool in fear, for the performance was now upon her. She must blow soul into the faces of her audience. She prayed for Durga to come. Without Durga, nothing was possible. Already the room had quietened, every eye now settled upon her. Rita took her arm, her fingers hard in warning, and pushed Sati down into the armchair. The three coloured glasses stood waiting before her, moths clustered thickly about the candle flames. The shadows of their beating wings flickered on the walls. Suddenly, upon orders from Demonteguy, the servants extinguished most of the candles. Night fell dramatically upon the assembled crowd, a smell of burnt wicks filled the air.

Now that the room was almost dark, Sati saw that some fireflies had settled upon a wall. They glowed before her in three points of light above the head of the Governor's wife. Below, in the dimness, Mrs Drake stared, her face drawn into shadowy valleys, the ridge of her nose and the plateau of her cheeks caught in a cross of light. Her eyes had a glassy appearance, anxious and severe.

Sati bent forward, covering her face with her hands. If she cut away the world before her, some strange force propelled her inwards. The momentum increased until she arrived before an inner door. There she floated into endlessness, suspended in a timeless world. There she was both found and lost. And it was there that Durga waited.

Slowly, then, she raised her head from her hands and leaned back in the chair. She was no longer part of the room. All she saw now were the fireflies, their fluorescence brightening then dimming, as if they breathed in unison with her, fuelled by her own throbbing pulse. And Durga had come after all, to guide her from one realm to another. Durga the bloody-minded, fierce as a warrior ready for battle. Her predatory force filled the room. She stamped her foot and her wildness was a dance Sati must follow. Durga knew what to do, what must be said, where the dance would lead. Sati gave a sigh of relief and relinquished herself. All tension ebbed away. Durga settled into her veins, deep as instinct, liquid as knowledge dredged up from forgotten lives. Immediately her breath became shallow and her eyes stared fixedly. A murmur spread around the room at this strange transformation. Rita and Demonteguy exchanged a look of satisfaction.

'She is ready.' Demonteguy whispered. He turned towards his audience to invite a first query through the glasses. Before he could speak, a loud voice rang out.

'Emily. Emily.' Durga's deep voice vibrated from Sati. Even as she spoke Sati saw Durga circle the room, making her way towards the Governor's wife. At the same time, Durga was still fitted tight inside Sati, filling her fingers, expanding her belly.

'Emily,' Durga repeated, flexing up and down on her toes impatiently, like a dancer. Sati trembled with the reverberations. Durga was not visible to the others in the room. They could only watch in growing terror as Sati's slight body contorted and stretched, releasing each growl of a word.

Emily Drake was split open by terror. She looked around for the invisible presence. About her there was only the night and the flicker of countless shadows. A whimper of fear escaped her. She had entered a world between worlds and its lush, wild shape closed around her.

Durga began to laugh, enjoying the shock of the audience at her terrifying presence. Her hoarse voice was that of an old singer-prostitute, worn bare by shameless projection.

'Jane. Let her tell you about her sister Jane.' Durga laughed in a knowing way. On the wall above Mrs Drake the fireflies seemed to grow larger. Their pulsating light lit up the room, lending energy to Sati.

'What does Jane want?' Emily Drake half-rose and then sank back again onto her chair. She stared fearfully into the night, twisting this way and that as tension filled the room. People sat forward, faces contorted in fear.

'Thief.' Durga laughed again. Sati thrashed about as the deep voice cut through her.

'I have had enough of such accusations,' Emily Drake struggled up again from her chair, looking around defiantly now. Durga took no notice but continued to laugh, the sound still convulsing Sati. People looked at each other in horror.

'Why have you come to torture me? Leave me my child, that is all I ask. You took the first; it was him you wanted. Is that not enough?' Emily's voice soared raggedly. She refused to relinquish another child to her sister's ghost. And she did not care now who knew her fear of Jane.

'Who is to judge what is enough?' Durga screeched.

'Leave me in peace.' Emily's voice tumbled from its brief peak, splintering as it fell. She stood up as if she would leave Demonteguy's house. The room appeared stalked by unseen predators, the air was sharp as glass. Beside her Lady Russell took her hand and pulled her down again.

Rita and Fabian Demonteguy exchanged looks of alarm; Sati was not meant to act in this manner. 'I told her exactly what to do,' Demonteguy hissed into Rita's ear, anger making him splutter. 'Your mother has put her up to this nonsense. It's her usual Black Town hokum pokum.'

'What about the glasses?' Rita whispered, seeking some way to control the situation. She shivered in terror. Things seemed to slither about the room. Dark, formless apparitions waited to attach themselves to her. Demonteguy stepped forward determinedly.

'What about the glasses?' he whispered, bending over Sati.

'What *about* the glasses?' Durga answered, sweeping them from the table with a single crashing gesture. Glass splintered and skidded beneath the chairs. Women lifted their skirts and drew back with choked cries. Men allowed themselves small guttural sounds of fear.

Durga lifted an arm and at her summons a bat flew into the room. It soared up to hit the ceiling, then dived to the candle with a vicious squeak. Its shadow swelled over the walls. A servant rushed forward with a broom to chase away the creature. In the chair Sati grew still as Durga's laughter suddenly faded.

Half hidden behind a curtain, old Jaya watched, her soft flesh tensed in horror. This was not Sati. The voice did not belong to her granddaughter. She could not speak in this deep mocking tone, like the *ferenghi* themselves. There was another creature inside her, a *ferenghi* devil. As soon as this terrible evening was over she would go again to the temple, Jaya decided. She turned her prayer beads faster, muttering an invocation to the Goddess in a desperate whisper.

It had been clear to Jaya for some time, since the moment these strange manifestations had begun to appear several years before, that her granddaughter was possessed. She had gone immediately then to a priest at the Kali Mandhir and he had taken money to exorcise the demon. Eventually, after some sessions with a brushwood whip, throughout which Sati screamed in a hair-raising way, he declared the devil gone. Now Jaya saw that her instincts were right; priest or not, the man was untrustworthy. And so was Demonteguy. He had stirred up that creature once more in Sati. Rita should never have married him. He would destroy them all. She must talk the whole thing over with her cousin, Govindram.

She stared from the veranda at the full, ripe moon. In the month no day was more auspicious than this particular one. The full cup of the moon held a confusion of seed that would sow itself as it wished. Man could resort to nothing but prayer. Jaya sighed. The future swelled heavily before her as she sat turning her prayer beads. Yet she knew that when the Goddess gave trouble she also gave strength to bear the trial. She had not failed Jaya in the past.

CHAPTER TWO

The news arrived late in Calcutta and was brought to the Chief Magistrate by the Governor himself. Relations between the two men were strained. For the purpose of work they managed a cool but civil environment, circling each other like two prize beetles that might one day be forced to fight. Governor Drake extended his evening walk within Fort William, descending by the East Gate to pass the Reserve Battery until he arrived at the Chief Magistrate's house. Given a choice he would not have skirted the cemetery at night, nor have been persuaded inside Holwell's house, which, by the placement of the Governor's apartments within the fort, he was forced to observe day and night. He was surprised to find himself doing both these things. It convinced him of the seriousness of the occasion.

At the announcement of the Governor, John Zephaniah Holwell rose from his chair on the veranda and came into the drawing room. He left a book and a glass of claret outside. Then, on an impulse, he retraced his steps and picked up the claret to meet the Governor with the insolence of a glass in his hand. He had not been pleased to hear the name of his visitor, nor to be called from his reverie on the veranda. Facing the river and a swollen moon, naked as a breast, he had sat with his hand cupped against the sky. His thoughts had been pleasantly far away, compiling an inventory of all the womanly orbs he had had the luck to clasp. A visit at this hour from Roger Drake could mean only an emergency or disturbing news. The glow of candles softened the room, deepening the colours of a fine rug spread upon the floor. Holwell stood before the veranda door, forcing Drake to cross the room.

'Dear God, Holwell, how can you live right opposite the cemetery? The moon is out full on those mausoleums. Sent the shivers down my spine,' the Governor burst out, standing at last before Holwell, mopping his plump, sweating face with a handkerchief.

'Many friends rest there. I shall no doubt be laid to rest there myself. Two monsoons are the Age of Man, and countless have died here to prove it. Best to gain a familiarity with the place now. A glass of claret or Madeira?' The Chief Magistrate stood a head taller than Drake and was the elder by fourteen years. He spoke lightly, for thoughts of mortality did not assail him to the degree they gripped Governor Drake. Holwell's longevity, although a matter of some mystery, was now taken for granted in Calcutta.

Drake took the claret Holwell poured and tossed back a large amount. Not for the first time he reflected that the Chief Magistrate resembled a gecko. His skin had the same yellow, rubbery quality, his small lashless eyes stared unblinking. The long cleft on his chin seemed only to define this secondary personality. Drake eyed the shadows behind the Chief Magistrate as if a tail might break free of the darkness.

The Chief Magistrate waited for Drake to finish his drink before indicating a chair. He noticed a light fall of powder from the Governor's hair had settled on his shoulders. Such a lack of care about one's person gave a slovenly impression. Drake rarely powdered his hair, and made a slapdash affair of it when he did. As with his dress so with his work, thought the Chief Magistrate. The man was ill equipped at every level to discharge the responsibilities of his position. In his excitable, yelping manner there was something pubescent about him. Thoughts seemed scrambled inside his head, like a half-cooked egg, running this way or that. The Chief Magistrate took pride in his own ordered mind, each polished thought stacked carefully.

'What is the trouble? I presume there is trouble to bring you past the cemetery at night?' Holwell asked when Drake was seated.

The Governor already regretted revealing his fear of cemeteries to Holwell. Now, the weary sarcasm with which the Chief Magistrate phrased his enquiry only deepened this feeling. In retaliation Drake announced his news about the nawab with a flourish he might otherwise not have attempted.

'That old devil Alivardi is dying, at last.'

The Chief Magistrate appeared unaffected by the information. He sat in his chair and sipped his claret. A familiar rage raced through him at the sight of Drake. The position of Governor was awarded by seniority. Men worked their way up to a seat on the Council of Fort William, then joined the queue waiting for the post of Governor. If the sweeping hand of mortality moved forward at an accelerated rate, which, in the climate of India, was not uncommon, this might arrive quite quickly. By right, the post should have come to Holwell four years before. Instead, Drake's uncle, who was on the Board of Directors in Leadenhall, had swayed the voting towards his nephew.

For a moment there was silence. The sawing of crickets in the dark undergrowth of the garden filled the room. The mournful, mud-bound boom of bullfrogs vibrated in their ears. The Governor did not want to break the momentum of his announcement by adding more details. The Chief Magistrate wished to make clear that he was unimpressed by the Governor's news. Holwell, with no effort, and Drake, with much effort, continued their silence in the noisy room.

'How many times before have we heard the same thing?' The Chief Magistrate spoke at last, judging the moment, stifling a yawn. 'The nawab has been dying for as long as I remember. He invariably recovers from whatever is wrong.'

'The man is eighty-two. He is not immortal.' The Governor sat forward in his chair. His breeches strained at the seams, his stockings sagged into wrinkles.

'From where did you hear this?' the Chief Magistrate asked with unconcealed forbearance, savouring the bouquet of his claret. His nostrils dilated like the gills of predatory fish.

'From the fat merchant Omichand, via his *banian,* Govindram. Omichand would not have sent such news late at night for nothing.' Drake watched a moth blunder into a flame and tumble, a minute incendiary dart, to the base of a candle. As its tufted body flared briefly, he felt a moth-sized sense of sadness. He thought of the arrogance of Icarus. He thought of his position as Governor and wondered if this also exposed him to an overdose of sun. In the dish the singed moth gave a last convulsion.

'With Omichand it is hard to tell.' The Chief Magistrate continued to sip his claret, a vision of Omichand reluctantly filling his mind. He had no love for the devious Hindu merchant who seemed to single-handedly control Calcutta.

'That is not untrue, but this news has been muttered by other sources for days. And I believe the word of Govindram. There is something about the man. He may be Omichand's chief assistant, but it is easier to tell when he is lying than with the usual Hindu.' Drake wiped his sweating face again.

'Do not be naive,' the Chief Magistrate advised. The image of Govindram, dark and spry, was suddenly before him, like an agile ant that persistently eluded the sole of a shoe. 'They're all a pack of monkeys.'

Drake mopped at his neck and the Chief Magistrate wondered, not for the first time, at the copius amounts of perspiration the Governor's body seemed able to expel. He never visualised Drake without a wet sheen to his face. And tonight was relatively cool, with an occasional breeze off the river.

The Governor shifted about beneath the Chief Magistrate's gaze. It was difficult to assert authority with a man fourteen years his senior, one who refused to make any deference to his position besides. It was nothing but envy. Holwell had seen himself as Governor of Calcutta. Instead, in far-away Leadenhall, the East India Company had appointed him, Roger Drake. Official confirmation of this decision, even after four years, had unfortunately yet to arrive. Drake's every order inevitably wobbled upon a shaky base. This was a cause of depression to Drake and a source of glee to men like Holwell. Still, a Governor was a Governor, even if not yet officially confirmed. Drake took another mouthful of claret, a smile on his lips.

'Omichand leaves for Murshidabad the day after tomorrow. Things cannot be good or he would delay. If we do not also go we may lose a last opportunity to settle our pending business. The nawab is dying, his coffers are empty and his precious heir and grandson, Siraj Uddaulah, wishes only to see an end to our Settlement.' Drake spoke with sudden force. The Chief Magistrate raised an eyebrow.

'We must see the way the wind is blowing in Murshidabad,' Drake insisted, wishing his voice would not rise to an effeminate treble whenever he felt under pressure. 'There are many that do not wish Siraj Uddaulah to come to power. The court is alive with intrigue.'

'When is it not? I cannot just drop all my obligations,' the Chief Magistrate argued, although he saw that they probably had to go. Thought of the formidable palaces and stinking alleys of Murshidabad always filled him with unease. Something lurked beneath the town that he could never quite describe. Something fetid and menacing that might, when his back was turned, reach up to devour him.

'We could sail with the evening tide the day after tomorrow, as will Omichand,' Drake suggested. Whatever the animosity between himself and the Chief Magistrate, the question of power tied them firmly together. The Council of Fort William and the workings of Calcutta rested in their hands.

'If you feel there is something to this report, then I suppose we cannot delay.' The Chief Magistrate's voice rose in annoyance. 'Whatever way the wind blows in Murshidabad, our trade is needed by all. Bengal cannot do without us.' He spat out the words, like the fibrous residue of a fruit he had eaten.

'The day after tomorrow then. I will have the boats ready.' Drake stood up, glad to leave. He hesitated a moment at the door, remembering the cemetery again. Then, determined to show no further weakness, he strode off in the direction of Fort William.

The Chief Magistrate returned to the veranda with the remains of his claret. Above him the Pole Star glittered with mysterious force. The star beamed down on the town, making one of its White and Black parts. He chose to ignore the bloated moon, whose rhythms, fickle as a woman, continually evaded him; there when not needed, invisible when desired, always veiling an inner life. Thoughts of his wife came to him and he could not suppress the anger that any memory of her brought.

He had built his great house in Calcutta in preparation for their marriage, but Rosemary had stayed in India less than four years, withering quickly like a picked flower. She had never recovered from the death of their first child. India's alien ways and the depression it brought debilitated her. Sometimes it had taken a year for a letter to arrive from home. This strange and unnatural isolation, where events closest to heart were viewed as if through the wrong end of a telescope, infinitely reduced and impossibly distant, distressed her more than most. She had learned of her mother's death eleven months after the event. And that bizarre juxtaposition of thinking her alive while she had been dead all the while seemed to crack her open. She had been ill for months. When a second child was eventually born, she had insisted on returning to England, fearful of losing another baby to India's rapacious ways. She had never returned again to Calcutta, leaving Holwell with a marriage that was living and at the same time dead. He thought of her now, and also his child, in the way he thought of dead friends.

Memories, like wet stepping stones, had led him into uncomfortable depths. He leaned back in his chair, listening to the soft slapping of the river at the bottom of his garden. He had chosen to build his house on the bank of the Hoogly not only for the coolness it afforded, but also for the bittersweet edge of memory. The thick odour of the water threw him back, if only for a moment, to the place where he had been born; he had grown up beside a river. On summer nights its scent had pervaded his dreams, with the distant rush of water spilling through the weir. There was no denying the pain when he had to put aside these memories and open his eyes to a ragged fringe of coconut palms. Exile obliged him to forget while forcing him to remember in order to survive. Holwell shifted in his chair. The lapping of water from the nearby Hoogly came to him again. The river was like no other he could remember.

Beyond the veranda the trees were alight with fireflies, the moon streaked the Hoogly bronze. Crickets and bullfrogs still battled in the night, but even this din sank into the silence of the great river. This monstrous silence both drew and repelled the Chief Magistrate, much as India itself drew and repelled him. The very soil of the place seemed possessed of a wily, murderous soul and his life was a battle against it. The river exuded the dank odour of decay, of things that festered, hidden away. The corpses of thousands were dumped in its waters, the defecation of millions coloured its tide. It ate its meal of death and rot and opened its mouth for more, as did India itself. In this land everything decayed. Flesh sickened, devoured by maggots, worms and parasites even as it lived. Death waited for its victims in the air, the grass, the sweetest fruit or the waters of the well. If not buried or burned within a few hours, a body would swell and sometimes burst with the speed of its own destruction.

This voracious need to destroy and assimilate was the nature of the country, thought the Chief Magistrate, and shivered in the balmy night. He remembered a native goddess with a long red tongue, black as a goblin, hung about with skulls, that personified the country for him. The evil creature was in the river and the night, in the birthing room and the cemetery, in the Courthouse and the mango trees, even in his glass of claret. She left her vile footprints upon life and death, dancing through both willy-nilly. Her breath moved dark trees to wildness. The Chief Magistrate was incensed by the sight of her, and such sightings were frequent and always obscene. The Old Hag, the Black Crone he called her, awash with his own bleak terror. If India and exile had taught him one thing, it was a view of his own identity he might otherwise not have learned.

Beneath the drone of crickets and the drumming of the frogs, the silence of the river rose about him again. Its silence had a waiting quality; eyes open even in sleep. The river was like a woman aroused, flushed with power, and filled him with fear. The Chief Magistrate found himself trembling with the unexpected range of his thoughts. He poured another glass of claret, fixing his gaze on Fort William, returning his mind to the tangible world and the events of that morning.

He had left his home before seven as usual. It was his custom to walk to the Courthouse situated on the Avenue. The Chief Magistrate found this morning exercise beneficial; his palanquin followed behind. In the coolness of the early hours the sun had yet to bite into the day and chew it to a pulp. Holwell walked carefully. His deliberation, unusual for a man of rapid step, was accounted for by the dust. Except when the skies opened, dust rose at the slightest provocation, endowing his shoes with the quality of soft moleskin. The dark eyes of vegetable hawkers, baskets on head, slid his way beneath the weight of aubergines, onions and jackfruit. On white-painted balconies servants dusted rails and peered down at the black velour of his hat. Untouchables, whose day was regulated by the straining bowels of White Town, slipped out of back gates with the first stinking buckets of effluent. They stared curiously at the cautious-stepping Holwell.

At intervals the Chief Magistrate stopped to look about him. His gaunt frame reared up like a long-legged bird, his attention deflected for an instant from the dust about his feet. In Calcutta they were never free of the eyes of spies. In Murshidabad Alivardi Khan was known to have scrolls that filled a whole room, inked thickly with knowledge of Calcutta's élite. This unseen violation of both his territory and his person filled the Chief Magistrate with rage. With narrowed lids he scanned the nearby architecture, meeting with a silent glare the invisible eyes he was sure must press upon him.

Eventually he turned into the entrance of the Courthouse. Here the day had already commenced. There was the buzz of activity in corridors, and the sweaty fuss of wigs. A close smell of warm wood, old food, armpits and privies pervaded the place; a comforting, manly odour of business, challenge and incrimination. Holwell made his way up a flight of stairs to the room of the Chief Magistrate. On the top step he collided with William Dumbleton, Calcutta's Notary. The collision knocked Dumbleton's wig askew and he straightened it with a laugh. Holwell returned the Notary's greeting, ignoring Dumbleton's rapier eyes.

The Courthouse was home to the Mayor's Court, at which, this morning, Holwell was to preside. The Mayor's Court heard the lawsuits of Christian Calcutta. It upheld the rights of not only the English and Europeans in the settlement but also those descendants of the Portuguese, now long intermarried with India, if they still professed to be Christian. The Mayor's Court called upon Holwell for a minimum of hours. As Chief Zamindar and Magistrate to the Cutcherry, or native court, it was with Black Town's petitions for justice that John Zephaniah Holwell was more closely concerned.

In his room the Chief Magistrate sipped a glass of sweet lime juice, squeezed freshly for him each morning. Its astringency washed through his veins, preparing him for the day. The Courthouse faced the Park and the cool waters of the Great Tank, surrounded by lawns and flowering trees, criss-crossed by dusty paths. The wide roads and great homes of Calcutta, set in large gardens, filled Holwell with a sense of rightness. It was as if the spacious plan of White Town had been deliberately conceived to repel the foul pressure of Black Town, always ready to spill upon them.

White Town dazzled with unnatural iridescence, rising above the

Indian town spreading malodorously about it. A paste of ground shell plastered all the walls and was set hard as zinc over the settlement, reflecting the sun like a mirror, luminous beneath the moon. So blinding at times was the effect of the *chunam* that many people now added some mud to the mixture, to lessen the strain on the eyes.

Already, from the window, Holwell could see a motley queue had formed to present petitions. With a start he looked at his pocket watch and, draining the last of the lime juice, walked down the corridor to the Mayor's Court.

Upon his entrance the first plaintiff was called. Holwell settled at his desk, observing the room before him. The Clerk of the Court stood up. The recorders readied their quills like a row of expectant hens, heads down, tails up.

'The Court will hear the case of Janet Jenkins versus Fabian Demonteguy.'

Holwell looked up with a frown from his papers. 'This is a case for the Cutcherry. On what grounds is this woman allowed to appear here? Her name is Jaya Kapur, no longer Janet Jenkins. This court is for the use of Christian people and this woman is not Christian.' The case, he saw from the document, concerned the custody of old Jaya's granddaughter, Sati. The woman's son-in-law wished to adopt her. He looked around but could see no sign of Fabian Demonteguy. Either the man did not know of this case, or had thought better than to defend himself against the flimsy allegations of an Indian woman, even if she was his mother-in-law.

Across the room the familiar figure of Old Jaya confronted him. As always, when faced with this immense and determined woman, the Chief Magistrate imagined the intractable body of India itself rearing up before him. He regretted that a past liaison with her daughter had put him in her grasp. His mind was suddenly filled with discomforting thoughts of Rita Demonteguy. Jaya's stance was defiant, deviousness lit her eyes. Her breasts and belly merged to a single shapeless heap beneath her bedraggled clothes. He could not make out what it was she wore, an outfit of Indian or European origin, or bits of both held together by brazenness. She appeared to have stepped forth from a circus. Soft pouches of flesh, resembling rudimentary breasts, settled on each side of her jaw. A hat with two feathers was perched on her hennaed hair like an unwieldy cockerel.

Behind her stood the girl, Sati, thin and sallow. Her breasts were flattened beneath a pink dress that appeared a size too small. Holwell stared in shock at the sudden maturity of her body. A feeling of panic rushed through him. Sati did not raise her eyes to him, but skulked in the shadow of her grandmother, half hidden from his gaze. She had not inherited the attributes of her mother, nor her father's milky skin, but had nurtured instead a surly gene, ripe with the traits of dark ancestors. He looked at her in distaste. Why Demonteguy should wish to legally adopt her was beyond his comprehension. Then his gaze returned to Jaya Kapur and rage filled him.

'Your Honour, she is here on the grounds of having had three European husbands,' the Clerk of the Court responded.

'But they are all dead,' Holwell roared, the insolence of the woman choking his words. Across the room the cockerel trembled belligerently, as if it might take flight. 'She is no more now than the sum of herself. State her full name for the record. Janet Jenkins *née* Jaya Kapur. From now on let her be called by her native name. Case dismissed.'

A murmur grew in the sticky air. He saw the cockerel pitch about. The face of old Jaya, impassive only a moment ago, now began to twist and work.

'My name is Jenkins. First Walsh, then Locke. But Jenkins now. All these are English names. All these Englishmen, and others besides have planted their seeds in me. I have borne Christian men's children. I am having every right to be here.' Jaya stood with her feet firmly apart, hands on her hips, and stared at him. The Chief Magistrate glimpsed a set of grimy toes thrust about the thong of a sandal.

'Case dismissed. I call you to appear before the Cutcherry.' He swallowed hard in rage and fear.

He refused to hear the words she screeched as they dragged her away out of earshot. The girl was pulled out with her, like a toy on a string, gripping the end of her grandmother's veil. She turned her head once, as if in appeal. For a moment her amber eyes met those of the magistrate and held him with a terrible force. He remembered again the way they had fastened upon him in the past. Then her thin body was sucked into the crowd and disappeared from the room.

'Next case,' Holwell called, relief flooding him at their departure.

Now, so many hours later on his veranda, the recollection of that scene still affected him. The memory of Jaya Kapur merged now with the black goddess and the wily river flowing before him. And that glimpse of the girl remained with him. Her yellow eyes and tortoiseshell hair, glossy as a cat's, stayed with him like indigestible food. A wave of unease passed through him and he took a quick mouthful of claret.

Holwell ignored the sounds of Black Town's evening bustle drifting to him across the Maratha Ditch and turned his attention to Fort William. The great bulk of the garrison stretched before him, seven hundred feet along the river, a town within a town. Day and night huge adjutant storks perched on its ramparts. Their silhouettes, massed against the moonlit sky, appeared like an army of gargoyles. The shutters of the Council chamber, where he spent a considerable amount of his time, gleamed dully beneath a cupola weighted down by birds. The Chief Magistrate's gaze moved to a balcony of flowering shrubs before the Governor's apartment. A hook of rage turned in him at the thought of Drake ensconced in those rooms. The man had no right to such luck. He sipped his wine and sniffed the heightened scent of the river, rustling through palm and mango trees. The damp air might fan pleasantly about him but pestilence blew on the Calcutta breeze. He wished it might find Roger Drake.

The sudden unravelling of so much emotion now thumped uncomfortably in his chest.

And still the day was not over. He had yet to face Demonteguy, if he chose to attend to the man's invitation. A message had come from the Frenchman in the afternoon, suggesting they meet for a business discussion. It could only concern Jaya Kapur and the custody case, the Chief Magistrate presumed. At least in the matter of this invitation there appeared to be a choice. Except that choice was often a fond illusion. Things had a habit of deciding themselves in a confoundedly secret way.

CHAPTER THREE

With an effort the Chief Magistrate pushed away the morning's disquieting memory of Sati and the Governor's tiresome visit that evening and reached again for his claret. Demonteguy's invitation now filled his mind as a further dreary weight. Night had already settled upon Calcutta. Moths beat against the lamp, bullfrogs pumped throatily in the darkness. To one side of the Chief Magistrate's garden the droop of palm fronds fanned darkly against the moonlit sky like black ostrich feathers. Behind them rose tamarind and mango trees. Screened from his sight by this thick growth lay the Maratha Ditch. The Ditch had been built long before to fortify Calcutta against attack. Now its sole function had become the demarcation of the city. On one side sat John Zephaniah Holwell, Chief Magistrate of White Town, replete with claret before the moon, while across the Ditch, only yards from his jasmine-filled garden, stretched the stinking miasma of Black Town.

The Chief Magistrate listened to the evening noise of Black Town slide into a lower key. The crying of babies had ceased. The smell of dung fires and frying onions, the voices of quarrelling women and the beating of a drum from a nearby temple drifted over to him. In the narrow alleys of thatched huts the cooking of numerous dinners had started. In his own area of Calcutta the trees glowed prettily with fireflies. The adjutant birds had retired for the night and the jackals had taken their place. There were considerably fewer of these creatures roaming White Town than there had been in the early days of the Settlement. Then, they had streamed in from the jungle at will, picking Calcutta clean as a bone, frightening children and old people who were without weapons or canes. Now, a patrol of sepoys, accompanied by a team of sweepers, kept down the numbers with clubs and guns. The adjutant birds had at once grown fatter and more numerous, for the bodies of the jackals were thrown into the Maratha Ditch, where they could more easily be consumed.

As Holwell drained the last of his claret, thoughts of Demonteguy filled his mind again. He did not want anything to do with the Frenchman, yet he knew he would visit him as he demanded. At last he rose reluctantly from his chair, his legs carrying him forward with a will of their own. Demonteguy's house, in an unfashionable area behind the jail near the Cross Roads, was a distance away. Followed by a retinue of servants, Holwell made his way to his palanquin. The runners squatting nearby chewing betel nut or tobacco, at once rushed to his assistance. The Chief Magistrate folded up his long body in a practised fashion, stowing himself into his palanquin. Soon he was lifted free of the ground and carried out through the gates of his compound. Torchbearers and guards ran before the litter to light the way and announce his importance to the world.

As the gates shut behind him, the Chief Magistrate noticed the moon streaming into the cemetery. For a moment he felt the same hesitation he knew Governor Drake must feel. Masonry of a grand and intricate nature was crammed tightly into the cemetery. The mausoleums, weathered black, resembled a decaying miniature town. Narrow lanes ran between edifices of a widely assorted nature, each larger than the next. Mughul domes augmented tombs that dwarfed a man, soaring Egyptian obelisks and sturdy cherubs topped massive sarcophagi. Grecian urns and Corinthian columns stood sentinel before many mausoleums. Flowering bushes and shady trees softened the place by day. Now the moon, shining down upon this third and silent section of Calcutta, lit the mouldering mass of stone with unearthly life. In the trees the fireflies clustered aggressively, jostling for space in which to flash their eerie fairy light. The place took on a glowing nocturnal power that made the Chief Magistrate shiver. He did not believe in ghosts. Yet he huddled in his palanquin as flares were lit to guide his way. The flame-bearers ran ahead, lighting the road beside the ditch that led to Demonteguy's house.

Why had Demonteguy asked him to call? And why was he, John Zephaniah Holwell, Chief Magistrate and Zamindar of Calcutta, acquiescing to the impertinent request? *Who* after all was Demonteguy but an upstart trader, an interloper? Few people even knew the nature of Demonteguy's business. Probably he dealt in gems, sending diamonds on Dutch ships to be sold in Amsterdam. Holwell too had made a respectable amount of money in this manner. Why had he not simply told Demonteguy to see him in his rooms at the Courthouse? Anger drummed through Holwell, even though the choice to go was his.

There were two new runners in the Chief Magistrate's employ who had yet to submit to the rhythm of the team. Within the palanquin Holwell endured the resulting discomfort in an uneven, bouncing trot, the confused nature of his thoughts only adding to his irritation. It was because of Rita that he found himself on this ridiculous journey. Why should the woman still have the power to draw him to her? Long before the coming of Demonteguy, he had used this same road to visit her regularly as she manoeuvred her way through widowhood. Against his will the old feeling of anticipation gripped his innards pleasantly. The road had acquired an illicit flavour drawn from his emotions in those days. He pushed out of his mind the uncomfortable scenes that had ended his relationship with Rita. He was never sure how much his wife had known about the affair. Even now he thought of the interlude as being her fault. Had Rosemary not been so intractable, he might never have strayed.

Soon they neared a bridge that crossed the Maratha Ditch into Black Town. The palanquin slowed to a halt behind the bony, swaying rumps of buffalo returning late to Black Town from a White Town dairy. Fresh cowpats splattered the road, their ripe odour filling the Chief Magistrate's nose. His liveried runners danced about to avoid them, dipping their torches to see the better. Within the palanquin Holwell was jostled around. At last the palanquin overtook the bullocks but was obstructed, this time by a funeral procession making its way to the burning ghat beyond the Maratha Ditch. Eventually the Chief Magistrate's litter pushed past the mourners on the narrow road. A wave of sorrowful chanting reached Holwell as the bier drew alongside his palanquin. Since the Chief Magistrate sat on the shoulders of runners, as did the corpse, they met at an equal level. The Chief Magistrate stared at the white-shrouded figure strapped to the bier beneath garlands of flowers. For some moments they moved in unison, the stench of death pervading Holwell's palanquin. The light from the flares of both parties waved wildly over the scene. The buffalo caught up with the palanquin once more and bellowed at Holwell's rear.

'Move on,' the Chief Magistrate shouted, wondering why a funeral procession was about at such an hour. The burning of bodies was done before sundown. Perhaps the man was too poor to pay for a pyre – as was most of Calcutta – and was about to be dumped in the river.

Crowded amidst the buffalo and the ragged cortège, Holwell's runners were forced to proceed as slowly as before. The corpse continued to travel in tandem with the palanquin, jostled about as much as the Chief Magistrate. Unlike the palanquin runners, the pallbearers were of varying heights and struggled to maintain equilibrium. The corpse lurched right then left, angled up for a time, then down.

'Move aside,' Holwell shouted, but with a row of oleander on one side and the ditch on the other, there was nowhere his runners could go. They looked at each other in consternation and began to shout at the funeral cortège. Such a show of disrespect for the dead angered the pallbearers, who heatedly argued their case. For a moment both the Chief Magistrate and the corpse were brought to a stop in the midst of this altercation. Holwell saw that the twine strapping the body to the bier had worked itself loose and the corpse now lay at an awkward slant. Before he could raise his voice in alarm, the dead man slid suddenly forward, coming to rest at the edge of the palanquin, as if he would join the Chief Magistrate. Holwell reached out in desperation and felt the stiff flesh beneath his fingers.

The touch of death moved through him. He was constantly stalked by the spectre. Not only from the strange fluxes and fevers that came without warning upon a man, but in the very verdure of India. From the impenetrable jungle, alive with all manner of fantastical snares, to the great vines that climbed in his own garden, rearing before him like muscular snakes. Death waited silently everywhere.

'Move on,' Holwell screamed. 'Move on.'

At last the palanquin runners broke free and took the centre of the road. The Chief Magistrate sat back in relief. The touch of the corpse still lingered on him, putrefaction filled his nose. The night was warm, but in his thick clothes Holwell was chilled by a weight of uncomfortable reflection. For a moment he could not deny that waxing and waning made an identical curve of each meagre life. King or pauper, humanity hurtled forward towards a single goal. In the secret hour of life's midday, death was born in everyone. There was no way he could protest the matter; God snuffed out existence without a glance in this fetid place. With an effort the Chief Magistrate controlled himself. Although he was not yet prepared to take his place amongst the mausoleum population, he saw now why death chose to haunt him this evening. On this day many years ago, a son of three weeks had departed. His grave was so small it could be forgotten, and this the Chief Magistrate had done with alacrity. Tonight he had passed by the cemetery without even remembrance.

Everything had started from that death. Until then, Rosemary had fulfilled her wifely duties in an admirable manner. The house was replete in every way. Servants were managed efficiently, guests were welcome and plentiful. Flowers graced every room. In her demeanour Rosemary reflected this decorum; never obtrusive but bound to her embroidery and a gentle sense of humour. To their conjugal life she passively acquiesced. All seemed satisfactory to the Chief Magistrate. Only Rosemary's dislike of India could not be overcome. Although she made efforts to accept her life, the swiftness of death, seen so cruelly and repeatedly, froze her good intentions. The true sweep of this spectre must, in India, be stared at open-eyed. Some could look and some could not. Rosemary wished for innocence; this India could not provide.

Eventually, their son arrived, a large baby with blue eyes. Rosemary had appeared complete, the future seemed assured. Yet after three weeks she had awoken Holwell in the middle of the night. The baby screamed, flailing small arms against her breast. She begged him to get the doctor. He had taken a horse and gone himself. The doctor was on furlough and his replacement was a casual man who said such vociferation was the way of babies. 'Wind in the stomach. Give it some rhubarb. I will call in the morning,' he said, and went back to sleep. Holwell returned with this news to Rosemary, much relieved within himself.

She heard him out silently, the child in her arms, before she said quietly, 'The baby is dead.'

The casket was tiny and the grave, under the shade of a tree, a trivial, flowery affair. It was just somewhere Rosemary went each day, as she might have visited her whist group. Yet, so small a death still had its way of working subterraneously. Rosemary closed her door to him. Embroidery lay idle in her hands. Servants pilfered and disappeared, food became inedible. Guests no longer came. After some time she rallied, as if a disease had run its course, but things were never the same again. She had moved beyond his grasp. Soon after this he had come to know Rita. He had handled the probate of her late husband's will. The estate was minuscule but included the house on the perimeter of White Town where they had lived. Rita's matters were soon settled, but the consolation she demanded for widowhood coincided with his own needs. That she sought this consolation with more gentlemen than himself he was ignorant of at the time.

The Chief Magistrate eventually passed the jail and entered a less fashionable area of White Town as he neared Demonteguy's home. The palanquin came to rest and the Chief Magistrate uncurled himself. Before him Demonteguy's small house stood in darkness, lit only by the moon. At this hour most homes in the Settlement were already extravagantly illuminated. Perhaps, thought the Chief Magistrate, the Frenchman saved on candles. He stepped from his palanquin and looked about, his pulse behaving erratically. Demonteguy had indicated the meeting concerned some lucrative business, yet Holwell knew the reason he had come to the Frenchman's house had nothing to do with this information. There were chunks of life that could not be got rid of but floated, like great icebergs, at the back of the mind. Occasionally the blast from that nether region broke through a forgotten door. Such a moment now seized the Chief Magistrate, rooting him to the ground. The image of Rita, naked beneath a négligé, pushed into his mind. Some invisible and arbitrary force seemed suddenly unleashed upon him.

He saw now that within the house a few candles were burning. There appeared to be a gathering, sitting silently in the dark. Why had Demonteguy called him for a business discussion when he was not alone? Was this a prayer meeting? Holwell frowned in annoyance as he stepped through the open door. His eyes searched out and settled on Rita. The candles threw distorted shadows on to the wall behind her. Her breasts spilt from her dress, as if offered to him upon her palms to do with as he wished. The memory of those golden orbs, quivering just above his chin as she sat astride him, would never leave his mind. The dark room continued to tremble about him, moving with the candle flames. He tried to step back but a servant ran forward, forcing him inside. People turned at the disturbance. Holwell sat down to escape further notice, discomfort boiling through him. He appeared trapped in some ritualistic meeting. Emily Drake, Lady Russell and Dumbleton, the Notary, he saw now were amongst the audience. He remembered his collision in the courthouse with Dumbleton just that morning. Soon, in the darkness, he spotted other familiar faces. Why were these people assembled in Demonteguy's home? The Chief Magistrate's eyes settled once more on Rita, and met her stony expression. At last he spotted Demonteguy and saw that the Frenchman observed him with surprise.

Holwell's confusion grew. He could make no sense of the proceedings. To his further horror he saw that the girl, Sati, faced them all from an armchair. Her amber-flecked eyes, luminous as phosphor, that he had fought to be free of all day, now burned relentlessly into him. He was terrified to drop his gaze. In his present state of vulnerability the girl might detect a crevice through which to shred his soul. Within that dark, icy place at the back of his mind, cold waves seemed to rise and fall. He braced himself to keep his balance before such a naked thrust of will.

One by one people turned towards him, as if the girl had the power to bend their gaze. Her eyes pinned the Chief Magistrate to his chair. Carved nodules of wood pressed into his back. The room seemed to darken about him. The flame of a candle wove sinuously about like a snake from a fakir's basket. The walls of the room had vanished, he appeared to be wandering in a dark cave, an unknown presence at his side. Sati was speaking, her voice deep and strange.

'He carries darkness into all his dealings. The river will be powerless to bear him away, even though he leaves. His lies will last.' The girl raised her arm, pointing at Holwell; her voice rang out in the room. A needle of pain passed through him.

'What nonsense is this?' the Chief Magistrate shouted, but the words sounded faint in his throat. With an effort he forced himself up, his limbs felt heavy as lead. About him the candles danced dangerously.

'Jane. Jane . . .' Suddenly the voice began to fade. Sati stood up abruptly, then collapsed on to the floor.

'About time too.' Strength pulsed through the Chief Magistrate's veins. As he pushed his way to the door, Demonteguy hurried towards him.

'How dare you bring me here, to this unspeakable charade, under the false pretence of business,' Holwell swore.

'I did not ask you here tonight. Our meeting was for tomorrow,' Demonteguy answered. His voice was unsteady and there was something unhinged in his expression.

The Chief Magistrate stopped in confusion and Demonteguy took control of himself. 'It is over. People are going. If you wish, we can talk now. Be so kind as to wait a few moments.' Demonteguy led Holwell to the veranda and a small table upon which was a bottle of arrack. Demonteguy quickly filled two glasses as Holwell sat down.

'The evening has been eventful.' Demonteguy gulped down the liquor with an apologetic smile, then hurried away.

A servant with a silver collecting tray was making a round of departing guests. Most people appeared bewildered and made no contribution to the evening. Demonteguy struggled to contain his fury. Not only would there be a lack of funds, but bad reports would circulate in Calcutta. Mr Dumbleton passed him without a word, hurrying out with a frown of disapproval, Lady Russell steered a dazed Mrs Drake to the door. Others followed her example, ignoring the collection tray. Demonteguy stood in the middle of the room, staring at the debris of the evening. Something he had appeared to hold in his hands had trickled through his fingers.

On the veranda the Chief Magistrate turned his back on the crowd filing out into the night. Through the open window shutters he saw servants lighting candles and oil lamps again. His fury increased as he observed old Jaya suddenly stepping into the room. That she should have seen him enmeshed in a charade indubitably of her own making was more than he could bear. The memory of her feathered hat across the Courtroom just that morning, trembling like a belligerent cockerel, came before him again. He watched as she and Rita bent over the prostrate girl, who now lay upon a sofa. Jaya covered her with a quilt.

'They are gone.' Demonteguy ran back up the steps to Holwell as the last palanquin departed. He had recovered his composure.

'And what was all *that*?' The Chief Magistrate's mouth was pinched in anger.

'The girl sees spirits. They speak through her. In Paris I attended a seance such as you have seen tonight. Many people wish to contact dead relatives or to know the future. Tonight the spirit of Mrs Drake's dead sister came into the room through Sati. We had not expected such a thing. Is it not marvellous?'

'Bah,' the Chief Magistrate exploded, and reached for the arrack. The liquor set his throat on fire. Everything within him was in disarray and now, face to face with Demonteguy, he felt an unexpected discomfort. Did the Frenchman know of his wife's reputation? But Demonteguy's mind was locked on more concrete matters than the Chief Magistrate's tumbled senses.

'Now that Rita and I are married, I have decided to adopt Sati. She can then be permanently with her mother. Already she is of marriageable age and can no longer be allowed to run wild in Black Town. It reflects badly upon us.' An oil lamp burned nearby and the light caught Demonteguy's watery blue eyes, as they confronted the Chief Magistrate.

'What is this to do with me?' the Chief Magistrate enquired.

'The girl's grandmother is filing for custody,' Demonteguy replied.

'Upon what grounds?' Holwell asked, as if he knew nothing of the matter.

'She has no grounds,' Demonteguy insisted. 'The only good she could do she has just now done, by making over to Sati a substantial inheritance.'

'An inheritance? Old Jaya Kapur?' The Chief Magistrate put down his glass. He felt inclined to laugh.

'Diamonds. She lived for a time in Murshidabad, in the *zenana* of some princeling there. Of course, I believe she did not go willingly, but was sold into concubinage. A sad story but a common one here. She escaped and fled with jewels the princeling had given her. Recently, she has made these baubles over to Sati to insure for her an adequate dowry.'

'It is possible, I suppose,' Holwell replied. There seemed no end to the day's eccentricity.

'How can a young girl take care of such an inheritance? How can an old woman be trusted not to lose such a valuable treasure? She might go senile and forget where it is. Will you be presiding over the case?' Demonteguy asked.

'Probably.' The Chief Magistrate became wary.

'If I were granted legal custody I could invest the inheritance to Sati's best advantage, perhaps double it by the time she married.' Demonteguy spoke in a coaxing manner. Holwell said nothing, for he felt at this moment silence was to his advantage.

'The diamonds are of a high carat. Shipped to Amsterdam, cut and polished, they would be of great value,' Demonteguy continued.

'How do you know all this?'

'I have seen the document making these things over to Sati. A scribe from the lawyer came to me. They were uncertain the old woman was of sound mind, or that the jewels even belonged to her.'

'I am told the girl is happier with her grandmother than with her mother.' The Chief Magistrate sat back to watch his words take effect.

'My wife is anxious to have her child beside her now that she can provide an adequate life.' Demonteguy gave a nervous laugh. 'If I were granted legal custody, I would make it worth your while. Some fine diamond buttons are included in the inheritance.'

'I believe the case is scheduled in the Cutcherry within a few days. I will let you know my feelings upon the matter before then.' The Chief Magistrate stood up to take his leave.

His retinue of servants came forward as he emerged from Demonteguy's house. He climbed into the palanquin and was soon jolted forward at a smart trot in the direction of his home.

Demonteguy turned back into the house. He glanced only cursorily at Sati, still asleep on the sofa.

'Sit with her until she wakes,' he ordered Jaya, rage knifing between each word. He strode to the inner room, where Rita waited.

His wife bent before an open cupboard, red hair streaming about her shoulders. She started as her husband entered and hurried to shut the cupboard door. Something furtive alerted him. Demonteguy stepped forward and pulled back the door. He saw a narrow shelf had been constructed inside the cupboard. Upon it stood several small brass images and a framed picture of the ugly goddess Rita had worshipped before their marriage.

'I told you to keep your heathen gods out of my house.' Everything burst in his head. The evening's humiliation seemed but a link in a continuing conspiracy between his wife, her mother and his stepdaughter.

'Soon you will destroy me.' Demonteguy pushed Rita aside.

She recovered her balance and began to shout. 'Several times I have told you, but you do not listen. The spirits come to Sati and they are real. In Black Town such things are common. I am requesting only protection from the Goddess, I am not seeking to destroy you.'

Rita was exhausted; the evening had been a great strain. Terror at her daughter's possession still echoed through her. On top of everything, Mr Holwell had appeared unexpectedly to stare at her in a lewd manner. Although not disagreeable it had been inappropriate and Demonteguy had noticed. The Chief Magistrate's sudden appearance had released a flood of uncomfortable memories that she preferred to put behind her.

'I do not believe in such nonsense. The girl is hysterical but her strange moods serve our purpose. Had she done as instructed it would have been a profitable evening. Instead she has made us a laughing stock. Tomorrow Calcutta will talk of nothing else.' Demonteguy was incensed.

'We have awoken forces beyond our control,' Rita whispered.

'I do not want your Black Town hokum-pokum here in my house,' Demonteguy shouted.

'I will tell my mother to call the priest from the Kali Mandhir. Once before he rid Sati of an evil spirit,' Rita replied in a trembling voice.

'Let there now be an end to this,' Demonteguy exploded. Reaching suddenly into the cupboard he swept the brass figurines from the shelf. He ripped up the cheap picture of the Goddess before his wife could stop him.

'You do not know what you have done.' Rita immediately dropped to her knees before the paper scattered on the floor.

'I have rid my house of heathen trash, that is what I have done,' Demonteguy fumed.

Rita's fingers trembled as she gathered up the brass images and the shreds of paper. The Goddess's eyes and part of her nose stared critically up at her from a fragment. Rita's heart beat fast in terror. What her husband had done was unconscionable. The Goddess would not overlook such treatment but would seek to exact her revenge. Rita knew she must immediately speak to her mother; the old woman would know what to do.

'All things are done through the Goddess, you do not understand.' Rita was sobbing now.

'I will not listen to any more of this heathen mumbo-jumbo,' Demonteguy yelled, incensed.

'You are seeing only profit for us in Sati,' Rita shouted, changing the subject.

'Once we have that profit she can return to your mother,' Demonteguy announced. He loosened the stock at his throat and pulled off his wig. Without it his balding head reminded Rita of a plucked chicken.

'We have entertained both the Governor's wife and the Chief Magistrate in our home. Is that not a good thing?' Rita reminded him, drying her eyes.

'Indeed, it is all that can be said,' Demonteguy responded.

Perhaps all was not lost. He had no interest in the Governor's wife, but something had been established with the Chief Magistrate. If Holwell participated in his plan they would be tied irrevocably together. There was no one more powerful in Calcutta than the Chief Magistrate. The Governor's power came through his position, which could be overturned at any moment by Leadenhall. The Chief Magistrate's power came through his guile. Perhaps, decided Demonteguy, the evening had not been entirely wasted.

Old Jaya listened to the sounds of argument between her daughter and Demonteguy. She applied a damp cloth to Sati's temples and smoothed back the girl's wild hair. At times her granddaughter murmured in a troubled way, but did not surface into consciousness. Jaya stared grimly in the direction of Demonteguy's voice. Terrible feelings rolled through her. Why had Hatman Holwell come here tonight? What business had he and Demonteguy to discuss for so long on the veranda? She had watched them together, faces shadowed by the oil lamp, pale eyes agleam, weighing each other up. The feeling of vulnerability she had carried about for the last few days had grown to new proportions. She remembered the magistrate's rage at the sight of her only that morning, and turned hurriedly again to her prayer beads. The seeds that were sown in an individual's lifetime never failed to be harvested, if not in this life then in the next. She would pray again to the Goddess, for there was nothing She did not see. When it came time for the Chief Magistrate to reap his harvest of worldly deeds, the Goddess would remember.

CHAPTER FOUR

From a window Emily Drake looked out over the bastions of Fort William and was surprised at her trepidation. Beyond the fort, The Avenue, as far as she could see, was crowded with camels, horses and elephants, all colourfully adorned. In their midst moved ornate palanquins and a richly covered cart. Dust shrouded the scene in a yellow haze. The procession turned towards the house of the merchant Omichand.

'What is happening?' she asked the old ayah, who had been with her since childhood.

'A nobleman has arrived from Murshidabad.' Parvati craned her neck from the window, then squatted down again by the cradle, toe rings clinking on the floor.

Emily fanned herself with a handkerchief. The hot winds blew fire on the town and beat in the shutters like rain. She always kept one tattie rolled up for a view of the Hoogly and the bougainvillaea she had planted on the balcony. She had no desire for the tame blooms of Europe, so fashionable in Calcutta. They did not remind her of home. Home was India for Emily Drake; she had never been to England. She had missed a garden most of all since the move into Fort William. Only the pots of bougainvillaea sustained her, overflowing the balcony, trailing bright magenta and orange. Grey

45

bricks, bugle calls and the drill of soldiers circumscribed her day. She rarely left the fort. To leave it was to invite hurt.

Beside her the baby whimpered. Emily placed a hand on the cradle, rocking it back and forth. Parvati moved forward to take over, croaking the discordant ditty with which she had once put Emily to sleep. In a far corner crouched the wet nurse, sent at the time of Emily's confinement by the redoubtable Lady Russell. Ill health forced Emily to use the woman's services against her best intentions. When the baby refused to settle, she beckoned to the woman, a young girl of twenty, neat in white muslin but with a vacant stare.

'Bibiji, visitors have come.' A servant entered the room and Emily rose in anticipation. There was a faint smirk on the servant's face; the Governor's private apartments were not usually the haunt of the riff-raff of Calcutta. Emily Drake knew the thoughts that passed through his mind. She sensed he did not approve of her; in some way she was not *pukka*. Arrogance was needed for the role of Governor's wife, and this she could not summon. The more arrogance displayed by employers, the more respect it produced in servants, according to her husband. It was he who had aspired to their present position; it had not been her wish at all. The wet nurse took the baby and Emily made her way to where her visitors waited.

She entered the room apprehensively, testing the air for intensity, glancing into the shadows for light. She gave only a cursory nod to Rita Demonteguy, her eyes fixing at once on Sati. For a moment she stopped in doubt. In the spacious room the girl seemed of no more substance than the saplings that lodged in the crumbling walls of Fort William. Before Emily there was only the empty room, the naive, shrinking girl and her vixen-like mother. It had seemed so different the other night.

It must have been the mother who had forced her to wear the garish, brightly trimmed gown, thought Emily. The girl fiddled with the ribbons at her neck, as if she would tear them away. Upon her wrists were glass bangles, at her neck a talisman such as Indian women wore. A gold nose-stud gleamed in the dim room. These

46

accessories contrasted strangely with the ill-fitting European dress. She appeared neither eastern nor western but a strange hybrid creature that struggled to be born. Her thin, dark face bore little resemblance to the brazen voluptuousness of her mother. Nor, except for her yellow eyes and tortoiseshell hair, could Emily find the genes of her English father. In contrast, the mother exuded the essence of a commodity. Rita Demonteguy's rouged cheeks, kohl-lined eyes and mane of hennaed hair appeared more appropriate to a *nautch* girl. The sweet, sticky perfume of attar of roses emanated from her. Her dress was of a glowing pink that flattered her honeyed skin. It must have been chosen by Demonteguy, Emily decided; such an eye for line could not be part of Rita Demonteguy's learning. The women diffused the essence of Black Town. Its tastes, smells and teeming vulgar life seemed suddenly to fill the room. To Emily Drake this sudden cracking of her silent world was not unwelcome. The flesh of her childhood expanded suddenly within her, like a dried fruit dilating in water. The river near her home was before her again, the sweet juice of the sugar cane wetting her tongue as she ran free with the servant's children. She thrust away the memories. They had no place in her present life and only impeded her further.

She returned her gaze to Sati, trying to find in the shuttered quality of her face the raucous creature that had mesmerised a crowd. Sati appeared more prey than predator now, more wistful than wild, more trusting than transformative. The girl was coiled deeply within herself and exuded nothing. Emily Drake gave a puzzled shrug; disappointment filled her. Perhaps the events in Demonteguy's home had been no more than a hypnotic dream. She had heard such a cloak of magic could be thrown by some adepts upon a crowd as to make hundreds hallucinate, but this girl, no more than fifteen, showed little maturity. The rough voice that still echoed in Emily's ears could not belong to her. It must have been a clever trick. India abounded with tricksters: fakirs and fanatics, snake charmers, spies, God-men, shamans and all manner of charlatans. The information the girl had spewed out the other night was not difficult to come by. Who in Calcutta did not know the gossip of Emily's marriage to her former brother-in-law? At these thoughts fatigue settled upon her.

'There has been a mistake. Things are not as I thought . . . There is refreshment in the other room. Please rest there a while before you go.' She turned towards the window and the blaze of bougainvillaea.

'You have called Sati here because of your sister. Now when you see her you do not believe Sati was saying all those things. But any time she can summon up those spirits. She will do it for you now.' Rita Demonteguy was all shrill persuasion.

Already the vision of herself dining at Fort William was slipping rapidly away. The terrible scene on her mother's Black Town doorstep only days before, watched by neighbours, chickens and watermelon vendors, became horribly clear once more. That tug of war for the girl and her gift, Rita saw now, was a fight for her own survival in White Town.

'They will not come just like that.' Sati pulled away from her mother's grasp.

'What are you saying? They came the other day with so many people watching.' Rita pushed Sati into a chair.

'Oh, please . . .' Emily protested, but Rita Demonteguy held up a hand authoritatively. Already Sati was covering her face, attempting to obey her mother.

For some moments the women stood side by side watching the girl's bowed head and hunched shoulders. At each slight trembling of her body an expression of triumph seeded itself in Rita's eyes and then faded as nothing happened. At last Sati straightened.

'I cannot do it. They do not hear me.'

'You *will* do it.' The expectation on Rita's face turned to anger. She leaned over Sati, whispering in her own language, 'Pretend, fool. Like the other day.'

Emily Drake, from her wild childhood, understood something of that language. At Rita's words she took a step forward and called for the servants.

'I have seen enough. I want you to go. I will not have her pretend,' Emily protested.

'Sometimes, when she pretends, they decide to visit her,' Rita answered with a shrug.

'Bibiji . . .?' Servants quickly entered the room at the sound of argument.

'Get out,' ordered Rita, turning upon them.

'You are in *my* house,' Emily retorted, stunned at the woman's audacity.

'They are disturbing my daughter. Just now her spirit people are coming to her, as you desire, and your servants rush in. How do you think the spirits must feel, forced to appear before monkey servants?' Desperation directed Rita.

'It is all right.' Emily weakly echoed Rita's order and the servants backed away.

'Now,' commanded Rita.

'Oh,' Sati breathed. She began to sway and clutch her stomach. She remembered little of her attacks and was uncertain now of how to behave.

'I am Jane.' Anxiety made her voice a trembling pipe. This name, she had been instructed, was the magic word. She had been told how Emily Drake's dead sister had appeared the night of the seance, and the effect it had had on the Governor's wife.

'I am Jane.' She could think of nothing more to say, yet felt something further was needed. In panic she left her chair and began to run about the room, hands held out before her. Rita Demonteguy stood a distance away, looking pleased. Mrs Drake wore a frown of confusion.

'Jane.' Above Sati the rafters of Fort William disappeared into the gloom. A sparrow flew in beneath the half-furled blind and beat its wings against the wall. At last it flew up to the rafters and perched on a beam. A great candelabra hung from the centre of the ceiling; Rita stood beneath it. Sati continued to dance about the room, wishing she too was a bird and could fly up to the candelabra. Then, from that inaccessible perch, she would send down enough foul droppings to cover her mother in a mountain of lime.

She whirled past the furled blind of the balcony but was brought to a halt by surprise. She had caught a glimpse of Durga in a forest of flowering shrubs, swaying about with ugly laughter. Durga had gone as suddenly as she had appeared, melting into the bougainvillaea. Sati was left to create her own mischief. She started off again.

'Jane. Jane,' Sati shouted.

'Hate you. Hate you,' she silently whispered as she danced past Rita, swallowing the words under her tongue. Above her the bird twittered.

'Hate her.' Suddenly the words coughed loudly out of her, as if someone had thumped her on the back. In a corner she saw Durga again and knew it was she who had thrown the words into the room.

Durga stretched out a hand from the shadows. Immediately pictures tumbled about in Sati's mind, of the red, blue and yellow glasses, of Demonteguy's garlic-tinged breath on her face as he had bent to instruct her. She felt again the pressure of her mother's hand pushing her down into an armchair before the pale candlelit faces. She ran to where Durga hid in the shadows, but Durga had disappeared.

'Hate her.' Now, even if she tried to swallow the words, they were tugged out of her. A luminous energy swirled through Sati; she was Durga's thoughts, the deserts she walked and the fiery winds that blew through her fingers. Durga spewed out of her like a firework; there was no way to contain her.

Emily Drake drew a breath, unable to evaluate what she saw. She smelled the vanish of fakery and yet, as she stared at the whirling girl, something quickened in her own veins. As if she herself was drawn towards a transformation. The girl seemed not to know herself. She had entered a state of ecstasy in the way that shamans, through dance and drum, are pulled deep into themselves. The girl spun around, releasing strange sounds, stamping her feet as if the rhythm of her dance drew her across a magical line into another realm. A wild energy spiralled from her, filling the room, reaching out to Emily Drake. Something formless seemed then to find shape within Emily. A sudden indefinable longing overwhelmed her, and took her by surprise. Where this powerful, bittersweet emotion sprang from and what it encompassed she could not explain, but her foot moved, as if she would dance after the girl. She controlled herself.

Once, in the house by the river of her childhood, she had gone with the servant's children to the hut of a shaman in the nearby village. This old crone had frightened Emily, for as she entered the hut, the woman had fastened upon her. The servant's children had crowded about, giggling and whispering. The dark hut had smelled of dung and mustard oil, chickens entered and pecked about. A thatched roof held the heat and released it around them. Emily's heart beat fast before the old woman, who sat cross-legged on the earthen floor. The woman's hair was matted and wild, strange animal noises escaped her, merging with the clucking of chickens. She drew Emily forward, gnarled black fingers curling around her arm. Then the old crone had begun to rock about, her eyes rolling up until only the whites were visible. Emily thought of the boiled eggs that had lain on her plate at breakfast. The woman rocked faster and faster. The strange grunts became the hissing of snakes, the squeaking of bats, the whistling of the wind. Emily tried to pull away but the old woman strengthened her grip. The wild energy that knocked about within her seemed to shake itself free. The woman seemed to grow tall and smooth-skinned; her boiled-egg eyes protruded from her head. The force loosed within the hut seemed to enter Emily, flowing hotly through her from the old woman's palms. The shaman still gripped her, fingers kneading rhythmically. Small as she was, Emily knew then that she had entered a crack between worlds, a place of miracles and imaginings. Her very substance ran free, dissolved. She was nothing but this inner knowing, ageless and older than the old crone, the source of the seen and hidden worlds; the source of her very self.

Suddenly, the woman had grown quiet and slumped in a heap. Emily's body stilled. She saw she was alone in the hut with the woman, and turned to stumble outside. The servant's children waited there. Fearful now of adventure, they drew back at the sight of Emily. Her feet seemed not to touch the ground but to move her fluidly forward. Her hair streamed against the sky. The leaves and trees, the dark dung soil, the song of birds and the flow of the river all now seemed manifest in her. For hours she lived in a daze, telling no one of the experience. She lay on her bed and let the mercurial feelings stream through her. Eventually her body ceased its thrumming. Once more her instincts turned inwards, like the petals of a flower at the end of day. The thunder passed, the flood dried. She no longer gazed at the world through a thousand eyes. Soon she was left with only the memory. Soon that too passed and she forgot the inexplicable adventure. Until this moment, before this strange girl.

Sati began to skip faster. Her head was full of whispers. Durga flamed within her until it felt as if the flesh fell away from her bones. On and on she whirled. The walls of the room disappeared. Durga was rapturous and shrieked with laughter, feeding on her own wildness. With a sudden twist Durga reached down and pulled up from the depths of Sati a further stream of foul words. Words absorbed from her mother's and grandmother's bawdy collections slipped from Sati's mouth like silk pulled through a ring. She chanted them like an invocation, her eyes riveted on her mother. All the words were aimed at Rita like a constant battering of small, sharp stones. *Hate her. Hate her.* Durga's laughter swelled in her head, like the beat of a drum with which she must keep pace. *Hate her. Hate her.*

Unaware of this silent drum, satisfaction grew on Rita's face as she watched her daughter dance about. The filth that poured from Sati's lips was as familiar to her as the raw taste of *paan* in her mouth, and lacking in true impact. To Rita things appeared to be going well. She turned and saw at once that she was mistaken in her judgement. In

Mrs Drake's face the colour was high, and a strange light burned in her eyes.

'See, she has made the spirits come, just as I told you,' Rita assured her.

'This is not how it was the other night. You told her to pretend.' Emily took hold of herself. The memories of shamans and her own yearnings should not blind her to the facts. She tried not to hear the vulgar words unreeling from the girl.

'That is not correct. The spirits have hold of her, just like a puppet. How otherwise could a young girl know so many bad words?' Rita protested loudly.

All Emily wanted now was for this harlot to leave. Rumour had it that half the men in Calcutta had lain between her legs. She only hoped Roger was not amongst them. But anything was possible and she was too tired to care. Life was like a narrow tunnel with the wind behind her, blowing her on.

'Go, please.' Emily turned to the window, her eyes on the Hoogly. She must free herself from the inexplicable hold the girl seemed to have on her. She had been drawn into the imaginings of an unstable child.

'Go? The girl brings your dead sister to you and you ask her to go?' Rita exploded. Anger gave her the courage to despise the Governor's wife.

As she spoke there was a crash. Sati had whirled into a Chinese vase perched on a marble base. She sat splayed on the floor, fragments of china about her. Rita ran to her but Sati shook herself free of her mother and dabbed at a cut on her wrist. The anger was hot in her face and her eyes were wild and liquid. Emily watched from a few feet away. She made no attempt to go near the girl. Sati was not the exhausted creature of the other night, drained of normal life. It took all Emily's strength to battle with the shame of knowing that she had been taken in by impostors. And yet confusion still filled her. A forgotten vein had opened within her. She stared at Sati's bent head as she sucked at the hurt on her wrist. Even now something about the girl cut through her anger and left her perplexed. When she looked at Sati she was filled with regret. The mother was another matter: gold-digging Black Town trash. She rang for the servants.

'See to them, a bandage, refreshments, whatever they need, then escort them out,' Emily instructed when a bearer entered, hardening herself and turning away.

'Give some money for her effort. We are coming so far, paying for a palanquin, exhausting ourselves for you. It is taking everything from her to summon up the spiritis. They feed on her, drain her dry.' Rita's voice flapped about hysterically.

Emily nodded and left the room, returning with some coins.

Even as they departed, Emily's mind refused to quieten down. She imagined the girl seated in a palanquin, imagined her journey on the road as Fort William grew gradually distant. Now, about her, the room was silent, nothing intuitive beckoned, no powerful residue remained. And yet her eyes still turned over shadows, seeking what lay behind. The girl's absence seemed only to heighten her presence in some unfathomable way. Why should she follow where the girl led? Why did the wildness of her face during that strange rhythmic dance not fade from her mind? She was filled by a sense of loss.

Yet even as she settled in a chair she saw that whirling, instinctual being, her skirts full, her hair blowing free, her chant a rhythm from the past, disembodied yet immediate. The root of light and the coil of darkness were centred within the girl. Emily knew there was also a place within herself where that same instinctual force resided. She understood her longing now, and her sense of loss.

The sounds of the fort and of the town came distantly to Emily. The lowered tatties dripped from their frequent dousing of water but failed to cool the high-ceilinged room. From her chair Emily stared at the river beyond the bougainvillaea balcony. Upon the water floated barges stacked with hay, rice or animals. A large raft ferried crowds of people back and forth. Great Indiamen were anchored in midstream and pleasure boats floated nearby. Corpses, discarded as easily as empty cocoons, also made their journey with the river to the distant sea. And there was something indefinable about the swift-running Hoogly, chasing towards its death and rebirth beyond a far horizon. There was no piety or profanity that the river did not know, and it treated both equally. It absorbed the ashes of murderers and witnessed birth on its banks. This wisdom it finally spilled into the sea. In heretical moments Emily sometimes thought God could well take the shape of the sea. She drew more strength from the river than from any church sermon, although she admitted this to no one. Beneath the river ran a silence deeper than the ocean that she listened to each day.

She had not always been like this. Once her blood had coursed through her like the river, with the same longing for the wild. Now, in the mirror she hated to acknowledge her face, marked by lines of ennui and a miserable existence. She still saw the nut-coloured skin and bare feet of an earlier creature. Six years of marriage had turned her from a defiant brown woman into an ethereal ghost. At these thoughts a sense of mourning filled her. Not a shadow remained of that earlier woman; it was impossible to know where she hid. It was enough now to know she did not love her husband, that in her mind he still belonged to Jane. She felt a kindness for him, but little more. For days they barely spoke. He relieved his frustrations in the grog houses, which did not help his reputation. She envied the luxury of his easy relief while she remained locked in herself. Duty calcified her.

Emily had grown up near Bombay on a large indigo farm that her father, John Coates, managed for the Company. The English population was negligible in the nearby town and Mr Coates was absent for weeks at a time. This had been a depressive weight upon her mother, who never ventured beyond her own malaise or the shadowy rooms that held her. The proper care of her daughters defeated her. It was the ayah, Parvati, who played the role of mother. It was to her that Emily ran after a fall, it was she who dispelled a fear of the dark even as her tales of gods and monsters sank easily into

Emily's mind. And Emily had played with Parvati's own children as if they were her kin. Their mother's thin pleas had pulled dutiful Jane to her side, but had meant nothing to headstrong Emily. Jane had tended their mother, embroidered, read and played the pianoforte. At her mother's side she had learned thrift, how to deal with thieving servants and keep an eye on the stores. She was five years older than Emily, from whom no such responsibility was required.

Some learning had been necessary, so their mother had roused herself to teach. Intermittently there had been governesses but nobody stayed for long. Emily had spent much of her childhood running wild in the sun with Parvati's children, only slightly lighter in hue than they. On the banks of the river she had watched the fishermen bring in their catch, her legs scratched by thorns, her feet bare and callused. She had thrived on the food in the servants' quarters and spoken the rough lilt of their tongue. On the banks of streams she had made whistles from leaves, climbed trees for mangoes and green almonds, cleaned her teeth chewing a stick of *neem*. Under the trees she had ripped off her skirts and run about in her shift, free to trap fish in her long-fingered hands. The sunset had flamed in her eyes as it lit the river. In those days her soul had run free. It had been easier for her mother to let her go than to find the stick of discipline. During her father's brief periods at home he had seen Emily for mere moments. All he had complained about was the state of her complexion.

Emily was fifteen when their mother died, Jane a mature twenty. It soon struck Mr Coates that an indigo farm was no place to bring up young women, and that Jane was already beyond marriageable age with no suitable man in sight. She was twenty-two by the time Roger Drake appeared.

He came to assess the farm for the Company. On his arrival Mr Coates began to woo himself a son-in-law. From the point of view of Roger Drake, the financial terms of Jane's marriage settlement were what he immediately needed. His future bride was plain, but he kept to the bargain. Yet against his will his eyes at times wandered to the sun-streaked sister, whose body struck restless postures. She held his gaze boldly, unafraid.

After the marriage, Emily had accompanied Jane and her husband back to Bombay. Jane had insisted her sister live with them; there were eligible men on the loose in Bombay that Emily might snare. They knew besides that their father kept the company of an Indian woman, set up in a home of her own with a brood of his half-caste children. He preferred to spend his time there, and was glad responsibility for his daughter now rested with Roger Drake. The sisters had taken Parvati with them, for her family was grown.

From the beginning the marriage was a tepid affair. The convenience of the arrangement was all that held it together. Soon, as if by silent agreement, Roger Drake crept into Emily's bed, leaving his frigid but dutiful wife. Brown-skinned Emily, her colour now fading beneath a wealth of petticoats, could still burst at a touch into wildness, however coarse that touch might be. She was heedless to anything but her own life force. Now, too late, she knew Roger was but the mirror in which she had seen herself. From the high-ceilinged rooms of Fort William Emily stared at the fast-flowing river.

Rita Demonteguy hailed a palanquin from a group waiting outside the Governor's house. The runners heaved themselves up from where they squatted, hawking and spitting red betel nut juice. Rita climbed first into the palanquin, Sati fitting herself as best she could into the remaining space.

'So clever you are. Because of you, one more time I am insulted in front of White Town people. That Mrs Drake will tell everyone about us,' Rita grumbled as they left Fort William.

Despite her disappointment, Rita was aware the spirits had deserted her daughter and left her bobbing helplessly like a cork upon the waves. It did not do to play too clever with the supernatural. Rita swallowed in trepidation.

'I have a headache. I need *paan*,' she announced as they passed out of Fort William. 'Find a *paanwallah*,' she instructed the runners.

They stopped a short distance later along the fort walls where an old man sat with his leaves and condiments. He parcelled ingredients neatly into a leaf and handed the *paan* into the palanquin. Rita ordered the runners to proceed and leaned back in the litter, mulching the *paan* against her cheek, where it made an unsightly bulge. She could not do this when her husband was around. He objected to the aromatic smell and the unsightly manner in which the betel nut stained her mouth. He sulked for hours if he caught her at it and demanded that she unlearn her ways. The tangy fragrance of the *paan* soon filled the palanquin and Rita revived. As her energy returned, the sight of her daughter, bunched up beside her in the swaying litter, irritated her once more. That self-contained expression, those critical eyes, connecting to silent thoughts, disturbed her. There was no way of knowing what went on in Sati's head. And now Rita was uncomfortably aware of her daughter anew. There was no explanation for the strange happenings of the other night, except that a spirit had entered Sati. Demonteguy refused to believe in such things, but Rita knew spirits when she saw them; everyone in Black Town did. In their gleaming White Town the Hatmen were lacking in any deep knowledge, clinging only to their one paltry God. Rita continued to stare at Sati as if seeing her for the first time. She knew so little about her daughter that it was difficult to believe she had produced her. A shadow of fear passed through her as she met Sati's reproachful eyes.

The palanquin bearers turned to take the narrow road beside the Ditch along which, on the night of the seance, Holwell had made his way to Rita's house. As they approached the White Town cemetery, they passed an imposing home of balustrades and balconies. It rose up like a tiered wedding cake, thickly iced with *chunam*. A large garden surrounded the house, half formal, half wild, with flowering trees, coarse-fingered palms and beds of canna lilies. To one side the Hoogly flowed into the Maratha Ditch, beginning its route about White Town. Rita stared at the house with interest, leaning out of the palanquin.

'That is Mr Holwell's house,' she said, nudging Sati with her foot. Rita had never visited the Chief Magistrate's home; he had always come to her during the days of their relationship. The sudden sight of Holwell's residence brought disconcerting emotions. The power she had felt as she straddled the Chief Magistrate at the time of their relationship she had rarely experienced again. He had personified more than his money or his meagre, tumescent organ. She had pinned him down and drawn out of his body the life sap of the man. There had been little physical about her satisfaction as she rode him voraciously to a climax. Every time she heard him groan his relief it was as if the town in which he lived splintered about her feet. He could not do without her.

At the mention of the Chief Magistrate's name a shadow passed over Sati's face. His tall, gaunt frame and expressionless face had made a fearful impression on her. At the time Mr Holwell had been a visitor to her mother's house, Sati had been living there as well. Jaya had been ill at that time and unable to care for her granddaughter as usual. The Chief Magistrate had reminded Sati of the adjutant storks, watching her from his small grey eyes behind the beak of his nose. Rita had been sharp and impatient with Sati, unwilling to be burdened with her child when her house was filled by admirers. Sati had felt herself an obstruction, but to what she could not say. She always seemed somewhere she should not be, at home when she should be at play, at play when she should be asleep. The toothless crone her mother had kept as an ayah had pinched her relentlessly. And there were the visitors. Gentlemen from White Town and sometimes Black Town seemed always to be coming and going. Each night on her pallet Sati listened to the tread of their feet across the room outside and their voices mingled with that of her mother. The house was not large and the sounds that came to her contoured things she could not explain. It had been the silences that frightened her most. Mr Holwell had stayed in her mind because of the manner in which he stared at her if ever she showed herself.

He had been there, she remembered, on her twelfth birthday. It was soon after that day that everything had started. Suddenly, objects in the room had moved about with a life of their own. A china ornament had flown past her and crashed against the wall. A book had lifted itself from a table. As she lay on her narrow pallet a hand had seemed to move across her body although she was alone. Then the voices began. Her behaviour became so strange that Rita soon returned her to Jaya. Her grandmother had at once called an expert on these matters. The holy man gave Sati a foul ash to eat and took money for some prayers. Afterwards he beat Sati with a bundle of twigs until she screamed for mercy. Eventually the priest announced that the spirit had departed. The voices stopped. For a long time there was nothing.

'Did you see Mr Holwell's house?' Rita asked again. 'You were so rude to him the other night. But he is a pig, he deserves it. All the time he was looking at me, seeing me like I was naked. He was so frightened by the things you said that he could not move.' Rita began to laugh. Her open mouth, still full of *paan,* was like a bloodied wound.

'I remember nothing,' Sati replied. Even if she pushed back inside her mind, she came up against a curtain. Rita looked at her strangely and did not pursue the conversation. In the palanquin there was silence.

At this hour the narrow road was congested with Black Town's traffic. Wide-horned buffalo laboured with carts piled high with vegetables and sacks of rice. A herd of goats on their way to the slaughterhouse trotted bleating amongst a detachment of sepoys off duty from the Fort William garrison. The soldiers pushed their way forward, battering the animals in their path with long wooden sticks. They stared into Rita's palanquin and made coarse remarks, their eyes on her cleavage. She yelled at them in language learned from her mother, raucous as the street. Her own father had been a half-caste Portuguese sepoy, although she barely remembered him. The sepoys stepped back in shock and then, recovering their wits, replied in like vein until the litter drew ahead.

Sati hid her face in shame, her knees drawn up beneath her chin in the cramped confines of the palanquin. She saw with relief that they had reached the bridge that would carry them back into Black Town across the Maratha Ditch. Soon White Town and its painful taunts would be left behind. To make the passage from Black Town to White Town across the wide bamboo bridge was to enter another dimension. However many times she made that journey, White Town still intimidated; its spacious tanks and park, its gleaming buildings set in huge gardens blazed with an unremitting glare that forced her to shut her eyes. Carriages and palanquins revolved through the streets, churning up dust, pushing her to the side of the road. Fashionable women in fashionable hats gazed at her dismissively. The blinding white walls of the town seemed only to echo the arrogance of its inhabitants. The place united to refuse her. Only the adjutant birds, perched in trees or massed on buildings, surveyed the town fearlessly. Beneath bald heads their beaks, three feet long over crinkled red chins, moved before them like swords. The birds had a presence that flattened all differences; they patrolled both towns as one.

Sati was bumped about uncomfortably in the palanquin as the runners negotiated the crowded bridge. She stared down at the slimy green water moving below, filling the Ditch like a sluggish reptile, and touched the amulet at her neck. Within it was an incantation to the Goddess, who must be awakened to guide her across this place of passage.

As they reached the other end of the bridge, Sati turned to stare at the retreating view of Fort William. The sad face of Emily Drake came before her again. The Governor's wife had been displeased. For some reason Durga had deserted Sati just when she needed her most. She wondered if she would ever see the Governor's wife again. Then the view of Fort William was suddenly lost and she was sucked into a different world.

CHAPTER FIVE

Jaya shut the door of her hut and began the short walk to her cousin's home. Govindram lived only a few alleys away, but his house was unlike much of Black Town. It was built on two storeys from small red bricks and faced inwards onto a courtyard. The house had been built with a loan from his master, the great merchant Omichand. It was one of the few *pukka* houses in Black Town and reared up amongst the mud-walled huts. It was not faced with *chunam,* as were the houses in White Town. Rain and humidity stained its walls, weeds lodged between the bricks, and upon the flat roof string beds could be seen. Goats grazed before its door. Govindram was a first cousin of Jaya's, as close as a brother, and she spent much time in his house. Without him her fate would be worse than a widow's. His position of importance in Omichand's business gave him much influence in Black Town and gave Jaya in turn a vicarious standing amongst her many neighbours.

As she approached Govindram's house she saw the gate was open. His wife, Mohini, stood outside, feeding the sacred cow led around all day for this purpose by an emaciated woman in a filthy green sari. Jaya stopped beside Mohini, who held a round tray piled with dry *dhal* and stale sweetmeats. Mohini took no notice of Jaya; she was absorbed in an argument over the price of a bundle of grass with which to feed the animal. The cow-woman's voice rose raucously. The grass was strapped to her back and trailed in long wisps about her. Since Mohini could not refuse to feed the cow for fear of the ill fortune that might ensue, the cow-woman had the advantage. But the day was incomplete for Mohini unless it rolled forward upon dispute. Eventually she turned with a nod of acknowledgement to Jaya, then yelled through the open gate to her husband.

'She is here again. She is your relative, speak with her. I have no time to waste.' Mohini pulled her sari further over her head so that her face was hidden.

Jaya ignored this rudeness and passed through the gate the *chowkidar* held open to face her cousin, Govindram. He rested upon a string bed in the courtyard, conversing with Sati, who sat cross-legged on a mat beside him.

'I am just now hearing about Sati's evening in White Town. Tell me why you permitted this disgraceful thing? They have tried to make money from her.' Govindram greeted Jaya with a frown. Since he and Mohini had no children, they felt proprietorial towards Sati, who, at fifteen, was the age a grandchild might have been.

'And why is she again dressed in your old rags? It is a shame to us all. Do I not give you enough money to clothe her? She should already be married with children about her,' Govindram scolded.

Sati wore a loose gold-edged *kameez* over wide trousers. The outfit was clearly one from Jaya's Murshidabad days, dug out of her old trunk. Sati's situation irked Govindram. Most girls were married at seven, entered their husband's home at twelve and bore a child before they were fourteen. Many girls of Sati's age were already widows. Soon, without even marrying, Sati's position would be the same as that of those discarded women. Govindram sighed loudly. He was a slight man beneath the bulk of his turban. A bushy moustache gave him authority, but he was younger than he appeared.

'So why do you not do something then?' Jaya retorted. The duty of wedding arrangements fell to Govindram as Jaya's only male relative.

The shame of her granddaughter's humiliating position was a weight Jaya had to bear every day. Her neighbours now openly wondered if Sati's *ferenghi* blood might not offer hope of marriage to a White Town sahib. It was well known that White Town women married when well past their prime. No one expected Sati to find a respectable alliance in Black Town. It was murmured that if she remained with her grandmother, destiny would deliver her to one of Calcutta's houses of ill repute. Jaya closed her ears to such whisperings and prayed harder to the Goddess.

Govindram sighed again and refrained from further comment. Given the reputation of her mother and grandmother, and Sati's own hybridity, what family would accept her? Besides, she was as tall as a man and unusual enough in colouring to provoke all manner of unflattering comment. A good dowry would be persuasive, but who would provide it except himself?

Sati shifted uncomfortably at this conversation but could not share their concern. The thought that she might not enter a bridal chamber or that no man would lift her veil caused her no disturbance. She belonged to no one but herself. She knew instinctively that her path was not the path of others. Her bones were filled with memories that she must follow to their ends. She touched the amulet at her neck. The dark moon might hide its light but the Goddess would be with her. It was She who eased the way from one realm to the next, through the perilous passage of life to death to life again. Through Her all things were created and were again dissolved.

Govindram gazed at Sati with an expression of tired concern. Her Indian attire was proof that Sati resided at present with her grandmother. The frilled muslin and ribbons of European fashion had recently become her identity if she was resident with her mother. It embarrassed Govindram to face the child when she was dressed in the foreign manner. There was nothing about her he recognised then; formality immediately stiffened him. And Sati too, in those strange clothes, was distant and withdrawn. It was as if she were two people who must inhabit the same body.

'He wishes to adopt me. I don't want to live with them. I want to stay here.' The words burst out of Sati.

'Who wishes to adopt you?' Govindram asked, his frown deepening.

'Demonteguy Sahib,' Sati answered, fidgeting with her bangles. The proposition of living permanently with her mother and Demonteguy filled her with unease. She would be forced to call the man 'Father'. Although she thought rarely of her own father, the idea of Demonteguy taking on that role filled her with distaste. She had no memory of her real father, who had died soon after her birth. Yet the legacy of his identity now set her firmly apart. All her life she had glimpsed him only in fragments. The large houses of White Town conjured him up. Sometimes on visits to the settlement she passed men in dark hats spilling from important buildings and knew that she almost touched him. His voice issued from bawdy taverns or echoed in the sails of Indiamen anchored in mid-stream. Unexpected things blew the feel of him through her. His essence lurked everywhere, untouchable, his ghost fading even as it appeared.

His name was Joseph Edwards, and his marriage to her mother had been short. He had taken Rita to England on the ship he captained. She had lived for some time in a boarding house near the docks while the ship was reloaded with cargo. On the return voyage Sati had been born. Since a ship was no place for a baby, Edwards left his wife and child behind when he next sailed from Calcutta. Within hours a fever caught him and he quickly sickened and died. He was fed to the waves three days' sail from the mouth of the Hoogly.

Govindram looked in enquiry at Jaya, who wore a dirty cotton sari, once white but now of an indeterminate colour, which she began to pull at in an agitated manner.

'Is this matter of adoption true? How can such a man adopt her? Why should Rita now want her back?' Govindram was puzzled. During Sati's growing-up, Rita had wanted only freedom from the responsibility of motherhood.

'It is true. You must give us your protection. That Demonteguy has made Rita mad. You think without reason I would come here, to bear your wife's insults? I have my self-respect,' Jaya replied.

The shadow of the mango trees beyond the house had lengthened to embrace them. Upon a wall monkeys waited to swoop upon food; in the sky sharp-eyed birds wheeled constantly. Beyond the wall urchins climbed mango trees to pull at the heavy fruit. The smell of soil and plantains, of excrement and hot mustard oil frying in the cookhouse rose up to fill Sati's nose. Thoughts of her father still occupied her mind.

She had only a single memory of him, woven for her by her mother. Rita had recounted the incident so often that it had entered Sati's consciousness as her own experience. She was floating above the earth, held high in her father's arms. Beneath her, spread upon the table, lay a map of the world. Her father had lowered her to the table and stabbed the map with a finger. Here, he had said, this is where you were born. His finger rested in the middle of an ocean, on a point where two lines met. To either side were continents where mountains, trees, people and histories massed upon the land. Her father pointed to a shape on the map that was her mother's country and to the island that was his own. Big or small, these places were defined by boundaries. Then her father's finger travelled back to her own source of being. No shape appeared to contain her. She stood alone, balanced precariously like a dancer upon the meeting of meridians. Beneath her father's finger there was nothing but the waves.

For years she had grappled with the meaning of her birth, in the middle of nowhere, at the crossing of two lines. She had sprung to life in a dispossessed place, far from her mother's great land and her father's tiny island. The knowledge hung suspended in her, like a bat in a tree through the blaze of day. At some hour this knowledge would awake, to live a life of its own invention. For now, that moment had not yet come. She hung suspended still, birthed neither in one world nor the other, pregnant with herself.

'Why are you sitting there like a blind creature? Go and help your

66

aunt. Just now she has gone to the cookhouse for refreshments,' Jaya interrupted Sati's thoughts. She was anxious to be alone with her cousin.

'I do not understand any of this,' Govindram sighed when Sati had gone.

'You do not understand because you do not listen,' Jaya complained. 'I told you everything last time I was here.'

'Then explain again.' Govindram spoke mildly. He reached for a box of *suppari* and chose a piece to chew upon.

'I have made my will, that is the root of the trouble,' Jaya burst out.

'Can a woman make a will?' Govindram looked at his cousin in surprise.

'In White Town such things are done. I went to a lawyer and paid much money. He was a *choor,* but everything is written down; it is legal now. There is a seal upon it,' Jaya replied.

'You are not about to die. Why are you doing this? And what do you have to leave? A few trinkets?' As far as Govindram knew, Jaya was destitute and lived on the charity he regularly dispensed.

'You know nothing.' Jaya ignored his question. 'How can I be sure my time is not coming soon? At this age such things enter our minds.'

'That is correct,' Govindram sighed. 'The one thing we can be sure of in this life is death.'

'Keep it with you.' Jaya pushed the heavily sealed document across the floor to him. 'In this town there are no secrets. How Demonteguy and Rita came to know of my will, I do not understand. Maybe it was that *badmash* scribe at the lawyers who told them. I have left everything to Sati, that is the trouble. I have not left my things to Rita. Oh no, not with that husband beside her now.'

Govindram scratched his head beneath his turban and refrained from further enquiries about his cousin's mysterious estate. Mohini returned to the courtyard with Sati. A servant followed with tumblers of sherbet and a plate of sweetmeats, which he placed before Jaya.

67

'Eat,' Mohini commanded.

Her sari had slipped and she pulled it forward again to cover her head in respect before her husband. It infuriated her that Jaya sat blatantly bareheaded before a male cousin older than herself. The end of Jaya's sari lay draped about her neck where it had fallen and she made no attempt to retrieve it. The hennaed ends of her pigtail faded into a head of white roots. In old age Jaya had lost all sense of propriety, Mohini decided. The teachings of childhood had worked themselves loose and hung as slackly about her as the rolls of flesh upon her body. Once that body and that face had been blessed and cursed in equal part with exceptional beauty. Mohini shuddered to think of the life Jaya had led. She no longer felt envy, only distaste. If she had her way her door would be shut to Jaya, just as other relatives had shut it. Only her husband's foolish sentiments forced her to keep it open. But she was fond of Sati. Mohini turned and walked off to supervise further household matters and Sati ran after her.

Jaya followed Sati's departure with a grim expression. 'I am bringing this lawsuit only for Sati's sake. I have a right to appear in the Mayor's Court. So many English husbands I have had. But that Hatman Holwell would not allow it.'

'What lawsuit are you bringing?' Govindram asked in sudden alarm.

'Do you understand nothing? For the custody of Sati, of course. If Rita and Demonteguy get custody, how will Sati inherit my things? They will take everything from her.' Her eyes brimmed with tears. 'My daughter is not a fit mother. Everyone knows that. Sati is happy with me.'

Govindram remained silent. Some parts of Jaya's tale began to clarify, yet he doubted she would be considered in White Town more suited to have custody of Sati than Rita. Whenever Govindram looked at Jaya now it was in fascinated horror that beauty could implode so conclusively. His own wife had merely faded and thickened, the process so gradual that he only now and then looked at her in mild disbelief.

'I knew no good would come from that marriage of Rita's,' Jaya burst out.

'You encouraged it,' Govindram reminded her.

'That Demonteguy is a sahib. I too, you remember, only married English sahibs,' Jaya argued.

Govindram refrained from reminding her that she had married common soldiers. One might even, he remembered, have been a sailor. And Rita's father was a half-caste Portuguese. How many other uncertain liaisons there might have been between his cousin's marriages he could not say. Such low-class men were not sahibs.

'Yes, Demonteguy is a sahib,' he sighed.

He had no wish to be reminded of Jaya's life story. All her troubles since he settled in Bengal had come to rest upon him. As children they had played together, brought up for a time in the same house in Delhi. Their families were not poor, but neither were they rich. Large dowries were out of the question. Jaya's great beauty had been used to secure her a widower husband of substantial wealth. The man had grown sons of Jaya's age, any of whom would have been more suitable as a husband. Jaya did not see her bridegroom until her wedding night and was shocked at the wizened man who came to her bed. He resembled an old dog at the end of a long bout of mange. Nobody else seemed to feel this way. They spoke of Jaya's luck at finding a rich husband. After the wedding, Jaya left with her husband for his home in Dacca.

Soon after this, Govindram had also married and left Delhi in the company of Omichand, for whom he already worked. In those early days the fat merchant was a seller of dried fruits and almonds and wished to try his luck in Bengal. Eventually they settled in Calcutta. After some time news reached Govindram in a roundabout way that Jaya's husband had ordered her from his house, divorced and destitute. She had been discovered in the arms of one of her stepsons. So shamed was Jaya's father by her behaviour that he refused to take her back. It was rumoured she had sought the protection of a famous singer. Next it was said she had entered the *zenana* of a nobleman in Murshidabad, sold into concubinage by the famous singer.

Govindram had already been in Calcutta some years when he found Jaya one day on his doorstep, already several times married and widowed. She had come to hear of him through the growing reputation of Omichand, and sobbed at the sight of him. He too had wiped his eyes in shock, for Jaya was greatly changed. The excesses of flesh and ravishment were already well in place. She had been the only woman to escape from the palace of Murshidabad during a bloody battle. Every woman in the nobleman's *zenana* had been slaughtered while Jaya hid in a chest of beaten silver. She had returned to the entertainment area of Calcutta and eventually married an English soldier of the lowest rank. From the moment she rediscovered him, Govindram had enabled her to escape her demeaning existence and live with dignity.

'Demonteguy did not want to make use of my Rita without marriage,' Jaya reminded Govindram.

'In this she is lucky,' Govindram agreed. After the death of Sati's father, Rita had lived on her own, hiring herself out as companion to several elderly ladies in White Town. Her small house on the edge of Black Town was also well known to the gentlemen of Calcutta. Many intimate friendships but no offers of marriage came her way until Demonteguy.

'My Rita is not as an Indian woman who must think of *suttee* or living a life like the dead. In the *ferenghi* world, widows remarry. I also have done it three times. Only my karma is bad, as you know. All my husbands are dead along with my other babies. English blood is not suited to this climate. Hardly did I marry my husbands than they got fevers and died. Only in Rita is my blood strong; it has kept her alive.' Jaya immersed herself in a new outburst of sobbing.

'I shall fight them in court.' She quietened suddenly. 'There was no trouble until this will.'

'Then why did you make it?' Govindram asked.

Soon Mohini and Sati returned, a trail of servants behind them carrying further edibles. Mohini fussed about her husband. 'Here is *prasad* from the Kali Mandhir. This afternoon I went there for you. It is time you also visited. Pray to the Goddess, it will take only a moment and please her,' Mohini ordered.

'We will also do a *puja* for Sati's health.' Mohini turned to Jaya.

'Then see it is done properly this time. Last time that *badmash* priest took only money and did nothing,' Jaya replied.

'How do you know he did nothing?' Govindram enquired.

'Because last time when you went to Murshidabad I gave money for a *puja* for your well-being and what happened? You came back sick from that place,' Mohini replied, pushing Jaya from the conversation.

'Murshidabad.' Jaya's eyes became dreamy with memory.

'What is so good about the place? When you lived there all you thought of was escape,' Mohini snapped.

'Some things were not so bad,' Jaya answered. Distilled by time, Murshidabad offered itself to memory now in a series of sensual images: clothes, jewels, caresses and the indolence of hot afternoons. There were the constant thrusting demands of the raja, the oiled hands of the masseuse and the perfume of unguents; flesh and its multifarious satisfactions had possessed the day and possessed her also. Above all his women, for a short time, the raja had desired her. At first she had fought these demands, but soon all she waited for, all she could think of, was that he should fill her body. Even now, as the flesh sagged about her, her insides were fired by the memory of those sensations. She could not explain this to a woman like Mohini.

'That is not what you told us,' Mohini replied. 'Before your eyes one hundred and twenty women were slaughtered while you hid in a trunk, and you say it was not so bad? I do not understand you.'

Jaya shrugged. It was useless to waste words on Mohini. She watched Govindram pick up her will and store it away in a small wooden chest, which he locked with a substantial key. She wondered if she should bring all her diamonds to Govindram to store safely for her in his home. But the thought of Mohini's sarcastic remarks abruptly ended this idea. She could imagine Mohini's expression if she ever saw the diamond jewellery Jaya had secured under her clothes as she fled the raja's palace.

Since that long-ago day she had managed, in one place or another, to hide the fabulous gems away. Now she had dug the treasure out of the mud wall of her hut behind which it had lain for so many years. None of her husbands had known of the existence of these rare gems, nor had they known of the raja or her incarceration in his seraglio.

The idea of a will had come to her suddenly and would not go away. The lawyer had demanded to see her assets so that he might weigh and list them correctly. After he had examined the diamonds, Jaya had re-buried them in the wall and gone immediately to pray at the Kali Mandhir, but the balance of things already seemed changed. Vulnerability stalked her. The gleam in the lawyer's eye as he turned her gems in his hand remained in Jaya's mind. Now she was forced to look constantly over her shoulder. She had never felt so exposed. Yet each time her eyes settled on Sati, the urgency of the matter overwhelmed her. There was nothing else in her life she could do for the girl. She looked up to the heavens as if for help, but saw only the white crescent of a waning moon in the still bright sky.

Sati sat down once more beside Govindram and met his solemn gaze. She saw her grandmother had been crying, although she had managed to finish the sherbet and the small plates of food set before her. On the wall above them two adjutant storks now perched where the monkeys had been chased away. There was comfort in the Black Town clamour, with its teeming lanes raw with stench and the odour of cooking between the closely packed houses. There was the soft shooting of greenery everywhere: bamboo, plaintain, mango and the pliant pampas grass. About cool ponds urchins splashed, women scrubbed laundry, and old men gossiped in the evening stretched out on string beds under the trees. Here kingfishers dived for minnows;

goats and buffalo came to drink. Lepers wailed for alms, women oiled their hair under the sun, shaking out a polished mass. Everywhere the press of bodies thronging the narrow serpentine lanes held Sati's life together. She could never be part of White Town; each step she took within that place threw her back upon herself. The pulse of Black Town throbbed deep in her veins, even if she was not to its liking.

She knew then that it was here she must stay. Although the blood of both towns ran in her veins, she saw that a choice was before her. Her mother, by marriage, had crossed a line to settle uneasily in an alien world. Yet wherever she went, whatever she did, however miscast, Rita carried the certainty of a past identity. She did not, like Sati, tread the soil of Black Town or White Town seeking a name with which to empower herself. She did not search for healing.

It came to Sati suddenly then. Just as she had been born where two lines met upon the ocean, so, where the seam of two cultures joined, there must be a crack. Thin as a hair, it ran right through her, denying her real wholeness. Yet it was through this crack, absent in those who grew all of a piece, that Durga squeezed. And in this place, like those cracks in the earth where springs take life, was something indestructible. Along that fault line within herself was a secret place of transformation. In that place she might at last be born, deep within herself. She looked up at the sky and saw the sun had set and the moon was but a sliver. Soon it too would roll from the earth to return again, reborn.

CHAPTER SIX

The Great Hall of the Durbar and its surrounding courtyard was ablaze with light. About the crowded place candelabra were massed like an exploding galaxy. Their radiance dispelled the night, tut could not illuminate the dwindling life of Alivardi Khan.

'See, he lies upon a bed,' Drake observed. 'It cannot be long.'

'This will be a last public view of the old man,' Holwell agreed, craning his neck to catch a glimpse of the shrivelled figure. Life flamed within the jewels upon the dying nawab.

'He is much shrunken,' Drake remarked. The old man resembled a mummified corpse he had once seen in Egypt.

'Any amount of pomp cannot amend that which must come to all men,' the Chief Magistrate observed.

'Nevertheless, he is a poor sight.'

'But an exceptional reign,' Holwell answered, unable to overcome a begrudging respect for Alivardi. 'Not like your other Moors; one wife and no drink or concubines. His *zenana,* they say, is filled with old women and the harems of those he has conquered. He touches none, but only offers sanctuary. For a Moor such behaviour is highly eccentric.'

'Not a life the grandson follows, for sure,' the Governor replied.

They stood within the huge courtyard, the precious inlay upon its walls agleam in the light of flares. The colonnaded hall, its arched walls open to the night, shimmering with mirrors and hangings of silk, lay up a short flight of steps before them.

Siraj Uddaulah sat some distance away, resplendent beside the supine old man. The light refracted upon his diamonds, rubies gleamed in his turban like pellets of frozen blood. Gold thread encrusted his robes in intricate patterns, set with precious stones. He was tall and hard-bodied, with a thin, ravaged face that, in repose, had the beauty of a woman. A face of weakness and hidden thoughts and unrestrained emotions. His eyes moved over the crowd, bored yet assessing. Something emanated from him, disquieting in its menace.

'An unstable fellow. Terrible tales are told of his cruelty,' Drake whispered.

'You cannot measure their heathen barbarism by our rules, for they have no rules in such matters,' the Chief Magistrate replied, his eyes upon the gleam of Siraj Uddaulah's jewels.

'Inbreeding results in unstable minds,' Holwell continued. 'Ali vardi has no son. Since his three daughters married their first cousins, Siraj Uddaulah is both grandson and great-nephew to Alivardi. The old man was besotted with the child and refused him nothing. The result is what you see.'

Although he spoke disparagingly, the Chief Magistrate, observing the pageantry before him, overwrought with ostentation, was aware of how little he could ever know of the convoluted life of the Murshidabad court. Here he was far from the centre of European power, and the dissipated depths of Murshidabad's intrigues were unchartable. He never liked these meetings with Bengal's nobles, dangerous, arrogant, arbitrary creatures, who looked upon him and his fistful of power as less than the sum of an ant. At the realisation of his paltry worth, the Chief Magistrate suddenly grew silent. The irritating whine of a mosquito bothered him more than he stirred the great body of India. He waved away in sudden rage a large moth that

75

fluttered about him. A great many winged creatures of the night flapped about the standing candelabra.

The air was perfumed with incense. Around him Murshidabad's noblemen spoke in a language he did not understand, underlining the Chief Magistrate's isolation. No place could be stranger than where he stood now, or more distant from all that was known. He remembered once, as a child, standing upon a beach, gazing at a boat far out upon the ocean. As it slipped from view over the horizon he had felt the strangeness of the phenomenon. He knew the craft sailed on, although he could see nothing. Now, remembering, confusion filled him. He had lived his adult life beyond that far horizon and was himself as good as dead to those who had stayed at home. And in this wretched place of exile he was no more than a transitional being, forced to live each day before the dense mass of India as if he faced his own shadow. Already the Chief Magistrate's linen was sodden beneath his serge coat at the extremity of his thoughts. He was glad to hear the Governor's voice returning him to reality.

'If the next nawab through all this interbreeding has holes in his head, we must expect less logic than ever from Murshidabad. It will not be easy with regard to Fort William's affairs.' Drake mopped his perspiring face with a handkerchief. The night simmered beneath the blaze of lights in the Hall of Audience.

'We must play our cards right. Siraj Uddaulah is full of bluff; not an ounce of real courage, unlike his grandfather,' Holwell answered.

'Let us make our way forward before the old man, bed and all, is taken away,' the Governor urged, for there seemed some indication that this might happen.

At a signal their band struck up, marching before them with pipes and drums. A detachment of red-coated soldiers, carrying the flag, followed to impress the court. Drake and Holwell made their way across the courtyard and up the steps to where Alivardi lay. The nobles drew back to observe them. Holwell held his head high as the sheen of silks and jewels slid past. As they drew near the royal dais, further progress was barred. Siraj Uddaulah held up a hand to deny them access to his grandfather.

The prince averted his eyes from the curled wigs of the Hatmen and stared at the chandeliers. He had no wish to recognise men he intended to wipe from the face of India. Within the opalescence of inlaid marbles and the fluid gleam of silks, the Hatmen moved in their heavy clothes, dark and stiff as a species of beetle. They embodied everything that was alien and unknown. With their upstart ways and naive minds they were dismissed by most with contempt. His grandfather's conciliatory policies had only encouraged these boastful men. Slowly, insidiously, like rot that begins at the edge of strong wood, these people had rooted themselves along the shore of the country. Although their Governor might come in pomp to Murshidabad, and in his own settlement assume the air of a deity poised between Heaven and earth, he was in truth an unexceptional man who had risen through the ranks. He was liable for dismissal or supercession with each dispatch from England. Siraj Uddaulah leaned back in his chair and continued to observe the chandeliers.

Seeing their dismissal, Drake and Holwell bowed carelessly; beside Siraj Uddaulah, Alivardi Khan appeared almost comatose. The old man's fair skin, proof of his Turkish origins, had a yellow pallor. His eyes were sunk deep in their sockets, his body wasted on the bone. A thin beard straggled over the jewels that weighed upon him like armour. The nawab opened his rheumy eyes as the Englishmen backed away. He turned to his grandson, whispering weakly to him.

Had they been able to hear the old man's words, the Governor and the Chief Magistrate might have had cause to congratulate themselves. As he strained his eyes to follow the progress of the retreating Hatmen, Alivardi Khan was possessed by a sudden clear vision that cut through his fading mind. He saw the Hatmen as one day possessing all of India. Words of warning rustled like dry leaves in his throat as he stared up at his grandson.

'Beware, my child. The Hatmen are like a hive of bees of whose honey you might reap the benefit. But if you disturb their hive they will sting you to death. Imagine a plain covered with grass. Should you set fire to it there is a chance of stopping its progress. But if you set the sea on fire, who can put that out? Such a fire would consume our whole world. Do not listen to proposals of violence.' A thread of saliva trickled from the old man's mouth.

Siraj Uddaulah continued to observe the dark-coated figures of the Hatmen moving amongst the crowd. 'They are dogs, to be kicked out of India on their backsides.' He looked defiantly at his grandfather. 'A slipper is all that is needed to govern them. Slap them with it whenever it is needed.'

'Do not forget the trade and silver bullion they bring,' Alivardi Khan cautioned, his voice a hoarse whisper. 'This we cannot do without. There must be balance in all things.'

Siraj Uddaulah looked away, his mouth hard. Upon his arm the old man's hand resembled the claw of a bird. Siraj Uddaulah knew the upstart Hatmen just as well as his grandfather. They abused the privileges they had been given to the detriment of local traders. Their taxes culled money from Bengal. He had an especial hate of Holwell. Since the man's appointment as Chief Magistrate and Zamindar, coupled with his seat upon the Fort William Council, he had accrued unprecedented power.

Upon his promise to Leadenhall to raise revenue, the Chief Magistrate had looked for ways to revise the existing taxation. He had employed a new structure of payment in the Cutcherry. He had done away with corporal punishment, imposing instead stiff fines. And as the issuer of not only trading permits but permits to farmers to till the land, and the sealer of leases and rents on all such land, the opportunities for bringing the resentful to court were limitless. His commercial agents toured the villages exacting dues, dispensing privileges, constructing monopolies of power. Even prostitution was no longer ignored but fruitfully taxed by the Chief Magistrate. He had quickly raised the yearly revenue of the settlement, as the Company demanded. Leadenhall was pleased with him, but the Hall of Audience at the Murshidabad court was crowded each day with the complaints of impoverished merchants and shopkeepers. Bengal's coffers were empty from years of warring with the Marathas, protecting the state and the lives of those Englishmen within it. And all the while the English grew more and more replete, like animals glutted upon a fat carcass. Siraj Uddaulah narrowed his eyes at the retreating Hatmen.

At the back of the hall a sudden disturbance began. The great crowd cleaved in two. The merchant Omichand, his retinue of attendants spilling about him in untidy fashion, waddled forward upon his short legs. He gave the impression of an ornately wrapped moving parcel, as wide as it was high. Servants followed him carrying bamboo cages containing a two-headed cat and a rare peacock, gifts for Alivardi's menagerie. It annoyed the Chief Magistrate that they had been forced to travel to Murshidabad in tandem with the greatest rascal in Calcutta. His lion-shaped craft had dogged their houseboats all the way up the river. And now, at court, his presence drew more attention than the Englishmen. Siraj Uddaulah reluctantly beckoned Omichand forward, much to the Chief Magistrate's disapproval. White Town was not even sure of the fat merchant's real name. Rightly or wrongly it rolled off the tongue as Omichand. No other Indian was allowed residence in White Town, but since Omichand had financed the building of the majority of Calcutta's great mansions, there was no way to deny him.

As agent for the East India Company, Omichand's hand steered all official business and the buying of native goods. His money brokered White Town's private deals. Gamblers at whist or five-card loo whose world was demolished in an evening were the next morning firmly enmeshed in Ominchand's net. Young writers of the East India Company, hot after fortune but bereft of capital, were forced to turn to him. The Company paid its servants no more than a pittance but condoned the profit of private trade that did not impinge upon them. This kept down all Company outgoings to a sensible level. It also allowed the scent of fortune to lure into employment young men who might otherwise catch a whiff of death from along the coast of India. Omichand understood this devious manner of recruitment, not far removed from his own turn of mind. Siraj Uddaulah frowned in resignation; he could tolerate Omichand little better than the Chief Magistrate, yet he ordered the bamboo cages placed before his grandfather, who held the fat merchant in high esteem.

'Already Siraj Uddaulah controls this court,' the Chief Magistrate growled, assessing the atmosphere once they were a safe distance away. He had watched Omichand's stumbling progress towards Alivardi Khan with dismissive amusement. His derision of the fat merchant was at least a familiar sensation and he clung to it now like ballast in a choppy sea. The sinuous cosmos of Murshidabad, slippery as silk and arch with knavery, was as debauched in mind as it was in body. Not a single known moral peaked above its duplicity. There was nothing to grasp or grapple with that the Chief Magistrate recognised. Not for the first time he marvelled at the place he had arrived at in his life.

He had been apprenticed as a surgeon at Guy's Hospital but was filled with an urge to escape his mundane life in England. Tales of fortune and the exotic made him determined to reach India. His father had speculated unwisely in business, leaving him nearly bankrupt. Overnight, the middle-class comforts Holwell had enjoyed vanished; struggle and the constant spectre of poverty took their place. The idea of India had come slowly to Holwell. Not far from his home on the outskirts of London was the grand house of a Company man. It was said he had gone out to India a pauper and returned with a bottomless fortune. Many disparaging remarks were made about the man and his new money, but the fact of his wealth remained. His home rose proudly, all turrets and gables in a great acreage of grounds. His wife's jewels turned heads and his stables were renowned. His sons were dressed like princes. Once Holwell had accompanied a friend to an exhibition of Indian artefacts, and stood in a daze before the opulence. Gold in profusion, beaten and studded with gems, silks sheer as water or encrusted with jewels, furniture of crystal or silver carved into the shapes of animals, and great sweeping fans of peacock feathers filled the cases around him. All this he knew had been gathered from the homes of those who had returned from India.

He took a post as surgeon's mate aboard a ship of the East India Company bound for Calcutta, but found it a loathsome experience. Before embarking, he had studied his medical books and prepared himself to deal with the unavoidable evil of scurvy. To the displeasure of the captain, he had laid out a small garden on board and harvested cress, lettuce, radishes and scurvy grass until a breaker had washed the garden overboard. The sufferers from scurvy had then immediately increased. He had advised the burning of damp gunpowder and juniper shrubs, and the spraying of vinegar to cleanse the air, all to little avail. But above all on that loathsome voyage the Chief Magistrate remembered the drinking water. It had been shipped with them in great oak tuns and not only began to smell but heaved with the bodies of worms. Each time a cup was dipped into the cask, the pink fleshy mass of bodies writhed like loose flayed skin. Eventually a glowing iron or a heated cannonball had to be immersed into the tun. Sometimes this cleared the water, the worms falling to cushion the bottom of the cask. Most of that voyage he had existed on beer or wine, the Chief Magistrate remembered.

The matter of the worms decided him to disembark at Calcutta, requesting a term on land at the Company hospital attached to Fort William. He found a town that promoted ingenuity and where a change of profession was not unusual if gain was to be found. His work as a lawyer for the Company soon exceeded his hours of purging and bleeding. Eventually his doctoring had ceased in favour of the law. He had never regretted the change.

Drake's voice interrupted Holwell's reverie. 'We must settle many issues with regard to Fort William before the old man dies.'

Holwell looked around. Across the room he saw the various knots of men surrounding the powerful figures of the Jagat Seth brothers, Mir Jaffir and his son-in-law Mir Kaseem. Above them all towered Raja Rai Durlabh, Alivardi Khan's chief minister and commander general of the army, surrounded by his sycophants. The commander's power was legend and his wily sense of preservation had seen him remain in his post longer than any other prince. It was rumoured that even Siraj Uddaulah treated the commander with respect. As the Chief Magistrate turned to draw the Governor's attention to Rai Durlabh, a man appeared at his side. He carried a message that a Murshidabad nobleman wished to see them. They would be taken to him later that night. Even when pressed with money, the man would reveal no names.

'Now what business is afoot?' Drake chuckled, wiping his face with his handkerchief.

'We shall soon see,' replied the Chief Magistrate, still observing the commander across the room.

Although the palanquin was large and accommodated both men, the Chief Magistrate was forced to sit with his chin upon his chest and his legs doubled up like a grasshopper. The Governor was pressed not for height but for breadth. Thick curtains of damask surrounded them. Holwell was bumped about by the rapid pace of the runners and his legs constantly tangled with Drake's as he sought to improve his position within the swaying litter. Already Drake was sweating profusely from excitement. The ripe smell of his linen charged their stuffy tent.

'Anything to see?' Drake enquired, as Holwell parted the curtains.

The Chief Magistrate stared out into the night. The bare shoulders of the runners appeared just below him, their breath rasping harshly. Holwell strained his eyes in the darkness. They had left the town behind; the runners' flares revealed fields and jungle. The howl of wild dogs and the shriek of night creatures came to them. Huts lined the road, a smell of nightsoil filled the air. A grove of mango trees passed, dissolving blackly into the night. Above them the moon glimmered through thin clouds, its light spilling over an expanse of water. Holwell could not push his head any further out of the litter for fear of losing his balance.

'There is a lake,' he announced. As he spoke he saw the dark shape of a building rising from its depths. Even in the darkness he could not mistake Motijil, the watery palace of Alivardi Khan's eldest daughter, Ghasiti Begum.

'Motijil,' Holwell informed Drake as they approached the narrow strip of land that served as a bridge across the lake to the Palace of Pearls. The silhouette of minarets stood out against the sky.

'Then it must be the Young Begum we have been summoned to see,' Drake confirmed as they were bumped across the bridge and through a further set of gates. Flares lit up the night as they entered the courtyard, and the gates swung shut behind them. They emerged from the litter and stretched their cramped legs before the heavily fortified palace. They were quickly escorted into the building and up a flight of winding stairs.

The walls and domed ceiling of the chamber they entered were set with designs in chips of mirrored glass. Oil lamps flickered, reflecting about them like a thousand stars. At first Holwell hesitated, for it seemed they were in an enchanted place. Taking a deep breath, he stepped forward. About him the smell of incense mixed strongly with that of charred wicks. He saw that a great many timepieces stood about upon tables of inlaid marble. Several ornate grandfather clocks were marshalled side by side at the far end of the room. Each clock was set at a different hour for reasons the Chief Magistrate could not comprehend. Their tinny hearts beat against the walls in a constant drumming echo. Mattresses and bolsters were arranged before a dividing wall of marble filigree.

As the Governor and the Chief Magistrate prepared to seat themselves, a small entourage of men crowded into the room. The Chief Magistrate at once recognised the Raja Rai Durlabh and behind him the equally powerful Mir Jaffir. That both men were present at this meeting confirmed for Holwell that the intrigue was of the

83

highest order. Two more wily men were hard to find in Murshidabad. Mir Jaffir was a brother-in-law of Alivardi Khan and the nawab's Paymaster General. From behind the filigreed screen came a rustle of silk, the light clink of bangles and a sudden wave of indescribable perfume. It was neither Rai Durlabh nor Mir Jaffir who spoke through the interpreter but the *diwan* of the Young Begum's late husband, a prince of some importance who it was rumoured was now established as her lover.

'Alivardi Khan is not long for this world. We must look to the future now. From the Emperor in Delhi there is as yet no confirmation for the accession of Siraj Uddaulah. Such a confirmation is needed in order to legally rule.' The *diwan* spoke smoothly, his eyes resting in turn upon the Chief Magistrate and then upon the Governor.

The incessant ticking of clocks hammered in the Chief Magistrate's head. The strong perfume about him appeared suggestive of the barbarities enacted in these rooms. A moment of panic overwhelmed him. Almost at once a grandfather clock began its deep strumming. The Chief Magistrate's hands turned clammy. In this fortress he could die and no one would be the wiser. His body could lie forever at the bottom of the lake, fodder for fish and water snakes. A lamp glowed behind the filigree screen and showed the outline of a seated figure, surrounded by wide skirts. The Chief Magistrate strained his eyes to assess the Young Begum better.

Everyone knew the story of Ghasiti, and her obsessive love for her father. On the death of her impotent husband, Ghasiti Begum returned to Murshidabad, to this palace on the lake, to be near her ailing father. She brought with her a treasure of considerable worth and also a sizeable army. Childless, she had adopted the infant son of Siraj Uddaulah's brother. She intended to surreptitiously rule Bengal once the child was on the throne. Suddenly the Young Begum began to speak and the *diwan* fell silent. Holwell knew it was unheard of for a woman to speak publicly in this way, but it was well known that Ghasiti Begum made it a habit to break rules.

'My nephew has little love for you Englishmen. He does not value your trade. If he ascends the throne he will throw you out of Benga.' The rasp of pent-up anger reverberated through the words.

'We seek your help,' the *diwan* explained. 'Only the merchant Omichand has knowledge of what we speak of.'

'What help can we be to you?' Governor Drake enquired, anxious to establish his presence before these nobles. To the Governor's frustration, the Chief Magistrate's haughty demeanour and seniority in years drew the attention of the noblemen for lengthy spans of time. Drake felt almost superfluous in the crowded room.

'Siraj Uddaulah prepares even now to put down all opposition. The Begum has her husband's treasure, which we now need to hide. This treasure will be used for the revolution to depose Siraj Uddaulah. We ask that you keep it safe within your fort at Calcutta,' the *diwan* announced.

'How is this treasure to be transported, provided of course that we agree to take it?' Holwell asked.

'My son, Kishindas, is already in Calcutta with the treasure. He is the guest of the merchant Omichand. For the moment the treasure is in his house. My son left Murshidabad on the excuse of a pilgrimage to Orissa,' the *diwan* informed them.

'In thanks, your licences for trade would be greatly increased and a part of the treasure will be given you. Such provision you will not get from my nephew. And, immediately, a gift of fifty thousand rupees will be made available to you both upon the promise of help,' announced the throaty voice behind the screen. Ghasiti Begum's words were almost lost beneath the crashing chime of another grandfather clock. Each stroke hacked deep into the Chief Magistrate's frazzled mind. Eventually silence settled once more within the room.

'You can be assured of our help and support,' Holwell responded, anxious to make their answer known before the next clock began to strike. He saw there was no choice in the matter; they could not afford to ignore a faction who tomorrow might be in power. Yet it was a dangerous business.

'We must act quickly. Time is not upon our side,' the *diwan* informed them.

At the mention of time, the Chief Magistrate thought suddenly of Alivardi Khan. Each impatient chime he heard might mark the last breath of the old nawab. And no less for Holwell himself. One wrong move or one loose word would see his head upon either the sword of Siraj Uddaulah or that of his aunt, Ghasiti Begum. Holwell turned to stare at Raja Rai Durlabh, who sat with a bored expression on his fleshy face, as if he took no part in the conspiracy. A thick beard was parted to meet in great wings on either side of his face like the whiskers of a cat. Already Holwell had an image of the man riding fearlessly into battle. Both Mir Jaffir and Rai Durlabh were deep in Siraj Uddaulah's camp; nobody else in the room had such access to the nawab, or the ability to arrange the prince's assassination. If either man decided to play the traitor, everyone's life would be in danger. The Chief Magistrate shifted uncomfortably against his silken bolster as Governor Drake repeated his avowal of help.

'Soon Siraj Uddaulah will see through this ruse of a pilgrimage. Spies will betray us. You must return quickly to Calcutta to secure the treasure. All other business can wait.' As the *diwan* rose to end the interview, a large brocade purse with a gold drawstring was placed before Holwell and Drake. It sat heavily upon the floor, the weight of its contents clear.

From behind the screen there was once more the rustle of silk and the clink of bangles as the Young Begum departed. Servants appeared and the Englishmen were led back down to the courtyard. As they left the room, a clock struck four, although it was past ten.

Outside, the Chief Magistrate gulped in the cool air and the heavy tang of the lake. In the confines of the palanquin again, the two men were at first silent, each ruminating upon the past hour, acutely aware of the silken purse that now sat between them in the litter. The Chief Magistrate lay back in exhaustion, no longer caring if his legs tangled with Drake's. The heavy bulk of the purse, although pleasant to contemplate, already filled the night with a sinister weight. The black shadow of the palace drew slowly away behind them.

'We will gain much by supporting the Young Begum.' Drake's voice was filled with the boyish bounce of a young man set on adventure.

'It is a dangerous business,' the Chief Magistrate warned. 'Never before has Fort William concerned itself with court intrigue.' The purse pushed coldly against his calves, the hard coil of gold coins thrusting through it.

'Rai Durlabh will do away with Siraj Uddaulah. I do not think Mir Jaffir is the man for such work. If he does this quickly there can be little danger,' Drake announced brightly.

'We English have been traders, not king-makers here. What if Rai Durlabh cannot or will not rid himself of the prince? What if Siraj Uddaulah hears we have the treasure and comes down upon us?' The Chief Magistrate was filled with doubts.

'What have we to lose? If the Young Begum's faction wins we will have accrued much personal money, and new power for Calcutta. And if not, well, let us think of that then. We can always gift the treasure to Siraj Uddaulah or keep it ourselves if we can,' Drake replied. The Chief Magistrate frowned at such flippancy.

'I do not think there is really any need for the Council to know of the Young Begum's personal gift to us. Clearly, the fifty thousand is to be divided between us two alone,' Drake continued.

'Certainly, no need. The treasure, of course, is another matter. The Council will have to be told and Fort William's reward shared fairly with them,' Holwell snapped, his nerves taut. Drake's very presence now annoyed him.

'We have nothing to lose on any front,' the Governor repeated, for once firm in his opinion.

The Chief Magistrate leaned back and closed his eyes in sudden fatigue. He remembered again how long ago he had stood on the beach, his eyes trained upon the horizon, watching the ships disappear beyond it. When eventually he had set sail for India, he found, however many miles he travelled, his distance from that elusive line never seemed to alter. The horizon lay always before him, always beyond his reach. When at last he arrived in India and, disembarking, turned upon that alien shore to measure the distance he had travelled, he saw the horizon had slipped behind him. He had the feeling then that he had passed imperceptibly through a strange portal to emerge on the dark side of a mirror.

He remembered too how on the deck of the ship carrying him to India he had stood before the noxious casks of water contemplating the precariousness of his life. The ship beneath him rocked, small as a thimble upon the great ocean, liable with every wave to spill him to a watery grave. And that strange horizon towards which he sailed came again into his mind. He saw now that it was like that invisible line that separates life from death. He had watched his father die, quietly, imperceptibly, with a single exhalation slipping across that mysterious divide. Who could tell where the dead went, what happened to them once they were sucked across that line? And in that same way, who could see the future, lying always beyond the same unmoving line? He remembered then that he had looked down into the vat of water with its wriggling mass of worms. When they had set sail there had been no sign of the creatures; the water had been clear. From where had they come? Had they lain invisible in the cask until the time to hatch was ripe? For the first time then a terrible fear had taken hold of him. Perhaps he had journeyed too far. What lay ahead he could neither forsee nor imagine. In the clearness of that long ago morning he had known only that experience waited for him, ready to hatch when least expected with the same vile flourish as those worms.

Now in the palanquin the Chief Magistrate felt again the cold weight of the purse against his ankle. The same fear he had felt on that ship long ago ran through him. Invisible seeds might already be germinating, preparing to endanger his future.

*

Once the Hatmen had gone, Raja Rai Durlabh finished the remains of his arrack. He had seen the Englishmen depart with relief and was now anxious to be free of Ghasiti Begum's palace. To have come at all was risky, but risk was the flavour of the times. Already, on every front, in every camp, there was a sense of realignment. There were no more than days or even hours before Alivardi Khan passed away. Already Siraj Uddaulah flexed his muscles. Already he manoeuvred into places of influence his drinking companions and cronies. He did not, like his grandfather, seek to spread administrative power equally amongst Hindus and Moslems. Alivardi had preferred the services of a high percentage of Hindus in every state office. Now, Siraj Uddaulah sought to overturn this by inserting everywhere Moslems of little calibre and questionable ability. Rai Durlabh was sure he would keep his own position in court, yet he was mindful of the future. He had no wish to serve a hot-headed young man who rarely showed him respect. He intended to play the game cautiously until he saw what destiny offered. As always he trod a path carefully, testing each stone before he put his heel down. If Siraj Uddaulah must be got rid of, then he would see that it was done. But he would not act in haste.

He drained the last of the arrack and stood up. The Hatmen, as predicted, had fallen easily into their place within the chessboard of moves already forming before them. As expected, the promise of money was all that was needed. They were easy pawns, and always transparent.

CHAPTER SEVEN

Emily Drake sat dressed in her loosest muslin, yet was unable to feel cool. Outside, the hot winds blew, like heat from a blacksmith's forge. As the day expanded, snakes disappeared into holes; dogs sought the shadows and lay comatose beside bullocks, goats and men. Urchins crept under verandas, risking scorpions, muskrats and cobra. Those flowers that could closed their petals tight. Wells were deserted, wet footsteps drying instantaneously as if beneath an iron.

Emily sat in a chair looking out at the Hoogly, passing the hours as she passed so many, silent with her tapestry. Today the needle dived clumsily, her stitches uneven. She was filled with shapeless impulses. *Do this. Do that. Go here. Go there.* The words whispered in her head. In his cradle Harry whimpered, the wet nurse moved towards him. The child had slept peacefully since the woman's arrival. Whenever he cried she hurried to him and immediately he was quiet. Emily herself seemed not to have this calming knack. Harry had gained some weight yet his stillness and the translucency of his complexion continued to worry her. The nurse placed the baby again in his cradle and silence filled the room.

Soon she heard Roger climbing the stairs and something closed within her. It was hard to believe that once she had waited for his step outside her door. Now there was only the draining away of emotion. They had slowly drifted apart, each upon their separate raft. Roger dealt with this void robustly, entrenched in work and social commitment. He lived besides, whenever he wished, a bawdy tavern life. He had a masculine strength that nothing seemed to rout. She had none of this; she lived a confiscated life. There was no one to blame but herself.

'It is time for tiffin, I am hungry,' Roger announced, rubbing his hands together as he entered the room.

'You are always hungry,' Emily observed good-humouredly, rising from her chair. Whatever her distance now from Roger, there were things in the past that could not be forgotten, whatever else might have been destroyed. There was besides no anger between them, just a growing space. Emily settled Harry with the nurse and followed him to the dining room.

The corridor lived in borrowed light from the rooms that opened off it. Roger walked ahead, impatient for his food. Emily noticed that an increased girth pulled his coat tight across his hips. The extra weight turned his short-stepping walk to an ungainly strut. He had been slim when they married, and open-faced, without the forced joviality he projected now. At times she felt a sadness for him. His wish for the governorship had been easily granted, but in return he had paid a price. He seemed now to have few friends, whereas before he had had too many. In the narrow corridor their hurrying feet rapped upon the bare polished boards.

'*Jane. Jane.*' The hot winds blew against the tatties to whisper the words in her head. Emily stopped and her heart flew to her throat. Something moved in the shadows. A large cockroach appeared to scuttle down the wall and disappear into a crack.

'What is it?' Drake turned at the sound of his wife's exclamation.

'I thought . . . it was Jane,' she whispered.

'We left her in Bombay.' Drake took hold of his wife's arm.

'If she were buried in Calcutta I think nothing could save me,'

Emily admitted. Drake sighed, letting go of Emily's arm as he turned again towards the dining room.

He continued along the corridor, Emily following, and once again the vibrations disturbed the cockroach. Deserting its seam in the panelling, it spread its wings to glide down upon Emily. She began to scream. The Governor turned and brushed the insect from his wife's breast.

She leant against the wall, her heart jumping about in her chest. Even though the insect was gone, she saw it still, black as a birthmark upon her.

'It is Jane . . .' She began to sob.

'Take hold of yourself,' Drake ordered, banishing his own fears in a show of impatience.

'She has appeared to me. She will not leave me alone.' Emily had yet to tell him about the night at Demonteguy's home.

'Such things they say sometimes happen to women after a confinement. It is all in your mind. Why do you not rest?' He spoke kindly now, taking her suddenly in his arms.

'What else do I do but rest?' She knew he meant well, but irritation flooded her. She could find no comfort in the damp pressure of his chin.

Suddenly he pressed her up against the wall, thrusting his hand down the neck of her gown, until he cupped her breast.

'Not here. The servants are everywhere,' she said, breaking free of him.

'You want me to go off to Black Town? How many days now has it been?' Drake complained with a scowl. Before him Emily stiffened and appeared not to hear, staring distractedly over his shoulder.

'It is the first of June,' she whispered. At once everything was clear.

'What of it?' growled Drake, drawing back from his wife.

'Jane died on the first of June.'

For a moment then Drake hesitated before speaking out firmly in a loud voice. 'We left Jane in Bombay, six foot under the ground with a stone obelisk to hold her down.'

The memory of his first wife, swinging dead before him from a rafter, was not easily forgotten. It had been he who had cut her down. Emily's obsession with her sister's ghost was not something he wished to examine. He felt again the limp weight of Jane's body as he held her against him while hacking at the rope. A monsoon wind had blown through the house, winding her hair about his face. The scent of rosewater and perspiration lifted from her and filled him to this day.

'Did you order kedgeree for me?' he asked, pushing away the memory.

'You cannot keep fish an hour in this weather, it is bad enough with meat,' Emily replied, following his lead, as if it was an ordinary day and nothing but kedgeree mattered. It was clear to her now that Roger could be of no help; she was alone with a ghost. Ahead of her Roger had already passed through the door of the dining room to survey the table of food.

Later, in the quiet of the afternoon as she tried to sleep, the old restlessness returned. The wet tatties dripped but did not cool the room. Bars of light around the blinds reflected on the walls. Sounds carried up from below; horses' hooves, the shouts of men, the bark of a dog, the cooing of doves near her window. The dim room about her, slatted with reflections, held her like a cage. She turned in panic and again the whispering filled her head. *Do this, do that. Go here, go there.* She knew she must do as the voice bid if she were to find any peace.

At last, as shadows breathed slowly into the heat, Emily Drake called for her palanquin. Once more she was driven to leave her home, as if to search for something lost. She gave instructions to the runners to take her to the Chandpal Ghat.

Often, from a high window of Fort William, she sat and surveyed the impacted mass of Black Town, turning her back on the Settlement. In this way she absorbed not only a picture of the Hoogly but also the life it so closely supported. Her view was distant as a bird's but the panorama held her. It was not just the tapestry of events, the funeral cortège, the wedding procession, the crying child, the bathing women or the work of the *dhobi* and the carpenter. This view of a seething world seemed proof of her own existence. Something came to her through the hawkers' cries, the beat of a drum, the bleat of goats or the shrill voices of washerwomen. These sounds floated up to move through her. And, fattened upon this view, she instinctively avoided the window behind her that commanded views of White Town pomp. The dazzling houses, the manicured gardens, the great water tanks kept clear of a single leaf, all stood before her like a desert she must trudge across each day. It was as if her real life were lived underground and showed no movement on the surface.

Now, in the palanquin, Emily Drake leaned back upon a bolster. When she told the runners her destination they looked askance at her. Then they set off obediently along the road beside the Maratha Ditch which carried Black Town's traffic. Every so often the palanquin was brought to a halt behind the swaying rumps of bullocks, or herds of bleating goats. Emily was unable to suppress her excitement, for already the life she documented each day from a distance pulsed about her.

At last they reached the bridge over the Ditch and crossed into Black Town. Emily looked down into the sluggish waters of the canal and knew she passed into an unknown world. In the litter she leaned forward eagerly. The palanquin was suddenly sucked into narrow lanes clogged with people, animals and carts. Cows ambled about in a world of their own. Men pushing overloaded barrows shouted either side of the palanquin. The runners raised the litter higher and thrust their way forward, adding their shouts to the noise. Emily slid about, clinging to the sides of her conveyance. The smell of dung fires and frying food and the acrid stench of urine mixed with the perfume of incense to fill the palanquin. The heat stewed these smells to intensity. Flies invaded the litter, settling upon Emily's face, hovering near her eyes. A mosquito bite itched upon her wrist;

another burned her ear. Wooden buildings lined the road, upper storeys ornate with carved latticed shutters and balconies. From these windows women peered out, faces veiled except for their eyes. Children pressed about them, like chicks looking down from an eyrie. Vendors struggled forward, baskets of fruit or vegetables balanced upon their heads. Thatched stalls and shops no bigger than cupboards were piled with spices, bolts of cloth or terracotta oil lamps. Purple aubergines gleamed next to the vivid splash of mangoes or mounds of flaming chillies. A barber squatted, razor in hand, attending to his client; a doctor of herbal remedies crouched upon a stool, a jar of pickled roots at his side. A tide of dirty muslin appeared to fill the road as people struggled forward. Emily flung back the curtains of the litter, as if inviting the tide to engulf her. She wished to discard her isolation as once in childhood she had discarded her dresses to run wild in a muslin slip. The notes of a long-forgotten dance sounded distantly in her head.

As they had entered, so, suddenly, they were free of the clamour. The narrow road was left behind. Now the glint of the river swelled before her. On its banks stood the Kali Mandhir and the Chandpal Ghat, which she had viewed distantly from Fort William. Soon the runners drew to a halt, and Emily stepped from her palanquin.

Before her was a complex of pagoda-roofed temples, busy with comings and goings. A large tank of water stood before it. Upon its steps children splashed while women immersed themselves in the water, emerging with their saris clinging to them revealingly. The ringing of bells and the chant of prayer sounded unceasingly. There was a smell of burning wood and incense, and a stronger odour Emily could not place. Some distance away, the bank of the river had been hewn into wide steps. A wall segregated this area from the temple. Upon it sat crows, vultures and adjutant storks. A glimpse of fire, roaring up suddenly, took Emily by surprise. From her window in Fort William the smoke of the burning ghats had appeared as innocuous. She backed away in revulsion, but the smoke curled about her, as if to draw her across an intangible line.

She saw her arrival had not gone unmarked. A crowd of beggars from the temple made their way towards her. Their progress was slow, for most were afflicted with deformities. Some hobbled on crutches, waving the stumps of amputated limbs. A legless man propelled himself forward upon a low-wheeled trolley. Lepers without noses or fingers guided forward the blind. A mewling growl was released from the crowd as they rolled towards her. Emily looked about in desperation and saw she was trapped between the burning ghat and the beggars.

Behind her was a hillock rising to a grove of trees. A tangled mass of vines almost hid a small building at its summit. She hurried up the narrow path. Her hooped skirts swayed awkwardly about her; shrubs caught at the silk and scratched her hands. She had scrambled up hills many times in the past, the taste of wild mint on her tongue, the arc of the sun ruling her day and roasting her skin. Memory blew through her, pushing her on. The late afternoon sun blazed in her face. At last she reached the top of the path and, looking back, saw the beggars arrayed angrily at the bottom, reluctant to make the climb upon their inadequate limbs. They preferred to await her return to the litter. Emily saw her palanquin bearers advancing in a determined fashion, intent upon dispersing the beggars. She turned in relief to examine the building before her.

It was difficult to see what lay beneath the knitted mound of creepers, but the entrance was carefully cleared. The place appeared hollowed out of the hill, part rock, part brick. Emily bent beneath a low portal and entered the cool interior. Although the blazing sun was left behind, it continued to dazzle, robbing her of sight. The chamber swam blackly before her, filled by strange rustlings and a fusty odour. She was forced to stand where she was, unable to see, afraid to step forward. In the dark cavern the sounds of life outside echoed distantly. Emily's heart began to pound. It was impossible to know where she was. She might stand on the edge of an abyss or before a pit of snakes. Her pupils dilated, her eyes grew large, but still she could not see. She was as blind as the beggar who sat outside the walls of Fort William wailing for alms. In the blackness she searched for an instinct that would tell her which way to turn. The past lay behind her and what was ahead could not yet be seen. Her everyday senses were useless and time appeared to hang suspended. She could not gauge whether seconds or minutes or hours had passed, bereft of her usual judgements. Then, slowly, her sight was restored, as if at last a door opened upon the strange place she had entered.

Creepers had thrust in from outside and taken possession of the chamber, twisting along the walls and the low domed ceiling. Above her, dark loops of vines pushed through the greenery like the sinuous coils of snakes. The filtered green light gave her the feeling of being in an undersea cave. Beneath her feet the floor was swept clean; no leaves or litter lay scattered about. However secretive it appeared, this was not a forgotten place.

As Emily's sight was further restored, she noticed the cave was bare of everything but a black-skinned idol standing in solitary command of the chamber. Her appearance was ferocious, her tongue protruding between sharp fangs. Her bare breasts and swollen genitals drew Emily's eyes immediately. The Goddess was adorned with a garland of skulls and stood upon a naked man whose phallus sprang up, avid as a new plant, beneath her. Her four arms held terrifying symbols of destruction, a severed head and a powerful sword, but also a bowl for alms and a lotus flower. In the dim green light her skin glowed pewter. The Goddess appeared to be cherished, for garlands of flowers adorned her and offerings of fruit were laid at her feet. Fresh incense perfumed the musty chamber. Once again rustlings stirred in the creepers; something moved through the twisted vines. But Emily Drake did not look up; the crude force of the idol imprisoned her, holding her fast. She was without fear or strangeness; she knew only a sense of return.

This Goddess had filled her childhood, unbeknown to her mother or Jane, hovering always at the edge of Emily's world. The servant's children had taught her to find the Goddess not only in temples but also in wayside statues or crudely daubed stones. She was found in hills rounded as a woman's breast spouting natural springs. She was there in the blood of a sacrificed goat or in the womb-like grottoes that pilgrims entered to be reborn. She was in sacred ponds and water containers, painted mantras and religious altars. She was in every dream of longing, the flight of birds, the notes of song and the dark at the bottom of a well. The Goddess was everywhere. In servants' huts Emily had helped to wash and feed Her and adorn Her in fresh clothes. She had held the small brass image in her hands and wondered at its power. *Shakti*. Emily remembered the potent word that encompassed the creative force of the world. She had bent in obeisance before her, aping the servant's children. The Goddess went by many names, each like the facets of a diamond, revealing her conflicting sides. Here as Kali the Goddess manifested a darker part of herself.

A piecemeal knowledge half heard long ago, seen only from the corner of an eye, returned to Emily now. Without this Goddess nothing moved in the world. Even Siva, over whom the Goddess stood, was but a corpse without her. At the touch of her foot, life filled him also. The Goddess was there at creation and at dissolution, in the birthing room and at the cremation ground. She was light and dark, the waxing and the waning moon and the bridge between that sustained.

In the dark grotto Emily stood transfixed before the small dark idol. She saw now that in her hands the Goddess held the implements not only of destruction but also of spiritual renunciation; she balanced life with death. The integrity of what she had heard so long ago was suddenly whole within Emily, like a seed that gestated in dark soil to sprout when least expected.

It was she who had whispered in Emily's ear, *Do this, do that, go here, go there*. In those cloudless days long ago, when the sun burned her skin as she had climbed for mangoes high in a tree, the Goddess had left her footprint upon her. Emily remembered the hut of the old shaman and knew the vibration that had passed through her then was no more than the touch of the Goddess. She only entered a soul at its wildest times. Now, again, in this strange grotto, something leapt in Emily, like the turning of an unborn child. For a long while she stood in the silent chamber, unwilling to leave. At last she forced herself to face the crack of brilliant light that would draw her once more into mundane life. The sun blazed in her face.

The smoke of the pyres rising up from below no longer bothered her now. After her meeting with the black goddess, the balance of things appeared changed. Above her vultures wheeled, waiting to snatch a half-burned morsel from a cooling pyre. A great squawking arose from the preponderance of crows. Beneath the sun the river swelled, awaiting its turn to devour the fiery remains. Three naked mendicants with long matted hair and bodies smeared with ash sat cross-legged near the water's edge. One held a withered arm in the air. His fist had been clenched for so many years that his nails now emerged from his knuckles. She watched as an old man, carried upon a stringbed, was manoeuvred down the steps of the burning ghats by a group of male relatives. The old man was not yet dead but had been brought to the temple to die. To hasten the moment, mud was pushed into his mouth and nostrils even as he struggled. Whatever her horror at this practice, Emily felt her smallness before the age-old patterns. The distant chant of prayer, accompanied by the sound of a bell, seemed somehow to complete a cycle beneath the indifferent sky. The place was busy not only with life but also with the business of death in an entirely emotionless way. The black goddess in the chamber on the hill stood at the door of life to facilitate in either direction the journey from one realm to the next. She was the Goddess of Perilous Passage. It was not for Emily to interfere. She watched the old man draw a last choking breath and then settle down to die.

Emily looked about her in confusion. From her window in Fort William she had seen the leap of flame at the Chandpal Ghat, seen the many domes of the Goddess's temple, but was unsure what had impelled her here. From the hill she looked back to White Town, to the window where she sat each day, viewing life vicariously. From where she now stood it seemed no more than a slit in a wall, as narrow as her life. The smoke of flesh and sandalwood rose about her; a crow alighted on a bush and cawed. There was a distant crack of thunder, although no clouds slid across the sky. At last Emily turned towards the path that would lead down to her palanquin.

As she stepped forward she was suddenly aware of a white shape against the trees. It appeared to move towards her in a cocoon of light. Emily turned in terror, preparing once more to fend off her sister's hungry ghost, but faced only a muslin *dhoti*, drying on a branch. Heart pounding, she stared at the flimsy cloth and sat down to regain herself.

It had been, she remembered, the beginning of the monsoon. Rain spat viciously into the veranda; a wind whistled through the house, beating angrily against the shutters. It had been old Parvati who had pulled her dementedly to where Jane waited. The wind had howled, whipping Emily's skirts and hair, blowing her towards her sister. A final blast had pushed her through a door into a curtain of muslin. The stuff had blown over her face; on her lips she had tasted starch and the grain of the cloth impregnated with lavender. As she tore the veil away, Jane's feet in white silk slippers had suddenly come before her, dangling unsupported in mid-air. She had looked up then and seen that Jane hung from a rafter before the door, dead. The wind rose again, lifting the muslin of Jane's dress, revolving her gently, first this way then that, like a mobile that had once, long ago, turned above Emily's bed. Nobody knew how long she had swung there, her face a dull blue, her tongue swollen. At once Emily's hand went to her belly as if to protect her unborn child. Already, for those whose eyes were sharp enough, the fruit of her wildness was visible. Parvati stood ashen-faced, her eyes fixed not on Jane but on Emily.

For months Jane must have known this moment was approaching, and prepared for it in her mind. The knowledge of the child Emily now carried, growing unstoppably within her, was there, unspoken, between the sisters. The balance of things was changed. To the outside world they appeared as before. Balls were attended, suitors appeared for Emily and were encouraged by Jane. Roger was attentive to his wife. But that unspoken knowledge loomed before them all, like the waiting edge of a cliff. Even as they stepped towards it there was no way to go back.

Roger had cut Jane down. She had been nailed quickly into a coffin, hastily prepared. No one knew what had occurred but the servants, and their whispers counted for nothing. Immediately, then, Roger had managed to get a posting in Surat, and quietly, within weeks, Emily had followed him with Parvati. They were married there by a clergyman who knew nothing of their history. Her body swelled freely then, and the life within it kicked and turned. Eventually the child was born, but died within a week. She had accepted that small death, glad almost to do penance. Within a few months they left Surat for Calcutta and the naked details of their history closed behind them forever. Emily pushed away the memories now and rose to make her way down the hill. As she reached the bottom, the beggars began to advance once more. She climbed quickly into her palanquin.

As the litter was jerked up upon the men's shoulders, Emily glimpsed two figures climbing the path up the hill to the grotto. A large woman was walking with difficulty, her weight spilling in rolls about her. A young girl pulled the older woman by the hand, easing her way to the top. There was something familiar about them. With a shock Emily recognised Sati. The pair reached the grotto and disappeared inside. Within the palanquin Emily hesitated, then ordered the runners to continue.

At last she returned to Fort William and old Parvati hurried to greet her. She waited for Emily as a mother would wait for her child.

'Where did you go to all by yourself? Running here and there like a wild thing,' Parvati scolded.

'I went to see the Goddess,' Emily replied.

'She can be seen everywhere,' the old woman mumbled as she helped Emily out of her dusty dress and brought a sponge and water.

'No need to go searching the world for her when all the time she is under your nose.'

'I had almost forgotten,' Emily replied. Soon she was changed and settled upon a chair. Parvati took a brush and began to pull it through Emily's hair.

'The *Devi* is not someone to forget. You discard her at your peril. Remember her and she will feed your soul.' Parvati handled the brush with practised strokes and began a tale about the Goddess. Emily leaned back in her chair. Parvati's voice wove about her as it had done long before. It was as if once more she was back upon the indigo farm. In the next room, as Parvati had put her to bed, she had heard the sound of her mother coughing or Jane's voice reading to her from a book. There had been the faint striking of a clock, or the notes of the piano as Jane played to their mother.

'In the beginning there were only male gods, and many terrible battles they were having with the demon *asuras* who were trying to conquer the world. Those male gods could not defeat the *asuras*, however hard they tried. They were feeling much shame as gods to be so humiliated. At last they decided they must find a new way to save themselves from the demons. They united all their energies in a great stream of fire. So great was this fire that it lit up the whole universe. And from that energy the Great Goddess Durga was born. The male gods were forced to create a goddess to save them from the evil forces. All their great powers were useless without her energy to ignite them. It is she who creates the world.' Parvati was pleased to think the power of a woman had been needed to save the world, despite the presence of so many strong men.

'Durga had more *shakti* than any male god. She was more powerful than any warrior. She stood before those gods in her armour, brighter than a thousand suns. Now, when they saw Durga those male gods were very pleased. Eighteen arms she had, with so many weapons and useful things, not only swords and shields and bows and arrows, but also beads for prayer, a lotus flower, a book of magic wisdom and a bowl for alms. Everything she needed she was carrying with her. And riding also upon a fierce tiger. No warrior was a more wondrous sight. And immediately the gods sent her off to battle the *asuras*. They knew already only she could stop the war between knowledge and ignorance.

'The world shook and the seas trembled as the Goddess fought the armies of demons. Each time the Goddess sighed, she created a battalion of female warriors. Very hard they all fought, and finally the Goddess defeated the Great Demon.' Parvati put down her brush and tied back Emily's hair. The evening was already upon them; the room was almost in darkness. Soon a lamp was lit and the moths clustered thickly about. Emily opened her eyes at the sudden fading of Parvati's voice.

'And then what happened?' she demanded, swinging her feet up on to a couch. Parvati pulled the loose hair out of the brush and wound it into a neat ball, dropping it into a waste-paper bucket. Then she squatted down on the floor beside Emily and continued with her story.

'Although this battle was finished, still other demons waited. The gods begged Durga to continue to fight. Now, the Goddess was seated upon her tiger on the high golden peak of a mountain, and it was there that the next army of demons found her. They drew their swords and bent their bows and rushed to capture her. Seeing this, Durga's anger became very great. She was tired of fighting and tired of seeing the evil faces of demons. She wanted an end to them all. In her anger she turned black as ink. All her rage was collected in her brow. So great was her fury that she frowned blacker and blacker until from her forehead the goddess Kali was born, black as Durga's frown. She is the manifestation of the Great Goddess Durga's purest anger. Garlanded all over with skulls, Kali was terrible to behold. But as well as the power of death, all knowledge and wisdom was also in her. That is why her *shakti* is so great. From her mouth her tongue lolled out and her eyes were red and sunken. She was a fearsome sight. Her voice was a deep roar, filling the skies. She stood before the army of devils and laughed. And while she was laughing, she was all the time eating up the demon army, flinging their elephants into her mouth, crunching up their horses and chariots, striking everywhere with her sword. Soon the army was defeated.' Parvati was growing tired; she gave a yawn.

'Tell me more,' Emily insisted. In just this way as a child she had spent so many absorbing hours.

'In the end the demons were defeated. Only that is important. Kali is always defeating all demons. Her *shakti* is very great. Durga gave birth to many other manifestations of herself, but no one is as strong as Kali. Durga's name is meaning "Beyond Reach". Such warrior women can belong to no man. She belongs only to herself.' However many times Parvati told the old tales, she still spoke with the same wonderment in her voice.

'Now you are no longer a child. There is no time to waste with these old stories. You have a child of your own to attend to.' Parvati turned towards the nursery, from where sounds of whimpering grew stronger. Emily rose from the chair to follow her.

CHAPTER EIGHT

At the arrival of Jaya and Sati, the beggars about the temple immediately geared themselves up for the usual assault on the pious. Jaya was used to such situations. She tossed a handful of coins over her shoulder so that they fell a distance behind her. The beggars raced to where the money was scattered and began to squabble. During this distraction, Jaya and Sati began their climb to the grotto on the hill. Here, near the burning ghat, the Goddess was at her most impartial. At this place of life's far boundary she stood revealed in the fullness of her terrible beauty. In the presence of death her touch transformed, removing pain, guiding each departing soul according to its needs. Here she was only compassion. At the top of the hill Sati and Jaya paused, then entered the grotto; they came here often together.

Soon they emerged again and descended the hillock by its steep path. Once more the beggars surrounded them, shouting rudely and waving the stubs of their amputated limbs. Once more Jaya tossed a handful of coins over her shoulder and the vagrants fell upon them. The women then quickly made their way across the compound to the main temple.

As they stepped into the shade of its arches there was a sudden roar from the jungle. At once the beggars sat back on their heels before Jaya's coins, muttering in fear. For some days a man-eating tiger had been terrorising Black Town. It slunk noiselessly out of the jungle whenever it needed a meal. Some said they had seen its amber eyes staring out of the foliage. Children were kept indoors. The old and infirm no longer slept on string beds under the trees. People adopted a guarded stance; while walking to the well women took a lighted flare at midday. At the Kali Mandhir the ash-smeared mendicants still sat by the riverbank, but their meditation was disturbed. Sometimes by the proximity of its roar the tiger seemed almost upon them. The mendicants reached for their tridents and moved closer together.

Now the tiger's roar seemed to echo upon the very walls of the temple. Jaya gripped Sati's arm, pulling her on. After the night in Demonteguy's house she had wasted no time in arranging to rid her granddaughter of the *ferenghi* devil.

'It is no *ferenghi*,' Sati had pleaded.

'No Indian spirit speaking like that to the Hatmen. It is a foreigner, a *ferenghi*,' Jaya insisted, remembering again the night of the seance.

They made their way past the main chamber to a small cell where a priest waited. The dark room smelled of old bricks and rodent droppings. At once Jaya began to speak. The priest nodded from time to time, without interrupting. He knew her well and so was aware that interruptions only prolonged her explanations. When at last he was free to speak he instructed them to sit before him. He began lighting sticks of incense. Soon myrrh and frankincense rose in a cloud, almost obscuring the priest from view. The perfume engorged their nostrils and glutted in their chests. Sati began to feel dizzy. Jaya coughed and fanned the cloud away with the end of her sari. Behind the smoke the priest was now a hazy apparition, a long beard covering his nakedness, grey hair flowing over his shoulders. His voice intoned hypnotically.

'*The power who is defined as Consciousness in all beings,*
Reverence to Her, reverence to Her, reverence to Her,

Reverence, reverence.

The power who is known as Reason in all beings,
Reverence to Her, reverence to Her, reverence to Her,
Reverence, reverence.'

Light sliced down into the dim room from a small high window. It fell in a burnished pool upon the priest and the accoutrements of *puja* before him: flowers, brass dishes of rice and carmine, a mound of powdered dung and sandalwood, coconuts, oil lamps and fruits. In a metal container he lit a small fire, igniting it with camphor. His hands reached out, palms up, as he intoned the hymns to Kali, eyes closed in concentration.

> *'Destroyer of time,*
> *Destroyer of fear,*
> *Who assumeth all forms at will . . .*
> *O Beautiful One . . ..*
> *Joyous one . . .*
> *Allayer of sufferings,*
> *To thee I make obeisance.'*

The priest sprinkled dung and sandalwood on to the fire. More camphor was added and the aromatic flames spurted up. The priest's deep-set eyes appeared lit from within and fastened on Sati, unmoving. His voice continued to intone. Jaya added a handful of fuel to the fire at a signal from the priest, and Sati followed. The flames spurted up again. On the window ledge above the priest a crow alighted and squawked, the sun running like oil in its ebony feathers. The aromatic smoke swirled and billowed about. Soon another crow joined the first. Their merciless eyes and brazen beaks were fixed upon the ritual enacted in the room. The birds and the priest seemed then to merge in Sati's mind into the separate parts of a powerful force, mobilising itself before her. She sensed the machinery of destruction closing in upon her. In the distance the tiger roared from the jungle again. Sati closed her eyes in concentration, willing Durga to come to her aid, but the room remained empty. Durga did not appear.

At last the *puja* was finished. The priest rose to anoint them with carmine and rice and to place consecrated bananas in their hands. Then Sati was led to a low brick shelf.

'Lie down,' the old priest ordered.

She looked for escape, but three younger priests had already entered the room. One gripped a cane of bamboo while the others held her down. Looking up, she saw the birds still shifting about, croaking hoarsely above her. Their beaks opened wide upon pink throats, eyes bright as beads of dew. As the cane came down upon her back, the birds released a clatter of sound, like the tumbling of pans about her. The pain of the bamboo drove through her flesh. She began to scream, calling out for Durga. The old priest continued to intone, taking no notice of her.

> *'Merciful,*
> *Vessel of mercy,*
> *Whose mercy is without limit,*
> *Who art attainable alone by Thy mercy,*
> *Who art fire,*
> *Tawny,*
> *Black of hue,*
> *Thou who increaseth the joy of the Lord of creation,*
> *Night of darkness,*
> *Yet liberator from the bonds of desire,*
> *Thou who art dark as a bank of clouds,*
> *And bearest the crescent moon,*
> *Destroyer of sin in the Kali Age,*
> *Thou who art pleased by the worship of virgins,*
> *Thou who art the refuge of the worshippers of virgins,*
> *Who are pleased by the feasting of virgins,*
> *And who art in the form of the virgin,*
> *Destroyer of fear*
> *Who assumeth all forms at will . . .'*

The pain ceased suddenly, although the young priest still lifted the cane, to bring it down upon her soft flesh. She saw then that some part of her appeared to have floated up near the ceiling, released suddenly from her physical self. It was possible now to look down and see herself writhing about beneath the thrashing. The sound of the cane ricocheted through her head but now she felt nothing. She saw then that Durga had come at last to pull her out of the cauldron of pain.

Durga cursed the holy men, her words torn out of Sati's tortured body. As her deep voice filled the room the priest hesitated, stumbling suddenly over his words. The young men drew back momentarily in fear. Sati continued to float, free of the scene below her.

The crows still stalked before the window but at Durga's cursing they took flight with a great flapping of wings. Where the crows had sat a filthy crust of yellow droppings remained. The window looked out at the hillock with Kali's creeper-lined sanctuary. From her strange vantage point Sati could see that a white cow had climbed the hill and stood pulling at the foliage that grew upon the shrine. She thought of the black image of Kali within. The Goddess was a warrior in the world, and her own Durga was no less, fighting for Sati, protecting her.

Durga was making a terrible noise; the priest was once more beating Sati with the bamboo cane. Although Durga roared like a lion the men now took no notice of her. The cane came down again and again.

The old man's words spun faster and faster. Smoke billowed about, filling the room with a thick, aromatic fog. Jaya strained her eyes in the haze, searching the shadows and the crumbling walls, her eyes watering with the smoke. But at last she saw the ugly spirit, crouching in a corner, naked, black, four-armed, her great vulva visible between spread legs, as if she would give birth to the world.

The old woman was sure she heard the rattle of skulls around the spirit's neck.

Jaya's head spun. Jumping up, she ran to the priest, shouting at him to stop his prayers, pulling at his arm. The old man wrenched himself free of her grip and returned grimly to his work. He knew the ways of spirits, and the manner in which they acted to prevent their exorcism. A young priest stepped forward and dragged Jaya away. She began to sob, but then stopped in confusion. The spirit had vanished. She looked about but could no longer see the creature that had just now appeared before her. Only its voice, deep and raw, still came forth from Sati, pleading now for clemency. Once more Jaya heard the tiger roar. Its howl was ripped from the jungle to resound in the room.

Sati still floated free of her body. She recalled a similar sensation once, long before. The memory was but a fragment. Yet whenever she tried to grasp it, it sank back into shadow. All she remembered was the sense of bursting free as she had done today. On that day long ago, she had had the feeling that her life was changed. This day too she knew would be no different.

From the window she looked down once again at the scene below. She had noticed her grandmother's sudden desperation but saw Jaya sitting quietly again, sobbing into her sari. Durga appeared to be tiring fast. She was now begging for respite. Sati felt a force pulling her down, back into the whirlpool of violence below, returning her to her body. Once again from the jungle the tiger roared.

CHAPTER NINE

Omichand's house was unlike any other in the Settlement, being neither Eastern nor Western in design. It lay behind The Avenue and was built in a style of great opulence. Corinthian columns soared up before latticed wooden balconies and fretted windows of Indian design. The Chief Magistrate passed through the gates of Omichand's home and his palanquin was lowered to the ground. He alighted, stretching stiffly and adjusting his hat. Pulling his waistcoat into place, he marched up the steps in a determined manner, preceded by a servant, preparing himself for the merchant's sly manipulations. Navigation of the serpentine route and hidden traps of any discussion with Omichand required all the Chief Magistrate's ingenuity. At the crack of dawn, before even the twittering of birds was heard, he had received a message from Omichand, demanding to see him that morning. In the six weeks since his return from Murshidabad, many things had happened.

Alivardi Khan had died even as Holwell and Drake made their way back to Calcutta. Now Siraj Uddaulah was flexing his muscles in an arrogant manner. Sensing a plot, he had arrested his aunt, the Young Begum, within days of his grandfather's death. He had confined her in his own *zenana,* from where escape was impossible. In spite of the Young Begum's incarceration, the plot to depose the prince still moved forward. Ghasiti Begum's treasure had arrived in Calcutta under the protection of the nobleman Kishindas. It had not been housed in the fort yet, but in Omichand's home. For the moment this was seen as less provocative by Fort William, for already the nawab knew about developments. A series of shrill letters had soon arrived from Siraj Uddaulah demanding the return of the treasure. If his demand was not met, the new nawab threatened to bring his army within sight of Fort William's walls. The fact that this treasure was not yet in Fort William allowed some space for argument.

Omichand received his visitors in an octagonal chamber walled with mirrors in ornate gilt frames. A large portrait of Alivardi, smelling a rose and gazing over the parapet of his Murshidabad palace, dominated the room. As he entered, incense filled the Chief Magistrate's nose, enclosing him inescapably within the merchant's domain. The room was dim and shuttered. Servants with fans of white yak hair stirred the air only slightly.

Omichand reclined upon a dais, propped up upon bolsters, drawing on a hookah. His face was bland as a mushroom cap, his features smothered by flesh. He was dressed in a robe of striped Murshidabad silk with a matching turban. Holwell parted the skirt of his coat and sat down on a chair fashioned from silver and crystal. Omichand's secretary, Govindram, already squatted behind a low desk to transcribe the interview. Holwell frowned in annoyance and met Govindram's gaze as the man sharpened his quill. Omichand pushed away his hookah to confront the Chief Magistrate.

'I was desiring to see the Governor. Why is he not with you?' Omichand's face was devoid of its usual ceaseless smile. Since the death of Alivardi and the new prominence of Siraj Uddaulah, the fat merchant was consumed by unusual gravity.

'Mr Drake has other urgent work,' the Chief Magistrate lied. Drake's digestion was troubling him and he had declined to see Omichand so early in the morning, insisting the Chief Magistrate handle the matter.

'The Governor refuses to keep me informed of his correspondence with the nawab,' Omichand complained, his scowl deepening. Missives from the new nawab now rained down upon Calcutta so thick and fast that neither the Governor nor the Chief Magistrate took great notice of them.

Omichand ordered a servant to offer his hookah to the Chief Magistrate. Holwell would have liked to refuse such an intimacy, but this would have been in poor taste. He took a short suck on the pipe and watched the water bubble.

'The situation we are finding ourselves in at present with Murshidabad is more fragile than a woman's heart. Any small thing can break it. In spite of knowing this, you have begun fresh excavations on the Maratha Ditch, as if you prepare to fortify Calcutta against attack. This has been most unwise. Siraj Uddaulah has come to know of this digging and it is not to his liking. He has taken it as a personal affront.' Omichand's expression now resembled that of a belligerent bulldog.

The Chief Magistrate looked at a point beyond Omichand's shoulder with studied disinterest. He had feared Omichand might raise this issue. At the direction of the Fort William Council, new excavations had indeed begun on the Ditch. There were rumours from Europe of war again with France. Should hostilities break out between the two countries, the French enclave upriver of Chandernagore could begin to threaten. This served as an excellent excuse to fortify Calcutta's defences against Siraj Uddaulah. The Ditch had been left incomplete at the time of its construction, and it was those undug parts of the original plans that were now being excavated. The Chief Magistrate had inspected the progress only the day before and found it unsatisfactory. The coolies lay asleep under the shade of a banyan tree without any sense of emergency.

'That we now look to our defences because of the French will also serve as a warning to the young nawab that we cannot be so easily threatened.' The Chief Magistrate tried discreetly to loosen the stock at his neck, the heat in the room was oppressive. He listened to the water in the hookah bubble.

'Any protection needed by your settlement is for the nawab to provide. You are but subjects in his land. You cannot take the law into your own hands. Mr Drake took it upon himself to reply to the nawab's enquiries in a most casual manner. You are familiar with his letter? It has not been written with proper courtesy and has upset the nawab.'

'The Governor writes many letters. I do not see them all,' Holwell replied. The soft bubbling of the hookah and the odour of incense knotted in his head. It was quite possible that in his cheeky, puppy-dog manner Drake had made some *faux pas*. His letters to Siraj Uddaulah were often dashed off in a cavalier way.

'Also, the nawab continues to demand the return of Kishindas and his treasure. My position is difficult as Kishindas resides with me,' Omichand continued. The Chief Magistrate detected panic in the merchant's words.

The heat in the room seemed to intensify. In spite of the servants diligently fanning the Chief Magistrate, his shirt was already damp. About him dull mirrors threw up unending images of himself and the fat merchant. Within the distorted glass Omichand swelled to even greater proportions, while the Chief Magistrate appeared diminished. He was pulled wide in the places he was thin, his head grotesquely elongated. Squashed up against the mirror frame, his shape appeared to waver about like a tapeworm stood on end.

'This letter of Mr Drake has incensed the nawab,' Omichand repeated, swaying on the upholstery of his massive thighs. 'The great Alivardi Khan was old and sick but still, by his wisdom, there was peace in Bengal. Now in his place there is a young hot-head from whom we have much to fear.' Omichand's usually impenetrable demeanour splintered to reveal a worried man. He pulled on his hookah and continued. 'Siraj Uddaulah has little trust in us Hindus. We are now out of favour at court.'

'This will mean you can no longer play Calcutta against Murshidabad. You will have to depend upon English favour.' The Chief Magistrate made no effort to hide his satisfaction.

'You do me much wrong with this judgement,' Omichand glowered, but a wily light entered his eyes as he made his next announcement.

'All this time I have given many excuses to Siraj Uddaulah for not returning Kishindas. Now time is running out. My life will soon be in danger from Siraj Uddaulah. I am having no choice but to blame you Englishmen for the situation.' Omichand sighed extravagantly.

'What have you said?' Holwell sat forward, sensing an obscure tentacle of reasoning beginning to emerge from the fat merchant.

'A slight twist to the truth is sometimes necessary to achieve a purpose. As you know, Kishindas left Murshidabad on the excuse of a pilgrimage to Orissa. I have now been forced to tell the nawab that on his arrival here you Hatmen discovered that Kishindas carried treasure to give as an offering in Orissa and demanded it from him. That is why he has been detained here so long. I have said that my life and that of Kishindas are in danger from you Englishmen. I have said that I am protecting him and his treasure from you until I can negotiate his safe return to Murshidabad. I have of course denied all knowledge that this treasure belongs to the Young Begum.'

'You have told the nawab this monstrous lie?' Holwell barked, rising in fury from his chair.

'Some game has now to be played if we are to retain this treasure and also Siraj Uddaulah's favour. The time for truth is over,' Omichand replied, assessing the Chief Magistrate shrewdly.

'You are only looking to your own safety. Soon Rai Durlabh and the Young Begum's faction will overthrow Siraj Uddaulah. You have no need to blacken the name of Englishmen. You are making it impossible for us to deal with the nawab.' Holwell was enraged.

'I am handling things in my own way,' Omichand replied, avoiding the Chief Magistrate's eye.

'This morning one further letter from the nawab has reached me,' Omichand continued casually.

Holwell, who had stood up to leave, sat down again abruptly.

'What does this further wretched letter contain?' He watched as the merchant tossed cashew nuts into his mouth.

'As you know, Siraj Uddaulah's position as nawab is not yet confirmed from Delhi. His cousin Shakut Jang in Purnea also contends for the *gaddi*. Naturally, this competition has not pleased Siraj Uddaulah. Therefore he has gathered together his army and begun the journey to Purnea to quell his cousin. Unfortunately for us all, Mr Drake's uncivil letter about the fortifications reached him on this journey and so incensed him that he has turned instead towards Calcutta to settle the matter himself. This is the news I have called you to hear. Already the nawab nears Kasimbazar.' Omichand sucked on his hookah in sudden anxiety. Kasimbazar was no more than a few days' journey from Calcutta.

'It is nothing but an act of bluff. How dare the young hot-head come down upon us in this impertinent manner. We must communicate at once with Rai Durlabh. He must have some say in this matter,' the Chief Magistrate exploded in shock. He did not think he had the strength to take any more news from Omichand, and stood up again to leave.

'We have not yet finished. Already I have heard from Rai Durlabh,' Omichand announced. Once more the Chief Magistrate sat heavily on his chair. Omichand drew on his hookah, then passed the pipe to Holwell. This time the Chief Magistrate had no compunction in refusing the merchant's offer.

'The commander cannot prevent a march upon Calcutta. Siraj Uddaulah has announced to all that he is bent upon teaching you Hatmen a lesson with regard to your manners and the repair of your defences. But the commander writes that he expects no battle, God willing. This can mean only that he intends to rid us of the young prince. The nawab's army is large. Once he reaches Kasimbazar he will sit awhile. An army of that size cannot so easily be got up once it has sat down. At that time Rai Durlabh will act,' Omichand comforted.

The smell of incense tightened unbearably in the Chief Magistrate's head. He shifted in his chair and found he faced the mirrors again. He saw himself stiff as a beetle in his dark frock coat beside the colourful heap that was Omichand. The reflection chased from mirror to mirror about the room in an unending circle, as if he and Omichand were bound together for eternity.

'It is not an easy job to do away with a nawab. But Rai Durlabh will find a way. He is not a man to be defeated once he has made up his mind,' Omichand assured the Chief Magistrate as he rose at last to leave. Holwell nodded in a dazed fashion, unable still to comprehend the unexpected turn of events.

As soon as he emerged from Omichand's house, the Chief Magistrate felt a great need for some claret or Madeira. He gave instructions to the palanquin bearers to cross the road to the home of Reverend Bellamy. Next door to the Chaplain's house stood St Ann's Church. It irked the Chief Magistrate, as it always did when he visited Omichand, that a heathen rascal of such indomitable power should place himself facing the house of God.

As he approached Bellamy's home he noticed anew the freakish appearance of the church. It had the look of an amputee. Its spire had blown off in a gale three years before and was as yet unrepaired. While talk stalled upon the financial conundrum of this repair, affliction further riddled the church. Its *chunam* peeled, white ants attacked rafters, and mould crept into prayer books, blotting out God's word. Since religion was not the moving force of White Town, this state of disrepair troubled no one unduly. The church was left to decay.

The Chief Magistrate found the Reverend Bellamy at home, surrounded by papers in his study. He looked up briefly from an open ledger at Holwell's unexpected entrance. His lips were pursed in concentration, a button was missing from his waistcoat and soup stained his linen cravat.

'A moment longer, John, if you please,' Bellamy apologised, frowning in concentration over the ledger.

As their friendship was of long standing and demanded a minimum of formality, Gervase Bellamy saw no need to disturb himself immediately from his work. The two men were drawn together by their long survival in Calcutta. Bellamy was Calcutta's oldest resident. At sixty-four, he had lived nearly forty years in the town. The Chief Magistrate, with twenty-four years in Calcutta, might lag some way behind, but nobody else could match these two exceptional terms of residence. India's cruel mortality rate not only gave the Chaplain and the Chief Magistrate importance in Calcutta, but was the basis of their friendship. They had stood together at more graveside services than either would care to count. Both had come silently to believe that God had singled him out for a special purpose. Why otherwise were they still alive when so many had gone before them?

Holwell sat quietly while Bellamy attended to his accounts, taking no offence at this casual treatment. A servant appeared with Madeira and placed it before the Chief Magistrate. Soon the spectre of Siraj Uddaulah faded slightly as the wine eased into his veins. Bellamy's home was, if anything, hotter than Omichand's, but no Oriental scents thickened the air. Instead there was the perfume of beeswax and baking bread drifting in from the cookhouse. The notes of a piano, slightly off key, came faintly to the Chief Magistrate from somewhere deep in the house. Bellamy's daughter, Anna, was at her practice. Holwell breathed in these familiar things and was slowly returned to himself.

The room was dim, the tatties already down to repel the glare of the sun. Only Bellamy, in need of light, was forced to sit in a searing beam, squinting at his ledgers. About him the room was in disarray. Stacks of books occupied all available places. Tattered hymnbooks and copies of the Bible of selected sizes were piled next to a variety of religious discourses. Alongside these stood ledgers containing a record of the Chaplain's years in trade.

The Chaplain spent the greater part of his day buried in the concerns of commerce. He was a cleric of the old school, not yet touched by new-fangled ideas about converting the Hindus. The Company policy was for a quiet life of profit, leaving heathens free to be heathens and chaplains free to trade if they pleased. Bellamy flew about in untidy fashion, his coat flapping open, his face wet with sweat, never a Bible to hand when he needed it, juggling the cares of trade with the cares of God. There was a well-stretched magnanimity about the Chaplain that came from the difficult art of balancing his religious duties to the Company's servants, his successful sorties into commerce and the responsibility of owning the best cellar of claret in town. Like everyone else in Calcutta, the Chaplain used the financial services of Omichand to underwrite his business ventures.

At last, with a sigh, the Chaplain blotted the page and looked up at Holwell. 'What is the good of accountants who cannot add up their sums? Here, you see, a single mistake and my stock appears to be lessened by a hundred and fifty bottles of claret.' Bellamy slammed shut the ledger and reached for the Madeira. As soon as he sipped it he frowned.

'This is of mixed vintage. Let us fetch another bottle,' he insisted.

'Siraj Uddaulah threatens to come down upon us,' Holwell confided as he followed the Chaplain out of the house into the baking sun. 'It is said that already he approaches Kasimbazar. He is annoyed about our excavations. And this business with Kishindas is the very devil.'

Soon they reached Bellamy's cellar, a low-roofed building beside the cookhouse. A servant ran ahead to light the flares in the chamber below.

'Kasimbazar?' The Chaplain stopped in alarm and turned to face Holwell. 'He must be stopped at all costs.'

Bellamy entered his cellar and began to climb down the narrow stairwell. Navigating the steep flight of stairs behind him, Holwell looked down upon the Chaplain's balding pink skull, and was reminded of a coconut. Then the sun was blotted out as the cellar claimed them.

Soon they reached the bottom of the steps. The Chaplain's cellar was extensive and was housed in a wide tunnel that ran from beneath Bellamy's home to below the church. Sometimes, whilst delivering a sermon in St Ann's, Bellamy's thoughts plunged down, straight as a plumb line between his feet, to the racks of wine laid out beneath him. He knew exactly over what vintage he stood, and whether it was claret or Madeira, Marsala or Shiraz.

Within the cellar Holwell could only just stand erect. The cramped confines of the place and the overpowering scent of soil and brick heated by the light of the flares filled him with sudden claustrophobia. He made an effort to control his feelings, but the confined space seemed only to echo the weight of the morning, still pressing upon his nerves. Once more his anxiety about Siraj Uddaulah overwhelmed him. Wherever he turned he was trapped.

The Chief Magistrate wished badly to unload himself of his difficult interview with Omichand. There was no one else he cared to speak to other than the Chaplain. Bellamy's advice was always of such a sensible nature and so in keeping with the Chief Magistrate's own thoughts that Holwell always marvelled that he had not himself thought of the things Bellamy pointed out. Yet now, for the first time, his tongue was tied. Besides the Council of Fort William, who had been told of developments upon Holwell's return from Murshidabad, and who would eventually have a share in the Young Begum's treasure, no one in Calcutta knew the real reason for Kishindas's presence.

'How is the nawab to be stopped?' Holwell worried.

'Cease all excavations at once,' Bellamy warned. 'And if this nobleman Kishindas being here irks the nawab, order the fat merchant to throw him out. Why cause bad feelings during this transfer of power in Murshidabad?'

Bellamy reached out and picked up a bottle, holding it beneath his bulbous nose, squinting at the label. He replaced the bottle and picked up another. Soon he found the vintage he wanted and they climbed back up the cellar stairs to emerge again into the sun. The Chaplain called for the bottle to be decanted immediately and brought to his study.

'Was this not worth the journey?' Bellamy sat back in his chair when the wine appeared and sipped testingly at the Madeira.

Holwell raised his glass to his lips but could not say he found a great difference. As they sat in silence, a gust of hot wind lifted a tattie at the window. A sudden wave of fetid air drifted into the room. The wind had changed direction and now blew the stench of the Salt Lakes upon them. The Chief Magistrate was again reminded that his future now sailed upon a similar corruption. He and Drake had not only accepted the silken purse of gold coins but already divided it between them. Whatever he did, wherever he went, intrigue and duplicity would stalk him now and could not be turned away.

CHAPTER TEN

Jaya Kapur squatted outside the room of William Dumbleton. Two Englishmen sat on a bench nearby, also waiting to see the Notary. They observed Jaya with affronted expressions, as if she no right to be in the Courthouse. Eventually they removed themselves to the furthest end of the bench. In the presence of the Hatmen it was aways the same. She must hold on to the knowledge of who she was as these men held on to their hats in a wind. Beneath the severity of their gaze she saw herself with the Englishmen's eyes, as a repository of malignant power, unrecognisable in all ways. She felt at once cut adrift from herself, an exile from her own soul. Outside the door of the Notary she seemed to shrink. She continued to glare at the Englishmen until they looked away.

One by one the waiting men were summoned by the Notary and disappeared through his door. Although the smell of the Courthouse terrified her, Jaya was determined to show no weakness. An odour of impenetrability surrounded her, of thick clothes, efficiency and heavy wood. There were things in this smell she could not even name and that now worked to diminish her further. She had seen the Notary the evening of the seance in Rita's home and taken little notice of him. The things that had happened since that evening had now led her to his room.

She rolled her prayer beads between her fingers, whispering the Goddess's name. Her greatest fear was that Chief Magistrate Holwell would suddenly appear and throw her out. As she had approached the Courthouse she had seen him standing before the building, talking to a group of men. She drew back behind a banyan tree and watched in trepidation. The Chief Magistrate's shadow spread out behind him, sliding smoothly over the road. In just such a manner, thought Jaya, the power of the magistrate moved over the town and could not be evaded. Perhaps in the place of grey skies where Mr Holwell came from shadows were faint or even unseen. But in the sharp, hot light of Calcutta they grew out of a man in a powerful way. The shadows of the Hatmen were tall and alien in shape. Sometimes the sun fell on to a knot of White Town men, merging their shadows together. Then this dark pool, devoid of even a crack of light, filled her with anxiety. If three or four men could produce a shadow of such density, the combined shadows of all of White Town would be longer and blacker than the darkest night. Soon the Chief Magistrate had entered the Courthouse, and after a safe interval Jaya had followed. Now, remembering his presence in the building, she clutched her prayer beads tighter and called on the Goddess again. Eventually, a *peon* stuck his head out of the door and announced her name.

William Dumbleton looked up from behind his table. The papers before him stated that a Janet Jenkins wished to bring a lawsuit against Fabian Demonteguy. The Notary had expected an English-woman. He tried not to show his surprise as Jaya entered. This was difficult, for her appearance could not be ignored. Above her sari she wore her feathered hat as a badge of her right to be in White Town. The hat had been acquired many years before, at the time of her marriage to a Mr Locke. There had been a riding habit to go with it then, and although Jaya had never sat upon a horse, she had worn the habit once or twice for the titillation of Mr Locke.

The hat was the first thing Mr Dumbleton noticed as Jaya made her way towards him. A stout cockerel appeared to bear down upon him. Looking hurriedly at the paper again he saw the woman was listed as *née* Kapur, also previously as Walsh, Locke and then Jenkins. Never before had an Indian woman approached him in his room like this. And what had she to do with Demonteguy, to whose home his wife had recently dragged him for some outrageous seance?

'You have many aliases,' he stated, keeping his eyes on the paper.

'All are the names of my English husbands,' the woman replied.

Dumbleton nodded. Few Englishwomen had the courage to venture out to India, risking both life and sanity. Dumbleton was one of the lucky few who had an English wife beside him. Others, with the Company's blessing, found varying solutions to the state of bachelorhood. Some wealthy Company men kept seraglios of native women in the Moslem style. A few married Indian women legally. Most, however, whatever their rank, were encouraged to take Indian women as temporary wives during their stay in the country. This woman, Dumbleton suspected, looking once more at Jaya, must have been the common-law wife of a low-ranking English or European soldier and lived in a hut near the barracks. The only idea of morality these poor creatures had was the rule that, whilst engaged in a relationship with one man, they should be faithful to him for as long as he lived in India. Once a husband died or left the country, they were forced for survival to form a further union with another European man or resort to the brothels of Black Town. And the children – Dumbleton did not really know what happened to the children, except that there now appeared to be a growing community of Anglo-Indians in Calcutta at every rung of the economic ladder. They seemed to fit nowhere in either Black or White Town but formed an island on their own. At times he had heard of certain Christian-minded Englishwomen in White Town attempting to establish orphanages for the more unfortunate children. The mortality rate was so high in the European community that many of these good ladies perished before their deeds took root.

'You may sit if you wish,' the Notary instructed.

The woman stood squarely before his table with a concentration that made him uneasy. Her flesh hung about her in such abundance that he was reminded of a mountain of soft sponges he had once seen harvested upon a beach. Ignoring the chair, she squatted down on the floor, rearranging her sari. Dumbleton leaned forward to keep her in view. His table was high and wide and all he could see of the woman were the long brown quills of her hat shifting below him in a threatening way. He felt this an unsatisfactory manner in which to conduct an interview.

'It might be better if you would sit upon the chair,' Dumbleton suggested.

After some hesitation, Jaya heaved herself up and sat on the chair. Her flesh spilt over the frame, like a pot of soup boiling over. Her short legs barely touched the floor and were spread wide apart beneath her muslin sari. Before Dumbleton could proceed with the interview, she began to speak in an agitated manner.

'They are taking the girl and now they are taking my things. I will bring a suit against them both.' Jaya's voice pitched about upon her anger. The tall feathers in her hat rocked perilously.

Mr Dumbleton looked confused. The woman's English was as raw as her voice, but he saw communication would be possible. 'Who is *the girl*, what are *your things,* and who are *both* of them? You must explain clearly to me.'

At the Notary's words and the unexpected patience in his voice, Jaya began to cry; she had anticipated ejection from Mr Dumbleton's room. She never cried but copiously, and now was no exception.

Dumbleton looked embarrassed. 'Come, come. How am I to understand if you do not explain?' Had she been a European woman he might have offered his handkerchief. There was clearly no need in this case, for the woman was already drying her eyes with the end of her sari.

'That night I too was there, sitting on the back veranda. I saw you then, Notary Sahib. They told me I must not come out into the room; no one must see my face. But my Sati wanted me there. She was so frightened. They could not make me leave her.'

'What night was this?' Dumbleton frowned.

'The night the spirits came into my Sati. She is possessed by a *ferenghi* devil, but I will get it out of her. Sati is my granddaughter,' Jaya explained.

'Ah! The night of the seance,' Dumbleton remembered, and began to make sense of the old woman's ties to Demonteguy.

'I saw both the Hatmen together then, that Chief Magistrate Holwell and Demonteguy. He is now my daughter Rita's husband. He has married her properly, not like my own husbands. That is the only good thing in this marriage, its properness. Her first marriage also was very proper. In this Rita is lucky, unlike me. You must also have seen how Hatman Holwell came into the room. And afterwards, when you were gone, for a long time they were talking together. So quietly, quietly talking and talking. And drinking much arrack also. And then after some days that Chief Magistrate Hatman, he sent his *goondas* to my house to get my diamonds. They made a great noise. They said they would beat me if I did not give them what they wanted. At last they found my things. All the neighbours came to watch. They will bear witness to what was done.' Jaya began to cry again. Dumbleton held up his hand, still very much confused about events.

'I think it would be best if you explain from the beginning, then I will understand things better,' he suggested. The mention of Holwell's name had immediately interested him. There were many like himself who had had enough of the Chief Magistrate's high-handed ways.

Jaya fell silent for a moment, then decided that the making of her will was the beginning of events. She was pleased to see the concentration with which Mr Dumbleton listened. As she talked, the Notary wrote quickly, the scratch of his quill underpinning her words. Outside the window there was a large tree. Monkeys sat in its branches peering into the Notary's room with bright-eyed curiosity, while picking lice from each other's fur. Crowds of monkeys had scampered about the Cutcherry on the day the Chief Magistrate had summoned her there. Jaya began to tremble as she recounted to Mr Dumbleton the scene at the native court.

The Cutcherry, being merely for the trying of native cases, had not the same grandeur as the White Town Courthouse. There were no plaster fleurs-de-lis or Doric pillars, no grand sweep or ornamented staircase. The Cutcherry was an airy building through which sparrows flew freely to nest in the raftered ceiling. Monkeys in their hundreds congregated in the compound and refused to be evicted, claiming the place as their own. They crowded upon the roof and occupied the windowsills like a squabbling, disinterested jury. It was a constant battle to keep them out of the courtroom. Each day the people of Black Town formed a never-ending queue about the building, standing patiently in the sun to speak to a magistrate. They were required to voice their business in a speedy, straightforward way when their turn came.

When at last Jaya had stood once more before the Chief Magistrate, her anger was well fermented. She had not come willingly, she had been summoned. She had seen no need to wear her hat for the lowly confines of the Cutcherry. As Mr Holwell spoke, reviewing her case, Jaya turned her back upon him, watching a mother bird feed its young in a wispy nest high above upon the rafters. Behind her the Chief Magistrate's voice stabbed the air in a sharp staccato. Jaya had decided not to understand his English, or the words of the interpreter. An old man with a child squatted behind her, waiting his turn with the magistrate. Jaya gave them an encouraging smile, drawing their attention to the sparrows. The old man pointed out the nest to the child, who moved up beside Jaya for a better view. The Chief Magistrate thumped his table with a hammer and glared. Jaya stood before him in a beam of sun; dust motes swirled about her as if circling her in magic light. For a moment she appeared unassailable. Since the evening of the seance, the Chief Magistrate's nerves were badly shredded, strange thoughts thrust into his mind. He brought the hammer down loudly once more.

'Aiee!' Jaya jumped in an exaggerated way as the hammer struck the table. Her hand flew to her throat in mock terror; the people behind her laughed. The Chief Magistrate thundered in new fury.

'You were ordered to hand over the inheritance of Sati Edwards, formerly in your charge but now to be under the legal guardianship of her stepfather, Fabian Demonteguy. Where is this inheritance? We have here ready the scales to weigh and assess its value. In the paper pertaining to the inheritance, mention is made of certain diamond items, the value of which has been put at considerable worth. Things of such value should be in the safe keeping of her legal guardian.' The Chief Magistrate's voice rose threateningly. Jaya made no answer but returned the magistrate's glare.

'If you will not produce the items, then I declare you in contempt of court,' Holwell roared.

'I made a will. Such a will is not for acting upon until after my death,' Jaya shouted.

'Do not shout in court. Can you read English? Can you write your name?' Holwell enquired, leaning forward over the table.

For a moment Jaya stiffened, smelling the brew of trickery. 'What is this reading and writing to do with a will?' Jaya faced Holwell squarely now, the sparrows forgotten. She had signed the will with a fingerprint.

'If you cannot read, then how can you be sure you made a will and not something else?' the Chief Magistrate asked, sitting back in his chair with a satisfied sniff.

He picked up a roll of parchment. 'I have here a copy of the document. Is this not your fingerprint? This is not a will; it is a making-over of your gems to your granddaughter. Whether before or after your death is not specified.' He waved the paper in his hand.

'This they did not tell me. *Badmash* lawyers.' Jaya grew red in the face. She saw immediately by the look in Holwell's eyes that this admission was something she should not have made. The Chief Magistrate pounced at once.

'Since you are no longer the girl's legal guardian, her inheritance must be handed over to that person, who is now Mr Demonteguy. You are presently in contempt of court. If the items are not brought quickly to me here, then I will take steps to secure them.' The Chief Magistrate sat back in his chair and sucked in his cheeks, staring hard at Jaya Kapur.

'They are my jewels. They belong only to me,' Jaya screamed. 'This is all a big play to steal my ornaments and to deprive my Sati of dowry.'

'Call the next case,' Holwell ordered.

He watched as Jaya Kapur was dragged away, cursing so loudly that the sparrows above flew out of the Cutcherry in a flurry. A feather dropped on to the Chief Magistrate's desk, brushing his cheek as it fell.

'The Hatmen and the *badmash* lawyers are all together in this,' Jaya sobbed as she described the experience in the Cutcherry to Mr Dumbleton.

'It will need to be sorted out,' Dumbleton comforted. Something seemed certainly amiss and he felt sorry for the ignorant woman before him. It was known that both Holwell and Demonteguy had business in diamonds.

'Hatman Holwell says it was no will, only a legal making-over of my ornaments to Sati. Can this be possible?' Jaya wiped her eyes.

'If you were not clear upon the matter yourself, and also cannot read what has been written down, then anything is possible. And there are such documents as you have described, to make over things before a death. How this should have come into Mr Demonteguy's possession without your knowing, is hard to understand.'

'He has bribed the *badmash* lawyer, what else? It is easy to cheat an old woman out of her only possessions,' Jaya replied.

'If it is a will you have made, then they can do nothing to you. If not, and you have gifted these items to your granddaughter as her inheritance in your lifetime, then your position is weak, for the law will not be upon you side,' the Nortary explained.

'They are all *choors*, thieves.' Once agin Jaya began to sob.

The violence of the day before, when the Chief Magistrate's *goondas* had come bursting into her hut, still flooded vividly through her. The men ware paid ruffians, and had woken her from sleep. They had abused her verbally with terrible *ghalees*, then thrown her into a corner while they tore up her home. They told her the Chief Magistrate wanted her jewels in his safe keeping for Mr Demonte-guy's stepdaughter. They kicked her water jar to smithereens. The sleeping pallet they ripped to a mound of white fluff that reminded her of the Chief Magistrate's wig. Her cooking utensils were thrown into the street and rolled about with a clatter. At once beggars had grabbed them and run off before they could be caught. Her big trunk was opened and the remaining clothes from her Murshidabad days had been strewn about the hut. The more they searched and found nothing, and angrier the *goondas* became. One held a knife to her throat. And then, just as they prepared to give up, they had seen the unevenness of the wall. They had struck the place repeatedly with a stick until the mud gave way and the bag of diamonds fell out of the wall.

She had since heard from Govindram through a paid spy that the jewels were in Mr Holwell's safe keeping. They had not even been given to Demonteguy. Mr Dumbleton's face, as Jaya recounted her tale, grew visibly sterner, especially at her last revelation.

'This is abominable.' Dumbleton frowned. 'What is the worth of this legacy?'

'How do I know about such things? Some of the diamonds are bigger than my thumbnail,' Jaya answered.

'It will be necessary for me to confer with my colleagues about the legality of this. There appear to be irregularities. I will also need to see a copy of the document you made. If it was a will then you can easily make another, reversing the first,' the Notary suggested.

'How many times can a woman make a will?' Jaya enquired.

'Any number,' Dumbleton replied.

'But each time I can only say the same thing. I want my Sati to have my ornaments,' Jaya insisted.

'Let me see the document first,' Mr Dumbleton answered, sitting back in his chair. The events were not without interest. In the Mayor's Court they had waited some time for just such a situation with which to clip the Chief Magistrate's wings.

'What about payment?' Jaya prepared herself for the worst.

'With irregularities like this it is possible you yourself might be paid some compensation in time. This could be a complaint against the Company Courts, not a legal suit. Let us leave it at that for the moment. An inquiry will need to be held.'

'No money needed?' Jaya was not sure she understood Mr Dumbleton's words.

'No money needed,' he confirmed, motioning to the *peon* to show her out.

'The paper I will send you tomorrow. My cousin Govindram has it in his safe keeping,' Jaya promised as she left the room.

The Notary wasted no time, once the day's procedures were finished, in summoning the Clerk of the Mayor's Court, Bartholomew Plaisted. He explained in detail the strange affair of Jaya Kapur.

'I was there myself that evening of the ridiculous seance. My wife insisted we go. I can certainly verify all the old lady has said. Holwell turned up that evening to see Demonteguy. It is yet another proof, Plaisted, that our Chief Magistrate's unlimited power has reached scandalous proportions. Now this naive old woman has been robbed by our Chief Magistrate and that low-class interloper Demonteguy. It is something I think the Board in London will be interested to hear,' Dumbleton explained.

'It will not be easy to break the Chief Magistrate's hold on things; he has accrued too much power,' Plaisted argued.

'He has taxed even prostitution. Any way he can tax the Indian, he taxes them. There is much discontent. The nawab's halls are filled with his people's complaints. Now I hear Holwell prepares to bring every half-caste Portuguese, Armenian and others who are Christian but not born of European parents under his *zamindary*. They will be forced to use the Cutcherry and taxed there as all Indians are taxed. The Mayor's Court has always upheld the rights of those who are Christian, whatever their birth or denomination. Now he seeks to exclude these people from recourse to our courts. He abuses his power. He seeks only revenues with which to dazzle our masters in Leadenhall. I believe, Plaisted, our Chief Magistrate lays the foundation not only for his own private fortune but for the Governorship itself. All at Calcutta's expense. He must be stopped.' Dumbleton's voice rose heatedly.

'We can try. Perhaps this old woman and her diamonds have given us a way,' Plaisted observed, but without conviction.

CHAPTER ELEVEN

The Council Chamber of Fort William was located in the Governor's House. It was a lofty room running the breadth of the building. Windows on both sides opened to the alternative views of the Hoogly and White Town. Outside, the blistering sun drained everything of colour. The silhouettes of trees were diminished as heat shimmered, distorting images. Shadows disappeared. Incandescent in their pearly plaster, only the houses of White Town competed with the sun.

In spite of the heat, a smell of mildew pervaded the Council Chamber. A library of leather-bound books ran the length of the room and gave off the odour of old paper. Upon the walls hung portraits of past Governors. After long battles with humidity, many of these eminent gentlemen now appeared afflicted by leprosy. The main feature of the room was the long polished table around which sat the Fort William Council.

It had been Drake's idea to call a Council of War, and Holwell had readily agreed. Siraj Uddaulah had not sat as expected in Kasimbazar but was pushing straight on to Calcutta.

'A Council of War will allow us to assess the strength of our defences,' Drake reasoned. It was more the bolstering effect of such a gathering that appealed to him at this moment.

'It will also give the impression of firm action on our part and avoid panic in both the Black and White Towns,' the Chief Magistrate pointed out.

Council meetings were a correct affair. Whatever the time of year, formal coats and wigs were worn. Dress swords had been dispensed with, for these were unwieldy when seated. No warning had been given for the calling of a Council of War and the sudden summons took everyone by surprise. The meeting had further been called at an hour when Calcutta sought to escape the heat in sleep, heightening the sense of emergency. The hasty arrangement allowed some men to arrive in light cotton clothes with skullcaps instead of wigs. Drake himself, realising the importance of the occasion, had chosen to wear a coat of the finest broadcloth, with elaborate silver facings. Already he was sweating profusely in this heavy attire.

Because of the hour the tatties were down, enclosing the Council Chamber in gloom. Servants revolved in a constant stream, dousing the blinds with water in an effort to cool the air. The wet matting gave off a mouldy smell and mixed with the scent of beeswax from the table. Hot winds blew against the shutters, rattling like rain in the louvres. There had also recently been a plague of red ants and the legs of tables and chairs now stood in cups of water to avert a further invasion. Beneath each chair was a low footstool, protected in the same way. The Council of War took their seats with difficulty. Some cups of water were overturned and immediately refilled by servants.

The Council of Fort William by law consisted of eleven members. No more than seven were ever present, for the four members who lived in outlying stations were invariably absent. Holwell sat to the right of Drake and looking about the table saw that William Mackett, the Paymaster, was in his seat. Opposite him sat Charles Manningham, the Export Warehouse Keeper, and William Frankland, the Import Warehouse Keeper. There was also Paul Pearkes, the Accountant, and Edward Eyre, the Storekeeper. Grouped about the further end of the table were an invited group whose opinions had been solicited for this occasion. Amongst them was the Chief Engineer, O'Hara, and Captain Minchin, the Garrison Commander. As Drake took his place an expectant hush fell upon the chamber.

The Governor cleared his throat. 'Gentlemen, this is a hypothetical meeting.' Even as he said the words, Drake realised his mistake.

'What kind of a meeting is that?' Minchin attacked, his pointed black beard giving him a satyric look.

'It is a meeting to determine what actions we have the option of taking in the event of a situation arising that has not yet arisen, and might not even arise,' Drake's voice dipped up and down like a bird trying to fly with an injured wing. He fixed Minchin with a belligerent stare. He had argued against including the commander in the Council of War, pointing out that the garrison had no knowledge of battle. Holwell had dismissed his remarks, saying they at least knew what to do with a cannon.

'Our Governor speaks in riddles.' Minchin gave a dismissive laugh. His scarlet military tunic was a blatant splash in the dim room. He had once had a tavern brawl with Drake, and animosity still remained between them.

There was a murmur of agreement about the table at Minchin's remark. Drake turned in distress to Holwell. The Chief Magistrate looked up, cleared his throat and reached for two packets of parchment. He was not averse to running the meeting if that was what Drake wanted. The Governor leaned back in his chair in relief. Everyone turned towards Holwell.

'As you know, Siraj Uddaulah has already captured Kasimbazar and our Factory there and is now making his way to Calcutta. The French have given us a most detailed account of the army as it passed through Chandernagore.' The Chief Magistrate cleared his throat and proceeded to read aloud from the letter that had arrived that morning from the French settlement.

The French informed Fort William that the nawab's army was of such immense proportions that it had taken more than half a day to pass. The nawab himself led his cavalry, eighteen thousand strong. Sometimes he rode at their head on horseback, sometimes he was carried in an ornate palanquin studded with silver. The artillery, announced the French, was unfortunately under the command of one of their own, which should make it a force to be reckoned with. The Marquis St Jacques was a renegade Frenchman who had been expelled from the garrison at Chandernagore. The number of cannon that had passed could not even be counted. Each was pulled by up to thirty yoke of oxen, while four hundred elephants lumbered behind. At a rough estimate there appeared to be thirty thousand foot soldiers with assorted weapons. Two thousand camels had also gone by, loaded with tents and stores. The rear of the cavalcade had yet to completely pass. This consisted of servants and cooks, workmen and concubines, besides seven thousand professional plunderers whose duty it was to strip each village lying in their path.

As he passed through Chandernagore, the nawab had demanded the surrender of the French garrison. The French had acted politically, pleading they were merchants with no thought in their head but trade. They had also offered financial atonement for any offence they might have given. The matter had been quickly settled at three hundred and fifty thousand rupees. Immediately, Siraj Uddaulah had lost all interest in Chandernagore and marched on towards Calcutta. The French begged the English in Fort William to act as they had done and not dwell on principle.

As the Chief Magistrate finished reading there was silence about the table. 'This army is little different from the armies of any other Oriental potentate,' Holwell attempted to comfort.

'It is coming for us, that's all,' Drake replied in a low voice. The sweat now ran in rivulets down his back, and beneath his thick coat, his shirt was uncomfortably wet.

'Let us pay then as the French have done,' Minchin announced.

Return the treasure and the nobleman, Kishindas. Order Omi chard to send him back from where he came. That is all the nawab wants. Already all the digging of the Ditch has stopped. Our very lives are endangered by sticking our necks out in this way.' O'Hara's voice broke hoarsely.

'We are not in the same position as the French. We have much to lose by capitulating to the nawab's demands. If Rai Durlabh can rid us of Siraj Uddaulah, Calcutta will have improved security and trading agreements. It will mean greater wealth for us all,' said Manningham. He had no wish to give up his share of the treasure, but the invitees at the end of the table knew nothing of the conspiracy between Fort William and the Young Begum's faction in Murshidabad. They knew only that intrigue was afoot at the Murshidabad court to get rid of Siraj Uddaulah and that Kishindas and his treasure were part of this intrigue.

'But what if he cannot get rid of him?' Mackett reasoned.

'You have put us in a difficult situation by giving protection to this Kishindas.' Minchin scowled at Drake.

'The nawab was not expected to set off for a battle. This is an uncalculated turn of events,' Drake turned red in the face. Beside him the Chief Magistrate cleared his throat in warning.

'We can relinquish Kishindas and his treasure even at the last moment if attack appears likely. The nawab will perhaps bargain a larger sum from us than from the French for our defiance of him, but that is all. We should not panic but wait and see the way events are shaping. I have confidence in Rai Durlabh. He has as much to gain by the execution of his plan as have we in the Settlement.' As the Chief Magistrate finished speaking, new arguments began around the table.

'Perhaps it would be best if we were to have a small dose of Madeira,' Holwell suggested, sensing the tension in the room.

Usually, during a break in meetings, men wandered about, glass in hand, chatting of this or that. Now, the Council of War took their refreshment where they sat. It was not easy to manoeuvre back the chairs, positioned as they were in bowls of water, but more than this, the letter from Chandernagore had had the effect of rooting people. Everyone now realised the enormous risk Rai Durlabh must take playing traitor to the nawab. Perhaps, as Mackett suggested, the commander would not be able to turn a sword upon Siraj Uddaulah.

The nawab was astute and must surround himself closely with guards, spies and tasters for poisoned food.

During the break the Governor sipped his Madeira glumly. He stared at the portrait of Job Charnock, founding father of Calcutta. Charnock's long nose and rippling curls, his loose mouth and Puritan collar confronted Drake in a critical way. He had been of a slippery, swashbuckling nature, flourishing like a weed in any water that reeked of corruption. He had survived thirty-eight years in India and his fame rested upon this longevity; he had had more years to get things done for posterity to hear about. He had been famous for his resourcefulness in tight situations.

A new anxiety overwhelmed the Chief Magistrate as he sipped his glass of wine. He turned to Minchin. 'How many men have we to defend Fort William should we be required, for any reason, to make a token stand?'

'It is difficult to give a precise number. We cannot match the armies of nawabs.' Minchin laughed unpleasantly.

'We must have a count,' Holwell insisted. Minchin shrugged.

'There is a constant fluctuation. Many die; they are always dying. The native ranks desert when and as they see fit and the hospital lays its claim upon large numbers,' he argued.

'This is preposterous,' the Chief Magistrate replied. His own orderly mind would have been able to account for every man. 'Find out how many men the garrison commands. Bring an exact report,' he roared at Minchin's second-in-command, Captain Clayton, who was also present in the room.

With Clayton gone, talk turned next to the physical condition of the fort. Everyone looked at the Chief Engineer, O'Hara.

'I gave a detailed report upon this matter some months ago,' O'Hara replied. The Chief Engineer was new to Calcutta and had been shocked upon his arrival at the condition of the fort. His report had received little notice from the Council and even less finance.

'If Council members wish, they can accompany me on a tour of the fort. They can then ascertain for themselves the true state of the defences,' O'Hara suggested.

'A good idea,' Drake agreed with alacrity. He had a great desire to vacate the tension of the Council Chamber, which, with each sentence spoken, only brought their precarious situation clearer into focus. Even if no battle were to occur, all this talk of defence was making him nervous.

Before the Council of War could accompany O'Hara, Captain Clayton returned to confirm that seventy European soldiers were confined to the hospital and twenty-five more had been sent to stations up-country.

'There are, of course, our black Portuguese and native troops,' Clayton reminded them, turning to the Governor. 'That leaves us, sir, with an available garrison of one hundred and eighty men, of which forty-five are Europeans.'

'Is that all?' Drake frowned. In his mind the nawab's thirty thousand marched towards him in a swirling cloud of dust. He looked again at the portrait of Charnock and remembered something.

'Once, a nawab surrounded Charnock on an island with an army of two thousand. Charnock had only a hundred men. Seventy reinforcements arrived and were dropped off where the enemy could not see them. Charnock had them march up to his fort cheering loudly. Then the process was repeated, the same seventy men marching round and round so that the enemy thought continuous reinforcements were arriving. They called the battle off.' Drake looked about the table.

'Times are different now,' said Mackett.

'Then, Charnock himself lived in a mud hut,' Manningham remembered.

'Let us proceed to view the defences of Fort William,' the Chief Magistrate suggested, his face set in lines of new sternness as he rose from his chair to follow O'Hara.

*

Although the afternoon was already well upon them, the heat still shimmered. Emerging from the darkness of Governor's House, the men gasped in the fiery air. The adjutant birds sat unmoving upon every convenient perch, like carved heraldic emblems. So great was the population of these birds, and so densely at times were they ranged upon the bastions, that at night their massed bodies gave Fort William a Mephisophelean appearance. Those near the entrance of Governor's House turned their heads sleepily as the Council of War emerged.

O'Hara strode ahead. The men trooped behind him reluctantly, some in full broadcloth and wigs and some in light muslin and curled Indian shoes. Upon the south-west bastion they stopped before the gun carriages. Numerous monsoons had eroded the metal, that now crumbled like biscuit. The group examined the beams upon which these decrepit guns must be mounted. With the help of a pocket knife, O'Hara tore away chunks of wood as if he sampled fruit cake.

'They are unusable.' Drake was unable to suppress his surprise after twenty-six gun carriages were found to be in the same state of decay. He was panting hard and had taken off his coat and unbuttoned his waistcoat. Other men in the group soon followed the Governor's example.

Next, they descended by the South River Gate to the Governor's Wharf to face a further mountain of rusting metal. Upon examination this turned out to be fifty cannon, along with a great many cannonballs. These had been unloaded upon their delivery three years previously, at the place where they still lay. The consignment had been ordered when the Marathas still threatened, but its eventual arrival in a decade of peace had appeared exaggerated. This immense delivery, which had filled the holds of an armada of Indiamen, was now completely useless. The Fort William party were silent, battling as much with the effects of the heat as with despondency. Almost to a man they had now removed their neckbands, exposing their chests to the sun.

O'Hara marched on around Fort William, pointing out an endless list of dilapidation. By the time the men arrived at the East Gate, facing The Avenue, shadows were deepening. In the sudden manner of Indian evenings, light was fast disappearing. This abrupt fading of luminosity paralleled the feelings of the Fort William group as they returned to the Council Chamber. So deep was the gloom and so great their exhaustion that the Governor ordered some claret to be immediately brought to the table.

'There is nothing more we can do for tonight,' said Drake. 'Perhaps tomorrow some line of defence will reveal itself to us.'

After everyone had departed and the candles were lighted, the Governor and the Chief Magistrate sat on at the table with their claret.

'Perhaps it would be best if you asked the Chaplain to attend tomorrow's meeting,' Drake suggested to Holwell.

Bellamy had not attended the Council of War, for Drake had argued with Holwell that the opinions of the representative of God were of little relevance to the secular matter of defence. It appeared to him now that God might indeed have a part to play in the future of Fort William.

'I think you are losing your hold on the facts.' The Chief Magistrate did not reply in the superior manner the Governor had expected.

'And what are they?' Drake asked as he poured himself more claret.

'That there will be no battle, or just the show of one at the most if we need to play for time. We have assurance from Rai Durlabh, and he appears to me a man of his word. He stands to gain much from succeeding in his mission. It is a gamble, but one we should bet on, I think,' Holwell replied. Letters to this effect had already passed between Rai Durlabh and the Governor.

'But what if things go wrong?' Drake worried. 'What if he cannot get rid of the nawab at this particular time?'

'It is unlikely. Rai Durlabh will see his chance and take it. Should there be some miscalculation, we will evacuate the fort. Do not forget, we have the river. The nawab comes overland; he will have no access to the river from his landlocked position. In the worst instance we will wait on the boats until it is safe to return. However, if we vacate the fort, we might lose it forever. There is much to be gained if things go as planned. Either way we shall be the richer,' the Chief Magistrate reasoned.

'The treasure is still with Omichand,' Drake reminded him.

'We must bring it into the fort,' Holwell replied, his face impassive before the Governor's agitation. 'If things go wrong, we shall evacuate and take the treasure with us.'

The next morning they assembled once more. Although it was early, the hot winds blew, spitting dust into the room. Calcutta now lived on a razor's edge, squinting each day at the sky, willing the rains to come. Nerves were taut as fiddle strings. Because the sun was not yet high, the tatties in the Council Chamber were still rolled up. Shafts of burning light skidded across the mahogany table to hit the portraits of past Governors. The legs of chairs were still immersed in their bowls of water.

The faces of the Council of War showed signs of a sleepless night. Only the Reverend Bellamy appeared his usual jovial self, the end of his nose like a crimson bud about to burst into flower. He had been given a synopsis of the previous day's meeting and an account of the fort's defences. Since his reliance upon God was of a less doubting nature than that of his colleagues, he saw no need to view the approaching thirty thousand with the same degree of dread. He beamed good will about the table. Unlike most of the men, knowing little, he had slept well the night before.

It was this sharpness of mind in the midst of the general exhaustion that caused the Chaplain to ask a pertinent question once the meeting had been called to order. Military matters were not his concern, but a thought had occurred and he spoke his mind.

'I have heard the situation with regard to our gun and cannon power is not of the best. But I have not heard from anyone what the situation is with regard to our ammunition. Do we have powder and grapeshot enough?' Gervase Bellamy smiled.

There was some movement around the table, like the weak eddying of a current in a shallow stream. No one had thought of ammunition. The Governor called immediately for a glass of arrack.

'Commander Minchin?' Drake managed an expectant smile.

'It would be best to ask Lieutenant Witherington. He is in charge of the powder store.' Minchin refused to be trapped by further responsibility.

Witherington was summoned and soon appeared, flushed with pleasure at being called before the Council of War. 'I think, sir, I am not wrong in saying that never in the history of Calcutta have we had such ample stocks of powder,' he announced to Drake. Relief echoed around the table.

'What is the position with regard to grapeshot?' asked the Reverend Bellamy, his mind still full of vigour.

'I will have to check, sir,' Witherington said, and hurried from the room.

Soon he returned, no longer smiling. 'With regard to the grapeshot, there is only a very small quantity. And that too is unusable, for worms have attacked it. Crumbles to dust when handled,' he reported.

'Why is there not more grapeshot?' the Chief Magistrate demanded with a frown.

'Well, sir, we have little actual need of it. We have never fought a battle,' Witherington reminded the Council of War.

'At least there is powder enough,' Minchin said in a businesslike way.

'Well, sir, there appears now to be a slight problem there also,' Witherington replied, looking nervously at the commander.

'And what is that, Witherington?' Minchin demanded, assuming a defensive stance.

'During the last monsoon the powder was not stored in a dry place.' Witherington gave an embarrassed cough.

'You are trying to tell us we have no powder?' Drake shouted.

'Powder we have, sir, but it is unusable. It is all damp. We have a very small dry stock, which we keep for gun salutes. There has never been a need for so much powder, that is the trouble, sir.' Witherington explained.

When Witherington finally departed, Drake turned savagely upon Minchin. 'You are not fit for your post,' he yelled. Others joined in the condemnation of the commander.

'Powder can be dried,' Minchin protested, as if it was a small matter. 'And if not in Fort William then in the large magazine in town there will surely be dry powder.'

The Chief Magistrate was silent during this angry exchange, but when the clamour died down he made his announcement. 'Since our garrison is so small and we face so large an army, we must form a militia to swell our numbers.' The originality of this suggestion was enough to bring silence to the table.

'We have amongst us a good number of responsible civilians to call upon, and we can request volunteers from the foreign vessels on the Hoogly. There are also large numbers of Dutch and black Portuguese mercenaries who are always ready to fight for a share of the spoils,' Holwell continued.

The Governor turned to Holwell. 'Chief Magistrate, you shall be captain in charge of the militia.' Out of the corner of his eye Drake saw Minchin glower, cut to the quick that a civilian should be promoted over a garrison commander.

Holwell at first seemed taken aback and then began to look pleased. The Chaplain had brought with him, as Holwell had hoped, a crate of Madeira from his cellar to fortify the Council. Glasses were filled and soon the men of Fort William began to feel more assertive.

'It appears to me now not so much a question of defending Fort William as of defending Calcutta itself,' Reverend Bellamy stated in a thoughtful voice, savouring his Madeira. The wine was of a good vintage and he was already regretting having to waste it on men like Minchin, or juniors like Eyre and Pearkes.

'It would only be possible to defend White Town,' Manningham reasoned. Everyone nodded their understanding.

'We have no choice in the matter,' the Chief Magistrate agreed.

'But we are still without any plan to defend the city,' O'Hara interrupted impatiently.

'And what do you suggest would be our best plan of defence?' The Chief Magistrate spoke coldly; he was tired of O'Hara's superiority.

O'Hara leaned forward in his chair and made a terrifying announcement. 'There is *no* way to defend White Town.'

Once he saw this statement had gained him attention, the Chief Engineer continued. 'There is only one chance for White Town should it come to a battle. We must demolish all the large houses about the fort, then fight from the fort itself,' he declared.

O'Hara's comment was met with a thunderous roar of dissent. Many men at the table had their houses in exactly the places the Chief Engineer wished destroyed. O'Hara thumped on the table for quiet and then turned to the windows, pointing to the grand mansions outside.

'Look there, gentlemen. Firstly, we cannot defend the long perimeter of the fort. And secondly, over the years the houses about the fort have come to stand higher than its ramparts. The enemy could fire down upon our garrison from those very houses and bring their cannon right up beneath our walls. If we destroy those residences we can then fire from a protected position, for they will have to advance towards us over open ground.'

'This is preposterous. What do you know of military strategy?' Minchin announced when O'Hara had finished.

'You really expect us to burn down our own homes?' Frankland laughed.

'Would you like us also to burn down the church?' the Chaplain enquired.

'It might come to that,' O'Hara grimaced.

'I shall pray for you,' Reverend Bellamy answered, peering sternly at him.

'The important thing is that there should be some plan for defence, in case things turn out for the worst,' O'Hara insisted. 'That is why we are here.'

'If things turn out badly, which is not expected, do not forget we have the river and can evacuate to our boats.' The Chief Magistrate now offered his contingency plan. A wave of relief swept immediately about the table.

'But we *must* have a plan of defence,' O'Hara insisted.

At last it was decided to draw a defence line through the houses of White Town, with batteries at the three main entrances. Smaller streets were to be palisaded, and a trench dug across The Park. Perrin's Redoubt at the far side of the fort was to be strengthened. The trench across The Park created the most debate, for to construct this fortification meant the destruction of all the trees.

As the Governor stood up to draw the meeting to a close, a servant came in with a man from the local bazaar. He approached the Governor fearfully. Drake listened quietly to what the man said and the colour drained from his face. His voice was grim as he turned to the waiting Council of War.

'Siraj Uddaulah has issued an order forbidding all native merchants and shopkeepers to supply the English with provisions.' Governor Drake sat down once more in his chair.

CHAPTER TWELVE

The moon hung low over Black Town, bloated with a yellow light. Outside her hut, Jaya Kapur stopped beside the water jar, staring up into the sky. As she lifted the lid of the container, the moon slipped quickly inside. Its light illuminated her hand and swam upon the water. She dipped in her scoop and the moon fragmented, then quickly reformed in the water. Jaya turned to look again at the sky. If the moon was aloof, forever beyond the touch of men, what was this silvery image in her hands that refused to disappear? She slammed the lid back over the jar and hurried into her hut.

On the pallet Sati moved weakly. Jaya helped her to sit and held the cup of moon-filled water to her granddaughter's lips. Then she peeled away the strips of cotton covering Sati's back and spread a fresh poultice of herbs over the raw marks from the exorcism, strange fears alight inside her. She was sure she had made a terrible mistake; the conviction grew stronger each hour.

A rat ran across the floor; the rustle of insects filled the thatch. Outside, bullfrogs and crickets hacked at the silence. Jaya stared at the patched-up hole in the wall that until recently had hidden her jewels. The loss of her gems sliced through her again, a wound that would not heal. A thread of hope still tied her to the Notary, Mr

Dumbleton. She remembered again her interview with him and his face, whiskery as a cat's. In India cats were evil creatures, so she was unsure if her association of this animal with Mr Dumbleton made him entirely trustworthy; he was, after all, a Hatman.

She stroked her granddaughter's hair, certain now of her mistake. The knowledge lay like a stone within her, its weight pulling everything tight. Jaya looked apprehensively about the hut, but nothing seemed out of order. Yet she knew she could no longer carry her anxiety alone; she must discuss the matter with Govindram. He would know what to do.

She heaved herself up and lit a fresh stick of incense before a brass image of the Goddess. On the wall above hung a picture of the *Devi* seated upon her tiger. Her many arms held auspicious objects. She was adorned with the crescent moon and her body blazed with the splendour of a thousand suns. For a moment, straightening up from prayer, Jaya met the stern gaze of the deity. Then, as Sati appeared to be asleep, she pushed open the rush door of her home and went off to find Govindram.

As soon as her grandmother had left the hut, Sati raised her head. She heard the scuttle of rats and the scratch of insects in the thatch. Outside the window, the distended body of the moon hung so low above the world it had caught in the limbs of a tree. Its white light drew together heaven and earth, knotting them in the branches. The tree had become a magic thing. It was all the work of Durga, she had pulled the moon down from the sky. Durga sat stretched out upon a branch, head sunk upon her chest as if sharing Sati's suffering. Fireflies were clustered in her hair, setting the moontree ablaze. Sati kept her eyes upon Durga's luminous presence and slowly the pain seemed to lessen. A spectral light pulsated from the tree, empowering whatever it touched. It was said that the moon was the cup from which the gods drank the elixir of immortality. Sati stretched out her arm and let the pewter light spill liquidly over her hand.

Jaya reached Govindram's gate and the *chowkidar* let her in. She found Govindram finishing his dinner. Beside him Mohini glared up at her in annoyance. Jaya took no notice, squatting down before Govindram.

'I have made a terrible mistake,' she announced, coming immediately to the point. Govindram finished his food, rinsed his fingers in a bowl of water a servant offered and looked in query at Jaya.

'For many years you have been making too many mistakes,' Mohini grumbled.

'Again there is trouble with Hatman Holwell? Your diamonds are returned?' Govindram asked.

'The trouble is greater than these small things,' Jaya replied.

'If those troubles are now small, then indeed the present trouble must be great.' Govindram exchanged a glance of amusement with his wife.

'My trouble is not of this world,' Jaya answered.

'Ahh!' Govindram sat back and prepared to hear his cousin's latest woe. Mohini gave an impatient grunt. She chose a mango from a dish of fruit the servant offered and began to cut it herself for her husband.

'All this time I have been thinking a *ferenghi* devil has entered my Sati. Now I am no longer sure.' A tumbler of sherbet and some sweetmeats had been placed before Jaya. She did not reach for them with her usual alacrity.

'You are without appetite?' Mohini asked with interest.

'If this trouble concerns Sati then tell it to us quickly.' Govindram frowned. He knew all about Sati's possession. Once, he had seen the strange phenomenon himself as the deep, rough voice emerged from the girl. He and Mohini had been greatly disturbed. Such possession was as intractable as disease. Although the treatment for the affliction was harsh, he had agreed to it and paid the money, wishing to see the girl freed.

'Why were you sure before that it was a *ferenghi*, a foreigner?' Mohini's interest was so great she forgot to edge her query with the usual sarcasm.

'Because that evening at Rita's, in front of those White Town *ferenghi,* the spirit was the same as the Hatmen. Same words, same voice, same way of thinking. Aiee, such things it said,' Jaya remembered.

'The spirits are too clever. They can appear as they want. They play with us for their own amusement.' Mohini cut the fragrant flesh of the mango free of its skin and placed it before her husband.

'But now I know it is *not* a *ferenghi,*' Jaya whispered. Mohini looked at her sharply.

'But only just now you were saying it *was* a *ferenghi,*' Mohini began to argue, but Govindram held up his hand.

'What is it then, if not a *ferenghi*?' he asked, leaning forward.

Jaya's pouched cheeks trembled, her chins rippled, she clasped her arms about herself. Mohini and Govindram waited. Jaya took a deep breath and began to tell her cousin all that had occurred in the temple.

'So many times she is calling the spirit, Durga. Now I know this Durga is not just any ordinary, common Durga. It is the Goddess.' Jaya's voice sank to a whisper. Then, with an effort, she continued her story.

'That day at the temple, the beating was so great the spirit was forced to come out of Sati. I saw it jump from her body into the room. It was terrible to behold, but I knew immediately it was the *Devi.* She was black as night and her tongue was so long it covered her chin. As Kali the Goddess has entered into my Sati. I tried then to stop that priest. I shouted that the Goddess had come. He did not understand. He is a fool. The Goddess is standing before him, and he can see nothing.'

'How can you be sure it was the Goddess?' Mohini whispered, her voice squashed beneath the marvel. Govindram sat silent, his brow creased in concentration.

'It was confirmed for me,' Jaya replied with sudden briskness. In spite of her emotional state, she had not failed to notice Mohini's unaccustomed respect.

'How was that?' Mohini leaned forward.

'As we entered the temple, a tiger roared. The *Devi* rides always upon her tiger. And at the very moment I looked upon the Goddess, it roared again. What other explanation can there be?' Jaya observed Mohini's awed reaction with satisfaction.

'If what you are saying is true, then this is no demon to be beaten from Sati.' Govindram frowned in confusion.

'I am also thinking the same thing,' nodded Jaya. 'The Goddess has come for some special reason.'

'If really the Goddess lives in Sati then she is above us all,' Mohini fell silent at the thought.

'The *Devi* has come to protect us from the Hatmen and from that Chief Magistrate Holwell who has taken my jewels.' This new revelation hit Jaya like a burst of sunlight. Suddenly, the loss of her jewels seemed a small price to pay for the presence beside her of the Goddess.

'It is not so much the Hatmen from whom we need protection. Siraj Uddaulah already marches towards Calcutta. All local merchants have been forbidden to supply the English with provisions. There is much fright in both Black Town and White Town. There could be death for those who help the English. Many people are preparing to leave, fearing for the future.' Govindram told the women the news.

Mohini gasped excitedly. 'Then this is why the *Devi* has come. She will fight for us like she fought the *asuras*. Remember how she manifested Kali so that she could devour the demons, laughing as she flung their elephants into her mouth, crunching up their chariots and horses, striking everywhere with her sword.'

'The Goddess easily rid the world of the evil *asuras*,' Jaya nodded. Everything had begun to fall into place. The one thing she could not get used to was the sudden lull in the animosity between herself and Mohini. It did not feel right at all.

'I must go back to Sati,' Jaya announced, heaving herself to her feet.

At the door Mohini stepped forward and pulled her unexpectedly into a close embrace. Jaya was taken by surprise; usually Mohini busied herself in some task that prevented a proper goodbye. She wondered how long Mohini's good humour would last.

Jaya walked the short distance to her own hut in a daze. The presence of the Goddess in her household was something she could not yet grasp. She turned into the densely packed alleys surrounding her home, which were filled with small shops. Her way was illuminated by the flares upon the stalls. Soon she came upon the itinerant vegetable woman who visited her hut each day; she was still hawking her wares.

'*Brinjal, gobi, bhindi.*' The woman sang out the names of her vegetables in a cracked contralto, stationing herself, basket on head, at a steady trot beside Jaya.

'I bought all I needed from you this morning. Who is fool enough to buy at this late hour? Look at the state of your vegetables, all day they have been in the sun.' Jaya pointed to the limp cabbage leaves and shrunken roots in the basket. 'Give it away to the beggars.'

'Have you heard? We are not allowed to sell to the English,' the woman whined.

The man at the fruit stall raised his voice. 'There will soon be no beggars left. They will be the first to run into the jungle when Siraj Uddaulah comes. They have nothing to lose and nothing to take with them.'

The road was suddenly filled by bleating goats. The goatherd's small son tried to round them up. The goats took no notice and pushed about Jaya. A kid stopped to urinate at her feet and then hurried after its mother. Two of the animals crashed into a stall selling terracotta oil lamps. The stallholder cursed loudly and shook his fist at the boy as a lamp fell to the ground. At last the goats were chased away and the lane returned to normal.

'Better to stay in Calcutta than to run. We will make money

providing for Siraj Uddaulah's army,' said the oil-lamp man, as he picked up broken pieces of terracotta.

In the dark alley the flares licked at the night. The moon illuminated the ragged fronds of palms. From the jungle came the rustling of bats and the calls of nocturnal creatures. Huge moths fluttered about. Jaya looked around apprehensively. She had walked at night many times down this alley and never thought the thoughts that came to her now. The Goddess was making her see everything differently. Mundane things seemed suddenly mysterious; the world was turned upside down. She stared at the sky, one foot still planted in the puddle of goat's urine. The moon had sunk so low it was cradled by trees and glowed within branches. Heaven had fallen to earth. The world seemed suddenly a place of transformation.

'Don't be a donkey. Siraj Uddaulah's army will burn our stalls,' shouted the man who sold spices, seated cross-legged before his heaps of dried chillies. 'I shall leave as soon as I hear he is near.'

'He will be a fool if he chases us into the jungle. He has an army of thirty thousand to feed. What does your brother in the big house say?' The fruit man turned to Jaya.

'Better to run. My cousin brother says the nawab has professional looters to strip your shops of food to feed his army.' Jaya shook her foot free of the putrid puddle. As the cousin of Govindram, her opinion carried weight.

'What you say is true,' said the man with the oil lamps. 'There is enough in life waiting to kill me, without Siraj Uddaulah. I will tell my wife to pack the cart tonight. Let it stand ready, then we can run at a moment's notice.'

'The Hatmen and their fort are here to protect the city,' said a man who was buying some mangoes from the fruit stall.

'Hatmen only protect themselves,' answered the spice man. 'They will lock themselves into their fort and leave us to our fate.'

'If Black Town people flee, so will the White Town servants. Soon the Hatmen will see how they depend upon us.' The oil-lamp man was pleased with this line of reasoning.

'I have also good *moong dhal*.' The vegetable woman began pestering Jaya again, anxious for a last sale. Lifting the basket from her head, she squatted down to search amongst the shrivelled vegetables. 'Make some *dhal* for your granddaughter. It will give her strength to throw out the demon inside her. How did it go at the temple today?' The matter of Sati's possession had been followed with interest in the quarter around Jaya's home.

'It is none of your business. You are obstructing my way. I do not want your *dhal*. The last lot you sold me was crawling with maggots, and you charged me for their weight.' Jaya tried to step around the basket.

'Next time I'll give you a discount. Here, see, this *dhal* is good.' The woman ran the lentils through her fingers, holding her hand to the flare at the fruit stall.

The fruit man leaned forward over a pile of watermelons. 'Buy *musumbi* for your granddaughter. Sweet limes will do her more good than *dhal*. Heal her wounds quickly. Their acid will burn out the spirit inside her. Do not buy from these itinerant people. Buy from us stallholders and you buy first class.'

'I have no rent to pay for a stall, so my produce is cheap and good.' The woman stood up and began to shout.

'You are obstructing me, get out of my way. My granddaughter is waiting at home.' Jaya herself began to shout.

The man who sold sandals was perched on the narrow shelf that was his shop, behind his merchandise. Rows of leather thongs were strung up like thick vines about him. He pushed his head out of this foliage. 'Make her drink lemon juice mixed with red chillies. Four sips every two hours. That chases out these spirits. My son also was possessed for a while, but we got rid of the devil that way.'

'There is no devil inside her,' Jaya informed them in exasperation. She raised her eyes again to the moon. The sandal man, the spice man, the vegetable woman and the man from the fruit stall all looked at her expectantly.

'It is the Goddess Herself who has come,' Jaya revealed. The importance of this announcement beat through her. In the trees the glow of the moon intensified. Light skated across a pond, turning it to pewter.

'How do you know this?' the fruit man asked, a new note of awe in his voice.

'It was confirmed in the temple. I saw the Goddess with my own two eyes. She jumped out of Sati into the room. Her tiger roared for Her from the jungle. I heard that too. It was the Goddess, there is no doubt,' Jaya informed them. 'Now let me pass, stupid woman.'

The itinerant vegetable woman drew back at once to the side of the lane, pressed her hands together and lowered her head in respect to Jaya.

'If the Goddess has come, it is for a reason. She will fight our battle with Siraj Uddaulah. We will be safe,' the sandal man announced.

'Here, take this ripe melon,' the fruit man insisted. 'Ask the Goddess to care for us in this difficult time.'

'Take these yams,' said the vegetable woman, not to be outdone. 'They are still good. Fresh things I will bring you tomorrow. We must keep the Goddess happy.'

'No harm can come to us if the Goddess is amongst us,' the seller of sandals agreed.

When at last Jaya reached home and pushed open the door, she struggled to enter, loaded down with the melon and vegetables, with a terracotta oil lamp and a pair of sandals. Sati lay with her eyes wide open. The flame before the Goddess had burnt out. The moon streamed in through the window, lighting the room mysteriously. Jaya peered nervously about; her home had acquired a strange new dimension. She hurried to the oil lamp. At this hour the Goddess must not be left in the dark. Pushing open the door again, she went to light a fresh wick from Pagal the albino who lived next door.

It was impossible not to tell Pagal the news, now that she had told the stallholders and the vegetable woman. He was after all her neighbour. Jaya explained the whole thing to him, adding details she would not divulge to a common shopkeeper. The albino's rabbity pink eyes blinked in confusion. He wore no turban and his flaxen hair fell about his face. His wife was out and his children danced around him, dark as the rest of Black Town, as if they were no relation.

'The Goddess has come to your house? Next door to us poor people? *Praise be to Kali. Praise. Reverence to Her.*' Pagal was overcome; he began to pray. The children, not realising the seriousness of the news, jumped about, chanting his words irreligiously.

'The Goddess has come next door. *Praise be to Kali. Reverence to Her!*' They sang out the words.

'Shut up,' Jaya commanded, lighting the wick from the flame in Pagal's house. As she turned, the albino roused himself and accompanied her. His children followed. Outside his hut he picked a frond of flowering creeper.

'For the Goddess,' he said.

In the door of Jaya's hut Pagal hesitated, as if afraid to enter. He stood staring at Sati as his children pushed about him. Then he bowed his head and pressed his hands together in obeisance. His children giggled as he stepped forward to lay the flowers at Sati's feet. Sati half opened her eyes and then closed them again, unable to find the energy to acknowledge him. She felt the feathery touch of leaves on her skin and heard the albino's breath pumping noisily in his throat.

As a child Jaya had told her the story of Pagal. Everyone called him Pagal, the mad thing; nobody knew what his real name was. One year there had been a monsoon when it rained so much whole towns were swept away. The albino was a baby then, and, unnoticed by his mother, who was busy cleaning rice, he crawled out into the rain. Soon he was lost and cried himself to sleep beneath a thorny bush. It was a while before his mother found him, and during that time, it had rained so hard upon him that all his colour was washed away. He had crawled out of his home a deep polished walnut and returned the colour of a maggot. His mother had never got over it. She sobbed

156

for weeks, refusing to nurse her baby. The horror of seeing his marble skin against her dark breast soon caused all her milk to dry up. Eventually she died of grief. The albino was then doubly cursed. He was left not only with the monsoon's freakish affliction but also with the burden of causing his mother's death.

'*Praise. Praise. Reverence to Her.*' The albino's white hair fell over his pink hands as he backed respectfully out of the door. His children crowded after him, still tossing his words about between them.

Once Pagal had departed, Jaya set the lamp before the Goddess again, bowed a moment in prayer, then started the cooking fire to heat a gruel of rice and *dhal*. She helped Sati up to eat the warm food. The girl coughed and pushed the gruel away, but Jaya was gently insistent. Soon the bowl was finished. Jaya settled down on the pallet beside her granddaughter.

'I have done a terrible thing. Tomorrow I am going back to the temple and asking forgiveness of the Goddess. I will take a basket of fruit to offer.' Jaya spoke in an agitated way.

'What is the matter?' Sati whispered. Any word of the temple now filled her with fear.

'I saw Her,' Jaya whispered. 'That fool of a priest could not see Her. Only to me did She reveal herself. There is no devil inside you. It is the Great Goddess who has come to you.'

'What are you saying?' Sati asked. 'It is only my Durga. I have told you about her many times.' To push the words out of her mouth was an effort; the pain reverberated down her back.

'The Goddess has come into you. She has come to you as Kali. In the temple I saw Her. I heard Her speak in that strange voice, deep as a man's,' Jaya told her.

'You saw the *Goddess*?' Sati whispered. Her grandmother's talk made her uneasy.

'I tried to stop that priest. I pulled at his arm and shouted but the fool took no notice of me. All he wants is money. The Goddess is before him and he can see nothing. But I, an old woman, can see Her,' Jaya scoffed.

'Why has She come to me?' Sati looked around for Durga. In spite of what her grandmother said, she could not see Durga as Jaya did. She looked at her in disbelief.

Jaya would say no more. Already her eyes began to close. It had been too long a day. She could not take in the momentous things that had filled it If the Goddess was in the room, She would know mortals must sleep.

Soon Sati heard her grandmother snore. She raised her head and looked one last time out of the window. The moon was still held fast in the branches of the tree, as if uniting heaven and earth. And in the midst of the illumination sat Durga. She held her head high now, and silver gleamed in her eyes. Fireflies made a fiery robe upon her as if her power were restored.

CHAPTER THIRTEEN

The Chief Magistrate left the Mayor's Court in a surly mood. He had been summoned there by Dumbleton and Plaisted, as if he were a criminal. As he passed Omichand's house in his palanquin, he turned his face away. He had no wish to stretch his tired mind to further complexity; his need was for a friend. He directed the palanquin bearers to take him to the Chaplain's house. The morning's events at the Mayor's Court had left him more disturbed than any threat from Siraj Uddaulah. He looked forward now to a glass of Madeira, and the steady atmosphere that always prevailed in the Reverend Bellamy's home.

The *chowkidar* was absent at the Chaplain's gate. It swung open at a push, groaning upon rusty hinges. The Chief Magistrate was too agitated to note the glances exchanged by his palanquin bearers. They lowered the litter to the ground with a practised swing of the arm. Holwell emerged, unfolding himself, pulling his waistcoat into place before turning to climb the steps. He was surprised to see no servant run forward to usher him in, but this irregularity was lost in the turmoil of his own feelings. He reached the door and rapped the knocker impatiently. Eventually it swung ajar to reveal a small part of Bellamy's face. When the Chaplain saw the Chief Magistrate he gave a cry of relief.

'Thank the Lord it is you, John.' Bellamy pulled Holwell quickly inside.

'What is all this, Gervase?' Holwell asked, detaching himself from Bellamy's grasp. There seemed something frenzied about the Chaplain. His hair stood askew, his black shirt hung loose about his breeches and was unbuttoned at the neck. He wore no coat or stockings. As he stared at the Chaplain's bare legs the Chief Magistrate was reminded of the pale pink worms in the drinking water of his first sea voyage.

'We are trying to light the stove. I was only by chance near the door just now,' the Chaplain explained over his shoulder as he hurried off into the depths of the house. The Chief Magistrate followed, swallowing his annoyance at finding his friend so preoccupied. A sudden idea, that Bellamy had gone mad, came briefly into his mind. There was also, he now noted, a perceptible difference in the house. Although the perfume of beeswax still lurked faintly, the sweet smell of fresh flowers and baking bread had vanished. Instead there was the odour of unemptied chamber pots. Tatties hung at the windows dry as a bone; a hot wind blew dust through the house.

The Chief Magistrate caught up with the Chaplain, and together they left the house by a side door and walked, as they had a few days before, in the direction of the wine cellar. Before they reached it the Chaplain stopped at the cookhouse and plunged inside.

'This is the cookhouse,' Holwell exclaimed, hesitating at the door. The Chief Magistrate had never once entered his own cookhouse and was surprised that the Chaplain should do so.

'Where else would the stove be found?' Bellamy's voice answered from within.

The Chief Magistrate shrugged and lowered his head to enter. It was dark and hot inside. The Chaplain's wife, Dorothy, and his daughter, Anna, were standing before a blackened stove. Both women had a dirty, dishevelled appearance. A servant child of about seven stood beside them. Why any of them were in the cookhouse was unfathomable to the Chief Magistrate. He looked about in confusion and began to feel annoyed. He had come for some Madeira and to unload his worries, not to stand about in the Chaplain's cookhouse.

'I have come directly from the Mayor's Court. The whole thing is an insult. They wish only to make a fool of me.' The Chief Magistrate's thoughts returned to the morning's humiliating appraisal of Jaya Kapur's will. The Mayor's Court had summoned him and there had been nothing he could do but obey. He had had to stand in the dock like a common criminal to face Dumbleton, Plaisted and company.

'I was forced to swear an oath upon the Bible and answer their impudent questions.' Just the memory made the sweat pour off the Magistrate's back.

'Why did you go then?' Bellamy asked in a tone of preoccupation as he tried to light a flint. He gave it to the servant child, but the boy was all fingers and thumbs and the Chaplain took it back.

'They demanded I turn over to them some trifling gems I have in safe keeping for a client.' Dumbleton had made a detailed examination of Jaya Kapur's will and found it a valid legacy of inheritance, not a making-over in her lifetime of worldly effects. The Chief Magistrate's blood began to rise once more at the thought of the Notary's impudence. He turned to see the effect this information had had upon the Chaplain, but Bellamy appeared not to have heard the Chief Magistrate. His mind was still upon the flint.

'Confound the thing,' the Chaplain roared, flinging down the flint in exasperation. His wife and daughter began to cry. Holwell frowned in annoyance.

'I will not be dictated to by Dumbleton. Do you know, he has had the audacity to overturn a case I have been trying, a custody case. Who does the man think he is, poking his nose into affairs that do not concern him? Why does he bother with a senile old native woman? Only because he can get at me through her. The man carries some grudge I know nothing of. . .'

'Do you know something of lighting a fire?' The Chaplain thrust the flints into Holwell's hand. 'Come to the stove, John. I beg you, make yourself useful. Perhaps your hand is better than mine.' Bellamy bent to haul a bucket of water up on to a tripod over the unlit fire. The servant boy ran to help and together they lifted the bucket.

'Add a little more paper and some of that charcoal, Anna. It'll burn up the better when we get it going,' Bellamy encouraged his daughter.

'For what reason, Chaplain, are we here lighting this fire?' Holwell enquired, looking down at the flint in his hand. He had had enough of the charade, whatever it was, being played out before him.

'Do you have a little claret or Madeira to hand, Gervase? The day so far has not been kind. I feel a great need of something, or I would not ask,' the Chief Magistrate continued when no answer was given to his previous question.

'We too have a need, John. A need for tea. We have not even had that today.' The Chaplain's voice was hard.

'Order the servants, Chaplain. I do not understand,' Holwell answered, controlling his anger. At his words Dorothy Bellamy's sobs grew louder. Anna gave a wild laugh.

'Dear God, John, where have you been today? There *are* no servants. Chaplain, Magistrate, Notary or Governor, all must light their own stove today. There are no servants left in White Town. Either they obey the nawab's order to supply us with nothing, or they prepare to flee into the jungle. This boy is still here only because he overslept and when he awoke everyone was gone.'

'My servants were there this morning. My palanquin bearers carried me here,' Holwell said with a frown. 'They are in general a well-disciplined crew. I would not expect them to desert.'

'Perhaps your servants are different from mine,' Bellamy answered tersely, taking the flint from the Chief Magistrate's hand. 'As of now I know of no one who has help. All are in the same pitiful position as us. All are attempting to make soup or tea. There is Madeira on my desk if you are so in need, but I cannot be spared to join you. Ah, here it comes,' Bellamy shouted joyfully as a flame crackled up against the wood. There was a sudden strong odour of smoke. The servant child jumped up and down in excitement.

'We can make a gruel of vegetables and rice,' Anna Bellamy said, after an examination of the cookhouse's deeper corners. She carried a rush tray with a few shrivelled vegetables on top of a mound of rice.

'There are weevils in the grain,' her mother accused, tears rolling down her cheeks.

'There is no grain in this country without weevils, Mother,' Anna replied. 'The servants spread the grain in the sun and the insects run away.'

'I thought that was what *they* ate. What *we* eat is surely kept in a cleaner state. How dare they give us such grain just because they think we do not know,' Dorothy Bellamy sobbed.

'Mother,' Anna sighed. She began to spread the dirty rice on a tabletop, picking out stones and weevils, crushing the insects beneath her nail.

'Do not excite yourself, my dear. See, the fire is burning up nicely now. Soon we shall have tea.' Bellamy tried to calm his wife.

'Take her back to the house, Father.' Anna's face, smudged with charcoal, turned grimly towards them.

The Chaplain sighed, taking his distraught wife by the shoulders and steering her through the door. The Chief Magistrate followed the Chaplain back to the house. It required some effort to control the impatience effervescing through him. Bellamy's haphazard ways and his wife's tearful hysteria were not the underpinning of an orderly house. It was no wonder the servants had run off at the slightest encouragement. The Chief Magistrate strode behind the Chaplain, his mind firmly upon the Madeira.

The Chaplain seated his wife in a chair in his study and hurried to provide her with some wine, holding the glass to her lips. Mrs Bellamy took a mouthful and began to cough, the wine spluttering over her breast. Unable to wait any longer, the Chief Magistrate stepped forward and picked up the bottle, looking about for a glass.

Several dirty silver tumblers stood upon the Chaplain's desk. Flies clustered over the sticky rims and fed within the bowls. The Chief Magistrate was acutely aware once more of the ripe odour of chamber pots. He had the sudden recollection that Bellamy kept a chamber pot in his study, hidden beneath the day bed that he himself was now sitting upon. He stood up quickly and opened a corner cupboard in search of a glass. There was nothing to be found. His need for a drink had now reached such a pitch that he picked up one of the fly-encrusted tumblers, took out his handkerchief, wiped it as thoroughly as he could and filled it to the brim with Madeira. With the first gulp he immediately felt better and realised that his wish, now the wine was under his belt, was to leave the Chaplain's home immediately. The sympathy he had hoped for was clearly not forthcoming. Bellamy had shown no interest in the morning's events at the Mayor's Court, and seemed cut off from Holwell. A world of domestic detail threatened to smother him. The Chief Magistrate's agitation had been intensified rather than mitigated by the Madeira and his view of Bellamy's depressing circumstances. He found a show of politeness beyond him.

'I shall get myself home now,' he said.

'Aye. You wanted your drink and now it is drunk,' Bellamy answered, his attention still on his sobbing wife. The Chief Magistrate looked up with a frown.

'I suggest you drop this business of lighting fires. Bring yourselves to my home and let me provide for the moment. This situation cannot last for long,' the Chief Magistrate replied.

'We may yet be forced to accept your offer,' Bellamy nodded.

'I shall send a palanquin for the ladies as soon as I return. I doubt you have any means of conveyance at the moment,' Holwell added, pursing his lips.

'We shall be grateful,' the Chaplain answered in an offhand tone.

The Chief Magistrate turned and left the room, making his way down the corridor. The latch of the door was stiff and took him a moment to open. At last he emerged into the sun. Below the steps his palanquin rested upon the ground, the runners nowhere to be seen. Holwell frowned and walked about in search of them. He had no doubt they had taken advantage of the wait and were chewing betel nut or tobacco in some obscure corner of the Chaplain's premises. After some moments of prowling around and calling out loudly in a stern voice, the Chief Magistrate was forced to conclude that he had suffered the same ignominy as the Chaplain. He returned to Bellamy's study. The Chaplain and his wife were now sitting quietly, side by side, each sipping a glass of Madeira.

'Those fools of runners are gone,' Holwell exploded. He suddenly noticed the predominance of flies buzzing about the Chaplain's study. He also noticed Dorothy Bellamy was still in her négligé, having had no one to lace up her stays. Her soft white body billowed shapelessly beneath the folds of muslin, like an overfed larva.

'It was to be expected,' Bellamy replied, raising his eyes briefly from the Madeira. His wife gave a long, shuddering sigh and held her empty glass out to her husband. He refilled it silently and topped up his own, then sat looking glumly into his tumbler, clutching the bottle to his chest. Holwell stepped forward, pulled the Madeira away from Bellamy and looked about for his glass.

'It is clear to me now, as never before, Chief Magistrate, how much we depend upon Black Town.' The Chaplain's voice was hoarse with emotion.

'Most certainly. The rascals see to our comfort and fleece us royally into the bargain.' Holwell was not prepared to hear a sermon at this moment from the Chaplain.

'My dear man, they do more than that. They have made us as weak and vulnerable as newborns. They tend to both ends of us at the same time. The going in and the coming out of us are dependent upon them. They nourish and cleanse us. They keep us afloat in this heinous land, whether they know it or not. They. . .'

'They are a pack of sly monkeys,' the Chief Magistrate interrupted. The note of hysteria in the Chaplain's voice, winding up like the spring of a rusty clock, alarmed him. 'What need have we of them?

Your Anna is managing well enough without them, as are you yourself.' Holwell was firm in his opinion as he stood up to leave.

'I shall return home and send you one of my own servants,' he announced, pulling down his waistcoat. He brushed dust from his tricorn as he left the room.

The Chief Magistrate was forced to walk home in the midday sun, picking his way up The Avenue. The sky was clear and cruel; a fire beat down upon him. Dust shifted about his feet and settled upon his lips. Wherever he looked he met the gaze of the adjutant storks lodged upon every available perch. He pulled his tricorn over his brow, but the heat knifed through his coat. Shadows were short and offered no respite. Sweat flowed in tributaries from him. He longed for a drink and looked about for a water carrier, but White Town was deserted of its usual underpinning of dark faces. The bustle and the call of hawkers' voices was gone. The place had a desolate feel. There had been many times in the past when the Chief Magistrate had stated aloud that Calcutta would be a more tolerable place if all the Indians could be deleted. Now, at last, he had his wish and it only annoyed him.

He decided to take the route across The Park, where the shade of large trees would protect him. Under their broad branches he could rest and recover himself. He turned in the direction of The Park and was brought to a sudden halt. All the trees lay tossed about at odd angles, brutally cut down. It was as if he faced a battle ground with an army felled before him. A long furrow, resembling the burrowing of a giant mole, traversed the elegant park. The cloudless sky was now blatantly mirrored in the burnished waters of the Tank, denuded of its usual leafy border. The Chief Magistrate caught his breath in horror at the desecration. It did not improve his mood to remember that it was upon the orders of the Council of War that The Park now looked as it did. In the open furrows, coolies worked like seething insects in an uncovered anthill. The Chief Magistrate continued down The Avenue, his heart pounding uncomfortably.

Eventually he reached his home. The *chowkidar* was nowhere to be seen. The usual orderly activity before the house, the bent backs of gardeners, the palanquin bearers squatting waiting in a row, the boy at the door, the *chowkidar* at the gate, was nowhere to be seen. Holwell was forced to struggle with his own front door, just as he had done with the Chaplain's.

The same air of abandonment as had filled Bellamy's home met him as he entered. The silence was intense. The buzzing of flies and the gritty taste of dust were now familiar to the Chief Magistrate. The Chaplain's words, opaque with panic, returned clearly to him now. What Bellamy had said was true. They were utterly dependent upon Black Town.

CHAPTER FOURTEEN

The first to arrive was Pagal, the albino. He bent in obeisance to touch the pallet upon which Sati lay. Placing a sprig of jasmine beside her sleeping body, he seated himself before her. His wife squatted beside him, her mouth hanging open, revealing rotted teeth. Their children squirmed, suppressing giggles and chanting in whispers the sacred words. *Reverence. Reverence to Her. Reverence to the Goddess.*

Soon the hut grew hot and crowded. The fruit man, the vegetable man, and the seller of spices joined the albino and his family. Others pushed in behind them, squeezing into the tiny room. It had not taken long for news of the Goddess's coming to spread. With the hut so full the growing crowd was forced to wait outside, talking quietly. Inside, only the albino's unruly children broke the silence. Sati still lay asleep on the pallet, her back to the visitors.

Jaya, returning from the dairy with a bowl of curd, stopped in amazement when she saw the crowd squatting outside her hut. People turned to greet her; some reached out to touch the hem of her sari in deference as she picked her way amongst them. She had acquired new status as grandmother of the God Woman. Jaya pressed the bowl of curd tightly against her breast for safety, the path was perilous to her front door. She thrust her way forward amongst the bulges of hips and the bony touch of knees. So great was the crush that people could move no more than an inch this way or that to allow her passage. Jaya pitched dangerously about. She gripped the curd closer and pushed on.

'Can a woman not enter her own home?' she cried out at last in frustration. Rolls of her flesh had dipped into the curd and wet marks now stained her sari. 'My granddaughter is ill. I go out to bring curd to nourish her and return to this commotion.'

'The *Devi* is ill. Make a way.' At last a narrow channel was opened. Jaya pushed through to enter her home. Once inside, she halted again in amazement.

'What nonsense is this? Only a short while I was gone and during this time the world has arrived in my hut.' She nearly stumbled over the albino's youngest child, crawling about underfoot.

'Look after your child. An elephant will squash him like an ant. All this must be your doing,' Jaya bellowed at the albino while surveying the crowd in her hut.

'I came only to see the *Devi*. If our neighbours also are wanting to come, what is the harm in that? I have spoken to no one. *You* told me of the *Devi*. You have told the stallholders too. And they may have told their neighbours,' Pagal replied.

'Sister, we are needing her *darshan*. We are poor people and her blessing can save us. Times are not good; many people are frightened for their lives as Siraj Uddaulah approaches. Already, the sound of his drums blows upon the wind,' the fruit man called out from where he squatted.

'You know the reputation of the new nawab. He will cut us down like rats for his pleasure. Only the Goddess can save us,' the seller of oil lamps argued from behind the albino.

'I have brought you good *subhsi* today. Here is bitter gourd and aubergine, yams and mustard leaf. Take what you want. I will charge nothing. Make the *Devi* her food.' The itinerant vegetable woman stumbled into the hut clutching her basket so firmly to her head that her brow was forced into wrinkles.

Jaya sighed in confusion. She had thought no further than the miracle of the Goddess's presence in her home. Now there were suddenly all these people, also demanding a part of the Goddess. Peevishness shaped her words. 'The Goddess has come to my Sati. It is nothing to do with you all.'

Laughter rolled around her. The seller of oil lamps stood up. 'Sister, the Goddess is not your property. She has manifested herself for us all. She is knowing times are bad and our lives may be in danger. She has come for the protection of everyone.' There was a murmur of agreement in the hut.

Sati turned upon her pallet. At the sight of the crowd before her bed she sat up in shock. She looked about but there was no sign of Durga. The dimness threw up only the pale face of the albino, glowing like the moon. As she stirred, a hush settled over the crowd. The intensity of the expressions before her was overwhelming. The need of the crowd swam towards her like desperate fish escaping the twine of a net. The same force of expectation she had felt in Demonteguy's home on the night of the seance came down upon her now.

The albino crawled on his knees towards her. His bare head, hair cropped that morning to deter lice, was now level with Sati.

'*Darshan*. Give me your blessing, *Devi*.' Pagal was bowed before her on all fours like a penitent animal. Beneath the corn-coloured bristles, his skull was pink as the morning sky.

Sati looked about but Durga was still absent. The albino reached out to clasp her ankles, the weight of his emotion pressing into her flesh. She feared he might cry, his hot tears falling on to her toes. The crowd before her caught its breath and Sati met their waiting eyes. She extended her hand to touch the pale bristles of the albino's head. The crowd released a sigh. The prickly stubble of Pagal's hair reminded her of the burrs in the brier patch behind the hut. She raised her eyes again and saw Durga at last, curled about the rafters. Sati's heart lifted at the sight. She closed her eyes and let Durga's strength surround her.

A deep voice filled the hut. 'Even though you do not see me I have been with you.'

There was a murmur in the room as the Goddess spoke through Sati. The albino drew back from Sati's pallet with a startled look.

'*Praise. Praise. Reverence to Her. Reverence,*' he chanted, staring up at the rafters, following Sati's gaze. Everyone in the hut raised their eyes to where he pointed.

'*Reverence. Praise be to Her.*' People pushed suddenly forward. Some managed to touch Sati's feet.

'Give us your blessings. Look over our children. Protect us.'

The powerful charge of so much emotion forced Durga to leave her perch, drawing her down to Sati.

'Ah!' Sati gave a cry as Durga poured herself into her veins.

'Ah!' the crowd echoed.

'Seek refuge in me and I shall protect you.' There was a new gasp from the crowd as the strange voice spoke again.

A man stood up and then threw himself at Sati's feet. '*Devi,* Siraj Uddaulah comes. We fear for our lives. He will kill us like flies. What shall we do?'

'Only believe in me,' Durga commanded through Sati.

'The *Devi* will slay Siraj Uddaulah's army, just as she slayed the *asuras,*' a man announced from the back of the crowd.

'See how the *Devi*'s light fills the God Woman,' people whispered.

'I will die for you, *Devi.*' A woman flung herself over the people in front of her to sprawl before Sati. Another woman gave a cry and threw herself forward in a similar manner. The albino's wife stood up, the emotions in the hut taking hold of her.

'*Praise be to Her.*' The crowd immediately echoed her words.

The albino's wife dropped to her knees, embracing the other two women. All began to sob at once. The albino crawled forward to join his wife and once more took hold of Sati's feet. Others also wished to touch the God Woman and began a new surge of pushing and shoving. At the frenzy the albino's children took fright and flung themselves on top of their parents. Jaya was pushed aside by the children hurtling forward like projectiles, regardless of obstacle. She lost her balance and fell into the crowd, who groaned beneath her weight. The bowl of curd spilt over people's shoulders. She was eventually set upon her feet again, like a great tree that the wind had uprooted.

Word passed from the hut to those squatting outside of the miracle enacted within. The news eddied briefly about the rocks of disbelief before swimming on up the narrow lane and flooding into the town. Those people who had at first refused to believe in the Goddess's presence in Black Town now left their ablutions or the drawing of water from the well. The goatherd deserted his goats, cows were left half milked, buffalo were abandoned to walk where they wished, some still trailing their ploughs. Stalls were suddenly unattended and prey to beggars' pilfering. The lame and afflicted emerged from their huts, carried on beds or relatives' backs. Seeing this trail of misery consolidating beneath the sun, the beggars reluctantly left the easy filching of melons, sandals and oil lamps. There was the sudden, discomforting realisation that the Goddess could see where others could not and might not approve of looting. Instead, they assembled and, upon agreement, followed the crowd towards Jaya's hut.

Now the crush had become intense. Word flew to the furthest corners of Black Town, to the Lal Bazaar and the Bread and Cheese Bungalow and the start of the road to the Salt Lakes. Like the swell of the tide rolling up the Hoogly, the population of Black Town turned towards Jaya's hut. Those who had never before heard her name now spoke in awed whispers about her granddaughter. Some snatched up fruit, a handful of flowers, the veil of a dying wife or the crutch of a crippled son to carry to the God Woman. Black Town now flowed in one direction, cousins stopping only to inform second and third cousins, nephews to reveal the news to their uncles, the money lender to enlighten those he had bankrupted, the Untouchable to reveal the coming to the Brahmin. Never before had news flushed through Black Town with this speed and portent. Roads were clogged, bullock carts brought to a standstill and palanquins overturned in the crush. Children were lost underfoot. Kittens lay squashed and old people fainted, smothered by the crowd. All whispered their awe repeatedly.

Reverence to Her. Reverence. Reverence. The sound blew on the wind through the streets of Black Town.

'*Devi,* have mercy.' The albino crawled forward again. His white face glowed in the darkness. Durga's weight seemed to increase within Sati. She felt her affinity to Pagal. The pain of the albino was to be forever different, to find his own strength, alone. They were both nothing but themselves.

About Pagal's hut were a profusion of plants that he tended carefully. Once Sati had seen him graft the stems of two plants together, splicing them through their root and binding them one to another. Soon, in the fertile earth about the hut, an unknown flower had unfolded. It was like no other bloom, rich in a mystery of its own. People had come a distance to marvel at its solitary strength. They stared as if the plant had some lesson to teach them.

'I am darkness and light. I am one in myself. I follow no shape but my own.' The strange voice spoke again.

'Ah.' The crowd bowed at the Goddess's words.

Now, the desperation of those outside had become intense and they pushed hard against the door of Jaya's hut, which was soon torn from its hinges. A woman stumbled in, holding a baby above her head. The infant screamed and screamed.

'Save my child, *Devi.* Save my child. It only cries from morning to night,' the woman sobbed.

There was a murmur in the hut. The woman was pushed forward with the hysterical infant until she fell awkwardly at Sati's feet, pitching her child over the head of the albino's wife into Sati's lap. Immediately the crowd became still, all eyes turned on the screaming infant.

The baby, shocked by this abrupt change of place, shut its mouth and looked up in amazement at Sati. Not seeing its mother's anxious face, nor finding itself subjected to a bone-shattering jiggling upon her knees in an effort to calm, it stopped crying. With a yawn and a whimper it fell asleep. A gasp went around the room.

The mother crawled forward. '*Praise. Praise to the Goddess*,' she cried, prostrating herself before Sati's feet.

The albino drew back in fresh awe. Behind him the crowd, stunned by the miracle worked on the baby, murmured in low voices. Some of the women began to cry, overcome by the weight of emotion. They stared in fresh wonder at Sati, whose hair was burnished by a shaft of sun to an unearthly halo. Those at the back of the hut pushed their heads out of the broken door and repeated in detail all that had happened with the baby.

Word was carried back up the crowded street, where people now jostled for place to stand within sight of the Goddess's abode. Parents lifted children upon their shoulders so that the full force of the Goddess's *shakti* might fall directly upon them as it radiated out from Jaya's hut. Those with lame or afflicted relatives or dying children limp in their arms pushed themselves forward, judging the force of *shakti* to grow in power the nearer they approached the hut. Those waiting for *darshan* stood their ground firmly before those in dire physical need. Soon fights broke out upon the subject of *shakti,* and whose right it might be to bask in its power. Word filtered back to the furthest reaches of Black Town of the details enacted in Jaya's hut. The words of the Goddess were magnified in the manner all things are altered when whispered many times. Soon it was told that the Great Mother, Kali, could be clearly seen, spears at the ready, fangs white in the sunlight against her black skin, ready to do battle with the Hatmen and the nawab. At the beginning of the road to the Salt Lakes, where the town petered out, word turned back upon itself, entwining new versions of events with the original story.

By the time news reached Govindram and Mohini, only minutes from Jaya's home, the story of events had reached epic proportions. Had Govindram lived in a hut, he would have heard of events much sooner. His large brick house, intent upon privacy, isolated him from the world at his doorstep. He was being shaved by the barber when he learned of the excitement. The barber mentioned the matter only to seek his opinion of things, unaware his client knew nothing. Govindram started up with such abruptness that he received a deep nick on his face. It took some moments to staunch the blood, and several more before Govindram and Mohini crossed the courtyard to their door. The *chowkidar* advised his master to remain inside, but Govindram flung open the gate. Immediately the crowd pushing against it fell in upon him. Mohini and Govindram retreated in shock as people flooded into their courtyard like a dammed-up river.

'Make way. The uncle comes.' A path was made through the crowd for Govindram and Mohini to reach Jaya's hut. As they passed, the crowd closed behind them, pushing them on, as if down a birthing canal. Eventually they were delivered before the God Woman. Jaya crouched beside the inert Sati, a look of bewilderment on her face. At once Mohini prostrated herself at Sati's feet. Then she turned to embrace the bewildered Jaya, who sat in a state between ecstasy and fear, riddled with nervous exhaustion. People stared in awe. Govindram looked about with a frown of concern, then turned his attention to Sati.

Her eyes were wide and staring. She had not spoken for some time and the hut was packed and waiting. Before her the crowd had grown quiet, their faces transfixed. People appeared oblivious of their surroundings. They drifted in bliss, absorbing the radiance of the Goddess.

Suddenly Sati stirred. Consciousness flooded back into her eyes, she looked about in amazement. Slowly, realising the Goddess had withdrawn, the crowd descended once more to an earthly plane, able to move at last. As they vacated the hut, those waiting outside at once pushed in to touch the feet of the *Devi*. Soon a long line had formed. Entering the hut was easy but no way could be found for so great a crowd to exit again through the same rush door.

The fruit stall man, who was still in the hut, seeing the immensity of the situation and the crowd stretching back to the end of Black Town, had a sudden idea. He gathered some friends and sharp implements and turned Jaya's small window into an extra door. Jaya gave a weak cry and started up as they began to hack at her wall. The albino held her back.

'It is for the Goddess,' he said. Jaya sat down at Sati's feet and began to sob.

Govindram looked about him in wonder. The world appeared to be collapsing, even as it was reborn. Already it was disconcerting to see the implosion of White Town after the withdrawal of Black Town support. At a stroke White Town had crumbled. Men and women who had called themselves superior now appeared as mortal as Black Town sweepers. The Hatmen no longer wore their hats. Kitchen soot smudged the weary faces of the marble-skinned women. The Chaplain and the Notary amongst many others had been seen emptying buckets of their own nightsoil. Into this strange and changing order of things the Goddess had appeared. Her appearance at this moment in time must have particular meaning, thought Govindram.

'It is for the Goddess,' Govindram repeated, looking at the sunlight streaming into the hut through the broken wall. He squatted down beside Jaya. Sati lay stretched out in exhaustion, tortoiseshell hair spread wildly about her.

Govindram saw now that this destiny had been waiting for Sati. She had always been a child apart, fragmented by cultures, born on the edge of the universe, on the meeting of two lines. Now the Goddess had come to reinvent her. He bent at last to touch her feet.

CHAPTER FIFTEEN

The Chief Magistrate sat upon his veranda with Drake and remembered the Governor's last visit: the easy consumption of claret, the warm glow of candles, the deferential tread of servants. He recalled standing before the veranda, glass in hand, forcing the Governor to cross the room. Such finely tuned insolence was impossible now. The Chief Magistrate must open his own front door, go in search of clean glasses and a jug into which to decant some wine, like a common servant. All that tied them to that earlier evening was the unaltered boom of the bullfrogs and an orchestra of crickets. Now desolation and dust carpeted the veranda and collected in a pattern of footsteps within the Chief Magistrate's home. The scuttle of cockroaches was suddenly apparent. Geckos clucked at night with the disapproval of a schoolmistress. Cobwebs hung from the balcony. But most of all it was the silence, the lack of hands, the growing odours that circumscribed the Chief Magistrate's fear. The silence of the empty house now merged with the silence of the river. There was nothing untenanted about this silence; it was of the watching kind.

The Chief Magistrate's house released a sour reek that had not gone unnoticed by the Governor. 'Don't know a home that has not the same odour the moment you enter the door. Those in the service of the Governor understand their responsibilities better than most. A couple of our people have remained. We have not to concern ourselves with gross matters. Emily is preparing our food with her own hands, but help is there to light the lamps and stove and to see to the disposal of nightsoil.'

'You are lucky,' the Chief Magistrate agreed in a terse voice, viewing with his usual distaste the Governor's sweating face.

Drake took a substantial gulp of claret and wiped his mouth with the back of his hand. 'Siraj Uddaulah draws nearer,' he announced.

'His army is already at Krishnagar,' the Chief Magistrate admitted. Shadows had at last begun to collect in the garden, softening the sun's harsh glare. An unexpected breeze lifted off the river, stirring the dust and ripening odours in the Chief Magistrate's house.

'Omichand grows nervous at the nawab's proximity,' Holwell told Drake. He had been summoned that morning to yet another interview with the fat merchant.

'As well he might,' Drake managed a chuckle.

'He requests that we arrest him,' Holwell announced.

'Arrest the rascal?' The Governor was astonished.

'I found the fat merchant much afraid. He desires that we arrest him and place him under our protection in the fort, along with Kishindas and the treasure. The merchant will then appear innocent of conspiracy with us in the nawab's eyes. The treasure will also be out of Siraj Uddaulah's reach,' Holwell explained.

'And we are to collude in this pack of lies for the sake of Omichand's life?' The Governor was indignant.

'It is not so bad an idea. The treasure will be in our safe keeping at last. If things turn out for the worst and we must flee, we shall take it with us. If Siraj Uddaulah is defeated, then the original purpose is served,' Holwell reasoned. The idea of taking charge of the treasure now propelled the Chief Magistrate.

'We will have full command of the situation once we have the treasure in our keeping. It will give us strong bargaining power with

Siraj Uddaulah, should it be needed.' Holwell looked across his garden to the river, but it washed past with its usual indifference.

'Omichand wishes for a showy arrest. He plans it like a play. Apart from ourselves and the fat merchant, no one, not even his many wives, is to know the arrest is but a charade,' Holwell continued.

'You think such a move is wise?' Drake queried, suddenly alarmed. Since the news of Siraj Uddaulah's approach, the Governor had found sleep impossible. Constant visions of battle and the beat of Siraj Uddaulah's tuneless kettledrums threaded through his dreams. His appetite had diminished and his digestion needed frequent doses of Seltzer to coax it through the day.

The sky over the Hoogly was now brushed by fiery light as the sun sank rapidly towards the water. The croak of bullfrogs and the rasp of crickets grew even more intense. A gecko clucked nearby. These sounds seemed somehow to entwine with unpolished mahogany tables, with cockroaches feeding on the remains of fruit, with the dust-laden veranda, the unlit stove and the general scrounging about for food.

'There is a strange feel to life without the native people around.' Drake shifted in his chair, trying to hold his anxiety in place.

'As if we are living in a ghost town. A door opens and you hear it creak, whereas before, in the bustle of life, such a sound might go unnoticed,' the Chief Magistrate agreed.

'Siraj Uddaulah expects the fort to surrender.' The Govenor's tone was half statement, half pleading enquiry. He reached for his wine again.

'That will not happen,' the Chief Magistrate answered. He knew the fears Drake's mind was prey to.

'We would all sleep better in our beds if Rai Durlabh would put a speedy end to the nawab.' The Governor was petulant.

'The essence of such matters is in their timing. We must trust in the commander.' As he spoke, the Chief Magistrate saw himself, sword at waist, gun in hand, welcoming a triumphant Rai Durlabh into Fort William.

'What if Rai Durlabh is killed?' The Governor could not stop the thought spilling from him.

'He will not allow such a destiny to overtake him,' Holwell answered briskly.

'There is a strange resonance in the air just here.' Drake leaned forward with a frown.

The Chief Magistrate nodded towards the Hoogly at the bottom of the garden. 'Probably a body is trapped in the reeds.'

It was not an unusual occurrence. Many Black Town families had either no money for cremation or less than was needed for a thorough conflagration. From their point of disposal at Chandpal Ghat, these unburned or half-burned bodies floated down river past Fort William. Occasionally, one of them drifted too near the shore and became trapped in reeds. The Chief Magistrate kept a special man whose job it was to free these rotting stalks of garbage from the watery bank of his garden. Up until this moment he had been unaware as to when these unfortunate cadavers arrived or departed. Now the man had gone, vanished into the jungle with the rest of Black Town, leaving Holwell to face the problem alone.

For some moments the Chief Magistrate sat immobile. He imagined himself in bed that night, the dark house silent about him yet alive with the stirring of nocturnal creatures. He saw the moon shining down upon the trapped corpse, the river lapping about it. Its stench would float up through his bedroom window and enter his dreams. He looked from the veranda to the yellow swell of the Hoogly, rolling past unconcernedly. It was another ploy on the part of the river to wither away his soul. He knew its tricks, its waiting silence.

The Chief Magistrate stood up abruptly. 'The sooner it is freed the better. You must help me, Drake.'

Drake rose from his chair but appeared to hesitate before the invitation. Holwell strode forward towards some outhouses, disappeared within, and then emerged with a wooden pole. Drake followed him down to the water's edge.

The overgrown grass and shrubs made Holwell nervous of snakes. A short distance away was a landing stage for visitors arriving by river. In the days when Rosemary had resided with him there had been boating parties and frequent shoots for waterfowl. Now the jetty lay in disrepair. The Chief Magistrate began to prod the clumps of reed along the bank, pushing the long pole deep into the water. At last, in the tangle of vegetation, he came upon resistance. He clenched his teeth against the stench and kept his thoughts upon the need to be rid of the corpse. Drake stood watching a distance away, unwilling to come any closer.

The rotting object was now visible. Partially covered by a shroud, it lay face down in the water. A hand dangled free. Holwell remembered his collision with the funeral bier on his way to Demonteguy. He looked down into the murky depths and man-oeuvred the pole until the thing was free of the reeds and pulled forward by the tide. Slowly then it bobbed away, leaving the scent of putrefaction.

Just at that moment there came a shout. The Chief Magistrate looked up to see a small boat arriving at the landing stage. The boatman secured the craft and a man disembarked. Holwell recognised Demonteguy.

The materialisation of the Frenchman, at such a moment and from such an unexpected place, took the Chief Magistrate by surprise. Demonteguy strode towards him with an expression of ferocity. He breathed heavily and was unshaven. His shirt was open at the neck, his coat was dusty and he wore no stockings. He had forgotten to put on his wig. In the boat a woman sat waiting. Demonteguy did not halt before the Chief Magistrate but reached out and took hold of him roughly by his neck cloth. Holwell was jerked forward until his chin nearly touched Demonteguy's nose. The Frenchman's sour breath covered his face. The Governor stood a distance away in interested observation; since he had never been introduced to Demonteguy, he saw no need to come forward.

'Damn you, Holwell. Where are my jewels?' Demonteguy shook the Chief Magistrate.

'Why are you here on my land, arriving in this manner?' The Chief Magistrate managed to free himself from the Frenchman's grasp.

'Where is my property?' Demonteguy shouted.

'Your property, sir, is with you.' The Chief Magistrate spoke smoothly.

'My diamonds are with *you*.' Demonteguy howled like a dog. 'I demand you give them to me, *now*.'

'If you have mislaid your mother-in-law's jewels, that is not my affair,' Holwell shrugged. Proof, he had found, was like fruit that had sunk to the bottom of a cake; its presence was undetectable until a thorough excavation was made.

'I have mislaid nothing. You took them forcibly from the old woman into your own safe keeping,' Demonteguy roared. 'I am now falsely accused of theft by that Notary, Dumbleton, and must flee my home with my wife. Within the hour it is said they will come for me, to fling me into jail.'

'None of this is my fault. I acted properly upon your behalf. It is the prying nose of Dumbleton that has brought you to this unhappy state.' The Chief Magistrate marvelled at Dumbleton's tenacity. At a time of such emergency, the Mayor's Court still appeared to have the energy and the means to pursue Demonteguy.

'I'll see you in your grave for this.' Demonteguy hopped from foot to foot in anger. The last pink rays of sun shone down upon his balding head. He had already the appearance, thought Holwell, of a fugitive: erratic, slovenly, desperate, his eyes feverishly aglitter. Who would believe his word against that of the Chief Magistrate?

'Did they see you run by the river?' Holwell asked. Observing Demonteguy's panic, he found he grew steadily calmer. It was Demonteguy's word against his. He had only to hold to his story.

'They will not catch me,' Demonteguy answered.

'They have seen you flee, then?' Holwell confirmed. His last fear of Demonteguy slid away.

'Better go quickly while you can. I will not alert the law. And if there are enquiries, I will say I saw nothing of you. This much I can do to help you. I do it only for the sake of your wife.' The Chief Magistrate narrowed his eyes, scouring the river. His gaze rested a moment on the tense figure of Rita awaiting her husband in the boat. Demonteguy followed his gaze. He began to back away.

'This is not the end of it. I shall have an accounting. You are no better than a thief.' Demonteguy turned at last towards his boat.

Shadows were now collecting fast. Bats already flitted about. The Governor stepped forward and stood beside the Chief Magistrate to watch the Frenchman's departure. Holwell kept his eyes upon Rita, but she gave no sign of recognition. She sat unmoving, her head erect. Darkness was settling on the river, although the sky remained light. Slowly, as the Chief Magistrate watched, Demonteguy's boat moved away from the landing stage and was soon swallowed by the dusk.

'What was all that about?' Drake enquired.

'The man is a lunatic. These are the hazards of legal work. Sometimes it is difficult to know the true nature of those one tries to help.' The Chief Magistrate's voice was filled with relief. He thought of the diamonds locked in the drawer of his desk, and immediately new energy filled him.

'If Siraj Uddaulah approaches further, we must expect even the coolies who prepare our defences to vanish before our eyes,' the Governor worried.

Drake's comments forced the Chief Magistrate to think again of Siraj Uddaulah. For some moments they stood in the growing shadows. The air was thick with the river; the smoke of dung fires drifted over the Ditch as Black Town prepared for the evening. A moth brushed against the magistrate's hand. The sky was darkening quickly as if sluiced down with ink. Holwell turned towards the house and the Governor followed, anxious to depart. As the heavy shape of the house reclaimed him, the Chief Magistrate gave a shudder. Silence once more surrounded him. He must soon scout about for a candle stub and find the remains of stale bread and cheese. And upon his bed, he knew already, the whine of mosquitoes would not disturb him so much as the memory of Demonteguy's face, and the corpse that had stopped by his garden. The stiff figure of Rita, fading slowly into the dusk, would also return, trailing devilish memories. The uncertainty of the future came down upon him suddenly. He turned at last to the Governor.

'Perhaps we would do well to call into the fort the women and children of White Town. Already their men are part of the militia and reside within.'

'Has it come to that?' the Governor asked in a low voice.

'We do not want panic. It is a precaution we must now take.' the Chief Magistrate warned. The Governor sighed and nodded.

Holwell accompanied Drake to the door and swung it shut behind him. Then he turned to face the empty house, dreading the long night ahead.

CHAPTER SIXTEEN

Emily Drake approached St Ann's Church in her palanquin. Its wounded spire seemed to encapsulate all that awaited her within. Each Sunday the same reluctance overtook her. She must force herself towards the open door of the church, her eyes on the deep and shadowy interior, as if she looked down the throat of an animal. The sun blazed upon her before the gloom of the church swallowed her abruptly. At her entrance there was a brief halting of voices, a suspension of movement. In the silence Emily Drake heard the hollow clack of her shoes as she made her way down the aisle. She did not have the arrogance to shrug defiantly; she had not acquired such learning upon her father's indigo farm. She moved in separateness and had done so since she was a child, a stranger in her own world. Observing her, people saw an intensity from which they recoiled. They were aware of something concealed. Her silence was disconcerting, and behind it lay a history different from their own. They watched her for the defenceless moment, for the crack that would expose. This knowledge swam in Emily Drake as she placed her hand on the rail of the pew and arranged her skirts demurely. She sat alone, the veil pulled forward over her bonnet. Roger had declined to come. He made the excuse of the Council of War and the emergency work this involved. There was a rustle of movement behind her as the congregation followed her lead and took their seats. Mrs Bellamy and her daughter Anna across the aisle inclined their heads politely. Mrs Mapletoft, so pregnant she rested her hymnbook upon her unborn child, looked up and then away. Mrs Mackett, also pregnant, pushed her mouth to smile. A difference she could not explain set her apart from these women. And, unable also to explain it, they tore at her outlandish marriage like dogs tear at raw meat.

The Chaplain entered with a smile, sermon notes and Bible tucked under his arm. When at last he reached the pulpit and surveyed his congregation, the Reverend Bellamy saw a large number of parishioners were absent. He noted the presence of the Governor's wife and the absence of her husband. His eyes rested a moment upon Emily Drake. She sat before him attentively, yet he was left with the image of something untamed. She was country born; everyone knew this. For people like Emily, born to the sun and the frangipani, to the screeching of parakeets and the smoke of the burning ghat, the shocking heathenism of India appeared of no consequence. She might hold herself apart from the heathen world like everyone else, but there was the suspicion that beneath the surface India had touched her in some fatal way. Bellamy cleared his throat and frowned. Whatever disturbed him about the Governor's wife was thankfully shut away. And let it always remain so, thought the Chaplain, looking beyond her to the back of the church.

In the empty pews the pious few of White Town stuck up like old teeth in empty gums. If it were not for a large group of Eurasians, the church would have appeared quite bare. Most people were home, foraging for food or carrying water from the well. The problem of nightsoil continued to plague. Through a stained-glass window a shaft of coloured light poured down. The other windows of St Ann's were devoid of glass and, but for louvred green shutters, stood open to the elements. The elevation of the pulpit brought the Chaplain level with these windows. As it was still early, the tatties were rolled tightly up, giving the Reverend Bellamy a view of Omichand's house and its extensive grounds.

As Siraj Uddaulah drew nearer Calcutta, Reverend Bellamy had decided to preach on John 10:11, 'I am the good shepherd.' He had considered a sermon from I Corinthians 1:23–24 on 'Christ crucified, unto the Jews a stumbling block, and unto the Greeks foolishness.' The sermon notes had begun, 'Now let me burn out for God.' He had the feeling it would do nothing to calm the present situation of heightening nervousness. The good shepherd would set the right tone.

As soon as the Chaplain began to speak and his sermon rolled effortlessly forth, his thoughts sank to the ground beneath his feet. This area of the church stood over the end of his cellar and his best casks of wine. He was directly above the prime vintage of 1746, a splendid year for claret. The Madeira beside it was no more than a tolerable breed which the Chaplain kept for picnics, fêtes and boating expeditions, events of a particularly gregarious nature where wine was not tasted but only drunk. On such occasions, once past the first drink when the brain became heated, any quality of wine was acceptable. Now, with the approach of Siraj Uddaulah, he was filled with anxiety for his cellar. If Calcutta surrendered there would be looting. If they were forced to evacuate to the boats, how would his wine be transported? These fears now kept him awake at night.

It was while he was dually employed in this manner, his thoughts running subterraneously while his words on God spewed forth, that his eyes became fixed upon Omichand's house. A squadron of soldiers from the Fort William garrison was marching down The Avenue, muskets and brass buttons gleaming in the sun, red coats like a streak of fire. With a shout of orders and a clanking of arms, the soldiers halted at Omichand's gate. Several empty bullock carts followed behind the squadron. The gates swung open and the soldiers and carts disappeared within.

'Let us pray,' Reverend Bellamy announced as the gates closed on the Fort William men.

When, once more, the Chaplain raised his head it was to see the gates swinging open again. Omichand's great carriage, especially built for his immense proportions, had been brought around to the door. The fat merchant waddled from his house and was helped awkwardly down the steps. A thin, bearded man followed behind whom Bellamy realised must be the nobleman Kishindas. Omichand ordered his armed guard to stand back. The Fort William soldiers swarmed closely around both men. Omichand's servants pushed about this tight cordon, trying to attend their master. Eventually the merchant climbed into his carriage, Kishindas behind him. For some moments they waited as many iron-bound boxes of the type used to hold money or valuables were loaded on to the bullock carts. Then, at last, Omichand's horses moved forward and the procession started back up The Avenue towards the East Gate of Fort William.

In the upper windows of Omichand's mansion his women and children crowded together and cried. The sounds of distress reached the Chaplain's ears as he craned his neck from the pulpit. Below, in the pews, the congregation had not the advantage of the Chaplain's elevated view. They looked up to find him distracted, calling for hymns or prayers in a preoccupied way, his gaze riveted on the outside world. Emily Drake turned to look up at the windows, as did the rest of the congregation, and saw nothing but the sky.

Unaware that the arrest of the merchant was a charade, consternation was great in Omichand's house. His armed guard, rendered helpless by their master's own orders, felt free to act once the soldiers were beyond the gates. They immediately opened fire. The Fort William soldiers ducked quickly for cover. They piled into the compound of St Ann's, hiding behind the wall. From there they returned a spirited volley, their muskets crackling heatedly.

Within the church the sound of guns took the congregation by surprise. Even the Chaplain, closely following events from his elevated perch, had not expected a fight. His parishioners, awash with pious thought, concentrating upon their prayers and hymns and the physical labour of kneeling and standing, knew nothing of the proceedings in Omichand's house. The crack of guns for them could only be linked to the nawab's army. It was presumed Siraj Uddaulah had arrived.

The shocked silence lasted only a moment, then the women began to scream. Mrs Mackett held her belly and rocked about. The Eurasians rose and rushed as one towards the door of the bell-tower. Lady Russell looked wildly about, opening and shutting her mouth. Several gentlemen of White Town stood up and sat down and stood up again in confusion. Mrs Bellamy and Anna fell to their knees. A great noise now filled the church.

From the pulpit Reverend Bellamy raised his voice ineffectively. His words of reassurance could not be heard amidst the general hysteria. The Eurasians only added to the din by drumming dementedly upon the locked door of the bell-tower. At last the Chaplain picked up his Bible and thumped it until the sound was heard.

'The firing comes from Omichand's house. The merchant has been arrested. It has nothing to do with the nawab. He is still some distance from Calcutta.'

Slowly the tumult quietened. Mrs Mapletoft and Mrs Mackett sat down, their twin domes of fruitfulness an instant reminder that the future must be considered. The Eurasians trooped back to their pews. The church door was opened and it was seen that although the soldiers still crouched outside, their muskets were now lowered. Yet even when seated once again, the congregation shifted uneasily. Before such agitation the Reverend Bellamy was helpless; God seemed entirely forgotten. A narrow gallery ascended to by a stair ran below the windows. To this vantage point the congregation now made their way, to determine for themselves the truth of the Chaplain's words. They stood pressed against the windows, looking down into Omichand's house. What they were now obliged to see was never to be forgotten.

To the thirteen women who were Omichand's wives, the emergency heralded their end. Their master had been arrested in such a manner by the Hatmen that his death appeared sure. Above all, one thing was apparent to Omichand's women: at the very moment of Siraj Uddaulah's arrival they had been left defenceless. For all they knew, the nawab was already encamped on the edge of town. Any woman falling into the hands of Moors must prepare for rape, murder or abduction. Hysteria swept through Omichand's house faster than a fire. His women, in their panic, thought only to save themselves and their husband's honour.

Under the protection of a trusted servant, the women trooped out into the garden. Thirteen women and three children walked in a docile file behind the old man to a coconut grove. There they formed a submissive row before the ancient servant. Without hesitation the first woman, who was also Omichand's senior wife, stepped forward. The old man drew his dagger from his sash and, raising it high, plunged it deep into her heart. She fell without a sound. As she slumped to the ground a second woman stepped forward. As she fell the next silently appeared before the faithful servant. Again and again he plunged down his dagger until the slaughter was over. Only the children lacked courage, and they were chased to their ends.

It took some moments for the White Town onlookers to understand the nature of events. Only the Chaplain, still resident in his pulpit and having seen the earlier enactment, comprehended something of the proceedings.

'Dear God. Stop, I beg you. They are innocent creatures, even if they cling to heathen ways.' Horror and pity tore through the Reverend Bellamy. Not for many years had he beseeched the Lord to listen to him with such a show of vehemence.

The women of the congregation were in no state to absorb further trauma. They twittered like a nest of terrified birds; some began to scream. The White Town men rushed down to the door of the church and peered out again into the street.

Emily Drake stood mesmerised, a cold chill creeping through her. Before her eyes the women were killed one by one, the children cruelly chased and felled. She watched the knife rise and come down again and again, as if powered by a force beyond that of a simple servant. She was unable to understand the terrible energy suddenly let loose. The scene was like a murderous pageant enacted on a stage. At any moment she expected the women to pick themselves up and wipe off the shocking stains. Instead, they lay unmoving. From behind a fan of plantains came the shriek of petrified children. Emily drew back from the window, a cry smothered in her throat. India was a cruel country where death was commonplace, yet she knew this scene would unfurl in her mind over and over again.

When at last she returned to Fort William she went immediately in search of her child, as if to reassure herself that the assault upon her senses lay far beyond her own life. She found Harry in his cradle as she had left him, his wet nurse in attendance. Along with Parvati and one old servant, the woman had stayed while the rest of the Fort William staff ran away. She was affectionate to Harry and sang to him constantly while he gazed up raptly into her face. Watching the wet nurse, Emily struggled with resentment at seeing Harry so attached to the woman.

As Emily bent over the cradle, the baby stirred. The movement brought colour into his cheeks and filled her with relief. He was not ill and yet his small face had the translucence of alabaster, so pale and unstirring it frightened her. In spite of the heat, his tiny hands and feet were always unnaturally cold. As she watched, Harry began to thrash about, his arms flailing like a windmill. The red orifice of his tiny mouth expanded to great proportions.

Emily picked him up but he struggled in her arms. It was always the same. Some nights she walked for hours with him, attempting unsuccessfully to soothe him. She did not like the wet nurse to constantly attend him, fearing he would forget it was *she* who was his mother. But now his agitation grew to such a pitch, Emily was forced to summon the woman. She took him in her thin dark arms and immediately Harry quietened. Emily was left feeling diminished, staring angrily after the woman. The sight of her child at the woman's breast always affected her deeply. There was the irritating clink of bangles as she rocked the baby.

It was only fear for her child that had forced Emily to keep a wet nurse. 'In this country, if you want a child to live, it must be nursed by a native woman for at least a year or more,' Lady Russell had commanded. It was she who had sent the woman. 'They themselves nurse a child until five or six, but this to me is excessive.' Her advice could not be denied, for she had outlived three husbands and borne a brood of children in India, most of whom survived. Yet whenever Emily observed the wet nurse, she saw the shadow of the woman's own infant, of whom she knew nothing. The milk Harry drank had been made for a different child. To ensure that Harry might live, that child would have dwindled and died or, if it were a girl, been put down like a newborn kitten. To Emily the ghost of that dead child hung about the wet nurse, like a face glimpsed fleetingly in a dark mirror. None of this seemed to bother the woman, but only Emily Drake.

She continued to listen to the rhythmic clink of the woman's bangles, and the sweet sound of her song. Within moments she knew Harry would sleep, dropping into a slumber from which little ever woke him. Emily could not deny the nurse's expertise, nor her own relief when Harry slept. Had the woman also fled into the jungle with the rest of Black Town, it would have compounded their difficulties. At last the nurse came towards Emily, the gold spiral of Harry's small crown aflame in the crook of her mahogany arm. As she lowered him into his cradle, Emily caught the odour of coconut oil from the woman's hair.

Before he could be placed in his cot, Harry began to cry again. The nurse straightened, the child still in her arms, and turned her back upon Emily. As she moved away it seemed to Emily that she placed her hand on the infant's face. Once again the rhythmic clicking of her bangles began; the soft melody stirred the room. Emily stared at the woman, unable to explain the sudden unease that filled her. The woman swayed from foot to foot, rocking the baby. A thick oily loop of hair lay against her head like a coiled snake. As the woman's soft singing began again, a sharp cry knifed out of Harry, as if a splinter of glass turned in him. Emily jumped up and ran to snatch her son from the woman's arms.

'What have you given him? What did you do?' Suddenly the reason for her unease was clear.

She forced open Harry's mouth but there was nothing to see. Yet she was sure the nurse had crammed something into Harry. She saw again the movement of her hand across the baby's face.

'I have given him nothing, Bibiji. See, now at last he sleeps.' The woman stood close to Emily. Already Harry's eyelids drooped; vacancy entered his face as sleep pulled him steadily downwards, fastening him in its sepulchre. Emily shook him gently, but he did not wake.

The anxiety would not leave her. She took a chair and sat by the cot, gazing anxiously from the window. Outside, on the parade ground the new militia performed its manoeuvres. The shout of orders and the metallic clank of muskets rose up to Governor's House. And beyond Fort William the sun beat down on The Park. Great trees lay about at odd angles, leafy heads shrivelled in the heat, roughly decapitated. Coolies were everywhere, chopping and sawing up the great trunks. Roped oxen pulled the logs away. Emily had watched the difficult job of hacking apart the great banyan tree that had, until recently, stood beside the Tank, spreading its shade across the water. Sometimes she had stood with her back pressed against the runnels of its massive trunk, looking up into a dark firmament. The great tree arched above her like the vaulted pillars of a cathedral. Now it was felled and the sun spun down rapaciously, drumming upon the naked water of the Tank. There was nothing now but a boiling plain. Emily surveyed the growing destruction and the hole of fear widened within her.

Beyond The Park the roof of Omichand's house could be seen. Once again, like a dream unravelling, Emily saw the knife raised as each woman stepped forward. She heard the shrieks of children behind the plantain trees and saw again the glistening pools of blood. There seemed no sense in what she had seen. She could not get the picture out of her head.

She thought again of the black goddess in the grotto on the hill, the Goddess of Perilous Passage. Had She been there to give the women the courage to pass into her realm? Did they hear the stamp of her foot by their side as she guided them towards her? Panic washed over Emily. Her life had hardened about her, like the shell of a chrysalis, crushing her within. She returned from her view of the empty park to the silent child, and a chill ran through her.

CHAPTER SEVENTEEN

The remains of the moon hung above the town. The weak light from its slender crescent no longer illuminated the pearly walls of White Town. Instead of emitting an unearthly gleam, the town now shrank into the night. To the Chief Magistrate, looking out from the balcony of the Council chamber, Calcutta appeared an unknown place. It was as if the Chief Magistrate stood the wrong side of a mirror and, from that dark place, viewed a town that no longer stood but lived only in his memory. A shiver of fear passed through him as he turned back to the Council chamber.

Before him winged insects swarmed thickly about the candelabra. Drake slumped morosely in his chair, Bellamy's concentration was upon the Madeira, Minchin yawned and as usual took no interest in things. The rest of the Council of War debated barricading themselves into the fort and bargaining their release with Siraj Uddaulah. Escape by the river was uppermost in everybody's mind. The arrest of Omichand and the nawab's proximity now frayed the strongest nerves. Siraj Uddaulah was reckoned to be a mere fifteen miles from Calcutta and could be upon them by the following day. No news had come from Rai Durlabh of the nawab's much-awaited demise. The Council of War now found their main comfort in simply sitting together. Arguments revolved and revolved again in an equally comforting way.

The Chief Magistrate returned to the balcony, taking with him a glass of claret. Above him, sleeping adjutant birds crowded the cupola of the balcony. The shifting sound of claws and the knock of beaks alerted him to their massed presence. Doubts about the raja Rai Durlabh had begun to enter his mind. Messengers secretly dispatched from the fort to Rai Durlabh always returned with identical letters. Rai Durlabh constantly urged Fort William to be patient. The smell of the river buoyed up upon the stench of the salt lakes drifted to the Chief Magistrate. The moon's slow withdrawal of light seemed only to echo the disintegration of his own structured life.

Below the balcony he was conscious of the sound of traipsing feet. The women and children of White Town were entering the fort. They walked quietly down The Avenue beside the denuded Park, trundling carts and carrying bundles. Children clung to their mothers' skirts. Most had buried their better possessions for safety from the nawab, but carried their jewels and some silver plate, pushing it along on the carts. It was impossible to stop the occasional clatter this made as their barrows traversed the rutted roads. They had been warned against creating a stir that might arouse the suspicions of Black Town, but so great was the general chaos in White Town that their departure had passed unnoticed. Everywhere officers galloped about on horses, powder trains cluttered the roads, troops swore loudly while pushing gun carriages into place and those coolies who remained dug ferociously to finish the trenches and barricades before Siraj Uddaulah arrived. All about, adding to the congestion, were large numbers of fleeing Indians. Still, the ladies of White Town took care to arouse no alarm. They arrived furtively, speaking in whispers, looking over their shoulders, passing into the fort with relief.

In the parade ground, in spite of the hour, there was still a great bustle. The militia and a large group of hastily recruited Dutch mercenaries drilled by the light of flares, sepoys hurried about dragging gun carriages or sandbags, brusque orders were continually shouted. To the women and children of White Town such activity appeared to signal security and they at once relaxed. They were quickly escorted to Writers' Row, where they were to be accommodated, the young writers of the Company having been turned from their beds.

On the balcony of the Council chamber the Chief Magistrate watched the file of women and children walk towards their temporary quarters. He passed a tired hand over his brow. He was aware of an atmosphere he could not define. Sometimes, before a monsoon, strange pressures played upon his brain, filling him with tension. He looked up again at the sky, but as yet no clouds marred its smooth expanse. Strange noises echoed distantly, making him wonder if, at last, the first sounds of Siraj Uddaulah's thirty thousand blew to him on the night.

Dry powder from the large magazine in town was being brought into the fort. Holwell gazed into the dark night but could not make out the tall pagoda-like towers of the magazine. The place had once been a temple to the black goddess he so despised. It had come into Fort William's hands inadvertently some years before through Omichand, who owned the land it stood upon. It had been the Chief Magistrate's idea to use the building as a weapons magazine. There had been a great protest in Black Town.

Across the parade ground, flares illuminated an arched colonnade along the east wall which served as barracks for the native regiments. Soldiers slept on tiers of wooden planks, protected from the elements but exposed to a view of the parade ground. A small part of this colonnade was bricked in and used as a cell in which drunken soldiers cooled their heels overnight. It was jokingly called the Black Hole. It was in this malodorous prison that Omichand was now held. The Chief Magistrate had visited the merchant soon after his arrival in the fort and found him full of complaints. As Holwell had expected, the food and accommodation were not to his liking. Words of fury had burst from Omichand like steam from a samovar.

'I was expecting to stay in the Governor's House during my arrest. Here I am held like a common criminal. In this cell, I hear you throw drunken soldiers. This is not a place for persons of station. And where is the treasure? Why is it not kept under our eye?' Behind Omichand, Kishindas whimpered.

'Arrest is arrest.' The Chief Magistrate shrugged. 'You asked for reality in this charade and we have adhered to your request. Believe me, this is far better than our common jail. You have light and air, a view of the parade ground, not to mention a guard to talk to.' The Chief Magistrate tapped the barred window of the Black Hole with his ivory-topped cane. 'As for your treasure, it is safe. You need have no worry.' The treasure had been kept beneath the fort in a safe-room with barred doors.

The Chief Magistrate made no mention of the death of Omichand's wives. He had decided that, in everyone's best interests, this was not the time to reveal to Omichand news of his family tragedy. The severity of the event might turn the merchant's mind, with disastrous results; he might hold Fort William responsible.

'One way or another, sooner or later, the manner in which we keep you will reach the ears of Siraj Uddaulah. How much better it looks for you if you suffer the discomforts of this cell rather than the comforts of the Governor's House.' The Chief Magistrate saw Omichand forced to swallow his fury before the verity of this reasoning.

Omichand was the only person in Calcutta who did not yet know of the dire happenings in his home. Beyond Fort William, news of his dramatic arrest and incarceration in the Hatmen's hive had produced a profound effect. A further large segment of Black Town had fled immediately into the countryside. This included most of the coolies who had been working on the new defences. Substantial pay increases had been offered, but only a small force had returned. They worked now by flares in shifts through the night to finish the trenches and palisades that would defend the town.

At Drake's request the Chief Magistrate had now moved into the fort. He had brought with him considerable baggage although he had buried whatever he could at the end of his garden. He had delayed a departing coolie with the lure of a large sum of money, and in a few hours the man had done most of the digging. There had seemed no end to his possessions however, and he became weary of the sight of things he had recently felt so necessary.

At one point in his labours he was reduced to envy of the Indians, who could disembark so easily from the physical structure of their lives. A length of cloth to wrap themselves in, a cooking pot, a jar for ablutions; they appeared to need nothing more. And also, thought the Chief Magistrate, people whose every step was sustained and surrounded by ancient customs that guided lives along a prescribed path, did not have to ask questions or frame decisions regarding conduct and goals. The Chief Magistrate was forced to remember that the weight he bore in possessions and sensibility was part of the texture of a civilisation he was sure set him above the heathen. He drew back his shoulders at this sobering thought and proceeded dutifully with his labours.

At last he trod the soil back into place over his possessions and returned to the house. A tower of his best plate was still heaped upon his drawing room floor, waiting to accompany him into the fort. The Chief Magistrate sat wearily in a chair and surveyed the sea of silver before him with a sudden feeling of nausea. It was only the thought of Siraj Uddaulah's looters swarming through his home that gave him the strength to carry on. He could already see the sweaty horde leering at portraits, ripping up furniture, kicking aside the chamber pots with a derisory cry. The shame of it all ran through him. He had loaded everything on to a barrow along with a box of cash and jewels. As all horses had been commandeered by the military, he had then been forced to trundle this barrow into Fort William himself.

Bellamy's arrival had created the greatest problem, for he had appeared with three large covered carts of his best wines that he refused to leave to looters. These had eventually been stored beneath the fort in its labyrinthine innards. There had been talk of opening the ballroom for the ladies of White Town, but then it had been decided that the small rooms of Writers' Row, however damp, provided a much-needed privacy and were to be preferred. The men of the militia could then also join their families in a continuance of domesticity. The ballroom was to be kept for use as a hospital should the need arise. The writers had bedded down wherever they could, loud and unruly, only too glad to be free of their cells. From the balcony of the Council chamber, Holwell listened to the sound of the young men's laughter and tipsy singing. There was almost a holiday atmosphere.

Drake had offered Holwell accommodation in Governor's House along with the Chaplain. As soon as he was settled, the Chief Magistrate had opened his box of valuables and lifted out old Jaya's diamonds. The small chest was filled with a collection of stones of varying size and quality. Bags of emeralds, rubies, opals and sapphires lay heaped within the box, but all paled beside Jaya's stones. The great necklace lay in the Chief Magistrate's palm, foaming with iridescence, the light refracting a thousand times within each shimmering gem. Holwell stared for a long time at the magnificent piece. Amidst the tension and uncertainty, the luminous stones appeared to him now not only endowed with magical qualities but the very cement of his future. In all his years of diamond dealing he had never possessed stones of this quality. Like all Indian jewellery, the diamonds were unfaceted, but, shipped back to Amsterdam, cut and polished, they would fetch a tremendous price. Yet, in spite of these thoughts, new fears filled the Chief Magistrate. On this strange and moonless night the future seemed more uncertain than ever. Already, he had left his home, surrendering it to its fate. What if, by some twist of destiny, looters entered the fort itself? When he allowed his mind to approach such perimeters, the blood seemed to drain from his veins. He looked again at the magnificent gems, then pushed them firmly back into their pouch. He strode from the room with them.

As he reached the parade ground he assessed his surroundings with a new eye for detail. At last, to one side of Governor's House, he saw a flight of stairs descending. Taking a flare from a sconce on the wall, he made his way down into the belly of Fort William. Beneath Govenor's House and the parade ground were the warehouses and storerooms of the fort. The Chief Magistrate looked about him. He appeared to be in some kind of entry room. A passage led away into the depths, but as he approached it he heard the scuttle of rats and drew back. Holding up the torch, he examined his surroundings and found at last what he was looking for. Kneeling down before a wall, he began to dig with a pocket knife at a patch of loose bricks. Within moments the bricks were dislodged, revealing a small space behind. Into this the Chief Magistrate pushed the pouch of diamonds, and reinserted the bricks.

Next morning the Council of War met early. There had been no further message from Rai Durlabh. It seemed increasingly likely that a battle of some kind might have to be fought if they did not evacuate immediately. Beyond the shuttered Council chamber the sun blazed down upon Fort William. Already a smell of cooking filled the parade ground from breakfast fires lit by the White Town women. After only one night in Writers' Row they were glad to escape their dank rooms, where sleep was impossible. Beyond the drilling of the militia, children played at hopscotch or skipping ropes. A camp atmosphere infused the place. Soon, breakfast finished, the women were set to work to make sandbags of waste cotton. Lady Russell had agreed to take charge of the children to allow their mothers to work. The ballroom was opened for this purpose and games were organised beneath chandeliers. Beyond Fort William's walls the sun blazed down upon an empty city. The wedding cake houses of White Town with their fretted balconies appeared suddenly vulnerable. Servantless days and accumulating dust already gilded them with decay. Now, as the cloud of sand that was Siraj Uddaulah's army rolled ever nearer, it was possible at last to imagine the danger the houses might pose for Fort William. They clustered about the walls, their upper windows looking directly down on to the parade ground. The Engineer's suggestion to the Council of War about setting fire to these homes now at last made sense. But as no one had the courage to take such an action, the houses remained, as if awaiting a new set of tenants.

At last, towards evening, the nawab arrived. The tidal wave of dust that hung permanently above his army now rolled on to swallow Calcutta. Suddenly grit filled every crack, sore throats and red eyes were complained about, a dirty powder carpeted floors and was found in soup and water jars. The nawab settled himself in Omichand's Garden, a retreat owned by the fat merchant two miles east of Fort William. Within the fort, tension was high. A great medley of sounds stretched across the town as Siraj Uddaulah set up his camp. Eventually, in the distance, a city of tents was seen. Bright pennants stirred in the breeze. The bellowing of elephants, the shouts of men, rifle shots and bugle calls drifted over the fort on the wind. Attack was expected at dawn.

'Why has Rai Durlabh not yet done away with the nawab? What are we to do?' The Governor grew petulant.

'Let us evacuate with the treasure,' Manningham said, for now reality pressed hard upon them all.

The Chief Magistrate voiced his worst fears to the Council of War. 'If we evacuate Calcutta, I fear it is possible all may be lost. Our homes may be fired and our fort commandeered. We may then be forced to live in our own town upon Siraj Uddaulah's terms. In victory he may prove even less reasonable. We must leave the option of evacuation until the very last. At that time we can try and bargain our way out.' Holwell spoke firmly, but beneath his words he saw events spiralling unstoppably towards him.

In the secret missives now going backwards and forwards at an accelerated rate between Fort William and the commander, Rai

Durlabh still indicated that he would soon successfully carry out his plan. Every moment Fort William waited for news of the nawab's dispatch.

'Unless Rai Durlabh does something before morning, it would appear at least one battle must be fought,' Mackett announced, his voice turning up at the end in panic.

'A further message has been sent to the commander,' Holwell wearily informed them.

Everyone now had trouble containing their impatience with Rai Durlabh. The last reply received from him had urged Fort William to prepare for the possibility of a short battle. If he was unable to act decisively before such an event, Rai Durlabh assured Fort William, he would persuade the nawab to attack at Perrin's Redoubt, a spot he knew was well fortified, which would be to the Hatmen's advantage.

'Let us hope he will soon do the needful. I suspect the commander is waiting for a moment in battle when confusion will be at its height and the nawab will be careless. I suspect also that the commander will see no great damage is done us. It will be a staged battle,' the Chief Magistrate tried to sound hopeful.

'Nevertheless, a battle is a battle. Had we known it would come to this we could already have begun bargaining with the nawab. Instead, we have sat around uselessly just awaiting the intervention of Rai Durlabh. I fear now we are hanging upon the word of an untrustworthy schemer.' The Governor was unable to control his anxiety.

In the silence that followed the Governor's words, the sounds of the militia drilling on the parade ground came clearly to them all. Shouted orders and the clunk of muskets echoed about the Council chamber. Those half-caste Portuguese and Armenians from the town who had volunteered for duty knowing nothing of military life were awkward with their weapons. It was found necessary to drill them constantly if some degree of proficiency was to be obtained. This was not the case with the Company's men or those who had volunteered from the Settlement or been drawn from shipping upon the Hoogly, who were all familiar with weaponry. And the band of Dutch mercenaries who had been persuaded to join them must be disciplined to control their recklessness. From wherever they had come, this influx of volunteers now swelled the garrison's force to five hundred and fifteen men.

'Are we sure attack will be at dawn?' Frankland queried.

'That is the way of Indian armies. Fighting will stop between noon and three, to allow each man to eat and sleep. It is ill mannered in the eyes of the Moors not to observe this siesta. All fighting ceases at six in the evening until the following dawn,' the Chief Magistrate confirmed.

'The *Prince George* with all its cannon is ready to fire from the Hoogly should we need it.' Drake had ordered the war ship to sail up river and it had arrived before Fort William the previous day.

'Of course, Fort William will be in no danger. The battle will be in the town. Should things get out of hand, we will wait no longer to evacuate,' the Chief Magistrate assured the Council of War.

The following morning, dawn broke with its usual magnificence. At the palisades and in the fort, in the redoubt and in the trenches across the denuded Park, the men of Fort William waited for the nawab to attack at the expected hour. Dawn came and went. The aubergine shadows grew lighter and faded at last. Flocks of parrots flew about screeching. The jackals returned to the jungle and the adjutant birds opened red-rimmed eyes in search of the day's first morsels. There was no sound from the enemy. In the heat, the Hatmen and their army waited, facing a wall of coconut palms fronting the impenetrable jungle. Soon the sun spurted fire more viscous than any cannon and heat rose shimmering from the ground. Men began to faint. The Dutch mercenaries and the Portuguese sepoys demanded a return to Fort William.

At the very moment they threatened to lay down their arms, the call of the muezzin rose suddenly from the enemy camp and floated through the jungle. The voice climbed steadily upon the hot air until it reached its zenith. There it stayed for some seconds, neither wavering nor falling. The sweet purity of the sound was such that everybody listened. There was something terrifying in such beauty, as if the voice of God were heard. Suddenly it stopped, and for a split second there was silence. Then, as if the world had broken apart, a wild battle cry came from the nawab's great army. A first wave of riflemen streamed out of the jungle, pennants flying, to form a line two hundred yards long. The Hatmen levelled their muskets. The Indians took up position, some lying, some kneeling, some standing behind, all without any cover. The Hatmen let fire at once and were relieved to find the returning fire not only ragged but harmless. Then, unexpectedly, a cannon ball crashed out of the jungle. It whistled over the Hatmen's heads to score a direct hit on Perrin's Redoubt. Smoke, dust, rubble and the cries of wounded men suddenly filled the air. Sunlight streamed through the redoubt's paltry walls, the dead lay in bloody heaps. From the depths of the jungle came an immediate commotion of wildlife. Birds rose from the trees in squawking clouds, jackals howled, hysterical monkeys fled their habitat showing yellow teeth.

The enemy screamed in triumph. They now ran at the Ditch firing wildly, flinging themselves into the sluggish water, scrambling out the other side for a final assault. At that moment the *Prince George* fired its first shots from the river. The aggressive boom from out of nowhere and the great spurts of dirt as each cannon ball landed had everyone confused. One moment the enemy was preparing for assault; the next the air was alive with flying bodies and limbs. Those left alive wasted no time in rushing back into the cover of the jungle. A thick fog of black smoke hung upon the hot air. It was twenty minutes past ten.

Soon the enemy regained some courage and returned for a further skirmish. The Fort William men in Perrin's Redoubt fought bravely. If an enemy hand gripped the base of a window it was sliced off. If a face appeared before them it was immediately run through. The fighting went on until noon. In Fort William the gunfire had been plainly heard and events just as plainly observed. Overwhelmed by the unexpected success, Holwell threw himself into the subject of strategy, the adrenaline pounding through his veins. While Captain Minchin sulked in the background, low on courage and advice, the garrison turned for leadership to the Chief Magistrate.

The distant sight of the redoubt in all its shambles convinced Holwell that a change of plan was needed for the afternoon. He ordered an eighteen-pounder cannon drawn up to Bagh Bazaar, the great market area of Black Town. Here the Fort William soldiers would be hidden while having a clear view of the Ditch. If this cannon, plus the men in the damaged redoubt and the *Prince George* on the river all opened fire at a given signal, the enemy would be attacked from three sides at once. It was not the habit of Indian armies to look in more than one direction at a time. And better still, the Chief Magistrate decided, Fort William would not observe the etiquette of waiting out the nawab's siesta until three o'clock. They would attack at two fifteen.

At the appointed time, oxen, horses and soldiers having dragged the great cannon the two miles to Bagh Bazaar, the enemy were surprised as intended. Cannonball after cannonball crashed down into the jungle from three separate sides. Firing continued for over an hour; no sound of defence was heard. This unnatural silence was because, unbeknown to Fort William, a lucky shot had smashed two cannon, blown up several kegs of powder and killed two of the nawab's French officers who were directing proceedings. Siraj Uddaulah's thirty thousand now refused to fight, sitting terrified amongst their dead. Two elephants, driven mad by the noise, broke their chains and stampeded out of the jungle to stumble into the Ditch amongst the dead and wounded. Vultures collected to wheel overhead. The smell of blood had also reached the jackals, who stuck their heads out of the cover of the jungle, braving daylight and crowds. Behind the screen of trees, sounds of retreat were heard.

Within Fort William the Council of War was jubilant. Lethargy was thrown aside. The unexpected victory had taken them all by surprise.

'We should not allow ourselves the luxury of jubilation so early in the day,' the Chaplain warned, looking about the table of the Council chamber. He had produced some bottles of his best claret in a sudden swell of generosity. At certain bald moments in the last few days the Reverend Bellamy had forced himself to face the fact that he might not survive the siege. Was it not right then to drink his best wines and leave the worst to posterity?

'The main assault, we are told by our spies, is set for the day after tomorrow.' Holwell exchanged a glance with Drake.

'By then perhaps the nawab will be dead, if we are to believe Rai Durlabh,' Frankland insisted.

'Rather than fight tomorrow, the enemy will prepare themselves for the main battle,' Drake observed.

A novel idea had struck the Chief Magistrate in the middle of his claret, and he voiced it to the table carefully, weighing each word as he spoke. 'I think, in order that we may more clearly see the enemy's movements, and also to deprive them of good cover, we need to rid ourselves of Black Town.'

'How is this to be done?' Manningham frowned, unable like everyone else to follow the Chief Magistrate's line of reasoning.

'It will have to be fired,' the Chief Magistrate answered. There was an immediate buzz of confusion in the Council chamber.

'But the natives still populate the place,' the Chaplain worried.

'Most have run into the jungle; the rest will follow their example as soon as the fire starts. The sacrifice of a few thatched huts is preferable to the destruction of Calcutta proper,' the Chief Magistrate announced, clear now in his mind of the necessity of his plan.

'We do not want the fire to result in unnecessary killings,' Bellamy frowned, remembering once more the slaughter in Omichand's house.

'We are in a difficult position. Some sacrifice must be risked for the greater good,' the Chief Magistrate argued.

It did not take long for a consensus to be reached at the table. The firing of Black Town was agreed upon and an order was immediately given. Yet the houses of White Town, clustered so closely about the fort, were still ignored as a potential danger.

Unbeknown to the Council of War, Siraj Uddaulah had at that same moment issued an identical order. He too had no use for Black Town. It impeded his vision of the fort, and the grand houses of White Town stood ready to provide any cover he needed.

Rai Durlabh entered the great pavilion of Siraj Uddaulah. The scarlet tent, sixty feet long and thirty feet high, was secured by gold pillars and weighed down with ornaments encrusted with jewels. Precious carpets covered the floor. In the midst of this splendour sat the nawab, a rope of pearls slung over a vest of chain mail.

'You have sent the message? Still they trust your word?' the prince enquired when Rai Durlabh stood before him.

'They wait for my direction.'

'They have the river and will run to their boats. They will take the treasure with them.' Siraj Uddaulah clenched his fist at the thought.

'The Hatmen will sit where they are hoping their God with my help will deliver them. When they find themselves cornered like rats in a trap, only then they will run to their boats. We shall soon recover the treasure. But the greatest treasure of all will be Fort William itself,' Rai Durlabh advised. Siraj Uddaulah rewarded him with a faint smile.

Later, as he left the tent, he looked up into the moonless sky. If the rains held off he had no doubt they could soon be within the fort. With the Young Begum's arrest it had been necessary to play a different role. It was important nothing was rushed, each step had to be considered. He had no doubt the young nawab would eventually destroy himself with his hot-headed antics. Rai Durlabh felt no need to risk his own life in power games: he had only to bide his time. Sooner or later, all that he wished would be his. He walked the short distance to his own handsome tent, where a small portion of

Omichand's Garden had been set aside for his enjoyment. The sawing of crickets filled his ears and the smell of the river came to him as he walked along. The moon had withdrawn from the world to begin its journey of transformation. When once again it was reborn, on what order of things would it shine? wondered Rai Durlabh. Mankind made plans, more fragile than a spider's web, but all things were in God's hands. Men were never in control of events, however hard they tried. Instead, events controlled the life of men. Rai Durlabh found new equilibrium with this thought. He sat down on a bench. The smell of jasmine filled the dark sky.

CHAPTER EIGHTEEN

At first the dire happenings across the Ditch in White Town did not disturb Black Town's day. It was noticed that lanes were clogged by a large number of departing families pushing overloaded carts. It was also noted that beggars immediately commandeered the many huts standing suddenly empty, but the true danger of events was not comprehended. The barber in the lanes near Jaya had vanished, and men complained there was no one to clean their ears or trim a moustache. The snake charmer and a group of acrobats no longer pestered passers-by. Some of the stalls had closed their shutters. The sandal man and the oil-lamp man were amongst the many who had disappeared. The fruit man and the spice vendor sat before diminishing piles of mechandise. Eventually nobody could deny that there was a lessening clamour, a slowing of trade, a thinning of crowds. Apprehension built slowly until it was like dry kindling, waiting only for a spark. Finally, most people who remained in Black Town did so at the ready, cooking utensils and other necessities tied up in carrying cloths. The old men stretched out on string beds under the trees talked in worried tones, ready to flee when the moment came. Stocks of rice and *dhal* were low. The itinerant vegetable woman now included some fruit and pulses in her basket and continued to pester Jaya.

'Here is a good *chunna dhal* and also sweet limes. Rice and *dhal* are now like gold; everyone is hoarding. The Hatmen are taking everything into their hive and closing their gates. They are leaving nothing for Black Town people.' The vegetable woman offered the *dhal* for inspection to Jaya.

'Always you are bringing me the same rotten things. See here, each bit of *dhal* is like a honeycomb. It has already fed an army of maggots.' Jaya pushed the pulses away.

'Aiee, Bibiji, nowadays who will care? Where will you get fine *dhal*? Only show me and I too will buy from there. *Dhal* is *dhal* once it is cooked; it will taste the same. I am not charging; it is a gift for the *Devi*. All I want in return is *darshan*,' the vegetable woman pleaded.

Every day Jaya's hut was crowded. It was known now as the Devi Ashram. People came from all ends of Black Town to pay homage to the Goddess. Those who believed She had come for a purpose at a critical moment in time remained unconcerned by events across the Ditch and the worrying swirl of gossip. Each day people collected about Jaya's hut, bringing offerings of fruit, a handful of almonds, a cup of rice or a few chillies. Those who could gave money. Many of the women and children who arrived each day were the families of the half-caste Portuguese sepoys of the Fort William garrison. Without their men, and beset with anxiety, these women found sanctuary in the Devi Ashram. A hut next to Jaya's had fallen empty in the exodus and the women devotees took it upon themselves to transform this into the ashram kitchen. All offerings of food were turned over to them. It had been agreed in the ashram that meals must be provided for the regular crowd of disciples, of whom some were sick or maimed. Whatever their condition, they had trudged across Black Town to the God Woman. Others insisted on carrying water from the well as a service to the *Devi*, or set themselves the task of sweeping clean the God Woman's hut. Some families took advantage of the number of vacant huts nearby and moved into these, saving themselves a daily trek. In this way there was now established a large circle of devotees about Jaya's hut.

At the very nucleus of the Devi Ashram Sati sat supreme. Even before the sun came up she awoke to sounds of the faithful gathering, of shifting feet and muted voices or the crying of a child. Then there arose the smell of cooking and the clank of pans. She ate the meal they served her and then Pagal opened the door. He had assumed the role of her attendant. For the rest of the day the faithful streamed through at regulated times. She sat silently while they touched her feet, and then gave her blessing over bowed heads. Govindram and Mohini directed the progress of things. With Omichand in prison and business slow, Govindram had many empty hours to his day, and was glad to take charge of the organisation. Mohini took charge of the needs of the women and children and Jaya governed the kitchen. Pagal, the albino, had proved himself indispensable, obeying willingly all commands. The Devi Ashram had already evolved a rhythm to its day. In the midst of growing turmoil it remained a pool of tranquillity. Its sudden birth in Black Town was whispered of in awe.

Even when the great cloud of dust that was Siraj Uddaulah and his thirty thousand came to settle upon Calcutta, the impact was negligible upon the Devi Ashram. Those who resided in its circle of huts maintained expressions of beatitude that nothing seemed to stir. When the departing crowds trundled past with carts of belongings and asked if they felt no trepidation, they replied as one, 'The Goddess will provide.'

Only Jaya, viewing the rolling cloud of dust, and tasting on her lips the first gritty particles, ran to secure the top of her water jar and drape a length of muslin over her window. This last precaution was useless, for immediately the sun was up, Pagal opened the door to the faithful and a continuous swirl of dust. It was towards evening, as the women devotees began preparing the evening meal, that Pagal, chewing tobacco outside the hut, saw the first wisps of smoke.

Soon, fired by the nawab and fired again by the Hatmen, Black Town was burning well. The closely packed huts, their thatched roofs dried by the sun, blazed up. Smoke billowed thickly and flames shot out. The fire quickly found momentum. The narrow lanes of Black Town were suddenly choked by stampeding crowds, behind them raced the holocaust. It reached out to touch a child's hair, drawing into its depths without discrimination geriatrics and newborn kittens, beggars and a moneylender who had paused to urinate. The old men who had gossiped under the trees were forced to abandon their string beds to the fire. Women left laundry and frying onions, stopping only to snatch up babies. Those who could jumped into the Hoogly, but they were few, for the fire blew landwards, cutting Black Town off from the river. Many jumped headlong into wells and died in consequence. The terror was added to by the nawab's men, who swept down upon the burning town, hacking at the fleeing crowds, plundering where they could. The dead and dying clogged the streets, slaughtered by soldiers or trampled in the stampede, suffocated by the smoke.

In the Devi Ashram there was panic at Pagal's alarm. Those who queued for *darshan* or an evening meal turned on their heels and ran. Only the most devoted stayed near the God Woman, hearts beating in their throats, aware of the danger of each lost moment. Govindram grew flustered and began to shout; Mohini clung to Jaya. The wives of Fort William's Portuguese sepoys clutched their children and began a hysterical debate. Although the fire had not yet reached the Devi Ashram, the smoke swirled densely, making people cough, and their eyes smart. Only Sati sat silent. Durga had appeared suddenly in the late afternoon, as if aware of trouble. She lay along the rafters under the thatch, chin upon her hand, observing the crowd. Sati kept her eyes upon her. Durga would tell her what to do.

One of the wives of the Portuguese sepoys pushed through the crowd until she stood before Sati. 'All the women of White Town are inside the fort. Their men already were there for fighting. So quietly quietly in the night they went inside, thinking we would not know. We too have a right to be in there. Our husbands also are fighting for the Hatmen.'

Another woman spoke up. 'Haa! They seek only to protect

213

themselves and their White Town. Our Black Town they are burning down for their convenience. Whether we live or die they care nothing. From one side came Siraj Uddaulah's men with their torches, and from the other came the Hatmen also with big torches. Everyone can bear witness to this.' There were cries of approval at this speech.

'Let us go to the fort. Why should our husbands fight for them if they care nothing for us?' the first woman demanded.

'Then let us hurry,' said Govindram. 'Inside the fort we will be safe.' There was new panic in the ashram as the heat of the fire drew nearer.

'Let us go,' Sati announced abruptly. One moment Durga had sat on the rafters; the next she was no longer there. It was clear to Sati that Durga had directed the sepoys' wives to advise them. As Sati rose, devotees immediately crowded about her like a hive of bees protecting their queen.

In this awkwardly bunched formation, the Devi Ashram began the journey to Fort William, moving amoeba-like about its precious nucleus. Smoke enveloped them, fingers of flame reached out towards them, hordes of terrified, fleeing people pushed against them. Roofs collapsed at their feet, fiery chunks of timber barred their path. The panic of flailing limbs and shouts and screams was deafening. Slowly, the Devi Ashram pushed forward, women holding their babies close, young children carrying younger siblings upon their backs. The albino and his family clung to each other and kept a firm hold on Sati's veil. Jaya struggled with the ashram's cooking utensils, trundling them before her in a small barrow. At one point the flames and the commotion became so bad that it seemed the barrow must be abandoned, but they pushed on, heads down against the smoke and pandemonium, as if they battled against a storm. Heat scorched lungs, smoke blinded eyes, but still they pushed on.

Eventually they crossed the Ditch and found themselves on The Avenue. Fort William stood before them. They had entered another world. The fire was suddenly left behind as if a door had closed on it.

Here, in White Town, the dusk descended gracefully, lit by Black Town's fiery sky. It was immediately clear that others besides themselves in Black Town had had the idea of reaching the fort. The Avenue was crowded with people all heading towards the garrison. As the crowd drew nearer Fort William, the Hatmen were seen looking down from the ramparts in consternation.

The first of the Black Town crowd to reach the fort were met with drawn swords. When the argument grew heated and forced entry was attempted, the great gates swung shut on them. Word of this rippled back through the crowd, now grown to a threatening size. Then, the wives of the black Portuguese sepoys inside the fort grew strident and, announcing the presence of the ashram to the crowd, began to push their way forward. People drew back in respect when they heard of the God Woman's presence. Still moving in a circuitous manner about their precious nucleus, the Devi Ashram arrived as one before the gates of Fort William. Sati, Jaya, Govindram and Mohini looked up at the fort with mixed feelings. The albino and his family drew back in awe. Only the wives of the Portuguese sepoys planted themselves fearlessly before the gate and began to argue with the guards. They shook their fists at the Hatmen, who still stood at the ramparts. The rattling of bangles on angry wrists rose ominously in the air. Soon, knowledge of the women's presence reached the ears of their husbands. On the parade ground, the soldiers threatened mutiny if their wives were not given refuge. They laid down their muskets and refused to fight, standing with folded arms. For some time debate raged, the women screaming on one side of the wall, the soldiers adamant on the other. Then the furious crowd suddenly overwhelmed the guards and burst through the gates of Fort William. They scrambled up the steps, spilling into the parade ground. The Devi Ashram were amongst the first to enter.

In spite of the excitement of an imminent reunion with their husbands, the sepoy's wives still moved in a protective formation about the God Woman, with the other devotees. People jostled past them, but the Devi Ashram climbed the steps cautiously, aware of their extraordinary status. In their midst Sati looked up at Governor's House, remembering the high-ceilinged rooms and the bird on the candelabra. Did Mrs Drake hover behind the tatties, staring down at them? Sati scanned the windows of the Governor's apartment. For a brief moment a pale face appeared in the failing light, but she could not be sure who it was.

For a while, once they had entered the fort, the people of Black Town seemed confused by their unexpected transposition. Many had observed the walls of Fort William for a lifetime and wondered at the world within. Few had business inside and even fewer aspired to enter the Hatmen's enclave. It had been thought by Black Town that the Hatmen's hive, shut away by high walls and mounted cannon, shaped and sustained by incomprehensible perceptions, must be as powerfully different as the world of gods was different from the world of men. It was a surprise to find this was not so. As they burst through the gates into the parade ground, as they staked out space upon which to settle, as they coughed out the acrid smoke from their lungs, the people of Black Town looked about furtively and found no reason for the Hatmen's disavowal of them. Fort William was not paved with gold, nor did the Hatmen breathe fire or show forked tongues. And as muskets could not be spared for use upon them, the Hatmen must for once bow to Black Town demands.

The old men who had gossiped under the trees and had recently watched their string beds burn now gathered together again in Fort William to survey their new location. The unexpected transition made the old men brave; they strutted about dropping snide remarks. The presence of the God Woman in their midst shored up their courage further. It was as they had always thought. Beneath their woollen hair and stiff, thick clothes, the Hatmen were insignificant men, no different from themselves. They climbed to the ramparts of Fort William and observed the world with the Hatmen's eyes. All about them the jungle flexed its muscle, hiding unknown terrors in its depths. And from its edge the Black Town world grew densely, like a colony of termites that would undermine foundations.

The old men scratched their heads and for the first time wondered if the Hatmen lived more in fear than arrogance.

It could be said, the men reasoned, that Fort William had been built upon the Hoogly's banks not so much to facilitate trade as to be ready for escape. With only a push, Fort William would topple into the Hoogly. The old men's laughter echoed across the parade ground. They swaggered about, pleased with themselves, confirming the sudden reversal of things. Soon the mutinous Portuguese sepoys arrived with rations for their families and something more for the Devi Ashram.

From his perch high upon the ramparts, the Chief Magistrate grew progressively agitated at the sight of the people of Black Town streaming into the fort. This sudden flooding of Fort William seemed to invert the order of things in a profound and disturbing way. In a moment the character of the fort was changed. The terrified women of White Town bolted themselves and their children into Writers' Row; the militia and the young writers sought refuge where they could. Never before in its history had Black Town invaded Fort William.

'Only musket fire can stop them now, but with the nawab on our heels, ammunition cannot be spared,' the Governor worried as he stood beside Holwell looking down at the crowd. In the distance, the flames consuming Black Town leapt into the sky. A dense black cloud drifted over Fort William.

'How can we now manage to evacuate the fort?' The Chief Magistrate's face puckered grimly. The sight of Holwell's anxiety filled Drake with new trepidation.

After the first fierce battle, the Council of War had decided that the women of White Town should be put at no further risk. The following morning they were to be evacuated to the waiting ships on the Hoogly. The sudden entry into the fort of so many Black Town people now made that operation precarious.

The Chief Magistrate turned back to view the growing tide in The

Avenue, and his knuckles grew white as he gripped the wall before him. The Governor stood silently beside him. At last Holwell turned to make his way back to the Council chamber. The parade ground was filling rapidly as Holwell and Drake strode forward. People who knew nothing of the Chief Magistrate pushed roughly against him. Ragged children trod on his feet; a group of arguing women made no effort to let him pass. Chickens ran between his legs, almost bringing him to his knees. Loaded barrows obstructed his path. A goat began nibbling at his coat. Already the dark was descending and a sliver of moon had appeared. The dust of the parade ground, greatly disturbed by so many feet, rose up to coat everyone even as ash from the Black Town fire floated down upon them. Holwell looked around in desperation. Fort William was unrecognisable. The people of Black Town, like the lava of some unstoppable volcano, now covered every inch, blocking crevices, squeezing through cracks, swamping all other life.

Beyond the fort, the smouldering town appeared like an extravagant sunset, lifting up a corner of night. Two water carriers had set themselves up in the middle of the square and now dispensed their wares to the thirsty. Mothers begged milk for hungry children from whoever had brought in a goat. Where would all these people sleep, how would they be fed? The Chief Magistrate looked wildly about, unable to comprehend these enormities. His brain was reduced to a scrambled egg.

He struggled on across the parade ground. The falling darkness, the shroud of smoke, the restless emotional crowd, all threatened to engulf him. Strange dark faces came at him, turned, then disappeared. Cries like the whooping of angry birds sounded in his ears. Warm naked flesh collided with him. He gave a sob and the sound of his own grief echoed within him. He was being stretched wider and wider, as if forced to swallow a river. The Hoogly at last had taken a form and exacted its punishment upon him.

Then, through the murky dusk, in the very midst of the throng, he saw a faint speck of brightness. He kept his eyes upon the one thing he recognised: a European face. He could not see whose face it was, agleam like a beacon in the midst of the swarthy crowd. Perhaps it was a Dutch mercenary, perhaps a member of the Council of War. In the smoky dusk it was increasingly difficult to see anything clearly. The Chief Magistrate set off, wading once more into the crowd. He was conscious of the Governor still trailing behind him. The pale face bobbed in the distance, occasionally disappearing from view. The Chief Magistrate pushed on.

Eventually he thrust aside the last obstacle to stand before the man. In the fading light he stared in disbelief at the white skin, pink eyes and stubble of yellow hair, unable to digest his mistake. Before him Pagal backed away in fear. Then Holwell let out a cry of such fury that the albino held up a hand to protect himself, fearing the Hatman would lash out.

Instead the Chief Magistrate turned away with a despairing sob, unable to hide his distress from Drake, who still followed close on his heels. Once more they turned back into the crowd, like weary swimmers far from shore. The Chief Magistrate pushed on again, oblivious now to the cries and the strange faces, and the acrid smoke billowing about Fort William. Eventually Governor's House loomed darkly before them. The Governor gave a cry of relief and pushed the Chief Magistrate forward. As they made their way towards the building, they found their path barred by a cordon of women.

The Devi Ashram, arranged in the usual protective circle about the God Woman, stood its ground before the Governor and the Chief Magistrate. Holwell was forced to a halt once more. Even in the near darkness, he could not mistake the faces before him. At first he thought his eyes deceived him, or that he was the victim of a malicious joke. Jaya Kapur stood before him beside her granddaughter, legs apart, arms folded across her massive breast. At her side the girl, Sati, stared at him with the same intensity she had on the night of the seance. Holwell groaned and retreated. His strength was waning. On this wild night, it seemed every harpy in hell had been let loose.

At last, the Chief Magistrate reached Governor's House and with Drake behind him stumbled gratefully up the steps. The flare in the porch lit up the familiar entrance, a guard stood to attention inside. Relief flooded the Chief Magistrate and his knees grew weak. Once inside the sanctuary, he sat down on the stairs to recover himself.

'The Portuguese are already demanding rice for their families,' the Governor panted, coming to sit beside him. He took out a handkerchief and wiped his wet face. The Chief Magistrate had not the strength to reply. Then, slowly, in the cool quiet of Governor's house, his thoughts began to order themselves.

'They must be given it or they will not fight,' he replied.

'But we do not know what lies ahead, how long our supplies must last,' the Governor argued. 'Already latrine facilities and drinking water are stretched to the maximum.'

'What does anything matter? Our women and children must soon be evacuated,' the Chief Magistrate answered, standing up determinedly, for he saw now that one way or another this must be achieved. He strode up the stairs towards the Council chamber. Drake hurried after him, his mind aquiver with questions.

The Council of War had left their seats about the table to stare down from the balcony in disbelief. The Governor and the Chief Magistrate joined them there. Holwell viewed from a distance the multitude through which he had just struggled and marvelled at his deliverance.

'At this moment, when the ground should be stripped for action, it is covered by this motley carpet. Tomorrow the nawab will attack again.' Drake's voice rose to an anxious squeak as he observed the turmoil below.

'How will we evacuate our women? As soon as they are seen departing to the safety of the boats there will be a stampede to follow them.' The Chaplain asked the question now upon everyone's mind.

'It will have to be done somehow,' the Chief Magistrate replied. It was now hard to remember the pristine condition of the parade ground brushed by a synchronised line of sweepers each morning.

Soon the Council of War left the balcony and returned to their places about the table. Once more the Reverend Bellamy opened bottles of his best Madeira. It was already late, but the Council of War had nowhere more comfortable to retire to. The thought of joining their wives in the primitive conditions of Writers' Row, oppressed by the stench of latrines and persistent flies, was to nobody's liking. They sat on in the Council chamber, fortified by dry biscuits, the Chaplain's Madeira and fruitless argument. The task of evacuation occupied everyone's mind, and it appeared impossible.

'It cannot be done in daylight, for the refugees will see what is happening,' Drake worried.

'We must wait until tomorrow night,' Holwell decided.

'Should we not provide rations to the refugees?' Mackett asked from the end of the table.

'We have nothing to spare for such a horde,' Drake frowned.

'We do not know what is ahead, we must conserve our stores,' the Chief Magistrate agreed.

'If no food is forthcoming, they may even be persuaded to leave.' The Governor's voice took on a hopeful tone.

'If we do not feed them they will starve,' the Chaplain pointed out.

'Let us assess the situation in the morning,' Holwell announced, unable to stretch his frazzled mind to any further thought.

'Then let us pray before we sleep. We do not know what the Lord has in store for us tomorrow.' Bellamy bowed his head to mutter well-worn words that had suddenly now acquired fresh meaning.

CHAPTER NINETEEN

In the high-ceilinged rooms that seemed to contain the sum of her life, Emily Drake paced the floor, her child in her arms. She had seen little of her husband; he was locked away in the Council chamber. His absence was a relief. She had seen the women of White Town enter the fort the night before. She had gone down amongst them with what food could be spared, offering help where she could. The conditions in Writers' Row were far from agreeable; she had demanded the latrines to be cleaned, but no man could be spared to do the job. To Mrs Mackett and Mrs Mapletoft, who were both expecting babies, she had offered shelter in the Governor's apartment, but they had declined, preferring to stay where their husbands could join them.

Like everyone else she had observed the roll of dust that heralded the arrival of Siraj Uddaulah. Even now she caught the tuneless sound of drums and reed pipes on the wind. Yet the violence of the day and the distant boom of cannon fire at Perrin's Redoubt had passed her by. Her life was without reality, hollow as a play. She looked down at the silent child in her arms and knew his life hung by a thread. In the night the doctor had come and shaken his head.

'It's opium,' he declared. 'These native women give it all the time to keep a baby quiet. Your wet nurse must have dosed him every day.

In my opinion, more of our children die in India of the effects of opium than from this dreaded climate.'

Emily had been ignorant of every sign. The silence and the small chill limbs, the transparency of flesh and the sleep from which he hardly woke were each a gate through which Harry passed towards the shores of death. In her ignorance she had done nothing to obstruct the journey. Yet in spite of what the doctor said, she was sure once again that it was Jane who was taking her child. The afternoon light was deep and mellow, shadows were lengthening and a bowl of roses loaded the air with perfume. In spite of the tension within Fort William, the day appeared full of deceptive beauty. It did not seem possible that threaded within it lay an evil detritus.

'What more do you want?' she whispered to Jane, laying her cheek upon Harry's soft hair. All about were unseen enemies that must be fought off every day. In the corner of the room the wet nurse, who had steered Harry to the brink of death, crouched sullenly. It was impossible to dispense with her; no replacement could be found and without her Harry would certainly die. Worse than this, a guard must now be kept upon the woman to ensure she did not run away. In comparison, the bearing-down upon them of the nawab appeared to Emily a flamboyance of unreal proportions.

From the parade ground the cry of a child carried up to her. Afternoon shadows collected in the corners of the room and moved across the ceiling. The scent of roses seemed to grow stronger. She clutched Harry tightly and watched the slow throb of his temples. The blue tracery of veins was etched more prominently, as if death already swam in his flesh. He must fight his fight alone, said the doctor; there was nothing they could do. Emily began to sing, a soft, lilting melody she and Jane had enjoyed as children. The child lay quietly in her arms, as if soothed by the sound. She took him to the window, so that the sun might warm him and the wild colours of the bougainvillaea, massed thickly before her, rouse him with their life. She lifted her head as she sang and looked out beyond the walls of the fort to a wider world beyond.

It was then that she first saw the Black Town fire. The dark smoke rose in a solid pillar. Soon the breeze took hold of the smoke, lifting it high, moving it forwards. It streamed out across the sky like a rapacious winged creature speeding towards her. At first she did not comprehend. Once or twice she had seen clouds of locusts moving over a plain, blackening the sky like night, and thought she saw again the same phenomenon. Then she heard the distant sound of screams and saw that beneath the dark cloud ran the people of Black Town, filling The Avenue. Soon they spilt into the fort. Emily Drake stepped nearer the window for a clearer view. This sudden invasion of Fort William seemed to invert the order of things in the same way that the sky, pinned to earth in a puddle, turned everything upside down. In the high-ceilinged rooms overlooking the fort, something stirred within the Governor's wife. The sense of separateness she carried within her now seemed an unbearable weight.

Stepping out on to her balcony, she leaned over the balustrade. Old men in *lungi* tottered around where before young writers had swaggered. Bare-bottomed children ran wild, women struggled with babies while unpacking meagre parcels of food. Barrows and cooking pots now littered the ground. The stench of Bagh Bazaar appeared to have entered Fort William. Flies swarmed. The adjutant birds, massed on their perches, squinted red-rimmed eyes as if surprised at the transformation.

In the stuffy rooms of Writers' Row, the White Town women struggled to maintain a structure that had long since disappeared. Their children cried, ill with fear, heat and exhaustion. Their bedding had gone to prepare for a possible influx of wounded, and they were left to make pillows of dresses and covers of petticoats. Thirst plagued them, along with diarrhoea. No medicines were available. Privies overflowed; no one could be spared to cart the contents to the Hoogly. Flies settled thickly in the latrines which punctuated the lines of cubicles in Writers' Row. The foul stench of these fetid holes sickened everyone. The whimpering of both Black Town and White Town children merged and swelled as one. Mosquitoes and flies attacked without prejudice the residents of both towns. Mothers in both encampments spent the night battling these vicious swarms as they crawled over the children, encrusting their nostrils, eyes and mouths. Soon, brought by the scent of suffering, a noxious army of stinkbugs appeared to worsen Fort William's plight.

At last, with the dawn, the shadows grew steadily shorter. In the grey light the refugees woke to stare at the still smouldering remains of Black Town. They climbed the ramparts of Fort William to gaze at the sky, unsure if dawn or the fire coloured it. Gutted shapes rose in the distance; a pall of smoke still hung in the air. The refugees discovered they were dusted with a thick grey ash. The crowd was packed even more tightly into Fort William, for through the night refugees had continued to enter the garrison. About two thousand people now occupied the parade ground.

As the shadows thinned, Emily Drake rose from her bed to settle the baby in his cot. Her dreams had been filled with the sounds of distress from the parade ground and Harry's shallow breathing. The thread of life within him appeared every moment more tentative. She had held him in her arms all night. Beneath the shroud of mosquito netting, the moon's measured light had seemed already to claim him. Now, as he slept, she placed him in his cot and watched him settle with relief. She left the stifling bedroom where the stored heat, trapped under the roof, reverberated through the night. She was unable any longer to bear the separateness her spirit placed upon her. From the balcony she could see now that women and children were the biggest part of the crowd. Dawn already curdled the sky; the hot white light of day waiting to boil over the scum of dark clouds. Throwing a wrap over her négligé, Emily left the Governor's apartment and made her way down the stairs and out into the early morning.

The guard was asleep at the door and she stepped quickly past him. A mist still hung over the Hoogly. Rats scuttled about amongst the sleeping refugees even as the light began to grow. Already, here and there, someone rose, picked up a child and began the journey to the water. The morning rituals and the waiting river made this no different from other mornings. The musty odour of the Hoogly drifted across the parade ground. Stepping carefully about the sleeping forms, Emily followed the line making their way down the steps of the Governor's Wharf.

The tide was out and a sticky black border of mud edged the Hoogly upon which squatted rows of the refugees. The men had retreated a distance away, leaving the nearer beach to the women and children. In a practised manner they were attending to the various rites involved each morning in the business of defecation. As they finished their chore, bare-bottomed children were cleaned briskly with a splash of water scooped up in an empty coconut shell. There were the purposeful sounds of the unravelling day: the screech of parrots, the scream of monkeys, the chat of the squatting refugees as they caught up with their neighbours' gossip. Others attended to their daily ablutions in the river, throwing ochre water over their limbs. Children splashed, shrieking with laughter. Everyone's strength had returned. Emily threw off her shawl and shoes and ran to the river's edge.

The scent of the river and the uninhibited splashing had unleashed a stream of memories from which she could not hold back. As the river swallowed her up, a flock of white cockatoos swung by overhead. Their raucous quarrels filled the air as they settled in the nearby trees. The Black Town children, infused with sudden daring, began to splash the White Town woman who had mysteriously appeared in their midst. Emily Drake beat the water, shouting at the Black Town children in a broken but familiar language. They drew back in surprise. Mothers turned in amazement, for Emily Drake's use of the language retained all the rawness of her own childhood. They edged forward in curiosity, conscious that their common wet and bedraggled state lowered barriers. Bold with questions, they surrounded her, enjoying the novelty of the contact. Beside Emily a child began suddenly to cry.

'There is no food,' a woman explained.

'What could we bring with the flames at our backs?' another scolded.

'Our children will starve,' yet another worried.

'We have had nothing to eat since the day before yesterday.'

'If the nawab does not kill us, the Hatmen will starve us.'

The voices rose up about Emily into the breaking day. As the sun pushed aside the last shadows, the first cannon was heard on the edge of town. At the sound there was instant confusion. The squatters on the muddy beach rose as hurriedly as they could. The bathers gathered their garments about them, wading quickly out of the water. Children began to cry again.

Emily watched them streaming landwards, until she stood alone. After some moments she too waded out and threw her wrap around her wet body. Her hair dripped down her back. As she turned, she looked up at Governor's House and met the eyes of the Council of War already assembled upon the balcony of the Council chamber to take a first breath of the day. She saw the looks of consternation as her husband pushed to the front of the crowd. She turned her back upon them.

Before Writers' Row, the White Town women were starting their cooking fires. The small store of rice and salted beef Emily had distributed the night before thickened the air with a savoury smell. The women greeted her and then fell silent, staring at her dripping clothes. In the distance came the sound of cannon fire and muskets again. She made her way across the crowded parade ground towards Governor's House. As she neared the entrance, she came up against the Devi Ashram. Behind a protective circle of women she saw the spirit girl, Sati, and stopped in surprise. The girl looked up and rose to her feet at the sudden appearance of the Governor's wife. The disciples of the Devi Ashram stared at the God Woman, trying to determine the reason she stood so respectfully before the bedraggled White Town woman.

'Come.' Emily heard herself speak as if in answer to a question. The girl nodded and moved forward, understanding.

Govindram looked anxiously at Mohini and the albino and then turned to follow Sati. The devotees of the Devi Ashram hesitated for a moment before hurrying after them. Emily Drake walked purpose-fully ahead of the crowd. Word spread across the parade ground, a way was cleared for her. People stopped in their tasks to watch the Governor's wife striding before the Devi Ashram. At last they reached the steps that led down into the warehouses beneath the fort.

'There may be rice down there,' Emily told them.

Above her she heard a shout and knew the Council of War still followed her progress. She saw an order given and knew soldiers would soon come for her. She turned back to Sati with new urgency.

A curious crowd of refugees had followed the Devi Ashram. The word *rice* was heard, and repeated back across the parade ground. It was also whispered that the finding of this rice was a miracle performed by the God Woman. Nobody would starve. Women with hungry children rocked their babies in anticipation. Old men grew suddenly cheerful. The crowd quickly swelled about the Devi Ashram and the bedraggled White Town woman.

'How is rice to be cooked? There are no pans.' Mohini pushed forward but nobody heard her.

Govindram, the albino and a crowd of men soon disappeared down the steps and returned after some time holding empty sacks and shaking their heads. The rice had already been devoured by rats.

'Search further.' Emily told them, ashamed at her inadequacy and the hope she had stirred in these people. She knew rice had been hoarded somewhere in Fort William.

'There are other rooms. We may find more,' Govindram agreed.

'There are no pans to cook it in,' Mohini shouted again. Already, in the distance, Emily saw soldiers, dispatched by her husband, making their way towards her. Before them ran Parvati, waving her arms about like a mad thing. Emily stared at her in confusion. At first she suspected a trick. Roger had sent the old ayah to draw her back to the house.

'The baby. The baby,' Parvati screamed, desperate before the advancing soldiers.

Emily turned when she heard the words and began to run to Parvati.

The breath stuck in her throat, the damp skirt stuck to her ankles, hampering her. The wind rushed in her ears while above her, a dark streak raced across the sky. A breath of heat touched her skin. From out of the sky a cannon ball dropped into the crowded parade ground. The ground shook beneath Emily's feet. A fountain of earth spurted up suddenly with a thunderous sound, showering those about it. Emily closed her eyes. When she opened them again, women and children lay lifeless around her. The soldiers who had marched to stop the looting of rice already lay limbless before her. Looking down, she saw she was covered not only with dirt but also with blood. At first she thought the blood her own, but she seemed unharmed. She was covered with the blood of the dead. A terrible wail of misery filled the air. Emily looked around, but the Devi Ashram had already fled the mangled piles of limbs.

She searched for Parvati, expecting to see her still running arthritically upon her thin legs. She began to call her name, turning right then left. No answer came and she was forced to inspect the mess of broken bodies. At last she found the ayah, face down on the parade ground, part of her skull blasted away, her lifeless limbs flung about at odd angles. Fear passed through Emily like the wash of cool water as she had entered the river. She knew they faced not only the enemy but also the workings of their own destiny. Parvati's urgency only moments before welled up before her once more.

She began to run again towards Governor's House, and when she entered, sped two at a time up the stairs. In her room the wet nurse crouched in a corner, almost hidden behind Harry's cradle.

She ran to the cradle, her breath sounding unevenly. Bending over the crib, she took Harry's small cold hand in her fingers.

'He will not wake now,' the woman whispered, looking up with a wide-eyed stare.

She saw then that Harry's silence was complete. In her absence he had been drawn at last across a waiting boundary. Before her the wet nurse still squatted beside the cradle, staring vacantly, her eyes fixed at a point beyond Emily's shoulder.

CHAPTER TWENTY

In the darkness of early morning, the Chief Magistrate mounted a horse at Fort William's gates and rode towards the newly erected defence. As commander of the militia, he could not shirk his duty at the East Battery, which now effectively blocked the enemy's advance on the garrison.

As he passed out of the gates of Fort William, the smell of the river filled his head. From the parade ground the wailing of a child could be heard. He turned his horse down The Avenue and its hooves echoed in the empty road.

Although, as he passed the cemetery, he could see no more from his horse than the tops of some trees, the Chief Magistrate observed the fireflies spreading a net of eerie light over the vegetation. The ponderous shapes of the mausoleums crouched in the dark like fantastical animals waiting to spring on the unwary. The moon was absent from the sky. It had begun its solitary journey of incubation and would return again reborn. The Chief Magistrate looked up at the heavens in trepidation. Although the moon's mysteries evaded him, one thought persisted: would he be there to see its new beginning? Perhaps a similar perilous passage of transformation awaited him with the morning light? For the first time the thought of death afflicted him and would not go away.

A further missive had gone out to Rai Durlabh, and the same bland plea for patience had been received. Now, as gunfire spluttered in his ears, the Chief Magistrate had been forced to conclude that Rai Durlabh might have led Fort William into a trap. Only the thought of the treasure, ready to be ferried to the Chief Magistrate's own boat, gave some satisfaction. He kicked his horse, and the animal started forward.

The East Battery now blocked off half The Avenue. The Courthouse made up its left side while on the right the wall of The Park supported it. Its earthen breastwork was several feet thick and a wide trench had been dug before it. Sandbags lined the three sides of the enclosure, which was open at the back to The Avenue and Fort William, a quarter of a mile away. Beyond the battery The Avenue continued for another five hundred yards to the crossroads and the jail, the last building in White Town.

The Chief Magistrate arrived at the East Battery to learn from Captain Clayton that Lieutenant Lebeaume and a small force of men had barricaded themselves into the jail in the hope of surprising the enemy. The Chief Magistrate announced his amazement at such a daring enterprise, but was also relieved. He looked up at the sky, suddenly hopeful of seeing the end of the day; the enemy might yet be routed. Small slits for muskets had been let into the breastwork of the battery and it was through these spy holes that the Chief Magistrate now observed the world. At the end of The Avenue the first faint light revealed the outline of the jail. The ragged silhouette of trees could just be seen, behind which waited the enemy. Unsettling noises carried to the East Battery, determining the enemy's presence, although little could yet be seen. Then came the soft, rhythmic pounding of feet as platoons of men took up their positions. These reverberations unnerved the Chief Magistrate just as they unnerved Captain Clayton, who, although a military man, had fought no more battles than Holwell.

Musket in hand, the Chief Magistrate peered out again through the spy hole. The shapes of trees and houses were now emerging progressively from the darkness. A pink glow suffused the sky, growing stronger by the moment. A sudden bustle of animal noises rose about the battery: the first jabs of birdsong, the cries of monkeys and the bark of jackals as they slunk back into the jungle. Light streaked the sky. Then, from the enemy camp, came the unearthly beauty of the muezzin's cry, a signal for the start of battle. The cry lodged deep within the Chief Magistrate, pulling at his gut. At such moments he could not deny an attachment to this lush and predatory land. It was like a woman he desired who constantly rejected him. He looked up again at the sky, and saw the stars were already fading.

He was so absorbed in the moment that when the jail was lit up in a flash of red light, he thought Siraj Uddaulah had attacked. The muezzin's call broke off abruptly. The Chief Magistrate saw that Lebeaume had sent a hail of red-hot grapeshot over the trees to shower the enemy before the sun could give them an advantage. The Chief Magistrate crouched down, realising the battle had begun. Almost at once there was a response from Siraj Uddaulah's men. A cannon ball shot out of the jungle and tore through the walls of the jail.

Soon the shadows disappeared and the sun beat down in full force on The Avenue. From then on the temperature rose rapidly, as did the pace of battle. The Chief Magistrate, behind the East Battery, felt trapped. He had not to fire a single shot and was in no immediate danger, as the battle still centred upon the jail, yet the constant proximity to death had a powerful effect on him, leaving him in a strange state of limbo. The Avenue might still lie deserted, but Lebeaume, only five hundred yards away, was taking a ferocious beating. Great bursts of light and sound came from a distance. From the safety of his position the Chief Magistrate watched the hypnotic dance of battle. The fiery movement swayed backwards and forwards as the enemy reached the jail and were driven off time after time.

The hours wore on but the sound of battle still spluttered fiercely. From the battery, the Chief Magistrate stared out at the machinery of death reaping its harvest at the end of the road, and for the first time realised the danger of the charade he had helped construct. About him men fought bravely, prepared to throw their lives away for something he had actively engineered. If it were not for the treasure and the benefits he conspired to gain, or for his secret involvement with the Young Begum's faction in Murshidabad, this battle would not be happening. The guilt of it overcame him. Several times the Chief Magistrate suggested Lebeaume be called back to safety, but a messenger, when sent to the jail, returned to report the Lieutenant's wish to fight on. Eventually the Chief Magistrate's guilt changed to annoyance at such foolhardy bravery. He could not accept responsibility for men who refused to be saved. He sat down behind the sandbags, the heat savaging his head.

The continuous crackle and boom from the jail now took on a monotonous pattern. The men of the East Battery lay slumped in the heat. At times the Chief Magistrate was ashamed to detect the pricking of boredom within himself. At other times he imagined himself within the jail, where, whatever the danger, there would at least be some shade. As the heat beat down on him, strange thoughts entered his mind. He fought them off as he would a mosquito, but they persisted. Rosemary loomed prominently in his vision, as did the child he had barely seen. He found nothing kindly in their presence; he had lost his place with them. He floated forever beyond their reach, dead while still alive. Rosemary might wait dutifully, but her dreams of him had scattered on hard ground. He too thought only occasionally of his wife, and always with resentment. He saw her amongst green fields, cool skies, plump sofas and the banked-up fires of winter. About her snow fell silently, filling the house with a clear white light. She lived where the wheat sank wet in the fields at a bad harvest, where summers were of a delicate weight.

He saw suddenly now that the inadequate shape of each individual life did not matter; its paltry content was of little importance. How a man embedded himself in his life was all that mattered. A person might flourish in the poorest of soil if his soul was properly nourished. But a man who could not see the richness of life would not grow in any soil, whatever the yearnings of his spirit. The Chief Magistrate was unprepared for such ponderous thoughts in so benighted a place. He considered himself as settled in India as it was possible to be in an alien land. In every way, to the best of his ability, he had recreated a familiar world. Yet whenever he sat upon his veranda, the sight of the Maratha Ditch and the sounds and odours that floated across it reminded him not only of the unreality of his life but of the fragility of its base. A sense of belonging evaded him. It was only in moments such as this, when his very existence was threatened, that he saw, as if looking into an abyss, the terrible truth of things. Exile and the gaudy splendour of his life in India made him a displaced person at home. And in spite of long residence, he would never be more than a transient creature in India. An inexplicable sadness filled him.

The morning wore on and the sun rose higher. Behind the protection of the East Battery men shaded themselves with whatever they could. Some, in desperation, sat with sandbags balanced on helmets or hats, the weight pressing their heads down into their shoulders, causing headaches. Hunger and thirst afflicted them badly; nothing had been forthcoming from Fort William but a bag of biscuits crawling with weevils. Time, in the mind of the Chief Magistrate, had now become elastic. It stretched then shrank according to his thoughts. Heat and tension seemed to compress his brain so that thoughts slipped about in a crazy fashion. Old memories were squeezed out of hiding places and the rational conclusions of the day were tossed carelessly aside. The sun was now high in the sky. At the jail the ferocity of the Indian onslaught appeared uncontainable.

Through the musket slits of the battery, the Chief Magistrate's view of the world was narrowed. He looked down The Avenue as if he looked down the barrel of a gun; at its end was the obstruction of Siraj Uddaulah. If he could be got rid of then not only the battle but the constant menace from Murshidabad would be gone forever. The

Chief Magistrate stood up, his destiny clear to him now. He must find a way to thwart the nawab and his plans. Nobody else could do it.

'Sit down. You'll get yourself killed,' Captain Clayton shouted.

The Chief Magistrate raised an eyebrow. 'I will not be killed. I have work to do. One way or another, we must hold the jail. The nawab must be shown he cannot do as he pleases. He must be stopped.'

'I fear that will be impossible. Soon Lebeaume must retreat,' Captain Clayton replied.

'If we allow Siraj Uddaulah to take the jail he can then infiltrate the town. Let me make an assessment first. Perhaps we should send a relief party,' the Chief Magistrate suggested as he mounted a horse. Ignoring Clayton's protests, he steered the animal on to The Avenue. He had the sudden conviction that if he transferred his energy to the besieged jail, the battle would turn and the nawab would retreat before the sheer force of his will.

His head throbbed from the hours of sun as he rode towards the fiery activity ahead. The din and flaming showers of grapeshot, arrows and musket fire falling about the jail appeared like some form of biblical wrath. Holwell swallowed his fear and willed himself to continue. At last he approached the back of the jail and dismounted. As he tied up his horse a sudden silence fell; the battle appeared to have stopped. The Chief Magistrate was taken by surprise and looked about in confusion. His first thought was that at word of his arrival the nawab had quickly retreated.

He strode into the jail, his pulse pounding, and was immediately appalled by what he saw. The dead lay everywhere. There had been no time in the height of battle to clear away a single body, and the stench was thick about them. The Chief Magistrate was relieved to see that Lebeaume and the Fort William men were all unharmed, there were casualties only amongst the sepoys.

The unnatural silence continued. Not a musket fired, not a cannon boomed. The walls of the jail were badly strafed, their soft brick riddled with holes. Holwell looked about, taking an inventory of the disaster, then peered at the nawab's front line. He was shocked to see a long file of Indians sneaking stealthily around the jail towards the large houses of Rope Walk. He turned at once to Lebeaume with the suggestion that he retire and a relief party take over.

'We cannot lose the jail. I will order reinforcements,' the Chief Magistrate urged. Before him the nawab's troops continued to openly enter White Town.

For the first time the possibility of the nawab actually taking the fort began to grow in the Chief Magistrate's mind. The besieged and crumbling jail, the heap of dead bodies and the ghastly stench forced him to face the uncertainty of the situation. As his thoughts careered wildly, the unnerving silence was abruptly broken. A cannon ball landed beside the jail, shaking the ground he stood upon, throwing up clods of earth. Holwell fell to his knees in terror, pressing himself against a wall.

As soon as he could, the Chief Magistrate made his escape. His knees were shaking to such a degree that he found it difficult to mount his horse. Once up on the creature, he turned to gallop along The Avenue, distancing himself as quickly as possible from the fury about the jail. Soon he reached the East Battery and entered another world. Men still lounged about concerned with questions of shade and how to while their time away. There were constant grumbles about the heat and the unavailability of food.

Eventually reinforcements arrived at the battery and began the march to the jail. As the Chief Magistrate set off to take news of the battle to Fort William, a house on Rope Walk was seized by the enemy. The nawab's flag was suddenly seen to fly from the roof of Lady Russell's mansion. As Rope Walk flanked the walls of the East Battery, Captain Clayton was forced to take his first action of the day. The Chief Magistrate turned in his saddle in time to see Clayton, with the zeal that comes after hours of boredom, train his eighteen-pounder on Lady Russell's home and blow off the first storey with a resounding roar.

Holwell urged his horse on towards the gates of Fort William and tried to remember The Avenue as it had been before the nawab's onslaught. He remembered the cool waters of the Tank beneath the shade of trees and the peace of the early mornings, when he had walked to the Courthouse, or the coolness of the evening, when he had taken a round of The Park with Bellamy. He wondered if Calcutta would ever be the same again.

Although the Chief Magistrate had been absent from Fort William for no more than a few hours, he returned to news that Mrs Mapletoft, the wife of the Chaplain's assistant, had given birth to a baby girl. Although conditions in the birthing room were wretched and Sarah Mapletoft was as badly plagued by the swarms of flies settling upon her as by the pains of labour, the child was a fine healthy girl. Mrs Bellamy and her daughter Anna had attended her as best they could. Anna had used her own underskirt as a blanket and Dorothy Bellamy had delivered the baby upon it. The child had been called Constantia. Although as yet no clear future could be seen for the baby, her cries of new life before the thunder of death had greatly cheered Fort William.

The Chief Magistrate joined the Governor on the balcony of the Council chamber, where Drake and members of the Council of War stood silently watching the nawab's advance through spyglasses. It was all as the Chief Engineer had foretold, everyone now remembered. The grandiose homes about the fort provided the cover the enemy sought; they moved forward almost invisibly to claim each new house. The Council of War, from their lookout post upon the balcony, only became aware a new house had fallen when Siraj Uddaulah's flag was hoisted. Soon the nawab's pennant was seen flying from Dumbleton's house in Rope Walk, and from its flat rooftop his soldiers fired down on the East Battery with disastrous effect.

The morning wore on, and with it the struggle for White Town's houses. The Governor and the Chief Magistrate were stretched as never before, rushing between the Council chamber and their lookout post upon the balcony, planning new strategy on the wing.

Men were ordered to move across The Park to drive the enemy out of Dumbleton's house. Then Minchin's palatial house fell to the nawab, as did Captain Clayton's. The nawab's troops cheered as they took a house; the Fort William troops cheered as they took it back.

The Chief Magistrate became increasingly anxious about the fate of his own great home, but there was little he could do. In the Council chamber, argument without resolution frittered the hours away. The Council of War looked down with growing consternation on the refugees packing the parade ground, loud with panic and pleas for food. They obstructed action and inhibited thought. Nothing was helped by the whistle of cannon balls alive in the air about the fort. When once more one fell over the walls of the fort and landed amongst the refugees, terror became uncontrollable. The Governor and the Chief Magistrate looked down in horror but could think of nothing to do apart from sending three European soldiers to cart away the dead.

'We must prepare to evacuate our ladies immediately. Somehow it must be done,' Holwell decided, the muscles of his jaw clenched in new determination.

CHAPTER TWENTY-ONE

Nothing now mattered to Emily Drake. When she looked from the balcony at the crowded parade ground, all she heard was the moaning of children. Above the distress, Harry's small cry seemed to float on the night from where she had been forced to leave him. She had slipped from the surface of reality.

At first she could not believe it. She had been sure that Harry took shallow breaths sleeping as deeply as usual. For a while she had sat beside the cradle, her hair and clothes still damp from her dip in the river, sure he would awake soon. She did not see the wet nurse go, but later, when no trace could be found of her, Emily became for a while hysterical, questions thrusting themselves upon her. Had Harry died silently, freeing the woman? Or had she put him down like a stray kitten in order to be free? It was impossible now to know and the doctor could not tell.

'Be thankful you knew the baby no longer than a few weeks. The pain is less, I assure you.' Lady Russell, well-meaning, consoled from experience. Emily had wanted to strike her. Suddenly, then, there were other women about her, tearing the child from her arms, laying him out, asking for clean clothes. They would not let her near him, even though she pleaded. She had wanted to prepare him herself; she did not want strangers to touch him. Instead she was dragged away.

Someone peeled off her damp dress and she saw glances exchanged. Her arms were thrust into a fresh gown; her hair was dried and brushed. Then she was forced to sit silently in a chair by the window while they busied themselves with the baby. He was small, there was little to do, she could not understand why they took so long. She sat dry-eyed and did not cry and knew they found this strange. She heard someone whisper that this was not normal; she was conscious again of conspiratorial glances passing between them. It was impossible to explain about Jane or the shadow of the wet nurse's dead child that still pressed heavily upon her. The women spoke of the will of God. How could she tell them that God had no part in this death, that it was all to do with Jane?

Roger came and stayed to arrange the funeral details. His eyes rested coolly on her and she knew later that she would hear from him about her visit to the river. For now his impatience centred upon the child, who had died at such an inconvenient moment.

'He must be buried at once, for when the nawab attacks how will we get to the cemetery?' This was all he said, although he patted her hand and stayed a while by her side. It was clear that Harry's death did not affect him unduly; things of larger importance now weighed on him.

'You are young, there will be others,' he said lightly, and for the first time she actively hated him. These words were repeated in one way or another by everyone she met.

In accordance with the Governor's order, arrangements proceeded at an indecent pace. A tiny coffin appeared from nowhere, as if it had waited for this moment, and within an hour they set out under parasols into the hot morning. Few people accompanied them on the short journey out of Fort William to that third and silent section of Calcutta. It was as she wanted. She could not have borne the curious looks prying deep into her soul. The iron gates of the cemetery swung back, creaking on stiff hinges. Before her, the town of ponderous mausoleums, weathered black, stood barring her way like an army of dark-robed giants at the entrance to the underworld.

They crowded before her, as if waiting to take the offering she brought. From this point she could no longer follow her child on his journey. That he must pass into a dark and unknown land alone struck her cruelly. Roger and the Chief Magistrate carried the tiny casket and she walked behind, to the very threshold of the world that would take him. In spite of the Chaplain's prayers, she sensed no one there to guide him; he must find his way alone. A hot wind scorched her cheeks, caking her lips with dust. The breeze soughed through trees; leaves rustled, disturbing bats in their sleep. Above the raw wound in the earth waiting to receive the casket, she saw the bats hanging like loosely furled umbrellas in the branches of a tamarind tree. That such creatures should now be Harry's companions grieved her painfully. The Chaplain hurried through his duty, glancing anxiously at times in the direction of the nawab's camp. Soon the tiny casket was lowered into the grave and they returned to Fort William. Soon Roger, the Chief Magistrate and the Chaplain disappeared again to the Council chamber. Emily was left with the empty cradle and for a while the company of Lady Russell.

Now, in the rocking chair before the balcony of bougainvillaea, Emily Drake looked towards the cemetery and wondered if the wisp of cloud trailing low in the sky carried the spirit of the child. Loneliness consumed her. Even Parvati was gone.

She no longer blamed Roger for deserting her. What could he know of a woman's life? A man, from birth to death, seemed to remain unchanged. His life ran along a single progressive line; nothing cleaved his soul from his body. He could leave his seed where he wished and know nothing of its growing. It was not like that for her. Something had grown within her that could never be uprooted. Her child might die, all her children might die, but nothing could take that knowledge from her. She had carried the child for nine long months under her heart, and under her heart he would stay.

Restlessness drove her from her chair out on to the balcony. In the distance, Black Town was nothing but a charred and flattened land now. Surviving cattle gathered at sooty water holes. The roasted carcasses of animals had been cleaned to the bone overnight by jackals and vultures and now reflected the sun like chips of *chunam*. Emily stared at the seared landscape, as if she could find some meaning of her own in its brutal annihilation. The morning grew before her and the sun blazed on her face, scorching her scalp, burning her wrists as if to cauterise her wound. In the distance the sounds of musket and cannon fire growing louder were but the ragged notes of a dream. Beyond Fort William's walls, the world had become unreal. The real world was carried inside her. The hot wind blew in an angry rush: the bougainvillaea stirred, the jasmine tightened its petals. The wind rattled through the green louvred shutters of Governor's House and hissed its papery words in her ear.

She looked again over the walls of Fort William to the place where she had left her child. Amongst the dry and dusty trees she glimpsed the dark, weathered heads of the mausoleums. In the branches of the tamarind the hot wind must rock the bats as they hung upon their perches. Lizards scuttled about, snakes sought the coolness of water. Would Jane and the wet nurse's child, unknown, unnamed, hound Harry on his journey, hungry for his tiny soul? Would Parvati be there beside him, as she had been in life? Already Emily sensed these shadowy beings weaving about her. How could she leave Harry to their ghostly ministrations? Her hand tightened on the balcony; her body stiffened against the balustrade. In the sky, vultures wheeled and she followed their silent, hypnotic spiral, homing in on death. If she spread her arms she was sure she too could fly. She had only to dare, only to trust. The wind would take hold of her, buoying her up, willing her after her child, as Demeter had followed Persephone to bring her out of Hades. She held her arms wide, gave a cry and was answered by a hundred voices.

The sound returned her abruptly to the paltry brick of the balcony. Beneath the parapet, Governor's House fell away to the parade ground and the sea of refugees. The people of Black Town looked up at her as she stood with her head flung back and her arms held open. They shifted uneasily as she leaned forward and shifted again as she leaned back, as if the movement of her body had its root deep within them. Looking down at the upturned faces, Emily felt she stood on a stage. Her audience waited for an extravagant gesture. She gripped the rail harder then, as if she would pull herself up upon it, but something stopped her. She began to scour the faces below. And at last she found the thing she searched for and knew immediately why she had not jumped. In the midst of the crowd she saw the girl's face, eyes fastened intently on her.

Sati stood alone, a circle of space around her, and did not move as she stared at the Governor's wife. Emily Drake drew back from the balustrade. The hot rasp of the wind seemed to die in her ears. Her thoughts became still. The girl waited for her. And she knew she must journey towards her, just as the child in his unseen world must continue on his way without her. She grew quiet then and sat down again in the chair beside the empty crib. All she saw now were the girl's eyes upon her still, drawing her down to the square. For a while she resisted, unsure of the future, unsure of herself. Then, at last, she stood up and made her way down the stairs.

Now, when she entered the parade ground, people drew back as if knowing already who it was she sought. Eventually, in a far corner of the square, she arrived at the Devi Ashram.

Even before she reached the place where the God Woman resided, messengers came out to greet her. A toothless crone with a basket of dried grasses and vegetable scraps. An albino, pale as the pink moon at sunset, with rabbity eyes and a skull of corn-coloured stubble. A horde of dancing children pushed about her, chanting. The messengers steered her on until she came before the girl, who stared silently at her. Guardians stood beside her, an immense-bodied woman and a small, wiry man in a turban. The foxy mother was nowhere to be seen; the girl now stood alone. And perhaps had always stood alone, Emily realised, only she had not been able to see it.

She had come on an impulse and did not know now what to do. She tried to explain about the death of the child. The man in the turban appeared to understand some English. He turned back to the crowd to interpret her words. Immediately there was sympathy; the women of the ashram drew close about her. They pressed her hands in sympathy to let her know they understood her pain, that they too had watched their children die. Emily felt their sympathy and took more comfort from these strangers than from anyone in Fort William. She sat down amongst them, conscious of their curiosity. A woman touched her hair, another felt the cloth of her dress.

'I have come for Jane. I want you to contact Jane.' She turned to Sati, but the girl only smiled in a vacant way.

'The Goddess has not returned to her. We are waiting for the Goddess,' the man explained, seeing Emily's confusion. Sati's eyes were now closed in deep meditation. As contact with the girl did not seem possible, Emily made her way back to the high-ceilinged rooms of Governor's House, where once more she would be alone.

CHAPTER TWENTY-TWO

The evening came down upon Fort William like the shutting of a door. With the dusk, the sound of cannon and musket fire abruptly disappeared. One moment it resounded about Fort William, and the next only the muttering of adjutant storks was heard, preparing for the night. The torching of Black Town had produced a dearth of perches for these large birds, who preferred the stability of masonry to the flimsy branches of trees. The sudden influx of birds into Fort William, along with the refugees, had done nothing to alleviate the multiple pressures within the fort. The crows were as numerous as always, undeterred by catastrophe, but the preponderance of fiery explosions had not only terrified the birds but also alarmed the monkeys in the jungle. Hordes of these creatures had made for the sanctuary of the fort. They battled with the storks to sit upon walls, and screamed in agitation. They showed no fear of the refugees and copulated shamelessly when not ridding each other of lice. Rats had come up from beneath the fort to further plague the fort.

Worst of all for everyone was the fight with all these creatures for food. Storks strutted about, crows dived audaciously, while monkeys looped down snatching at morsels or rummaged about amidst sleeping bodies. The small quantities of stale *chapati*, dry biscuits or rice that had been scooped up in the stampede to the fort were, if not already finished, being eked out in the most pitiful way. That these few crumbs must now be consumed before a hungry zoo was for some the last straw. Fighting broke out amongst the refugees. Fear, starvation and the heat began to drive people mad. Children died, a man slit his throat, a nephew killed his uncle. Dysentery added to this toll.

In the garrison, things were no better. The want of provisions and the fatigue of battle caused a mutinous situation. The arrack and toddy in the liquor store had been looted by the Dutch mercenaries and the half-caste Portuguese. The Chaplain's store of claret and Madeira had also been found and ransacked. Drunkenness was rife and the Dutch mercenaries were rumoured to be hunting for women amongst the refugees. Lurid stories were passed around of young Indian girls being raped.

In the Devi Ashram, the severity of the situation was brought constantly before them. Without food, and forced to peer excessively at death and violence, people thought all the more of God. A never-ending queue of desperate souls braved the sun to touch the feet of the God Woman. For many, her presence in Fort William was the only thing that made the siege tolerable. It was not everyone who, even once in a lifetime, could come so near a deity. Everyone understood that circumstances must be of the most extreme to entice a god to earth. This was the view of the old men who had sat on their string beds under the trees in the peaceful days before Siraj Uddaulah. This group had taken up residence in the Devi Ashram and now served the God Woman devotedly. Before the enemy surrounded the fort, one old man had ambled out and returned with hanks of green banana. Another collected coconuts, a third produced some medicinal herbs, others stood as bodyguards around the Devi Ashram. Ancient though they were, the number and irritability of these men made them a force to be reckoned with. Pilferers and undesirables kept their distance.

For Govindram, incarceration in the fort gave him access to

Omichand. He had not been able to enter the fort after Omichand's arrest but could now visit him every day. The conditions in which his master and the nobleman Kishindas were held in the Black Hole had come as a shock to him. Unaware that Omichand was still ignorant of the death of his women and children, the first thing Govindram had done when he saw his master was to offer his commiseration. Omichand sat down, dumbstruck, and began to wail and tear at his clothes. Govindram had stood outside the Black Hole, peering into the place through the bars, helpless to do more than beg Omichand to remember God. He knew that once the enormity of the shock wore off, and Omichand was re-established again in his life, other women would be found and new children quickly made.

'It is all the work of Hatman Holwell. The nobleman's treasure also he has taken,' Omichand roared.

The fat merchant's misery was greatly compounded by his need for food. Govindram had tried to gather some scraps for his master, but Jaya and Mohini put a stop to this.

'For what are you feeding that elephant? Is not the Goddess of more value than he? And what of the children who are here with us, do not they deserve first to be fed?' Jaya enquired.

'He will see us all dead from starvation, but that elephant must be kept alive,' Mohini admonished in agreement with Jaya.

Govindram returned empty-handed to Omichand. If he could not offer food, he could lend an eye on the world to the merchant. His day then quickly picked up purpose as he divided his time between the fat merchant and the Devi Ashram.

Sati sat, as instructed by her grandmother and Govindram, under a ragged canopy that had been hastily constructed from an old *lungi*. The sun, filtering through the dirty muslin, gave off the scent of warm cloth, but at night its pale shroud obscured her view of the stars. About her the ashram slept. Pagal, the albino, had stationed himself at her feet, and neither his wife nor his children were able to tear him away. Day and night, the itinerant vegetable woman shadowed Jaya and slept beside her. A goat had nibbled at her basket, now empty at last of its tired vegetables. The goatherd's small son, cut adrift from his family in the fire, had taken refuge with the goat and her kid in the Devi Ashram. The vegetable woman's anger at the goat's audacity had been overlooked before the value of the creature's milk at this difficult time. The fruit stall man and the seller of spices slept beside their women, but their children had joined the children of the wives of the half-caste Portuguese soldiers. All these infants lay together in a large group while their mothers formed another. Only Sati lay awake, savouring the solitude. To be the nucleus of so much veneration had become a weight. Her every need was anticipated, her every action watched. Where once dismissal had isolated her, attention now cut her adrift.

She lay with her arms behind her head and stared up at the sky. The moon had disappeared to work its transformation. The stars might blaze as usual, but their impetus was gone; the world had been left in darkness. To what solitary chamber had the moon withdrawn in order to seek rebirth? Worst of all Durga too had disappeared. Everywhere she searched, Sati was met with silence. The shadows lay empty. Leaves curled dustily against the sun, lizards scuttled to hide in the cracks of walls, but Durga was not to be found. In the ashram the devotees waited. Sati proceeded through her circumscribed day, a vessel for the emotions of others, but without Durga, she was without her guide. At times panic overwhelmed her. Above her the sky appeared without colour, and nothing in her thrived.

The darkness was intense. Only the candlelit windows of Governor's House spread a meagre light upon the parade ground. Sati scoured those windows with even greater diligence but could not see the pale face of the Governor's wife. She remembered her just that day, perched high upon the balcony as if she would jump to freedom. The Governor's wife appeared to live in a captured state. Sati could not explain what drew her to the Englishwoman. Except that it seemed Emily Drake, like herself, had begun a journey towards an unknown destination.

The moans and stirrings of countless women and children came to her in the night, filling her with new restlessness. The sounds moved through her and the scent of the river blew upon the hot wind. And as if it blew to her from a great distance, she seemed to hear the echo of Durga's voice carried upon the breeze. Sati stared into the darkness and heard Durga call again. Her heart leaped and at once she stood up, stepping around her sleeping devotees, following the sound to the river. No guards were about as she slipped down the steps to the wharf.

Immediately, the coolness of the water and its thick animal smell wrapped about her. The night vibrated with the hollow drumming of bullfrogs from the muddy bank. In the distance, from the camp of Siraj Uddaulah, came the trumpeting of elephants, the roll of a drum, a voice, a song. She could smell the movement of change and it frightened her. Within herself, too, there had been a change. All her life she had reached out, seeking a place in which to dissolve, to become a part of something whole. Now Durga had taught her to know that she belonged to no one but herself. As did Durga, who could turn from tenderness to destruction in the blink of an eye. Sati might never enter the bridal chamber but she had entered the darkness of herself, for Durga demanded a frightening reverence. She required a journey towards experience, the deep knowing of herself. Where that destination was, Sati did not know. It waited for her, just as Durga waited for her, beyond the edge of time. She looked up again at the starry sky, filled by a brightness that shed no light. She listened but the voice that had called was silent. There was nothing before her but the running of the tide. Yet the wash of the current came to her now as a life-giving silence. She closed her eyes before the river and heard it whisper her name.

She knew then that Durga resided within her still, in that crack between spirit and matter. She knew too that Durga swam before her in the wild and solitary force of the river, and that by the river all things were sustained. Its tide rose and fell in seasons, it caused the birthing and the dying-away of everything at its right time, over and over again. Whatever the river touched was fed by its force. She took a breath of the thick muddy air and swallowed it deep inside her. She knew now that Durga was everywhere.

She became aware then of other sounds and looked up. A short distance further up the wharf there was movement and the light of flares. A crowd of women and children were descending on to the quay from the fort. There seemed something furtive about the women as they huddled together at the river's edge. The crying of infants was immediately hushed, the loud voices of boatmen were lowered. Even the number of flares seemed frugal for so large a party. Sati saw then that the women and children were being piled into small boats. One by one these set off towards two Indiamen waiting out in mid-stream, ablaze with lanterns upon the dark water. For a while she watched the boats row back and forth and the waiting group on the wharf grow steadily smaller. The sound of running feet eventually disturbed her.

'*Devi*, everyone is worried. You were not to be seen. Some said the drunken Hatmen had taken you.' Pagal hurried her. Jaya, Govindram and Mohini followed a short distance behind with a group of devotees. They streamed down the wharf with cries of relief to surround her. Jaya immediately burst out crying and cuffed Sati about the head.

'Everyone is looking for you.' She wiped her eyes on the end of her sari.

'Many bad things are happening; all the Hatmen are drunk,' Mohini explained, pushing in front of her.

The relief of the Devi Ashram resounded loudly upon the wharf until Pagal, who had wandered off on his own, returned shouting and waving his arms.

'Hatmen's ladies are all leaving. All are going to the big boats to escape Siraj Uddaulah. Only we have been left for the nawab to slaughter.' The albino collapsed at Sati's feet.

'Aiee,' Jaya cried out, and beat a fist upon her great breast in fury. Her cry was a signal for confusion. The women of the Devi Ashram all began to speak at once in a hysterical manner. The old men raced off along the wharf as fast as their arthritic legs allowed. The Devi Ashram streamed after them towards the departing boats. Sati was borne along in their midst.

At the water's edge before the River Gate the Devi Ashram halted in shock. The last boats had already pushed off from the quay to carry the women of White Town away. Not a craft was left for the refugees. Some of the wives of the sepoys waded into the water as if to follow the boats, screaming out curses and bewailing the fate of their children. The Fort William soldiers still standing about on the quay began immediately rounding them up with bayonets.

Word soon spread back into the fort of the happenings on the waterfront. Refugees from the parade ground immediately poured out of the fort to swell the crowd of devotees on the wharf. Others peered over the ramparts at the departing boats.

'The Governor is still here, and also all the other Hatmen. They have sent only their women away,' someone yelled.

'If their women are going, then truly danger is near. It is no longer in their power to defend us.' The fruit stall man pushed his way forward to stand next to Govindram.

'Already the nawab has control of so many big White Town houses.' The seller of spices spoke up from behind the fruit stall man.

'All the Hatmen soldiers have now come into the fort for safety. Very few are left fighting in the town. The nawab will come into Fort William to chase them out. Bang, bang, swish, swish. Soon we will all be killed.' The itinerant vegetable woman jumped about in anxiety.

Sati had been pushed to the front of the crowd to stand at the water's edge. The tide was high and the river washed over her bare feet. Darkness spread before her. Upon the water a lantern illuminated each departing boat. They bobbed slowly away on the tide into the night, the calls of the boatmen drifting back over the water. In the distance the two Indiamen waited, their lamps stars upon the river. One by one the small boats were lost in darkness, but for a pinprick of light.

The last boat of evacuees was already some distance from the quay.

It bobbed about, its lantern swaying precariously. Beneath the rocking lamp the pale faces of terrified women and children were tossed in and out of the shadows. Sati saw then that a woman stood agitatedly at the end of the boat. A Hatman appeared and gripped her firmly, forcing her down. Sati stepped forward and did not realise how deep the water was about her until Govindram reached out to draw her back. The lantern on the boat had illuminated a familiar figure. There was no mistaking the Governor's wife, poised as if to jump from the boat. Her hair hung loose about her shoulders, desperation clawed at her face. About her the women held on to her skirts as if they pegged down a billowing tent. Emily Drake's voice echoed back to Sati over the water.

'Set me free.'

The lantern continued to rock, throwing Emily Drake backwards and forwards between shadow and light. Then, for a moment, she stood quite still as her eyes alighted on Sati, knee deep in the muddy waters of the Hoogly, held back by Govindram.

'Set me free.'

The cry came again and fell into the fast-flowing Hoogly. The Governor's wife stood silhouetted against the dark night like a cameo. Then, suddenly she sat down in the boat. The lantern was steadied and the shadows grew deeper, swallowing up the craft.

CHAPTER TWENTY-THREE

The Chief Magistrate felt his life was unravelling. Nothing was going right. Except for a few isolated White Town houses in which beleaguered troops still battled away, the militia and garrison were now locked into Fort William. Siraj Uddaulah's army was poised to shoot down into the fort just as the Chief Engineer foretold. Within the fort the Dutch mercenaries and the Portuguese were running amok in a drunken state, having looted the liquor store and the Chaplain's cellar. Sickness had struck Bellamy down in a heartless way at the very moment of this loss. The makeshift hospital in the ballroom of Governor's House was now filled with wounded and dying men, and neither bandages nor medicines were available. The cemetery was unreachable and the question of what to do with the dead grew daily more important. Temporary graves were being dug in the furthest reaches of Fort William. Although the women and children of White Town had been successfully evacuated, the refugees were now on the point of rioting. Worse than this, Manningham and Frankland, who had accompanied the women to the Governor's Indiaman, refused to return to Fort William on the excuse that some guard was needed for the ladies. Several members of the militia, including the Chaplain's assistant, Reverend Mapletoft, had also reached the boat and turned their backs on the fort. The only bright point was that along with the women the treasure had also been loaded on to the *Dodaldy* and the *Diligence*. Throughout the day small craft had plied back and forth between the Governor's and the Chief Magistrate's ships and Fort William, carrying the treasure to safety unobtrusively.

It was now increasingly clear that the men of Fort William must also soon depart. How a second evacuation was to be manoeuvred, now that the refugees were alert to procedures, was beyond the Chief Magistrate's frazzled comprehension. Letters continued to be smuggled to Rai Durlabh, but the tone of the commander's replies made it increasingly clear that something obstructed him in his mission. Yet all these things diminished before the towering problem of gunpowder. Once more, the store of powder brought into the fort from the main magazine in town was damp and not fit for use. Without powder Fort William could not be held.

The Chief Magistrate was encamped in Governor's House in a small ante-room leading to Drake's office. The Chaplain was installed in the guestroom. Although surroundings were more amenable than Writers' Row, the advantage of the latter quarters was their proximity to water. Without servants to lug buckets up and down stairs, the luxury of Governor's House soon deteriorated to the level of squalor elsewhere in Fort William. The stench of excrement was little less than in Writers' Row. Water was rationed and heat lay trapped by dry tatties. Rats and cockroaches roamed about aggressively, gnawing at overstuffed sofas, stores of biscuit, official documents and bags of sugar and tea. Lizards and bluebottles infested the house. A plague of flying ants had joined their earthbound brothers to irritate everyone further.

The Chief Magistrate made his way to Bellamy's room and found him lying upon his bed, the linen heaped untidily about him. The Chaplain was weak but slightly recovered from the fever that had afflicted him. Empty bottles of claret and Madeira stood about the room. His grief at the looting of his claret continued to affect him. A half-filled glass of wine stood beside Bellamy's bed and he reached for it as the Chief Magistrate entered.

'It took an armada of Indiamen to fill that cellar. It grieves me more than I can say to think of those ruffians consuming my bottles.'

The Chaplain still looked poorly, but the Chief Magistrate had his own troubles and could not find time in the present situation to discuss the trivial loss of some wine. Since the Chaplain was the oldest man in White Town, the Council of War had requested the Chief Magistrate to seek his advice.

'These are extraordinary times.' Holwell answered before broaching the issues he had come to discuss. He decided not to tell the Chaplain of Mapletoft's desertion to the Governor's ship, as it would unnecessarily upset the old man.

'I fear the mutiny worsens. Refugee women have been molested. The soldiery have established their tabernacles in the very rooms where your liquor is deposited. They are rowdy and refuse to hear the call to duty. The refugees grow hourly more restless. Everything hangs upon Rai Durlabh, but I fear now he will not act as promised.'

'The refugees grow restless because they are not fed,' Bellamy pointed out.

'We have rice and wheat enough for six months but few pots to cook it in, that is the problem,' the Chief Magistrate explained.

'Then you had better depart to the ships with speed,' Bellamy murmured, his mind still upon his wine.

'We are forced now to think either of departure or surrender. Either way it is likely we may lose Calcutta. We are now without much powder,' the Chief Magistrate admitted.

'Without powder we cannot fight.' Bellamy looked up in alarm.

The Chief Magistrate nodded, the strength draining rapidly from him. He sat down to mop his brow and caught sight of himself in a mirror. Like everyone else, he had been reduced to discarding unnecessary clothing and wore only his breeches and shirt. He was unused to such informal attire and felt as vulnerable as if he walked about naked. He stared at his pinched face in the glass, at the eyes drawn small with anxiety, at the grim line of his mouth and at something more that swam up from within him to fill his face. That a piece of glass could reflect his soul suddenly disturbed him.

At the Chief Magistrate's news the Chaplain had grown thoughtful. 'Why not offer a bribe to Rai Durlabh? Perhaps that is what he is waiting for. Get Omichand to write the next letter to the commander. His influence still remains very great.' The Chaplain threw out his advice in a careless manner while refilling his glass with wine.

'What good can the fat merchant do?' the Chief Magistrate had almost forgotten Omichand, still held with Kishindas in the Black Hole.

'Who knows? His voice has a stronger effect on his people than does ours,' the Chaplain remarked, and returned to his claret, unable to contemplate any further disagreeable twists of fate.

'If we evacuate the fort, all will be lost. If we can surrender honourably it is possible we may be able to bargain some concessions, most importantly to remain in control of Fort William,' the Chief Magistrate confided. Bellamy nodded weakly, closed his eyes and lay back upon his pillows with an exhausted sigh. Soon he gave a light snore.

The Chief Magistrate left the Chaplain to sleep and made his way back to the Council chamber. He found it in the usual disarray. Apart from deteriorating conditions, its members now showed the strain of constant discussion. Most were inebriated with Bellamy's wine and waited only for departure. They gazed longingly from the windows towards the Hoogly, where the Governor's ship, the *Dodaldy*, waited with its cargo of women and children. Beside it the *Diligence*, the Chief Magistrate's own vessel, already loaded with his valuables, waited for the Fort William men.

The Chief Magistrate sat down and gave the Council a brief synopsis of his discussion with the Chaplain. He refrained from mentioning the powder situation. Instead he ordered a letter to be prepared for Omichand to sign, promising a large bribe to Rai

Durlabh to rid them of the nawab. Then, at the insistence of the Council of War, the Chief Magistrate proceeded on to the Black Hole to visit Omichand with this letter.

As he set foot upon the parade ground, the suffering crowd of refugees shifted before him like an angry ocean brewing up a storm. The late afternoon sun now threw the shadow of Governor's House over the ground. The refugees huddled within this shade, the first respite they had known that day. Once more no food had been forthcoming. Misery swirled about the Chief Magistrate as he left the steps of Governor's House. Women begged for food, children clawed at his clothes, emaciated goats stood in his path and excrement soon smeared the soles of his shoes. Eventually he reached the Black Hole and Omichand.

The Chief Magistrate had not seen Omichand since his arrest and he could not contain his surprise. He peered in through the small barred windows of the cell and saw what appeared to be a heap of rags at one end. A guard threw open the doors of the prison upon the Chief Magistrate's orders, and the fat merchant sat up. Behind him Kishindas stirred, his hair wild and matted. At the sight of the Chief Magistrate, Omichand let out a spluttering sound, his breast heaving up and down.

'You have grown thin,' the Chief Magistrate said in amazement as Omichand came towards him. The fat merchant's robes trailed extravagantly over the floor; deprived of corpulence, his cheeks lay flat against his bones, and his eyes appeared suddenly larger.

'Only dry biscuits. Sometimes not even that. And for water we have also to beg,' Omichand exploded.

'We too have only dry biscuits. We have rice and wheat for six months but few pots can be found to cook it in. The Chaplain's wine is all we have in abundance. I shall have some sent to you, and whatever odds and ends of food can be found.'

As the fat merchant seemed slightly cheered by the promise of sustenance, the Chief Magistrate broached the subject of the letter to

Rai Durlabh that Omichand must sign. 'It might end this ordeal peacefully for everyone,' Holwell reasoned.

'If such a letter fell into the wrong hands I should lose my life,' Omichand shouted, and turned back into his cell, ignoring the Chief Magistrate's protests. Kishindas hurried behind him.

'If you do not sign, we must surrender. We will then have to live in our own town upon the nawab's terms. It will be insufferable,' Holwell admitted, stepping into the cell after Omichand. At once the sun was shut away and the fetid smell of old brick enclosed him. The Chief Magistrate halted at the entrance and proceeded no further into the gloomy interior.

'Perhaps that is what Raja Rai Durlabh is wishing. Perhaps he has decided *not* to do away with the nawab,' Omichand replied, sitting down heavily upon a plinth built along one wall of the room.

'What have you heard of the matter?' The Chief Magistrate took a step forward in alarm.

'I have heard nothing. I only surmise,' Omichand replied.

No amount of persuasion could convince Omichand to sign the Chief Magistrate's letter. Holwell raised his voice, then called the guard at the door to hold a musket to Omichand's brow. Nothing softened the fat merchant. In the end Holwell was forced to leave with the letter unsigned. As he stepped out of the Black Hole he caught a sly gleam in the merchant's eye before the door swung shut upon him.

Once more the wails of women and children filled the Chief Magistrate's ears as he faced the parade ground. He plunged resolutely into the mass of people to make his way back to Governor's House. At once his balance was threatened when a child clutched at his shirt, dragging it from his breeches. Then an old crone started up before him, screaming abuse. He stepped back in shock and trod on a goat that protested by biting his leg. All he saw was the dark, toothless cave of the woman's mouth spewing upon him its bitter fury. She reached up a long-nailed claw and fastened herself to his wrist. It seemed as if an immeasurable force had risen to consume him. Behind the old hag he had a vision of thousands of faces, all turned at this moment towards him. In a spasm of horror he tore himself free and stumbled on towards Governor's House.

At last he reached the doorway. His heart pounded uncomfortably. The sight of that gnarled and filthy claw fastened upon him would not leave his mind. He was reminded suddenly of Rosemary. Soon after her arrival in India, in a spirit of misguided adventure, she had gone with her ayah into the Black Town bazaar. There she had become parted briefly from the woman and stumbled on a ritual that intrigued her. A group of gaudily dressed young girls were gathered about two women, who painted their hands with delicate designs in a thick black mud. Before she was able to refuse, Rosemary had been drawn into the group. The women took hold of her hands to demonstrate their art. Soon she appeared to wear a pair of ornate lace gloves and looked in fascination at the finely drawn designs. The ayah eventually found her and drew her away, saying the women were prostitutes. Rosemary had been horrified and immediately wiped the henna from her fingers. The mud had rolled easily off but a pale orange filigree remained beneath. Rosemary had returned to the house in a hysterical state, her fingers made raw by rubbing. For days she scrubbed at her hands, but nothing removed the dye. It lingered deeper than memory and stained her to the core. The Chief Magistrate had shown no sympathy at the time for the manner in which she felt marked. He was only concerned about the impression the crude stains would make upon their friends.

Now, sympathy for his estranged wife flowed generously through him. However hard he tried, he knew he would never forget the demeaning sight of the parade ground. It was as if not just Fort William but his very person had been invaded. He knew now how Rosemary must have felt.

The Chief Magistrate soon recovered himself and made his way back to the Council chamber. The Council of War turned their lethargic gaze from the Hoogly to stare at him bleary-eyed. The Chief Magistrate's announcement of Omichand's stubborn behaviour shattered the inertia. The commotion was so great and lasted so long that Drake was forced to bang on the table for quiet.

'We must think clearly,' the Governor announced. Even as he said the words he doubted his mind would move other than slowly, rusted over with exhaustion and fear. He looked towards the Chief Magistrate for enlightenment, but Holwell was mopping his brow. In need of immediate inspiration, Drake gazed up at the portrait of Job Charnock. Clusters of flying ants had settled upon Charnock's eyes and gave him the appearance of blindness. Drake turned away in fright.

'There is no way now but to evacuate,' Mackett shouted. There was a roar of approval from around the Council chamber.

The Chief Magistrate raised his voice. 'Our retreat must be orderly and, most important, after dark. Already night is upon us. Nothing can now be properly organised for today. We must wait until tomorrow. During the day the wounded can be evacuated, and also the last of the treasure. Even if this is seen by the refugees it should not raise alarm. Messenger boats are regularly coming and going from the ships and it will be seen that all we Europeans are still here.'

The Chief Magistrate had hardly finished speaking when a whistling noise was heard overhead. The Council of War looked up. The candelabra above the mahogany table trembled, its glass flutes tinkling as if the monsoon had suddenly arrived. The whistling grew louder and ended abruptly with a deafening crash. The sickening groans of breaking timber and crumbling brick followed the thunderbolt.

The Council of War sat in stunned silence, watching a cannon ball drop through the roof of the Council chamber and land a few feet from their table. They looked up at the roof in disbelief. Beside the candelabra, which now swayed violently at a precarious angle, the sky showed through a large hole. The first pale stars could already be seen and the last red streaks of sunset. They were brought to their feet by the creaks of the swinging chandelier that soon threatened to fall on them. The Council of War hurriedly fled the chamber.

CHAPTER TWENTY-FOUR

The next day dawned with terrifying briskness. The enemy now occupied the East Battery and had also mounted cannon there. As the early mist rose, the sun sucked up shadows and the heat pressed down upon Fort William. Soon the hot winds began, whipping up dust, rustling through foliage like falling rain. As the refugees rose to make their way to the river for the day's ablutions, the enemy opened fire. A splattering of muskets was heard, cannons boomed and from the ramparts of Fort William the enemy were seen swarming everywhere below. Shot suddenly flew about the eastern wall of the fort. The adjutant storks rose from their perches with a violent flapping of wings, parakeets screamed and departed in a yellow cloud. In the parade ground hysterical refugees clutched their children, raising fists to Governor's House.

In the damp, rat-infested passages that led to the strong rooms and warehouses under the fort these sounds echoed distantly to Sati. The ashram had found a providential place in which to hide the God Woman during the heat of battle. The problem of protecting the Goddess had grown as bands of drunken mercenaries roamed the parade ground looking for women. At first a large number of the ashram had tried to accompany Sati beneath the parade ground. The cramped conditions in the small space at the bottom of the stairs had forced them down the dank passages. There, darkness, the constant journeying of rats and the fear felt by the children of the Portuguese soldiers forced many again above ground. It was decided that only Sati and her attendants should make use of the underground protection.

As dawn shattered the darkness over Fort William, it was clear that the day, although hardly begun, had already developed a sickening momentum. Soldiers continued to retreat into the fort from outposts, carrying their wounded. The enemy yelled and charged recklessly about below the walls of the fort. Now and then volleys of lighted arrows sailed over the ramparts. Although these fell short of the parade ground, waves of fresh panic ensued. Conditions in the makeshift hospital in the ballroom of Governor's House were appalling. Dysentery was rampant. The dead lay beside the living in pools of vomit and excrement. Pans and bowls were non-existent and space was unavailable for new contingents of wounded. The constant exiting of corpses from the ballroom into the parade ground upset the refugees further. Bales of broadcloth had been brought up from the warehouses. Groups of men worked to erect traverses about the bastions of the fort to resist cannon balls and grapeshot. As they worked they sang, drunk on illicit liquor. Soon Fort William assumed a macabre holiday air, decked out in yards of dark bunting. The refugees became even more desperate at the sight of such revelry in the midst of attack.

The dank cellar below the parade ground filled Sati with depression. She argued to stay in the sun but her grandmother pushed her downstairs.

'Still so many drunken soldiers about. Better you remain out of sight. The Goddess must be protected,' Jaya insisted.

Each day now, for hour upon hour, Sati was cut off in near darkness from the world. And Durga, who had run in her blood like mercury, continued to evade her. To the Devi Ashram, Sati was a container for the Goddess and so was herself contained. And by transforming the Goddess from spirit to reality she was herself transformed. They could not see that Durga was uncontainable. Or that, weighed down by the restrictive vision of so many, she refused to show herself.

Sati turned on the makeshift pallet. The light from the top of the stairwell dissipated quickly and dissolved within the dark passages before her. The scent of soil and brick and animal droppings pressed closely about her. There was the constant scuttling of insect life and the squeaking of rats. She heard the noise of someone descending the stairs and thought Pagal must have returned to crouch again by her side.

She turned to greet him and saw a European man clambering awkwardly down the stairway. He stopped in surprise before her. Sati drew back against the wall in fear, remembering the tales she had heard of rape. The man appeared to be drunk, swaying unsteadily on his short legs, the odour of spirits about him. For a moment they stared at each other in silence, the man's round, bulging eyes never losing their expression of surprise. Sati faced him like a cornered animal. Then, to her relief, he turned abruptly to stagger away towards the labyrinth of passages. Sati prepared to run to the stairs just as the man, after taking a look at the dark, dank tunnels beneath the fort, decided against proceeding. She drew back again against the wall as he looked about him in agitation. Then his eyes settled upon a filthy trunk pushed into a corner. Without a word he sat himself down upon it and, leaning back against the wall, immediately fell asleep.

Within a moment Govindram and then Mohini and Jaya made their way down the stairs to stare anxiously at the intruder, who had now begun to snore.

'Get him out,' Jaya demanded, positioning herself before the man.

'Better not to disturb him. He will bring others and then who knows what trouble we will face,' Govindram reasoned.

'He has come here to hide,' Mohini declared.

'Already if one has found this place others may follow. There will be many that do not wish to fight,' Jaya worried. She stepped nearer the sleeping man and prodded him with a finger. He gave a grunt but did not stir.

'We cannot leave the *Devi* alone,' Mohini announced, sitting down beside Sati. Jaya nodded in agreement and followed Mohini's example. The women made themselves comfortable upon Sati's rag pallet; their great bodies stretched out like protective ballast either side of the girl. Govindram squatted down beside them and continued to stare at the man as if, by keeping his eyes upon him, danger would be averted.

Dishevelled by circumstances and anxiety, it was impossible to recognise Governor Drake. Wigless and hatless, his shirt and breeches filthy, unshaven and redolent with the scent of spirits, it was easy to mistake him for a Dutch mercenary. The tension of the Council chamber, which he had stoically born for so many days, had suddenly uncoiled like a spring within him.

As he hurried across the parade ground from a visit to Writers' Row, a hail of enemy fire-arrows had fallen about the Governor. He had looked up to see the sky emptying fiery rain upon him and stood transfixed, feathers of flame falling around him. Looking down at the smouldering sticks spread about his feet, he knew he had come to within inches of death. He turned in panic and hurried on towards Governor's House, pushing his way through the hysterical refugees. The wretched crowd seemed only to exemplify the adversity against which he struggled each day. An unbearable fatigue washed through him. If he could close his eyes in some dark place for even a moment he was sure his strength would return. As he approached Governor's House he drew suddenly to a halt, unable to face the lethargic squabbles of the Council chamber. He made for the steps that led down under the fort to the warren of warehouses. All he wanted to do was sleep.

For an hour the man dozed, watched minute by minute by the Devi Ashram. He snored and turned but nothing more. Govindram had made a detailed examination of the intruder but as the man carried neither dagger nor sword there appeared no immediate danger, except that others might follow.

'All soldiers are drunk. Soon all will want to sleep and hide,' Jaya continued to worry.

Before Govindram could reply, a further noise was heard on the stairs and yet another Hatman climbed down and came to stand before the sleeping man, leaning forward to shake him.

Lieutenant Witherington, in charge of the powder train, had been searching for the Governor. A sepoy had seen Drake descending the stairs and pointed Witherington in that direction. The Lieutenant made his way down into the darkness beneath the parade ground and looked blindly about, waiting for his sight to clear. Then, seeing Governor Drake asleep on the trunk, he stepped quickly towards him. He cleared his throat loudly but Drake did not stir. Eventually the Lieutenant took hold of the Governor's arm and shook him apologetically.

'Governor Drake. Excuse me, sir,'

'Witherington?' Drake sat up, rubbing his eyes.

'Sir, everyone is looking for you.'

'I am tired, Witherington. The job of Governor is not easy.' Drake was inclined to close his eyes again but Witherington, who still held on to his arm, shook the Governor gently once more.

'I thought it best to find you, sir, to report the news to you myself. We don't know what to do, sir.'

'Stop blabbering, Witherington. What is your news?' Drake asked. He had no wish to hear *any* news, all of which he was sure must be bad. He wished to go back to sleep.

'There is no more powder, sir, we have now reached the very end. If we have enough for even a few hours of battle tomorrow we shall be lucky.' Witherington spoke in a low voice. Drake leaned forward with a frown.

'Speak up, Witherington, I cannot hear.'

As Witherington turned back to Drake, Govindram moved

forward, for if he had understood correctly, the sleeping man was the Governor, improbable as it seemed. As Witherington repeated his news in a louder voice, Govindram gave a gasp.

'What is it?' Jaya and Mohini asked together.

'There is no more powder with which to fight.'

'The Hatmen can no longer fight?' Mohini wailed.

'The nawab will come and we shall be slaughtered,' Jaya gasped.

The women turned and made for the stairs, struggling upwards as fast as their bulk allowed. The sound of their cries and their stricken expressions made it clear to Drake that his conversation had been understood.

'There will be a panic, Witherington, if those women spread the news.' Drake's brain was forced suddenly into gear.

Witherington immediately threw himself at Jaya's feet as she ascended the stairs. She kicked herself free of his grasp and with Mohini emerged into the sun of the parade ground to warn everyone of the new danger.

Soon the parade ground was alive with the terrifying news that the nawab was coming to slaughter them and the Hatmen had no defence. Refugee women ran about screaming, children still suckling at their breasts. Goats and chickens, terrified by the hysteria, set up a great commotion. Old men shouted advice that nobody heard, children shrieked in a heartbreaking way. Within moments everyone began to run towards the river, set upon escape by the Hoogly.

At last Drake reached the Council chamber with Witherington. The Council of War stood before the windows that faced White Town. Much of the town was in flames, fired either by the enemy or now by the garrison for their own protection. They stood helplessly, trying to determine whose houses had been fired and whose had not. At the Governor's noisy entrance, the Council of War collected once more about the table while Drake imparted his news. At once the Council transferred to the windows of the chamber which overlooked the Hoogly. As the refugees reached the River Gate, the sentries raised their muskets, attempting to quell the hysterical crowd. For a few moments they were seen jerking about like puppets before being thrown aside by the crowd, which then flowed on to the river.

It was at this moment that further bad news was received. The enemy were now in possession of the Company House to one side of the fort and were trying to force the fence to the river. From the upper storey of the Company House they were firing directly into Fort William. Retaliation was impossible, for the men of the garrison were picked off by the enemy like clay pigeons. Attention was diverted from events at the river by this new development. The Council of War immediately moved back to the windows looking out over White Town. Within moments they saw a lucky cannon ball from Fort William put an end to the ferment from the Company House.

When the Council of War returned their attention to the river, they found a disaster of tragic proportions already in the making. An army of hysterical women had fled down the steps of the quay to a large but dilapidated ferryboat. With children held high above their heads, the women waded into the water towards the boat. It had been built to hold fifty people but soon several times that number of women and children had managed to cram themselves into the craft. Even as it floated away, more women tried to climb in over the bows. They were pushed viciously back into the water by those already aboard.

The Council of War now hurriedly made their way out of Governor's House and up on to the ramparts of the fort to assess the situation the better. The first thing they saw was that Siraj Uddaulah's army was still thick about the river fence. Slowly the overloaded boat of women drifted towards the enemy upon the Hoogly's strong current. As soon as they came within range, a stream of fire-arrows was let loose upon them. Volley after volley hissed through the air and fell upon the boat. The women left on the banks began to scream as stray arrows landed amongst them. They turned and hurried back into the fort. No such escape was available to the women in the boat. Within moments the craft burst into flames and lurched over on its side. Women and children, their garments aflame, jumped into the water, forced to choose between drowning and roasting.

The Chief Magistrate watched the unfolding tragedy in grim silence. The Governor trembled and began to blubber in fright. Below them, refugee women fleeing back into the fort were met by a crowd of deserting, drunken troops staggering towards the river. The thought of escape swept through Fort William with the force of a hurricane. The wharf was soon choked by a hysterical crowd of soldiers and refugees. As the Governor, the Chief Magistrate and the Chaplain leaned over the ramparts they were shocked to see amongst the mass of desperate deserting men Captain Minchin, commander of the garrison, clambering into a *budgerow*. O'Hara, the Chief Engineer, climbed in beside him and seized the oars. Far out in midstream the *Dodaldy* waited. O'Hara turned the craft towards it and began to row rapidly away.

On the ramparts, Governor Drake gave a furious roar at the sight of the departing Fort William men. Others of the Council of War raised their voices in equal anger, helpless to prevent the desertion. As Minchin's boat drew away from shore, new energy seemed to catapult through the Governor. He gave a further shout, deep and loud as a war cry. The sound welled up and burst out of him in a torrent of anguish and wrath. The Chief Magistrate looked at him in surprise and was at first nonplussed when Drake left the ramparts with considerable speed and made for the Governor's Gate. Bellamy moved closer to Holwell, and both men stared down at the crowded wharf.

'He goes after Minchin,' Bellamy announced as Drake was sighted below the walls. 'And it is the right thing to do. A Garrison Commander cannot desert.'

'Minchin is a coward,' Holwell replied, his eyes upon Drake's portly, hurrying figure. Already Minchin's boat was gaining distance,

O'Hara pulling hard on the oars. Holwell wondered what Drake could do now to stop him.

The Governor was seen to force a path through the crowd, pushing out strongly with his arms. He began to run along the wharf towards the mudflats a short distance away.

'Where does he run to?' the Chief Magistrate frowned.

As they watched, the Governor jumped down on to the river shore. The Chaplain and the Chief Magistrate saw that he made his way towards a boat that waited on the mudflats. By the crest on its bows the Chief Magistrate recognised the Governor's own *budgerow*. A soldier with a drawn sword guarded the boat and turned at once to assist the Governor. As Drake scrambled into the craft, the man pushed off after Minchin, towards the waiting ships. It was now seen that wind billowed in the *Dodaldy*'s sails and it pulled on its anchor as if already preparing to sail. The Chief Magistrate saw now that his own craft, the *Diligence,* a short distance behind the *Dodaldy,* had also unfurled its sails.

'The Governor himself makes to escape to the boats. He does nothing to delay Minchin.' The Chief Magistrate roared. He grabbed a musket from a nearby soldier and fired it after Drake. The shot arched through the air then fell into the Hoogly, a great distance from the departing Governor.

Eventually Minchin and then Drake reached the *Dodaldy,* and in the distance the tiny figures were seen being helped aboard. Almost immediately the ships began to move downstream, accompanied by a flotilla of boats. The Chief Magistrate was forced to watch his own ship follow the others.

'We are stranded. How now are we to evacuate?' The Chief Magistrate howled with rage.

'God will find a way,' Bellamy advised, but in a tired voice that carried little conviction.

Below the parade ground, the Devi Ashram had not seen these momentous events. Jaya and Mohini returned to spread their terrifying news and to urge everyone to flee. Govindram was of the opposite opinion, and voiced his views decisively.

'We shall remain here. It will be safest. Up there it is no better than a stampede of elephants.' He insisted everyone in the ashram gathered below ground.

'Always you think you are knowing best, that I as a woman know nothing,' Mohini argued, so frightened she did not care who heard this disrespect for her husband.

'Many boats are waiting upon the river. They will take us away from this hell. On the water we shall be safe,' Jaya yelled at her cousin, equally furious at his pig-headedness. The wives of the half-caste Portuguese added their agreement in loud voices. Govindram stood his ground.

'We shall stay here,' he ordered.

He left Pagal to guard the devotees and returned above ground to assess the state of affairs himself, taking the old men with him. When he returned to the Devi Ashram it was to report the dire events that had decimated the refugee population.

'Already two hundred and fifty women have died. We shall remain here,' Govindram repeated, unmoved by the argument swirling about him.

'To be slaughtered by the nawab,' Mohini answered in a faint voice.

'All escape is now cut off,' Jaya sobbed in terror.

'The Goddess will save us,' Govindram replied.

Everyone turned towards Sati.

CHAPTER TWENTY-FIVE

From the deck of the *Dodaldy*, Emily Drake looked towards Fort William. As the Governor's wife she had been allocated a makeshift cabin, hurriedly partitioned off, in the roundhouse on the upper stern deck. She had given this to Mrs Mackett, who had suffered a miscarriage before evacuating the fort, and Mrs Mapletoft and her new baby, Constantia. The other cabin she had insisted be given to the weakest children. She refused to sleep below deck, where conditions were unbearable. The *Dodaldy* had been built to carry fifty passengers, but there were now well over a hundred terrified women and children on board. All, like her, after one look below, immediately settled themselves on the deck. This was a feat of some manoeuvring, for the place was crowded with wildlife. Ducks and pigs, chickens, turkey, sheep and goats, a cow and her calf, all these animals, besides the ship's cats, must share the deck with the passengers. Time and the cooking pots would reduce their numbers, but for now the menagerie bleated and crowed. It was as if they lived in a farmyard. Since the *Dodaldy* was an Indiaman and must traverse hostile seas, the deck was also fitted with cannon and all the paraphernalia these needed: canisters of powder, ramrods, water buckets, cannon balls and grapeshot. Little room was left for passengers. Manningham and Frankland, as well as the Reverend

Mapletoft and several members of the Fort William miltia, were also on board. They had been forced by decency to sleep below deck but emerged at times gasping for air. Ships' passengers were always required to carry with them their own furnishings: a bed, linen, pillows, footbath, washstand and chest of drawers, besides lamps and candles and supplies of food. The women on board the *Dodaldy* possessed only the clothes they stood up in.

None of this worried Emily Drake. She looked down into the Hoogly's sinuous currents and listened to its many voices. As the boat rocked on the tide she leaned on the rail and its rhythm moved through her. Behind her were sounds of misery and yet she marvelled that about the ship the hot winds blew unconcernedly, the tide ebbed and turned and birds wheeled and cried in voices like stones skimming over the water.

Women came to crowd about her at the rail. Far away, over the water, Fort William appeared diminished. Fire still flared in White Town. The women sobbed, pointing out whose house was aflame and whose still stood. Only Emily had no wish to climb back into the life left there. Nothing now held her to the town. Its burning left her unmoved; something obsolete was being cleared away as already something was cleared within herself. Even Harry's small grave did not draw her. He was gone from her, embarked upon a fathomless journey where neither voice nor touch could reach him. Nothing now seemed of importance but the pinprick of time in which she now stood. Roger was as distant from her as Harry, embarked upon a different journey. He had no need of her, nor she of him. This knowledge flowered within her in an emotionless way.

Before Fort William, figures small as tin soldiers could be seen strutting about. At the quay a collection of boats had gathered. The moments when she had stood upon that quay, forced into an overloaded barge, seemed already to belong to another life. Then, all she had wanted was to return to Fort William, for in the uncertain light of the flares she was sure she saw Harry. His small face was buffeted within the shadows and stared out from below the dark waves. The sound of his crying reached her from the cemetery.

'Set me free,' she had pleaded, struggling to stand in the precarious boat so that it rocked violently. The women screamed and pulled her down. She had wrenched herself from their grasp but already, she remembered, the stretch of water was widening. All the while the lantern danced above her head, fingers of light swinging over the river. Again they had pulled her down. Again came the crying that she knew must be Harry. It seemed nearer, as if he had reached the water's edge and held out his small arms for her return.

'Set me free,' she had shrieked as they pulled at her skirts. The whimpering came again. For a moment the boatman seemed to hesitate; the craft lost its rhythmic pull.

'They will come on to the boat if we stop now,' someone screamed from the back.

Then, in the light of the rocking lantern, she had seen the crowds of refugees spilling out of Fort William, wading into the water after the boat. She saw mothers with babies at their breasts, and knew it was the cries of these hungry children that she had heard, not Harry.

She drew back then in the boat. Harry's face had disappeared beneath the weight of other faces; his cry was swallowed by the screams of other exhausted infants. Women fought on the wet steps, stumbling forward into the water, holding their babies out to her. Then, beyond the desperate crowd, standing apart beneath the illumination of a flare, Emily had seen the spirit girl, Sati. As the water widened between the quay and the boat she had watched the girl grow smaller until at last the darkness claimed her. Then Emily Drake sat down in the boat, suddenly without emotion. She was filled with the memory of the girl's wild dance again and how her own feet had itched to join her. She knew then she was hungry for whatever might bring her alive.

She had turned to gaze at the *Dodaldy* waiting out in midstream, its lanterns ablaze. In the overloaded barge there had been silence but for the watery swish of the oars and their occasional knock against the bows. Far away on the quay, beneath the flares, the refugees could be seen returning to the fort. Blackness and silence enveloped the barge, as if the river now possessed them. The boat was sunk low in the water and pulled forward with an effort. Emily trailed a hand in the water and the current ran through her fingers. The river sang into her flesh. She knew then she would have no control over the future. She would do as she would do.

When at last they reached the *Dodaldy* she had climbed passively aboard. Above her the great masts of the ship rose into the sky. In the darkness, the cries of night animals drifted over the water; the howl of jackals and the croaking of frogs came to her as the disembodied voice that entered all her dreams, calling to her from beyond the rim of consciousness. Eventually she slept, but the sounds echoed in her sleep as if to awaken her to herself.

Her dreams that first night on the *Dodaldy* had been of the river. She was wading across it. The moon sailed in the sky, lighting the water about her. As she reached midstream the Hoogly's strong currents suddenly gripped her. She looked into the water and saw long, oiled sinews twisting about her. At first she seemed powerless against this force, however much she battled, but eventually she freed herself. On the bank there were people who helped her out of the water. They told her she was lucky to have escaped. Look at what you were fighting, what was after you, they said. She turned to where they pointed and saw on the bank beside her the burnt remains of a body. She had expected to see some terrible creature but faced instead a heap of bones and ash. It had now become very dark. And look up there, the people said, pointing in fear to the sky. She looked up, searching, but saw only the moon and stars.

She had woken then upon the hard deck to the violent beating of her heart, filled by a terrible fear. Above her the sky was still covered by night. She had lain on her back, looking up at the moonless expanse, her heart slowly regaining itself. The dream stayed with her; she knew it had come for a reason.

In the morning the heat rose in a mist, hovering over the water as if the Hoogly were a steaming cauldron. The business of battle had already begun on the distant shore. The sound of cannon and musket fire resounded; the showers of fire-arrows were as spectacular as a fireworks display. About the fort the wedding-cake houses of White Town were blazing. On the *Dodaldy* a great anxiety blew up. Messenger boats plied backwards and forwards so that news from shore was regularly received. It was in this way that the women on board the *Dodaldy* were able to make sense of the jerking frieze of events upon the banks of the Hoogly. Their concern was for their men, which the constant shattering noise of cannon did nothing to assuage. Soon Captain Minchin arrived on board to confirm the hopelessness of conditions on shore.

Suddenly, a strong vibration shook the ship. Looking up, the passengers saw that the craft's huge sails were being unfurled with a great rippling and flapping and roars from the crew. At once the hot winds took hold of the canvas so that the sails billowed and creaked in a terrifying fashion, assuming a life of their own.

The ship, now full of the urge for flight, tugged hard upon her anchor chain. The impatience could be felt by those on deck. It was then that a craft rowing out from the mudflats was determined by those with spyglasses to carry the Governor himself. The *Dodaldy* got ready to receive its last passenger and move downstream to safer water.

Until now it was as if time had stopped. The close proximity of the great river upon whose back she rocked had filled Emily with new certainty. All that seemed real was the river stretching before her, the unending arc of the sky and her place between these things. Her soul seemed to swell, as if at last it emerged from long hiding. Now, suddenly, that one small boat pulling slowly away from the shore seemed to threaten her existence, diminishing everything once more to the scale of petty concerns. When her husband clambered aboard the *Dodaldy* she would be seen again in the old perspective. She must remain silent when she was on fire; once more she would be the

Governor's wife. Once more she would be bent to resemble the people about her.

Already it was happening. Roger Drake had reached the boat and was being helped aboard. Already she made her way towards him, as did Manningham and Frankland and Captain Minchin. Already Mrs Mapletoft and Constantia and Mrs Mackett, who grew sicker each day, were asked to vacate the roundhouse cabin for the Governor. Emily's protest at this treatment of the frail women was carelessly swept away. She was powerless to make her voice heard but must climb the steps behind her husband, fettered to protocol and the mindless actions of others.

Above her the wind blew stronger in the sails as the ship prepared to move. Wood creaked, canvas groaned, the voices of wheeling birds screeched above the *Dodaldy*. A hot breeze blew about the ship, the voice of the river floating to her upon it. Screaming birds and thrumming sails ate up the disembodied words, but Emily knew to whom the voice called.

CHAPTER TWENTY-SIX

In the dark, the Chief Magistrate looked out at the river. A further nightmarish day had ended, and throughout it, he now realised, the Hoogly had commanded each hour. He stared at the river in hate.

There were not many of the militia now left in Fort William. Of these, the Dutch mercenaries could no longer be looked upon as a viable fighting force. They lurched uselessly about in an inebriated state whenever their expertise was needed. In their rare moments of sobriety they were mutinous. A large number of sepoys had already left the fort and gone over to the enemy. Those Portuguese that remained had stayed only because their wives and children still filled the parade ground. And they had to be berated constantly to fight. All will to attack had drained away in whatever contingents survived.

The Council of War sat around the table in the Council chamber. Above them the damage wrought by the enemy had opened a window to the sky. Rubble from the ceiling lay as it had fallen in a dusty heap, and members of the Council were forced to pick their way about it. The cannon ball had rolled a short distance and now lay against the wall under the portrait of Job Charnock.

The Chief Magistrate, anger ripe within him at the cowardly desertion of Minchin and Drake, swore loudly to continue to fight for an honourable settlement. The Chaplain, still looking pale and ill, seemed now to find more solace in his claret than in the word of God. Instead of a Bible, he walked about with a bottle under his arm. From the Council chamber he stared at the empty vista of the Hoogly, devoid of the ships that would have removed them to safety, and gave a shuddering sigh.

'The *Prince George* has sailed back up river, but we must send a message to Captain Hague to return to evacuate us all immediately,' the Chief Magistrate suggested. At the table the men at once looked hopeful, and young Pearkes offered to row out to the boat.

After Pearkes's departure, the thought of the *Prince George*'s imminent arrival carried them through the day, with its further shattering onslaught of cannon. There was an attempted scaling of Fort William's walls by the enemy which was, with difficulty, repulsed. The houses surrounding the fort were now all occupied by the nawab's soldiers. This made it impossible to fire from the bastions without being blasted by enemy muskets. Another score of the garrison's diminishing force had died in this manner.

At last, in the mid-afternoon, the *Prince George* sailed serenely into view, her great sails billowing in the hot breeze, sitting easily astride the wilful Hoogly. A cheer of relief went up in Fort William. The nawab's forces at once retaliated by firing at Fort William again with the garrison's own discarded cannon. When the Council of War returned its attention to the *Prince George,* it was to find it heading for disaster. The treacherous Hoogly tried even the most experienced pilots. Ships were thrown about within its currents and tossed on to its sandbanks at will. One moment the *Prince George* appeared to sail smoothly along; the next it spun about as if heading for the shore. As the men of Fort William watched, it was brought around with difficulty, only to drive into a sandbank. The ship shuddered and lurched and began to list, spilling rigging and men overboard. Each frantic effort to right it proved useless. Within an hour it was boarded by the enemy, plundered and set on fire. It burned brightly on the Hoogly under the gaze of the garrison.

In the dark, the Chief Magistrate stood with the Chaplain on the south-west bastion above the river, silently observing the blazing ship. Fort William was filled with solemnity. There appeared now to be only a choice of death or surrender; all hope of escape had gone. About the Chaplain and the Chief Magistrate a red glow lit up the night as the smouldering remains of White Town suffused the moonless sky. Holwell's own great house a short distance from the fort was now unrecognisable. The charred frame of the upper storeys sat like a humiliating crown upon its once gleaming exterior. All day the Chief Magistrate had tried not to see the figures on its great balconies and within its many rooms, prising open cupboards or drawers, looting it of its finery. The sight of these men in his home left him sick with violation.

At the Chief Magistrate's side, the Reverend Bellamy seemed almost too tired to stand. For a while he supported himself on the wall of the bastion and then sat down beside a cannon. He had suffered badly, not only from the looting of his liquor, but in the manner the enemy had treated his church. Three field pieces had been dragged into its interior and fired at Fort William to great advantage. The church was held hostage by the enemy, its broken spire a sullen reminder of Calcutta's neglect, its walls brutally pitted by cannon but unable to fall. The Chaplain made a small sobbing sound.

'It is like a woman that you have taken for granted, not caring even to outfit her properly. Now I must watch as she is ravaged and understand at last what she means to me. It is the Lord's punishment. And it is a just one. I have neglected my duties and must now know remorse. That is why I am here and not upon that boat I believe, Chief Magistrate, there is a reason the Lord has kept us here in this hell. He has a purpose for us all.' As he spoke, Bellamy searched his pockets for the flask of Madeira he carried.

Holwell nodded; he was of the same mind as the Chaplain. He was equally perplexed at his own continued presence in the fort when he might have followed Drake. Now, like the Chaplain, he was sure the

Lord had a firm hand in things. God might need to put lessons of remorse before Bellamy, but for himself, the Chief Magistrate decided, He might well have other plans. With Drake's surprise departure, Holwell, as the senior Council member, was at last in the position of Acting Governor. The Chief Magistrate was acutely aware that at this moment history would judge his every action. His life played out before him, crowded with incidents that had never made sense. Now he saw that everything fit a pattern that had conspired to bring him to this day.

'Rai Durlabh is a traitor. He has betrayed us.' The Chaplain's face crumpled in despair.

'As the Young Begum's treasure is now safely aboard our ships, we may be able to make an honourable truce with the nawab. The longer we hold out, the stronger we appear when bargaining for surrender. Above all, we must not show weakness.' The Chief Magistrate advised. Already he saw himself negotiating with the intractable nawab, the destiny of Calcutta in his hands at last.

Far away, almost lost to sight from Fort William the lanterns of the *Diligence* and the *Dodaldy* twinkled like distant stars in the night. The Chief Magistrate looked out at the remains of the *Prince George* and the Hoogly washing about it. He realised now that the river had steered every disaster. Over her waters Drake had run, as if hearing the Siren's voices. The refugee women had sunk and burned. The flotilla of rescue ships had been drawn away against all logic on her tide. Her moonless water was now lit by White Town fires. And when the Chief Magistrate had played his trump card of the *Prince George*, she had crushed the ship before him. Holwell listened, as he had done each night on his veranda, to the incessant booming of the bullfrogs. It was as if those slimy balloons of foul air had set themselves up as attendants to the river's genie. Beneath their ugly croaking, the sinuous silence of the river lay in the troubled night. He sensed the river still watched him, waiting to destroy him. Anger seized the Chief Magistrate; this was his moment, and he would not be denied it by the wily designs of the Hoogly.

The Chief Magistrate's resolution was so fierce and his gaze was so determinedly fixed on the river that he failed to notice the fifty-six Dutch mercenaries deserting Fort William. They dropped silently over the walls of the fort and ran off to the enemy-occupied church. There, the nawab's emissaries awaited them. When at last this further act of betrayal was brought to his notice, the Chief Magistrate shrugged resignedly. He knew suddenly that his battle was not with these mutinous men, nor even in some strange way with the waiting enemy. It was with the river and the heathen black spirit that lay buried in its depths. This realisation, and the new perception of his role in Fort William's destiny, filled him with fresh certainty. History was his to form now from the balance of each moment.

He slept fitfully, rising at times to pace his room or stand upon its balcony staring at the river. The dank odour of the water mixed now with the stench of the corpses piled up in Fort William. In spite of Siraj Uddaulah's cannon fire, in spite of the distant sight of charging figures and the rain of fire-arrows, whenever the Chief Magistrate closed his eyes the enemy became a shadow. It hovered on the edge of sleep, black, amorphous, uncertain in its predilection, containing a darkness he recognised as connected to himself. He always awoke with fear raging through him; fear that was as much of the enemy as it was of himself. On his bed he tossed and turned as through the open window the smell of the river and the smell of death entwined within the hot night.

The following morning, his dreams forgotten, the Chief Magistrate rose early, ready to claim his place in history. Entering Drake's bedroom, he found a clean shirt in a tallboy. Although the neck was too large and the sleeves too short, it served its purpose. He made an attempt to shave but the soap would not lather and he cut himself. Still, he had the feeling he had gathered together some necessary threads, and in the darkness of the early morning, he made his way to the Council chamber.

The new confidence shown by the Chief Magistrate was noticed at once by all. Before the sun came up and the first cannon could thunder, Holwell summoned the remainder of the garrison to a corner of the parade ground and exhorted them to fight. The refugees were forced to make room for them and looked on curiously as Holwell began his oration. The Chief Magistrate spoke in the manner of a preacher buoyed up by God, an ethereal lust in his eyes. The small group of bedraggled men listened, and the dream-filled night, when death had hovered upon the ragged edges of sleep, faded from their minds. The Chief Magistrate's certainty grew as he spoke.

'However many times they may assault us, we will show no weakness.' The Chief Magistrate's words rang out, breaking through the cobwebs of mist that hung over the Hoogly.

He was well aware of the Indians' psychology. If the moment came for surrender, the enemy must believe a formidable fighting force still remained in Fort William. If not, and if surrender was unconditional, a bloody vengeance would ensue, for the Moors had no respect for weakness. Holwell raised his arms before the tattered garrison, exultant. And the exhausted men before him buried their misgivings, glad to place their terror upon shoulders so ready to bear it. Soon they went back to the shambles of their barracks, to a breakfast of thick *chapati* cooked over a fire of broken-up furniture from Writers' Row. The Chief Magistrate walked to a meal of weevily rice cooked in pots commandeered from a wealthy refugee.

The Chief Magistrate's speechifying was all before the sun arose or the first cannon had sounded. In that peaceful, misty silence it was easy to drift in hope. But as the morning dawned, it was clear the enemy was just as exultant as the Chief Magistrate. They had heard many truths from the deserting Dutch mercenaries and saw the great holes their cannon had wrought in the supporting walls of Fort William. They knew also about the Hatmen's diminishing powder supply and, having no such troubles of their own, fought with new intensity. Their losses were not insubstantial, but with an army of thirty thousand, these casualties were but a piffling number. It was not so within Fort William. By mid-morning, twenty-five of the remaining garrison had been killed and seventy more were wounded. All but fourteen gunners were dead. A great clamour now arose in Fort William for an immediate surrender before any further men were killed. The Chief Magistrate held out against this decision. Even when Witherington again rushed into the Council chamber to repeat the one piece of news he seemed destined to bring, that they had finally exhausted all the dry powder, the Chief Magistrate would still not give in.

As the morning progressed, the Chief Magistrate's belief in his own destiny no longer communicated itself with such strength to his men. Anxiety and dissent ruffled the atmosphere in the Council chamber. The sun blazed down through the hole in the ceiling upon the remaining Council of War. The growing stench of unburied corpses ripening rapidly with each hour carried deep into the room. This odour now permeated everything and was a constant reminder of an omnipotence beyond the Chief Magistrate's exhortations.

'Siraj Uddaulah *must* be made to believe we can withstand a continued siege,' Holwell insisted. The sun fell in a shaft upon him through the damaged ceiling. The buzzing hordes of flies and the layer of dust motes in the filthy room were illuminated, floating around him like celestial bodies.

'Without powder nothing is possible,' Mackett answered. 'We must wave the white flag of surrender.'

'Why not try once more to persuade the fat merchant to write a letter to the nawab? He may do it now, for he must be impatient for release from that prison. Let him argue our strength and demand an honourable settlement.' The Chaplain spoke up in a trembling voice. Holwell regarded him with admiration; even in his frail state, Bellamy's wisdom could still be relied upon.

Once again Holwell faced the parade ground for the journey to Omichand in the Black Hole. Since his last crossing, a great number of the Portuguese soldiers had laid down their lives for the garrison. The wailing of their widows and children now pressed hard upon the Chief Magistrate. The frenzy that had filled his last crossing of the square had been replaced by lethargy. Children did no more than whimper; dazed women no longer grasped angrily at his clothes. Rats scampered boldly about. The goats had gone to keep the living alive. The stench of death was horrifying. Men, women and children lay where they had been felled. Rats feasted on rotting flesh. Hungry vultures, crows and adjutant storks made a continual nuisance of themselves, and had to be waved away from the corpses by grieving relatives. Above the parade ground, on the ramparts of Fort William, men still stood at their posts manning cannon and guns. Even from a distance, the Chief Magistrate could see that they were tired. Eventually he reached the Black Hole and demanded Omichand be brought out.

Extra days of imprisonment had wrought further changes upon Omichand's physique but the Chief Magistrate had neither the time nor the inclination to dwell on the fading bulk of the merchant. He came at once to the matter of writing a letter.

'On both sides casualties are heavy and trade is at a standstill. Mr Drake, who has so upset the nawab, is gone from Fort William. I am now Acting Governor. A new start can be made in our trading relationship. In Fort William we have the means to continue to fight, but for both sides it would be wise to avoid further bloodshed and come to an arrangement. All this you will tell the nawab. We will, however, only agree to a ceasefire upon the promise of honourable treatment for the garrison, and a negotiated settlement. Our ships lie ready in the Hoogly, and reinforcements are expected at any moment from Madras,' Holwell finished. He dared not admit the state of affairs in Fort William even to Omichand.

The fat merchant said nothing as he took up the quill that Holwell offered. He was anxious for release and was sure no suspicion of conspiracy could now be pinned on him; things had gone too far.

The response from the nawab was almost immediate. An envoy was seen to approach Fort William, walking slowly up The Avenue. The Chief Magistrate climbed to the ramparts above the gate and guardedly watched his approach. The man advanced up The Avenue through the ruins of the embattled town and the wreckage of battle; broken gun carriages and discarded cannon lay everywhere, the carcasses of bullocks and horses and the bodies of men were thickly surrounded by vultures. A short distance from Fort William's walls, the envoy came to a halt. The Chief Magistrate climbed higher to reveal himself. The envoy bowed. He spoke English. His message was that the nawab also wished the fighting to stop and would accept Fort William's surrender. Having delivered his message and heard the Chief Magistrate's demands, the man bowed again and returned the way he had come. Holwell ordered the white flag of truce to be raised as the emissary retreated down The Avenue. He continued to stand on the ramparts staring out over Calcutta.

Alone, high on his lofty pinnacle in the hot breeze, the Chief Magistrate felt he stood astride the gulf of time, spanning triumph and disaster. Before him were the charred remains of Calcutta and beyond them the nawab's camp. He saw none of this but looked only at the horizon, stretching to eternity. His spirit winged towards it. From where he stood, the earth and its miserable happenings seemed a great distance away. On the parade ground, the men of the garrison and also the refugees stood waiting, eyes upon him. At last he turned towards them.

'Lay down your arms. Rest and refresh yourselves.' His voice rang out over Fort William.

Immediately, jubilation broke out. Once the news of the ceasefire reached them, even those in the garrison's hospital on the point of death rallied to cheer and contemplate recovery. It was noon, time for the nawab's siesta. His emissary was to return at three o'clock with terms for the ceasefire. During these intervening hours there was an air of euphoria in the garrison. The nawab might enter Fort William in triumph but there had not been the humiliation of unconditional surrender. This strengthening thought was in every-one's mind; honour would be upheld.

Such euphoria did not take hold of the refugees once they knew the way things were going. Their knowledge of their Moslem rulers was based on a different experience. Since their exposure in the parade ground to illness, starvation, cannon and arrows had whittled down their will to survive, most resigned themselves to certain death at the hands of Siraj Uddaulah.

Three o'clock came and then passed without any sign of the nawab's emissary. At four o'clock, sounds of activity outside the fort brought the garrison expectantly to the walls. Instead of the orderly movements of troops for a ceasefire, they were confronted by the enemy emerging in a rowdy fashion from the houses of White Town. They crowded beneath the walls of the fort, shifting about in a menacing way, shouting incomprehensibly. No shots were fired. This sudden dearth of combustibles left the garrison unsure of the nature of the enemy's overture. On the ramparts of Fort William, muskets were raised and readied. Holwell called immediately for caution; he felt sure the demonstration must be good-willed, in view of the morning's proceedings. He ran back to his perch on the ramparts where he had so recently stood in triumph, for a better view. The moment he set eyes upon the restless crowd, the Chief Magistrate knew he had been mistaken in his evaluation. Below him, The Avenue seethed with angry men.

A young officer by the name of Baillee scrambled up to stand beside him. 'It is better that you come down, sir. We do not know what is in their minds, or even why they are here.'

The Chief Magistrate stared down from his perch at the enemy, and was filled with sudden rage at such contrary behaviour. 'Nonsense, Baillee. Brute strength is all these people understand. If I retreat they will sense our fear and all will be lost. I do not fear them. Let them see who is in command.'

Holwell laid his hand upon the hilt of his sword and stood unmoving, chin pushed out and shoulders drawn back defiantly, high above the disquieting crowd. He did not look down, fearing eye contact, but stared out at the crushed and looted remains of White Town. The sun no longer reflected upon its dazzling parts. It had been brought to its knees in a mire of soot and ravishment. For a moment the Chief Magistrate felt the pain he knew Bellamy must feel when he looked at the violation of his church. His hand clenched the hilt of his sword as he stepped up to the edge of the ramparts. From The Avenue then a single shot rang out, hissing near his ear. Holwell drew back in surprise, stung by such audacity. He was suddenly aware that young Baillee had dropped to the ground beside him, blood spurting from his head. As the Chief Magistrate bent towards the wounded man, a sickening realisation washed through him. The shot Baillee had taken had been meant for him. Already, as if a thread had broken, bullets and arrows began to rain once more upon the walls of Fort William. The men of the garrison swarmed up beside Holwell to begin firing again at the enemy.

It was at this moment that the Chief Magistrate was alerted to further treachery at the River Gate. The gate had been forced open by the Dutch mercenaries who had deserted Fort William the night before. Already, the nawab's thirty thousand were entering the garrison and yet others, unstoppable now, scaled Fort William's walls. Soon the fort swarmed with the enemy, who made straight for Governor's House.

As the enemy cascaded over the walls, the Chief Magistrate was forced to leave the wounded Baillee. He ran to the bastion above the gate and ordered the sepoys there to discharge the cannon and fire their small arms at the enemy now flooding into the fort. The men took no notice of Holwell's frantic commands. They prepared to flee before the nawab's army.

'I order you to fire,' the Chief Magistrate screamed.

'We will be dead before we can fire a shot,' a Portuguese sepoy shouted, cowering behind the cannon.

'Fire or *I* will shoot you. We must show strength.' Holwell aimed his pistol at the men as the noise of the mob rose about them.

Under threat of the Chief Magistrate's gun, the men moved reluctantly into position. One by one they stepped forward with their muskets. Before they could even raise their guns each was felled by enemy fire. Within moments the men lay writhing at Holwell's feet, their blood collecting in a pool that trickled towards him.

The Chief Magistrate stared about wildly. Not a single shred of order remained. Wherever he looked he saw the dark force of the nawab's men, yelling and slashing with their swords. The refugees were running about in a terrified manner, attempting to escape the slaughter. On the river wall of Fort William the nawab's colours were already being hoisted. Holwell began to run in the direction of Governor's House. In the afternoon Bellamy had retired to his room, too ill to keep up with events. The vulnerability of the Chaplain's situation now came forcefully before the Chief Magistrate. As he neared the entrance he saw a handful of Fort William men clash with a further yelling mob. The Chief Magistrate raised his pistol. He fired and reloaded and fired again as quickly as he could.

CHAPTER TWENTY-SEVEN

As conditions in Fort William deteriorated and drunkenness amongst the soldiers increased, the Devi Ashram grew progressively nervous about the safety of Sati. They continued to hide her beneath the parade ground. It was as if she were buried alive. The worse things became in Fort William, the less Sati was allowed to emerge above ground. At times a thick piece of rush matting was thrown over the steps down to the warehouses to camouflage the entrance, leaving her in darkness. Now, when she thought of life above ground, of the changing light of the sky or the lengthening shadows of afternoon, it was to feel that when she re-entered that world she would be as if reborn. Once, she had climbed the stairs, longing for air and contact with the ashram. As she came up into the parade ground the light dazzled and the stench had sickened her. The corpses of soldiers and refugees lay where death had struck them down, without anyone to cart them away. Rats scuttled about the bodies, intent on feasting. The world Sati imagined lay above her seemed to have disappeared. She had returned to her underworld as if shrinking back into a cocoon.

Time had no meaning in this dim place. Her eyes had grown so used to the shadows that she could see depths where before there appeared to be nothing. Either Pagal or Jaya remained at her side, but even they now made excuses to sit at the top of the stairs. Pagal worried for his children and Jaya insisted a better guard must be kept upon the entrance and trusted no one to do this but herself. Sati was left alone. The dank scent of mud, stale air and rat droppings grew steadily more pungent. The walls crawled with insects she could not name. Rodents scuttled about near her pallet. Through the beaten earth above her head, sounds echoed down in an impacted way.

All morning she had listened to the boom of cannon and the cries of terror above. A terrible restlessness filled her and the fetid odours of her prison fizzed within her head. She felt she could stand it no longer and must reach light and air whatever the risk. As she prepared to climb the stairs to the parade ground, the sheet of matting covering the stairwell was pulled aside and the morning sun shone down. Pagal's face peered down and behind him was Govindram.

'All is lost with the Hatmen. The nawab's army are everywhere. People are leaving to return to Black Town and the nawab takes no notice of their departure. It is better we also go,' Govindram called down.

She followed them up the steps, coming at last into the air perfumed with death. The Devi Ashram immediately formed a protective cordon about her. In the sky above Fort William, monsoon clouds had begun to collect.

'The nawab will enter from The Avenue; his troops already cheer loudly there. We must avoid that place, for the crowds will be thick. We will go out by the River Gate,' Govindram decided.

Slowly they moved across the parade ground, pushing their way through the mass of people. Siraj Uddaulah's pennants were everywhere, streaking the fort with unaccustomed colour. Platoons of his soldiers marched about, muskets gleaming in the sun. The sepoys of the Fort William garrison had already been pardoned and were busy changing sides and vowing allegiance to the enemy. The nawab's army took no notice of the ragged Black Town crowd, streaming out of the gates. They were interested only in the Hatmen.

As the Devi Ashram approached the river gate, they were caught in a sudden crush and pushed back into the fort. The nawab's bodyguard, in indigo *dhoti* and turbans, were clearing the gate for the arrival of the nawab. It now appeared Siraj Uddaulah would not enter the fort from The Avenue but through this smaller gate, after he had made an inspection of Fort William's walls.

'Get back,' Govindram shouted as the crowd pushed against them. He pulled Sati up the steps of Writers' Row. The indigo turbans formed an impenetrable barrier before them. The noise of cheering troops was deafening as Siraj Uddaulah, in an immense silver litter, was carried triumphantly into Fort William at last.

While the nawab was in the fort no movement of people was permitted. The Devi Ashram was forced to wait in the broiling sun until the nawab returned from his tour of the garrison and was set down in the parade ground. It was then that Sati, peering out between the fence of muskets and indigo uniforms, saw the Chief Magistrate. His hands were bound and his clothes hung untidily about him. His wig sat at an odd angle, giving him a rakish appearance. Beneath it his face was grim. He walked forward held by a guard and was pushed down to kneel before Siraj Uddaulah. The nawab's voice drifted in angry snatches over the waiting crowd. Sati was near enough to see the shadow of a beard on the Chief Magistrate's face. Whenever she was confronted with him, the same inexplicable confusion filled her. Then people pushed in front of her and the view of Holwell was gone.

With the exit of the nawab, the Devi Ashram prepared to move forward again, only to find themselves before a wall of flames. It appeared the nawab had given an order to burn Governor's House. Fresh hysteria swept through the departing refugees. The gates to The Avenue were blocked by the desperate crowd, and the nawab's army, tired and victorious, were now in a touchy mood. A further fire had been started along Writers' Row and the buildings adjacent to it, making progress to the river gates precarious.

'Better to hide underground until all is quiet. Then we can leave at first light when most of the soldiers are sleeping,' Govindram suggested.

He led them back the way they had come, giving the blazing Governor's House a wide berth. The flames lit up the parade ground, eating into the darkness, and sounds of crashing timber were heard. Soon the Devi Ashram reached the entrance to the underground passages and slipped down, unseen by Siraj Uddaulah's guards.

The dirty pallet on which Sati had been confined still carried the indentation of her body. She seated herself on it once more and Jaya and Mohini sank down heavily beside her, exhausted. The rest of the Devi Ashram were forced down the rat-infested passages, where they cowered in fear with their children. From the parade ground strange booming noises filtered down the dark labyrinth. There was a faint light from the fire above. Those who could, pushed into the small space about Sati's pallet.

'Tell the Goddess to come. They are needing her now,' Jaya whispered, looking at the anxious faces about them. Sati shook her head sadly.

To the ashram Sati was the *Devi*. They had made her the God Woman, breathing into her whatever they willed. Many times in the past few days the women had fallen to their knees before Sati, their tears wiping the dust from her feet. Their children were dying, husbands and friends were already dead. Confused and distraught, they feared the future. She could do nothing, yet the touch of her hand on their heads immediately lightened the weight of emotion within them. They drew back and wiped their eyes, better resigned to their fate. It was as if Sati had been captured. As amber sets about something that has once known life, so now the torrent of need that was poured upon her petrified in her veins. Durga had not deserted her. It was Sati who had lost her way to that place within herself where Durga waited for her.

Jaya Kapur did not know how long she slept, but when she opened her eyes the whimpers of babies and the snores of old men filled the small space at the bottom of the steps like scuffling animals. She pulled herself up and leaned back against the wall. Beside her, Sati slept and Mohini dreamed uncertain dreams punctuated by noisy grunts. The stairwell was now filled with grotesque red light from the burning of Fort William. She turned to look down at her granddaughter and stroked the wild mass of her hair. Behind her, a loose brick in the crumbling wall pushed hard against her spine. She turned in annoyance and found that the brick came away in her hands at a touch. Immediately a heavy object fell into her lap. At first she thought it must be a dead rat and was about to scramble to her feet. Then a sudden extra flare of fire from above sent more light down the stairwell. Old Jaya looked down in disbelief. Although she was poised to stand, she sank back on her bed in amazement. In her lap was a small cotton sack of considerable weight. She pulled open the drawstring with trembling hands and tipped out the contents. It did not seem possible, she was sure she was dreaming. Upon her wide lap, sparking like ice in the light of Fort William's conflagration, were the gems the Chief Magistrate's *goondas* had dug from the wall of her hut. Jaya rose up with a piercing cry that awoke the Devi Ashram. Babies began to howl, women rubbed their eyes and sat up in fear. Jaya stood before them, arms outstretched, her hands filled with a mound of shimmering light. Slowly their fear subsided and the ashram rose in curiosity to draw near the unearthly fire cupped in Jaya's hands.

'It is the work of the Goddess. She has returned to me my diamonds.' Jaya's voice was hoarse with emotion. The miracle pulsated through her.

'Even though she has not shown herself to us for so many days still, she is wanting us to know she is with us. That is why she is giving me back my ornaments.' Jaya began to sob, tears dripping upon the gems. The Devi Ashram pressed about Jaya in wonder. Govindram took the stones in his hands, incredulous, turning them this way and that. Beside him Mohini stared disbelievingly at the jewels and then at Jaya.

'You are sure these are the same ones that were stolen?' Govindram asked.

'Same ones. If you are not believing me, then look at that *badmash* lawyer's paper. Everything is listed there,' Jaya answered.

'Such things you had in Murshidabad?' Mohini queried in a whisper.

Pagal crept forward on his knees towards Jaya's laden hands. *'Reverence. Reverence to Her.'* He swayed backwards and forwards in prayer.

Sati looked at the jewels and then at the hole in the wall behind her grandmother. 'Someone has put them there,' she whispered in Jaya's ear.

'The Goddess has put them there. She is choosing this way to show me she is near,' Jaya reasoned in a low voice that only Sati could hear.

'She is near. Reverence to Her. She is near,' Pagal chanted and his words flowed back down the dark labyrinthine passages beneath the parade ground of Fort William, echoing into the distance.

For some moments the ashram stood as if stupefied before the miracle in Jaya's hands. The meaning of the sign reached each person in different ways, but its effect was always the same. In the rush of wonderment, fatigue was forgotten.

As they stood about Jaya, wrestling with the miracle, there were sudden sounds above. Mothers tried to hush their babies, who only screamed louder. The fiery light at the top of the stairs was suddenly blocked out by the entry of the nawab's soldiers. Jaya quickly thrust her jewels back into their bag and hid them beneath her sari. Then soldiers descended, filling the passages below Fort William, prodding members of the Devi Ashram with musket butts and wooden spears, rounding them up like goats. Soon everyone was pushed up the stairs to face the fire they had fled.

'You are free to go. The nawab has pardoned everyone but the Hatmen,' an officer told them.

The Devi Ashram looked at each other in relief as they were

herded into the parade ground. They tried to form the usual protective circle about Sati, but the soldiers demanded they walk two abreast. They were forced to stand so near the blazing shell of Governor's House that the heat almost seared their flesh. The blaze lit the parade ground like a fireworks display, spitting out light and sparks. Sati looked up at the fiery shell and thought of the Governor's wife. She wondered if the black papery petals of ash that fluttered down upon them were the charred remains of Mrs Drake's petticoats, slippers or books.

Jaya placed herself beside Sati, taking her arm in a protective way. Govindram and Mohini walked ahead and Pagal and his family trailed behind. Before them the officer in charge marched about shouting orders. He frowned as he stopped before Pagal, whose pale presence illuminated the Devi Ashram. Then his eyes moved on to Sati. The light of the blaze fell upon her, sparking in her yellow eyes and her wild tortoiseshell hair.

'Step out here,' the officer shouted in an agitated way. Another soldier at once appeared.

'They are Hatmen, disguising themselves to escape,' the first officer shouted to the others.

Immediately the soldiers thrust the sharp blades of their sabres into the Devi Ashram, cleaving it open. Then, from its midst, as a stone is prised from a piece of fruit, Sati was pulled away and Pagal was dragged out beside her. The women of the ashram began a wail of protest. Govindram stepped forward in fury. Jaya threw herself at the officer in charge, who turned in surprise at her audacity. She shouted to no avail, her voice rising above the crackle of the flames. Govindram attempted to reason with the officer but received a sharp blow with a musket butt. The Devi Ashram was marched away under the threat of guns to the East Gate. Sati and Pagal, under a separate guard, were escorted to the arcade along the east wall.

CHAPTER TWENTY-EIGHT

The Chief Magistrate had not imagined that his meeting with Siraj Uddaulah would take such a humiliating form. He had refused to hand over his sword when the nawab's men entered the fort, although he had relinquished his pistols. His hands had been tied like a common prisoner while he stood in the sun awaiting the nawab. Finally, at the approach of Siraj Uddaulah, the Chief Magistrate had been marched to the top of the ramparts to stand in full view of the nawab's palanquin. The irony of this struck him, for it was at exactly this spot that he had stood so recently in triumph before Fort William. Now, from this same pinnacle, he was forced to watch, like a ceremonial deflowering, the nawab's final penetration of Fort William. The Chief Magistrate pulled himself up and tried to project dignity. This was not easy, for his shoes had been divested of their buckles by looting soldiers, and they flapped about him as he walked. The formal coat he had put on to meet the nawab had similarly been stripped of its silver buttons and hung in a slovenly manner about him. While dressing that morning he had hurriedly donned a wig but the officer who had accompanied him up to the ramparts had accidentally knocked it askew. The Chief Magistrate was aware that every eye within and without the fort was on him. As the nawab's entourage halted before the gate, the Chief

Magistrate at last relinquished his sword before the crowd to a turbanned officer. Although his hands were freed for the ceremony, Holwell knew he must cut a ridiculous figure. He suddenly remembered the fleeing Demonteguy and his fugitive appearance. The nawab approached and the Chief Magistrate made the customary salaam. Looking down from the ramparts of Fort William, Holwell observed the arrogant face of Siraj Uddaulah peering out of his palanquin in open curiosity. The nawab returned the Chief Magistrate's greeting with a casual wave before his litter proceeded towards the fort. Behind him on horseback sat the treacherous Rai Durlabh. The Chief Magistrate had a great desire to throw himself from the ramparts upon the man, but his hands were quickly tied once more. He was marched back to stand again beside the Chaplain and the other survivors of the siege. As they watched, the nawab was carried up the last steps to enter Fort William. His palanquin was set down in the square before Writers' Row.

The Chief Magistrate had expected, as Acting Governor, to be granted an immediate interview with the nawab. Instead he saw Kishindas and then Omichand escorted forward. Kishindas, as a nobleman of royal blood, went first before the nawab, who received him graciously, even presenting him with a ceremonial dress as a sign that all was forgiven. The fat merchant followed, and although he received no gift, it was clear that Siraj Uddaulah did not view him as a conspirator in Fort William's affairs. The Chief Magistrate noted the expression of satisfaction on the merchant's face. Both men were escorted from the fort with considerable pomp.

The Chief Magistrate prepared to step forward but instead found himself ignored once more. Siraj Uddaulah's great palanquin was lifted up again to tour the interior of the fort and enter the Governor's House. The tour was extensive and took much time. The nawab was particularly interested in Drake's private apartment and the manner in which the Governor had lived. The Governor's cupboards were opened and his waistcoats and wigs displayed. The stays and petticoats of the Governor's wife were held up for the nawab's inspection. He had taken a liking to a mahogany coat stand, and secured it as a trophy, along with a set of Mrs Drake's stays. A harpsichord, a fine marquetry table and several sets of chairs, were also carried out. Finally, Siraj Uddaulah returned to the parade ground.

Beside the Chief Magistrate, Reverend Bellamy grew faint as they waited in the heat, and swayed precariously. Although his hands were tied, Holwell turned to the bodyguards in anger, demanding a seat for his friend. The men took no notice, and when he continued with his requests, he was struck in the small of the back with a musket. Eventually Siraj Uddaulah returned from his tour of the defeated fort and the Chief Magistrate was brought before him.

Evening was falling quickly. The last fiery rays of sun licked the beaten-silver birds that covered Siraj Uddaulah's great litter. The Chief Magistrate stood grimly before the nawab, and his bow was a paltry affair. The bodyguard prodded him hard, forcing Holwell to prostrate himself. His wig fell off, revealing to all the closely cropped hair on his head. The dust of the parade ground filled his mouth and he spat out the grit with some force. For this insolence he received a further kick from a guard, so that he sprawled ignominiously before the nawab. Eventually, the Chief Magistrate heard Siraj Uddaulah give a command. Immediately, the bonds about Holwell's wrists were loosed and he was pulled to his feet. He stood up to meet the eyes of the nawab.

'They do not extend the right courtesy to an Acting Governor and for this I apologise.' The nawab spoke through an interpreter.

'We have surrendered in an honourable way. I request honourable treatment for my men and a negotiated settlement,' the Chief Magistrate demanded, brushing the dust from his coat, settling his wig on his head once more. At these words the nawab snorted with anger.

'What is honourable about standing in my way? What is honourable about concealing my treasure? Where is it hidden? Have it brought out.' Siraj Uddaulah leaned forward within his silver litter.

His eyes were of exceptional brightness and glittered now like black quartz. For a moment the Chief Magistrate was taken aback by the sheer force of the nawab's anger.

Rai Durlabh stood silently beside the palanquin, his head held high, his gaze unconcerned. Holwell kept his eyes upon the commander, willing some sign of recognition, but Rai Durlabh was unyielding. He turned his face away, as if the proceedings bored him.

'What treasure we have is in our treasury. Take it if you wish,' Holwell answered; if the mercenaries had not already looted the treasury a few chests of insignificant coins might still remain.

'You have come over the seas to plague my country. The merchant Omichand and my relative Kishindas were imprisoned in this fort and divested of the treasure to satisfy your greed.' The nawab began to grow agitated.

'I know of no treasure, search if you wish.' Holwell stuck to his story. Unbeknown to him the fort had already been searched and the paltry amount of plate and bullion found did not cover the nawab's expectations.

'My treasure is on your ships with your cowardly Governor. I shall pursue it. Did you see him take it when he left? How was it loaded? In how many boxes and chests? It came into this fort from Omichand's house at the time of his arrest; there are witnesses to this. I *will* have what is mine,' the nawab screamed.

The Chief Magistrate lowered his head. The words rained down on him as he knelt before the nawab. The shadows had deepened and already flares were being lit, but Siraj Uddaulah's tirade continued. At last the nawab became silent and looked angrily about him, seeking a way to place his stamp permanently upon Fort William. Turning again to Holwell, he pointed to Governor's House.

'That is the residence of Drake is it not?' he queried, squinting up at the building with an expression Holwell could not interpret.

'It is the Governor's residence,' Holwell confirmed, following the nawab's gaze. A sudden wave of regret trickled through him.

Whatever dreams he had had of eventually taking his place in that mansion must now be temporarily shelved.

'If that is his residence, then burn it,' ordered the nawab as he lay back in his litter. The Chief Magistrate began to protest that the house did not belong personally to Drake, but felt a musket butt strike him again. As he sprawled once more in the dust, Holwell saw the nawab's great litter lifted free of the parade ground for the return to his camp.

'Tonight you will think very hard where the treasure might be. In the morning we shall talk again.' The nawab's voice drifted to Holwell as the litter was borne away.

The Chief Magistrate's hands were not bound again, for the nawab had given orders to treat him and his men with respect. As he returned to Bellamy's side, the first flames shot up the walls of Governor's House. The Chief Magistrate reached out to support the old man who had begun to tremble at the sight of the fire. For some moments they stood silently together, unable to speak for emotion. The guards moved away, and they were left alone. Within reason now it appeared that the Fort William men could wander about, although a strict eye was kept upon them. For a wild moment Holwell wondered if he could retrieve old Jaya's diamonds from their hiding place, but the constant vigilance of the guards made this plan impossible.

A confused crowd still filled the parade ground. Refugees continued to leave the fort, looters went assiduously about their job, gravediggers carted away the piles of rotting corpses left from the siege and vast numbers of the nawab's army drilled wherever they could. The Dutch mercenaries who had betrayed Fort William were now swaggering about the parade ground again, more drunk than ever before. The Fort William men stood about uncertainly, kicking the dust and discussing their chances of escape. They were thirsty, hungry and exhausted. The Chief Magistrate looked about him. So few familiar faces were left. During the last of the fighting all that remained of the garrison had been twenty-five men, and many of these had already departed Fort William, slipping through the nawab's indifferent security. Many in the groups about the Chief Magistrate were, like Bellamy, already sick, touched by fevers or dysentery or badly wounded like young Baillee, Witherington, Blagg and Captain Clayton, all of whom had shared the East Battery with Holwell on the first day of the siege. They were no more than ten men altogether.

Soon the nawab's soldiers approached with a group of sepoys and a few Europeans who had volunteered for the militia from the boats on the Hoogly. Trailing behind were three young writers, Court, Burdet and Walcot. The soldiers began to round up the Fort William men and finally ordered everyone across the parade ground. The Chief Magistrate took the Chaplain by the arm to help him forward. Bellamy leaned heavily on Holwell and his breath came in short, laboured gasps. In spite of the warm night, his hand on the Chief Magistrate's arm was cold.

'They are taking us to the open barracks along the east wall. There we shall have a passable night.' The Chief Magistrate tried to cheer the Chaplain as they proceeded towards the area where Omichand had been confined.

Fire now circled them wherever they looked. There appeared to be no building in Fort William that had not been torched. 'They wish to burn us. That way we can then be got rid of without trace or explanation,' the Chaplain panted. Behind them the men of Fort William followed, those few like the Chief Magistrate who were in reasonable health helping forward those who were afflicted by illness or wounds.

Eventually they reached the colonnaded arches of the east wall and sat down gratefully on the wooden benches there. The Chaplain leaned back, breathing hard. A short distance away a group of Dutch mercenaries were fraternising loudly with the nawab's professional looters. All had been drinking hard. By now the Fort William men were sitting comfortably. The wounded were helped to stretch themselves out, and what little could be done for them was done. It seemed as if a destination had been reached at last, and the morning light would bring a turning point of more positive dimensions.

'We have been left unmolested. Probably when this army is fed, which must be soon, we too shall be given food. After all, dead men cannot lead the nawab to his treasure. Besides, he needs our trade too badly to be rid of us,' the Chief Magistrate reasoned to Bellamy.

Before them the parade ground was filled with distorted shadows and the fierce, garish light of the fires. The sound of the muezzin calling the army to prayer rose above the crackling and the crashing of falling timber.

The men of Fort William began to relax. Their thoughts turned now to the food they felt sure they would soon receive. Some had already fallen asleep. All were unprepared for the musket shot which rang out suddenly a short distance away. They sat up with a start, peering into the night. The trouble appeared to be with the drunken Dutch mercenaries, who had taken a quarrel with the nawab's looters to dangerous extremes. At the intervention of a soldier, the mercenaries had became even more riotous. One had pulled a pistol from his belt and shot the soldier at point-blank range. The man now lay slumped on the ground in a heap. Immediately a crowd of officers ran up and an argument began. The dead man was dragged away and the five Dutch mercenaries were escorted to the Black Hole and locked away within it. They banged on the door and yelled from the barred windows, all to no avail. The men of Fort William sat on their benches, observing the scene with interest.

'They may be common mercenaries, but their behaviour reflects upon us. In the nawab's eyes we are all birds of a feather. The fools have done us no good,' the Chief Magistrate grumbled. He was worried for Bellamy, whose fever raged. The groans of Baillee, Clayton and Witherington, who were all afflicted with musket wounds, filled him with foreboding.

The nawab's soldiers walked back to their posts, giving the men of Fort William no more than a cursory glance, so that they settled down again to await the food they hoped would soon appear. Some dozed off once more. The young writers, Burdet, Walcot and Court, played five-stones to pass the time with some chips of brick found beneath the benches. Bellamy began to mutter deliriously but there was nothing Holwell could do to help him. The evening wore slowly on. No food appeared, although smells of cooking drifted to them, aggravating their misery.

Although the evening appeared dull, the Fort William men were unaware that word of the Dutch mercenaries' drunken bawl had been relayed to the nawab. His advisers counselled that if a single Hatman, even if of a lesser caste than the Chief Magistrate and his men, could cause such trouble then a large group, left at liberty through the night, might eventually prove disastrous.

The nawab was tired after his exhausting day. Now that he had viewed the inside of Fort William and the home of the irritating Drake was destroyed, he had no energy left to think further of the Hatmen. He too was waiting for his dinner and had already consumed copious amounts of wine in celebration of his victory.

'Where in the fort are prisoners usually confined?' he asked in a weary voice.

'In a cell they call the Black Hole,' his officer replied.

'Confine them there then, until the morning, when I shall see that Chief Magistrate again.'

Eventually this message returned to Fort William. The officers in charge of the fort were relieved to receive clear instructions. A group of Hatmen sitting about like honourable visitors had been a worry to them all. Immediately, soldiers with muskets advanced towards the seated Europeans and ordered them to the Black Hole.

'What is the meaning of this? We have sick and wounded amongst us who are in need of attention.' The Chief Magistrate placed himself before the men, refusing to take a step forward.

'The room is too small for so many,' Holwell protested once more as the nawab's orders were repeated. But before a plethora of swords, clubs and lighted torches, there was little further appeal to be made. The men gathered together, supporting their sick and wounded.

'What exactly is the nature of this place?' the Chaplain whispered hoarsely to Holwell. He leaned heavily on the Chief Magistrate as he stumbled forward. The Chief Magistrate said nothing for fear of alarming the Chaplain.

'Let us stay where we are,' Bellamy pleaded querulously. His words were lost in the general protest as soldiers began to prod the group towards the waiting cell.

The doors of the Black Hole stood open and the Fort William men were pushed inside. The Dutch mercenaries rose at their entrance and showed great annoyance at being pressed to the walls by the influx of so many men. As the Chief Magistrate had placed himself at the head of the group, he was the first to enter the Black Hole. Behind him Fort William men fell over one another as they were pressed in roughly behind him. Including the five Dutch mercenaries, there were soon thirty men or more wedged tightly into the inadequate room.

The Chief Magistrate at once took charge of the situation, ordering men to arrange themselves in such a way that all might sit in some small space. This seemed possible only if everybody drew their knees up beneath their chins and allowed their feet to be sat on. The Chief Magistrate was deeply involved in these manoeuvres, which were made doubly difficult by the darkness, when the sound of bolts being drawn alerted them all once more. The cramped conditions behind the door made it almost impossible to open. It swung inwards on its hinges and crushed those in its way unbearably. The guards pushed from the outside until the space were enough to thrust into the room a young girl and a fair-haired man. Beyond the barred windows the burning torches of the guards threw a flickering light into the Black Hole. The man and the girl stood pressed up against the door, looking helplessly about.

'Here.' The Chief Magistrate beckoned to the woman, anxious to show some courtliness to a vulnerable creature, although in the darkness he could see little of her. The fair-haired man wore a tattered *lungi*. The Chief Magistrate did not recognise him, but many of the young writers took to wearing Indian fashions at home in the worst of the heat. With great difficulty the pair, stepping over the squash of seated men, made their way towards the Chief Magistrate.

'There is a sleeping shelf here, sit yourself upon it,' Holwell said to the girl. A few inches of space was made for her to sit by those already wedged upon the plinth, and the man squatted down as best he could beside her.

The Chief Magistrate wondered briefly how a woman came to be amongst them, but there was so much of a threatening nature to be considered that he let the thought pass from his mind. Then a guard, pressing his flare up to the window to monitor conditions inside, lit the room briefly for a moment. The Chief Magistrate found himself staring straight into Sati's yellow eyes.

Raja Rai Durlabh turned the silver cup in his hand. Hours of victorious drinking had blurred his mind. Beyond his tent the sounds of revelry pushed deep into the night. As soon as he could, he had left the celebration. He had drunk with the nawab and his coterie until they were too inebriated to notice his departure. Things had not turned out as expected, but there was nothing he could do. The sense of realignment that Alivardi's death had brought about still reverberated through Murshidabad. It was too risky to take a stand against the nawab in the way the English expected. Even so much as a glance in the Hatmen's direction would be to doom himself. Patience was now the essence of the game, for events had moved too quickly. Before long Siraj Uddaulah would be deposed, he had only to bide his time, Rai Durlabh decided. Yet the sight of Holwell prostrated before the nawab had filled him with strange feelings. Rai Durlabh had felt no pity for the man, so full of petty ambition; seeing the Chief Magistrate sprawled so ignominiously in the dust had only brought home his own vulnerability. The course of events, like the currents of a river, could never be predicted.

Except for the occasional ascetic, all men desired money and power; the English were no different. Yet they were like children, going straight towards a goal, looking neither right nor left. And in this, like children, they were dangerous, thought Rai Durlabh. When a lie might serve them better, they naively told the truth. They did not see that truth should be used with caution, a little at a time.

The image of Holwell, forced down in the dust before the nawab, came to Rai Durlabh again. He lifted his cup and drained it quickly of wine. In the sky a new moon had emerged and the build-up of clouds already heralded the monsoon. He could take but one step at a time.

CHAPTER TWENTY-NINE

The hours stretched before the Chief Magistrate in a nightmarish way. He stood with his back pressed against the wall,
unable to sit for the pressure of bodies about him. With so
many confined to so small a room, the heat grew quickly intense.
The Chief Magistrate was glad he had divested himself of his wig and
coat while sitting outside on the bench. For some reason he had kept
hold of his hat and found a new use for it now as he began to fan
himself. On entering the Black Hole, he had immediately positioned
himself beside one of the two small windows, and whatever the
pushing and shoving about him, he clung to the bars determinedly.
His visits to Omichand had given him the advantage of knowing
beforehand the sparse geography of the room. He pressed his face to
the bars and the smell of fire filled his nose. Space was at such a
premium that the sick and wounded could not be made comfortable
and their distress was pitiful to hear. Those still wearing coats had
taken them off and rolled them up as pillows for the afflicted. The
metallic stench of blood seeped from the wounded and the Chief
Magistrate worried that they must pass so many hours unattended,
for their wounds were of a dire nature. The Chaplain too, weak and
feverish, could no longer sit and had sunk awkwardly between the

knees of those behind him, his eyes closed and his mouth hanging open.

The Dutch mercenaries had made their way to the door, trampling indifferently on whoever sat in their path. They attempted to force the entrance open but their endeavours were fruitless. Since he was at the window, the Chief Magistrate called to the guards outside. They yawned and turned away. Only one old man shuffled forward and, holding up his lighted flare, gazed in at conditions within the Black Hole.

'Release us. We will give you as many gold mohars as you want,' the Chief Magistrate offered in a pidgin language.

The old man drew back into the darkness to confer with his friends. Soon he returned, shaking his head. 'It cannot be done but by the nawab's order. Now he sleeps and no one dares wake him.' The man vanished into the darkness again. In the Black Hole, men began to panic. The Chief Magistrate attempted to restore some order again.

'The night ahead will be uncomfortable, but we shall get through it if we remain calm and do not unnecessarily exert ourselves. We are in need of more air and this we can produce if those few of us with hats use them to stir the atmosphere.' The Chief Magistrate fanned himself to demonstrate. Those who could followed his lead, and for some moments a slight draught circulated about the Black Hole. This effort could not be continued in an effective way, for the men were generally dehydrated and were unable to support such continuous activity. The Dutch mercenaries jeered loudly when the fanning eventually dwindled away.

The Chief Magistrate's main concern now was for Bellamy, who appeared almost comatose. Holwell had placed him near the window, propped up against the wall. The Chaplain opened his eyes as Holwell fanned him, but seemed not to recognise him.

'Water. Water.' The call now swelled within the room. The Chief Magistrate turned again to the window to summon the guards. At his insistence the same old man shuffled over once more and listened to the new request, nodding in sympathy. He withdrew and after some time reappeared with a water skin. The sight of the wet leather, gleaming in the light of the flares, had an immediate effect upon the incarcerated men. Those who had managed before to control themselves now gave way to hysteria. The greatest obstacle to assuaging their thirst was getting the water through the bars of the window. It seemed that the only means of doing this was by way of the few hats that had earlier been used for fanning.

The Chief Magistrate, and those others who were near the two small windows, held up to the bars the three or four hats that were available. Although the old man outside with the water skin filled these containers in an affable manner, the ferment within the Black Hole was so great, and fights to possess the soggy cups so vicious, that most were overturned before even a sip could be taken. The velour quickly absorbed what little liquid remained. The result of this activity was that everyone became even thirstier than before. The sight of water that could not be reached drove the most sanguine of men insane. Outside the window there were now guards who had not the sympathy of the shuffling old man and who, for the pleasure of seeing the Hatmen struggle, brought further skins of water to repeat the process until they grew bored. The Chief Magistrate was able to bring a little water, cupped in his own palm, to the Chaplain's lips. Bellamy was unable to swallow and the liquid dribbled down his chin.

All about the Chief Magistrate men groaned in new despair. The temperature in the small room had taken on the element of something solid, pressing upon them like a pillow that would suffocate them all. The Chief Magistrate concentrated on his breathing and tried to think in a positive manner. Although the Black Hole was cruelly cramped, they were not without some air. Men had been confined in worse conditions. He had recently read of a privateer captured by the French. The crew of this ship had been confined in the hold for two days with neither water nor air. It was said those who survived had been forced to drink their own urine collected in the heels of their shoes, and had sucked their own shirts for perspiration to alleviate their thirst.

'Only keep calm and all will be well. We have some air and enough space to be seated,' Holwell reminded them all. His words renewed a fragile hope.

The Chief Magistrate still clung to his place at the window, but he wondered now if he could risk a change of seat to rest his weary limbs. He looked towards the wooden platform, already crammed with men, that ran the length of the Black Hole, and longed to stretch out on it. No sooner did he think this than he saw the dim outline of Sati, illuminated by the flare of a passing guard. All the while, whatever anguish filled each moment, he had been conscious of her presence. It was as if fate had brought her here with the sole purpose of tormenting him further. He peered into the blackness, and although he could make out little in the dark and palpitating room, he sensed her yellow eyes upon him. He had built his life of solid blocks, but she was like a weed growing within the interstices that might one day undermine foundations. He did not want to remember that long-ago day, buried now beneath the years, when her amber eyes had fixed upon him in a way he would never forget. He had sealed away the memory of that day but it welled up now to claim him, like a tentacle uncoiling in the darkness.

He remembered how he had gone to Rita as usual, but earlier than expected. The servants were reluctant to admit him but he had pushed his way in. He had found her naked upon her bed, head thrown back, her slim thighs wound about a dark and ugly specimen of a man who was working himself upon her. The bald, loose cheeks of his buttocks heaved and thrust before the Chief Magistrate's affronted gaze. Holwell had backed hurriedly away, closing the door, his mind in turmoil. Yet, against his will, he was horrified to find the blood rushing through his veins, hardening his own body. He pressed his back against the wall as if to control his fury and despised himself for still wanting to suck at Rita's dark nipples, for needing her oiled and supple limbs to draw him to her centre. Until that moment he had had no idea that she even saw other men. He had thought himself the only one. His rage grew with the shattering of this conceit. If he had arrived when expected he would have innocently bathed in the juices of the grunting creature who had peceded him. Everything in him exploded in revulsion. He hated what she did to him.

His anger pounded within him like a creature that would burst its way out of his body. As he stepped away from the door of Rita's room he found he faced her daughter, already now twelve years old. With her yellow cat's eyes and unruly tortoiseshell hair, she would soon be ready for the whorehouses of Black Town, thought the Chief Magistrate in a wave of fresh agitation. He had been trapped by the evil of these lustful women who knew nothing of Christian morality. He had stepped forward, he now remembered, and had taken the child's arm in sudden resolution, dragging her after him. Even now, remembering his shame at Rita's door, his anger rose like the after-effects of food sodden with chillies.

At the sudden release of these long-buried memories, the sweat flowed copiously from the Chief Magistrate. He perspired now not from the heat pressing about him but for something he experienced within himself. A new wash of terror consumed him. He slid down to crouch between the comatose Chaplain and a panting Mr Eyre, the Storekeeper. He was trembling with emotion. The memory of Rita, so unexpectedly awoken, stayed with him, and the yellow eyes of her daughter locked upon him from across the fetid cell would, he feared, never now be banished.

The guards outside the Black Hole had withdrawn a short distance and the occasional glimmer of light their torches shed through the windows of the cell had vanished. The blackness, pressing about the Chief Magistrate, was filled with tortured groans. Something seemed to push deep into his body, searching as if for the thread of his life to pull until it unravelled. His heart thrashed in his chest. It was as if something within him, bigger than himself, now unfolded to split him open. He feared the very force of his life would seep from him to mix with the darkness about him. There was a species of spider in his house that if squashed oozed an umber blood, as if bleeding its own store of evil. Long after it was cleared, a dark shadow remained on the floor. The Chief Magistrate dropped his head into his hands. The door to a dungeon within him had opened and the mess of his life trickled out.

He stood up again and pressed his face to the bars of the window, gulping in the still air. Someone tried to push him aside, but Holwell clung to his hold. The Reverend Bellamy slumped heavily against his legs, making balance difficult. The strong odour of burning entered the cell and filled the Chief Magistrate's head. Across the parade ground Fort William continued to burn. Holwell stared at the heaps of blackened timber visible through the flames, and drew a shuddering breath, for overriding even the smell of burning, the scent of the river came to him again as if locking on to him at his weakest moment. For a moment he had a vision of the black goddess dancing like an ugly goblin in the dark. Wherever death lurked, the dreadful creature appeared. Such an anger rose up in the Chief Magistrate then that he feared his head might burst. He was at a loss to know what spawned such hatred. He stood with his face pressed against the bars of the Black Hole and knew at last that he was defined by what he hated. He was not ashamed; the emotion had kept him strong in a place that would long ago have destroyed him.

In the darkness now the Chief Magistrate began to see shapes that were not of this world. He reached out a hand in fear, as if something tangible floated before him. A guard with a flare came again to peer through the window. The sudden glow illuminated the far corners of the room. The Chief Magistrate turned and, as he knew he would, stared straight into the yellow eyes of Rita's daughter. A fresh wave of panic filled him. Against his will he remembered the grotesque voice that had issued from the girl the night of the seance in Demonteguy's house. He remembered the diamonds he had stolen from her. And now the memory of that day long ago in Rita's house when the girl was twelve years old was before him at every turn. Perhaps the girl was possessed, just as they said. Perhaps, as they said, the black goddess resided within her. Now fate had placed her here in this prison, as if to put her in charge of his suffering. The heat of his thoughts beat against his skull. He turned from the window and began to stumble across the cell. His mind ran liquidly now.

CHAPTER THIRTY

S ati sat where the Chief Magistrate had placed her, too terrified to move. Pagal was slumped at her feet, one side of his face a bloodied mess where the guards had beaten him. The heat and stench in the cell were unbearable. Occasionally the flares of passing guards threw a weak light into the Black Hole. As far as Sati could see, there appeared to be no other women besides herself. Hatmen and rough soldiers filled the place. Many were wounded, and, with the heat and lack of attention, appeared on the point of expiring. The Chief Magistrate had a place at the window. The light of the fires outside illuminated his shape dimly. She wanted to turn away but felt forced to keep her eyes on him in order to protect herself. Her fear at the suffocating crush of desperate men faded to nothing before the sight of the Chief Magistrate. At her feet Pagal now appeared to have fallen into a troubled doze. She shook him gently but he did not stir and she let him sleep. At times he called for water, muttering and groaning in delirium. A guard passed again with a flare and stopped to stare through the window. By the light of the torch she could see the severity of the wounds to Pagal's head. The soldiers had beaten him mercilessly before throwing them into the prison. She feared he might die in the night, leaving her alone. New panic filled her and, looking wildly about, she met the Chief Magistrate's eyes once more.

For a moment he stared at her, then, stepping unsteadily between the crush of men, he began to push his way across the room.

The guard with the torch moved away but the faint light of the fires outside was enough to show Sati the Chief Magistrate moving towards her. Fear tightened in her throat. Soon he would stand before her, his shadow merging with the blackness to envelop her entirely. A fragment of memory thrust suddenly into her mind. Once, long before, she remembered the Chief Magistrate's shadow had fallen upon her. She had been standing in a long bright room. She recalled the whorls on the floorboards and a picture on a wall. In her mind there was a boundary to the pool of light, beyond which, however hard she tried, she could not see. It was as if some knowledge was denied her. This sliver of memory frightened her whenever it appeared, moving like something unhinged in her mind, filling her body with weight. The Chief Magistrate had manoeuvred the last few yards of the tightly-packed room and finally stood before her. She drew away in terror but the brick wall pressed hard against her back. The Chief Magistrate towered above her.

'Durga.' For the first time in days she whispered the name and touched the amulet in her neck, willing the spirit to come.

Immediately obedient to the summons, Durga showed herself. Sati saw her dancing on the bodies of the suffering men, surrounded by light in the dark cell. As she watched, Durga sailed out through the window and circled above the guards. When she dived back into the room, there were sparks of fire in her hair. She flew towards Sati, diving deep within her, lifting her away from the Chief Magistrate's grasp just as in the temple she had lifted her away from the bamboo cane. Sati felt herself float free of her physical body again, light as gossamer. Looking down from a height, she could see herself, cowering fearfully in her corner. Above her the ceiling of filthy bricks was shiny with moisture. A gecko ran across it, a spider sat in his web in a corner. At the window Sati breathed in the still night air and observed the smouldering heap of embers that had once been Governor's House. The flowery balcony Mrs Drake had stood on was gone. Sati stared at the smoking rubble. She searched the distant river for the *Dodaldy*'s lanterns but there was nothing to see. Mrs Drake's ship had moved down river, away from the dangers of Siraj Uddaulah.

Thoughts of the Governor's wife still lingered in her mind. She was tied in some way to Mrs Drake, just as she was tied to Durga. Karma was a strange thing. She knew that sometimes soul wandered in the lives of a worm, an elephant or a moth, and in whichever of life's mazes it struggled, karma bound a soul to others. Something she would never understand bound her to Mrs Drake. At last Sati turned her gaze away from the window to observe the Chief Magistrate. Something drew her gaze to that sinister shadow, just as her mind bent to the thought of Mrs Drake. It was as if he waited for her. The very darkness of the Black Hole seemed to spread out from the Chief Magistrate's body, like a billowing cloak. Hidden beneath it wrestled things too gnarled to risk the light. Far below she saw herself cringe against the wall as the Chief Magistrate leaned over her. As she knew he would, he reached out a hand and touched her.

His thin fingers burned her skin. Until now, suspended far above her body, Sati had looked on, detached from the things that happened in the room. But the shock of the Chief Magistrate's touch ricocheted up to her. She felt herself plummet downwards then, back into her terrified body. She found herself staring up into the Chief Magistrate's face.

'Durga,' she screamed.

And immediately Durga was alert, preparing to fight Sati's battle. Sati felt herself slip away within her own body, giving Durga the space to live. Durga's deep voice rose above the whimpering men, loud enough to stir Pagal from his stupor. He raised his battered, bloody head at the familiar sound and smiled.

'The Goddess has returned,' he whispered.

Under Durga's direction Sati stood up, uncurling slowly like a bud, until she faced the Chief Magistrate. From her mouth Durga's raw voice flowed out.

In the room men stirred, trying to comprehend what was happening. Pagal managed to get up on his knees.

'The Goddess is here. *Reverence. Reverence to Her. Reverence.*' He dragged himself forward, dipping his head to Sati's feet.

The Chief Magistrate understood enough of the language to catch the meaning of Pagal's words. He gave a low growl of fury, and turned on the albino. Pagal's pale face confronted him, as it had on that night of confusion in the parade ground.

'Goddess? What goddess? I'll show you what she is.' Holwell gripped Sati's arm, shaking her like a dog.

'No!' Sati screamed, and the cry was her own.

In just this way, with just this degree of terror, she knew now she had stared up at him once before. At last a door swung open in her mind, she remembered it all. The bright room was before her again and now there was no dark boundary hiding knowledge in its shadow. Filled with the afternoon sun, the room stretched away to the brilliance of a long window. In this illuminated place, she remembered, she had looked up to see the Chief Magistrate coming towards her. His shadow had suddenly fallen on her, cutting off the flood of light. She had looked down at the warm polished boards of the floor and seen the darkness of him stretching out as far as she could see in an elongated shape. He had reached out and gripped her arm, propelling her forward, his fingers digging deep into her flesh. She had been forced to cross the bright room enclosed within the Chief Magistrate's shadow. She had been twelve years old.

She recalled entering a further room and then the slamming of a door. She remembered how her hands had fastened on a book and then on a china figurine, hurling them at the forbidding figure before her. These items had fallen ineffectually at the Chief Magistrate's feet. Her screams had filled her ears, blocking out all other sound, but nobody came. The Chief Magistrate clamped a hand on her mouth. She remembered next the feeling of falling, and of the brightness about her vanishing. A weight sank down on her; something so heavy it pressed her flat, like a delicate flower trapped in the leaves of a book. She could not breathe, she could not move. No voice came from her throat. The darkness tumbled about her, smelling of sourness and sweat. The Chief Magistrate appeared to hang above her like a spider, waiting to devour her. She was drowning in the darkness of his shadow, already it ran in her flesh. His chin dug into her shoulder, his bones grinding upon her own. She tried to fight but could not lift the weight of him off her. The great wrestling force of the Chief Magistrate pushed her further into darkness, tearing her limbs apart. Soon she was sure she must die. Yet at that moment when she thought death must come, life returned in a great searing pain, ripping her body in two. She began to scream and heard again the sound of her own voice. Suddenly then, she felt herself soar up, free of the Chief Magistrate, free of her body.

There had been no Durga then to guide her. She had floated, a fragment of herself, high above the scene in the room, looking down without emotion. She knew instinctively that what she saw had nothing to do with her. She was safe above it all. Far below her the Chief Magistrate was splayed on the floor in such a way that she thought him dead. But then he moved and with the litheness of an animal gathered himself together and stood up. She saw then that something lay beneath him, pitifully squashed. She saw with surprise that it was herself. The Chief Magistrate straightened his jacket and pulled his breeches into place. He turned and left the room.

She had known then of no way to return to her body. Instead she had listened to the soughing of the hot wind in the shutters and the cries of birds and animals. She had watched the day disappear over the river and darkness stream in with the stars. Below, in the room, that other half of her made no movement at all. She did not recall the moment of her return, when her ripped and oozing body summoned her back into its shell. She had woken in her grandmother's arms, the old woman's tears falling copiously on her.

Much later she had woken again to darkness and seen through the window a solitary star. She no longer remembered the pain, but only the feeling of her own solitude, cold as that distant star. At that moment she knew she had broken in two and would never be whole again.

Now, as she stood before the Chief Magistrate in the stinking cell they called the Black Hole, the knowledge denied her for so long flooded her again. At last she was once more in possession of the bright room in her memory. Nothing was now refused her and would never be again. This sudden revelation flooded through her and was immediately sensed by the Chief Magistrate. He let go of her arm and drew back, his breath still sounding hard in his chest. As light is deflected from a bright surface, he felt the strength of her will turn against him.

She knew now she was free of his power. Something had unravelled and in the darkness she burned suddenly with new fire. The night would soon end and she would be free to give birth to the wholeness inside her.

'Reverence. Reverence to Her.' Pagal's voice flapped up and down deliriously.

There were Portuguese soldiers in the room whose European blood, over generations of intermarriage, had been diluted to such a degree that they were now a fierce ebony. Although they pronounced themselves Christian, they could never shed, however hard the Church tried, the voluptuous comfort of ancient ways instilled by their Indian mothers. They had heard from their wives of the Goddess who sheltered with the refugees and now they pushed forward in the darkness, stumbling over compatriots and Hatmen, the wounded and the newly dead to reclaim their souls. They began uttering unfamiliar words, moving rusty ancestor thoughts, trusting suddenly in old gods.

'Reverence. Reverence to Her.' They tried to fall to their knees beside Pagal, but in the confined space, they succeeded only in trampling on distraught men.

Sati turned away from the men crowding at her feet and leaned back against the wall to wait for the morning light.

The Chief Magistrate might stand before her still, but she would never again be in fear of him. Durga too had suddenly vanished and might never return; she was free of all her fears.

Sometime that night Pagal died. The Reverend Bellamy, young Baillee, Clayton, Blagg and Witherington and the several wounded militiamen followed shortly after him. For Pagal, at least, the Goddess had waited to guide him through the perilous passage from one realm to the next. He died with her name upon his lips.

At six in the morning the nawab, in his camp of tents, had enquired after his prisoners and been given a report of the difficult night passed by all in the Black Hole. He had been surprised and upbraided his men for causing the Hatmen so much discomfort. He ordered all but Holwell and three other Hatmen – to be randomly chosen by the guards – to be released. At once the door of the Black Hole was opened. The remaining Hatmen trooped out, followed by the Dutch mercenaries and the Portuguese sepoys, who were now much subdued. All were ordered to sit on the benches outside the Black Hole. The fresh air and the sun, a drink of water and the fist of bread they were now given soon restored vital energy. The Chief Magistrate's concern now was that a proper respect be shown for Bellamy's corpse. He got up, intending to return to his dead friend, but was pushed back into place by a guard.

Soon the bodies of those who had died in the night were dragged out of the Black Hole. The Chief Magistrate saw Clayton and Blagg and then Witherington pulled out by their feet and heaved on to a cart. Next Baillee's body and two Indian militiamen, humped over the shoulders of soldiers like meat from the abattoir, were dumped on top of them. Bellamy was then brought out and, however much the Chief Magistrate protested, was flung into the cart over Baillee. Pagal, the flaxen stubble on his head bright in the morning sun, was thrown on top of them all. There was nothing the Chief Magistrate could do to stop the albino's inclusion in the funeral cart. The troops clearing the bodies from the Black Hole had mistaken him for a European. This troubled the Chief Magistrate, for now it appeared the man would be buried with them. The Chief Magistrate rose to protest once more but was pushed back on to the bench with a musket. The thought that Bellamy and the other men would not get even the briefest of funerals filled him with fresh horror. Once the carts were full, they set off, trundled by oxen towards The Avenue. There, the Chief Magistrate was told, the bodies would be buried in the trench that had been dug across The Park. The Chief Magistrate followed Bellamy's stiff pink legs – all he could now see of the Chaplain – until the cart disappeared from sight.

Within a short while guards came up. They stared at the Fort William men, conferred briefly, and then pulled out from amongst them the three young writers, Burdet, Court and Walcot. It was announced that all but Holwell and these three young men were free to go. The Chief Magistrate was forced to sit outside the Black Hole and watch the men with whom he had shared such a nightmarish time quickly depart Fort William. Beside him on the benches, Burdet, Court and Walcot searched once more for chips of brick with which to play five-stones. In the interval the Chief Magistrate's thoughts turned again to old Jaya's diamonds. From where he sat, he could see the dark hole upon the parade ground that was the entrance to the warehouses. The thought of the gems shut away in their sepulchre now filled the Chief Magistrate's mind. He stood up as if to go to them and then sat down once more. How would he reach them unseen by the guards? How would he keep them safely upon his person? Questions buzzed painfully in his mind like an insect that could not get free. There was no choice, the Chief Magistrate decided, but to leave them for the time being in their grave. He would find a way to return to them later.

Before long, Siraj Uddaulah arrived once more in Fort William to interrogate the Chief Magistrate on the whereabouts of the Begum's treasure. The Chief Magistrate was marched to the parade ground to stand before the nawab's silver litter again. His dishevelled appearance and obvious fatigue took the nawab by surprise. He ordered a chair brought forth for Holwell, but was told all the Hatmen's furniture had been destroyed in the fire. Eventually a set of folio volumes discovered in a heap of plunder were found and piled up for the Chief Magistrate to sit on. Immediately, Holwell recognised them as part of the library housed in the Council chamber. He placed himself reluctantly on them, yet even when seated, the Chief Magistrate could no better oblige with information than the night before. Siraj Uddaulah grew incresingly testy.

'Then you shall remain under my command until you remember better,' the nawab at last declared.

The Chief Magistrate stood but his knees trembled so badly he was obliged to sit down again on the leather-bound books. He looked up at the sky but was immediately blinded by sun. A guard approached with fetters.

Sati had followed the other prisoners from the Black Hole and walked with them from Fort William. Once out of the gate, she looked towards the charred mess of Black Town and then at the remains of The Avenue. She began to make her way towards Omichand's house, where she was sure Govindram would be.

CHAPTER THIRTY-ONE

Emily Drake watched as the *Dodaldy* drew steadily further away over the water. The small boat in which she sat rocked upon the tide. In the early morning light the *Dodaldy* acquired the quality of a Chinese ink painting, half folded into the night. The sound of the waves splashed against the craft. She trailed her hand in the water until the river ran in her flesh, as if it was one with her.

She had stood in front of Mrs Mackett and Mrs Bellamy and made the arrangements herself in the local language, showing the man the money beforehand. The women gave her no more than a desultory glance. She could not believe they did not recognise her beneath the turban and dirty face. It immediately gave her hope.

Hanging on a makeshift washing line she had found a *lungi* and a shirt and then a length of cloth for a turban. Roger Drake slept heavily in the roundhouse; the morning light filtering through the window had not yet disturbed him. Behind a screen Emily discarded her dress and stays and put on the strange new clothes. She had untied her hair and cut it off roughly close to her head, then wound the turban about it. She had wrapped her hair in a piece of sacking, stuffing it into a bag with a few other necessities. Then, hesitantly, she had looked in the mirror and been surprised; even in the brightest light she might not be recognised. She left a letter for her husband propped up on his mahogany washstand. Once the shock and humiliation were digested she doubted he would look back. She turned once at the door and watched as he snored, his face squashed loosely in sleep, then hurried to the stairs. Many small craft came about the ship at this time of day, bringing fresh produce, taking off washing or men. She had been confident from the start she could persuade one of the boatmen to take her to the shore.

Now, as Calcutta edged closer, the first doubts seeped into her mind. The water was cool upon her hand and the force of the current against her fingers brought her back to herself. Something had been captive, held to ransom in her life. Now a creature separate from herself had taken command of her. Upon the gently rocking *Dodaldy*, that she had fought so hard against boarding, this wild woman had insidiously emerged. Day or night, the heady scent of the river spiralled in Emily's head. The sight of the water stretching about her, flowing always anew upon its journey seemed to enter her body. She could not take her eyes from the river, leaning constantly upon the rail. The wash of its waves and the smell of the water were forever in her head. And all the while the slap and creak of the billowing sails seemed to lift her out of herself. It was as if another river ran beneath this river, and within it flowed her life.

The same voice that had whispered in Fort William, *Do this, do that. Go here, go there,* whispered again to her. But now that strange woman was out in the open, billowing like the creaking sails, luscious and powerful to behold. Emily Drake grew weak before her. This woman, discarded, devalued, in every way unacceptable, had lain in darkness planning the jump to freedom. If Harry had not died she might never have felt the moment ripe to boil up from her shadowy place. Now that she was prancing about so recklessly, there was no way to put her back. Emily was like the tail of a kite, winging helplessly through the air behind her, powerless to do more than follow. She had trusted to something inexplicable, just as now, without trepidation, she had handed herself to the river. Whatever it was that commanded her was wiser than she was. She reached out a hand to cup the river in her palm and watched it run through her fingers. The same essence that flowed through the river flowed in the veins of the woman steering her now to her fate.

The mist on the river had lifted. The morning was already spilling out its fierce heat. A net of dark clouds drifted forward slowly, a harbinger of the monsoon. The boatman did not give her a second glance as he chatted. She had told him she was from Afghanistan, for this would cover any oddity of speech or paleness of skin and eyes. The *Dodaldy* drew further away and the figures on the deck no longer seemed real. On the shore cooking fires smoked into the morning. Now at last she drew from her bag the parcel of hair. A sudden revulsion filled her. The hair was weightless and yet in her hands she held the very thread of her life. She was impatient to be rid of it. As the boat drew nearer the shore, she cast this obsolete part of herself to the waves. Water quickly flooded the soft sacking and drew the parcel down. For as long as she could she followed its descent as it journeyed amongst the dark bodies of fish. It gave her a strange satisfaction to know some part of her would now swim with the river, dispersing in a million fine filaments to mix at last with the sea.

She drew a breath and the scent of the river knotted in her head. The grotto on the hill above the Kali Mandhir came suddenly into her mind. As she had left the blazing sun to enter that dark cave she had been robbed of sight, waiting blindly between two worlds, unable to see her way forward. She had trusted then to something larger than herself, and slowly the darkness had cleared and she had passed to where the Goddess waited. On the river now she knew herself to be in that same place of passage. This journey across the water was a journey of return. And yet the land before her was not the place she travelled to. Already she was as if dead to that world, but death's road seemed to lead to life's door. She looked again towards the shore, to the growing coils of smoke from early morning cooking fires and the smell of burning cow dung lifting strongly over the water.

Eventually they reached the quay. The boatman set her down near

Fort William. No one took any notice of her as she walked along the wharf. She had not planned to return to the fort, but the boatman had landed here. Already the sight of Fort William's grey walls, pitted by cannon, filled her with heaviness. She dreaded the moment she must turn into the fort, forced again to face her old home, to touch the cradle, to open a drawer, to run a finger over a book. The past lay upon her like armour, within which she might be caught forever.

The fort bustled with activity; the nawab's soldiers ambled in and out. Everywhere she looked was familiar and yet something appeared to be wrong. She entered the fort without difficulty but came to a halt in shock. Fort William was nothing but the sum of its walls. The proud life it had enclosed was gone. Charred mounds of burned rubble were all that remained of Governor's House, the armoury, the laboratory and Writers' Row. She stared about disbelieving. Someone pushed roughly against her but still she did not move. All that she had been was now wiped from the earth. Not an article remained, not a book, a glove, a ribbon or a letter. The child's cradle was gone and his small muslin robes, her tapestry, her footstool, her flowery balcony and its view of the Hoogly, all were gone now from her forever. Only the residue of memory remained. She owned nothing but a man's stolen *lungi*, a turban and a shirt. Even her gender had been misplaced. She was thrust roughly across a boundary, as if something were recast.

There was nothing to stay for. She left by the East Gate, coming down on to The Avenue. There was a lightness now in her step. She walked quickly along Fort William's walls until she came to the cemetery. A short distance away stood the remains of the Chief Magistrate's house, charred and deeply gashed, its innards revealed for all to see, looted of its finery. The gate to the cemetery swung crookedly on its hinges but its peace remained untouched. The cemetery had survived, an oasis in a shattered world, its trees still knitted into shady tunnels. Emily walked along a dappled path. On either side of her, rows of weathered mausoleums stood like stout matrons at a ball, exuding disapproval. Monkeys and adjutant birds had found sanctuary from fire and flying cannon balls about these gloomy tombs. The still and statuesque nature of the birds made them appear part of the masonry.

Emily arrived at Harry's small grave and was relieved to find it deserted of wildlife. A bush of jasmine grew nearby and its scent was heavy in the air. As she squatted down to clear away dead leaves from the grave, her eyes fell on the bright and coarsely woven cloth covering her knees. For a moment she was filled with a confusion of fear and exultation. She sat back on the grass beside the jasmine. The peace of the place came down upon her. The singing of birds and the rustle of the coming monsoon stirred in the branches of trees. Always, in the silence here, she pulled into herself a new strength. A door seemed to open within her and through it she passed to a timeless place that she had now learned existed within herself.

She looked down now and saw that a thick line of ants ran before her. Some carried bits of refuse, and when she investigated she found they swarmed about a dead cicada, systematically dismantling it. For a while she watched them running backwards and forwards, relentlessly set on their business. Each moving speck contained a brain, each body its limited emotions and the boundaries of fulfilment. Yet, what could an ant know beyond this one small grave? Perhaps it might explore some nearby area of the cemetery, but beyond the cemetery lay a town, beyond the town a country and beyond the country a sea. And over that sea lay further countries and yet again further seas. And beyond all this was the limitless sky. How could an ant comprehend such vastness or the cohesion of all these things?

Similarly, how could she comprehend the mysteries that lay beyond her life, or the universe within her? Her horizon was as limited as an ant's. And like the searching of that tiny insect she too had only instinct to guide her. She sensed the cycle of life running always before her, life, death and life again knitted seamlessly together. And she saw then that in order to live she had decided to die, for in loss she knew she must gain. The pattern was there for her to see. The sun set only to rise the next day. The apple fell for the seed to sprout. Winter was reborn as spring. The past died to bear the future. Each frail death carried its own transformation.

At last she rose and turned to leave the cemetery, looking back once at Harry's small grave. She sensed a new finality, as if his spirit was gone and no longer hovered about her. And she sensed too the sudden absence of Jane now that the past was soldered against her. Emily left the cemetery, walking back towards The Avenue. The wreckage of The Park lay before her. Beside it The Avenue was still littered with the refuse of war: abandoned cannon, pieces of sacking, the carcasses of horses picked clean by scavengers but not yet cleared away. She walked on until she arrived at St Ann's Church and turned to face Omichand's house. It was not until she was before it that she realised where she was.

In one place the wall of the compound was shattered. Through this gap she looked straight into the garden where she had seen Omichand's wives meet their end. She heard again the screams of the children behind the banana trees and saw the dying women, blood soaking through their clothes. It was as if she saw herself lying there beside them. Then she shook her head and the picture was gone. Before her again were flowering trees and the empty ground beneath them.

She took a step forward and passed through the broken wall, passing from the dishevelled atmosphere of The Avenue into a silent, overgrown world. She stood at the place where the women had fallen. She expected their ghosts to gather about her but there was nothing now to see. In the days since the slaughter, weeds had grown to cover the spilling of blood. There was nothing but silence and the thick, hot smell of the undergrowth.

Banana trees stood to one side, and before her was an orchard. The aroma of ripe fruit folded about her like the scent of her own intuition. She walked on and the trees seemed to bend towards her, offering their fruit. She reached up to a low-hanging bough and pulled down a thick-skinned golden pear. A breeze rustled suddenly through the trees, stirring the dry, dusty leaves. Already the smell of the monsoon burrowed into the heat. There was a wildness in this garden. Roses grew unpruned beside flowering bushes of jasmine and bougainvillaea. Banana and coconut palms spread their ragged fronds beside fig, apple, pear and mango trees. A peacock stood suddenly before her and raised its great tail in a fan of iridescent crescents and moons. She sat down on a marble bench and watched it silently while she ate the pear. Already she had passed, as she had in the grotto of the black goddess, from one world to another. She must wait now for the blindness to clear.

CHAPTER THIRTY-TWO

The Chief Magistrate was trundled over rough ground in a large-wheeled bullock cart. The horns of the animals, stained red by henna, were all he could see from where he lay. The rouged tongues protruding from the heavy heads gave the creatures a fiendish appearance. The Chief Magistrate had a sudden vision of being drawn towards an underworld where unknown fates awaited him. At any moment he expected darkness to overwhelm him. Instead, he glimpsed a town of tents. He tried to raise himself upon an elbow but the fetters weighed him down. He lay back again on the rough, bumping boards, powerless to protest the journey. Above, drifts of dark cloud piled up in the sky, heralding the monsoon. He longed for the heavens to open upon him and cool his burning skin, but the rain still appeared a distance away.

He saw the ornate pinnacles of tents against the sky and managed at last to pull himself up. Across the plain tents adorned with bright pennants spread out as far as he could see. Guards stood before each of the larger tents, for these housed the army's senior officers, along with their servants, harems and wine. A short distance away, Siraj Uddaulah's great scarlet pavilion rose majestically. The Chief Magistrate expected to be taken again before the nawab to be pummelled by questioning, but the cart bumped on and did not stop in this area of magnificence. Soon the tents they passed grew smaller and meaner and began to peter out. Eventually the cart stopped and Holwell, along with his three companions, was helped down and thrust into a tent that was no more than a blanket thrown over stakes.

The shelter did not cover their shackled feet, and if they sat up it threatened to topple upon them. So great was the exhaustion of the four men that these discomforts appeared nothing when compared to the suffering of the night before. Although the life of the camp bustled about them, nobody approached and no food was forthcoming. Soon they fell asleep.

The Chief Magistrate awoke with a start to darkness. At first he wondered where he was, and then remembered. The tent was filled with a sudden flash of brightness, as if someone passed with a flare. He saw the sleeping forms of Court, Walcot and Burdet pressed up close about him. Then the crack of bullets filled the air. The Chief Magistrate ducked down, his heart pounding, his mind torn open by fear. Not for a moment of the siege, nor even through the horrors of the Black Hole, had he quaked with this kind of fear. Only once, when as a small child he had watched the flickering of a candle on a wall and realised in those shadows he faced his own death, had he felt such emotion. Then, his mother had entered the room with comfort and a glass of warm milk. Here, he was far from his moorings. His teeth chattered and his body trembled in uncontrollable spasms. A steady trickle of water ran over his feet; he thought he had lost control of himself and was drenched with his own urine. Then the tent was once more illuminated and he saw that the sky was broken by lightning and the bullets were no more than thunder. The first monsoon shower bathed his feet. In sudden relief he realised then that he would continue to exist. He turned on his back and listened to the rain spitting down heavily upon the tent. The thunder cracked and grumbled, lumbering after the lightning. In a while the Chief Magistrate began to feel cold and the ground beneath him turned to mud. Yet in some way he could not understand, the rain appeared a comfort, washing away the past few days. He closed his eyes and slept.

He was shaken awake in the morning. Although broken by cloud, and sky was hot again with sun. The parched earth had sucked up the rain and there was little evidence of the monsoon's arrival but a thin wedge of freshness in the air. The Chief Magistrate's joints were stiff, his head ached and his eyes hurt. He was shocked to see large boils appearing on his naked legs and arms. When he stood, the chains about his feet filled him with shame and anger. He demanded water for them all and was surprised when the water-carrier immediately appeared with his wet skins and allowed them to drink their fill. Soon the Chief Magistrate began to feel stronger. He was able to walk when soldiers once more appeared to prod him with the end of a musket. He presumed they were to be served up with breakfast to the nawab. Instead they were marched through the camp.

They set off from the tent, clothes muddied and torn, the sun roasting their heads and bare feet. Holwell had long ago lost his shoes; without buckles to fasten them they had soon come adrift in the Black Hole. He kept his head down as he walked, the three young writers trailing behind him. All he heard was the clanking of their chains as they were forced down long avenues of tents. The iron chafed against the Chief Magistrate's ankles and the weight of the fetters diminished his stride to a shuffle. His toes were bleeding from the cuts of stones, and filth formed a crust upon them. With sudden nostalgia he remembered how, in what now appeared another life, the sight of dust upon his shoes had appeared a demeaning invasion.

Lining the road between the tents was a large part of Siraj Uddaulah's army, called out to view the Hatmen prisoners who had dared to stand against them. The Chief Magistrate threw back his shoulders in defiance, thrusting out his chin. Either side of him was a wall of men; the rumble of their curses sprayed him with hate. The chains on his feet grew heavier, the rhythm of the fetters following the chant of the nawab's army.

'Hatman. Hatman.'

Beneath this weight the Chief Magistrate stumbled. He clutched at the soft cloth of a tunic and grazed his hand on the muzzle of a gun before he was pushed back on to his feet.

'Hatman. Hatman.'

The Chief Magistrate lowered his head once more, not in shame or fear now but from a different emotion. His shoulders grew hunched and closer together, he condensed his tall frame and crossed his arms upon his chest as if to hide an emptiness, or to protect a precious core, his own hands cradling his terrified body. The darkness pressed closer about him until it seemed to shut out the sun.

They did not stop at the nawab's great tent but were forced to march along the same route they had taken in the bullock cart, the rough ground bruising their bare feet. Occasionally they were given water. They marched all day and passed people already returning to Calcutta to remake their lives in Black Town, trundling carts and carrying babies. Once more women walked to the well, brass pots upon their heads. All turned to stare at the Fort William men clumping along in chains. Eventually, as the afternoon shadows lengthened, they reached the river bank and were ordered to sit on a landing stage jutting out into the water.

'Where do you take us?' the Chief Magistrate enquired.

'The nawab's order is that you are taken to Murshidabad.' The guard had brought water but no food.

'When do we depart?' Holwell asked. No craft appeared to be in sight.

'When there is a boat.' The man shrugged and went back to his friends.

Their chains were not loosened, and without food the Fort William men grew faint. As darkness fell the guards lit a fire and began to eat their dinner. Eventually the Chief Magistrate and the young writers were brought a few handfuls of leftover rice. The guards pitched a tent but no shelter was provided for the Hatmen. The bamboo slats of the landing stage were hard beneath the Chief

Magistrate's back. He looked up to the sky and saw the slender finger of a new moon slip away behind dark clouds. The scent of the river rose powerfully about him now, the water lapping beneath him. The incessant croaking of frogs was only inches from his ears. The creatures rose out of mud to hop about him; their dissonance resounded everywhere like a victorious braying. He turned and groaned, for he knew he was powerless now before the brutal will of the river. Whenever he closed his eyes the black goddess seemed to hover before him, ready to draw him to herself.

On a low hill a distance away the ruined walls of an old fort were silhouetted against the sky. The crumbling mass rose before Holwell in the dark, the haunt of jackals and ghosts, the secrets of its forgotten life buried by time. Few knew and even fewer cared who had lived or died there. The stoic loneliness of the remains struck a sudden chill in Holwell. India was full of such ruins. They stood everywhere. And for whatever little still stood above ground a whole history lay buried beneath. Under his head the rungs of bamboo pressed uncomfortably and the smell of wet mud filled his nostrils. He had a sudden vision of the earth beneath him, filled by the rubble of countless ruins descending layer upon layer far back into time. Time covered everything with its thick dust, obliterating the achievements of kings and the mundane doings of paupers. Time now appeared, to the Chief Magistrate, to be the mysterious essence of India. It out-waited everything. This thought filled him with fresh unease. India was a land of buried things. His insignificant mark on it would not even be recorded.

CHAPTER THIRTY-THREE

So strong were the Hoogly's currents that when the tide flowed against the barge, the rowers were compelled to pull the boat forward with ropes from the shore. The Chief Magistrate had made the journey many times to Murshidabad and knew each curve of the river. On those journeys he had occupied a spacious houseboat and busied himself with work. Wherever they stopped, peasants had hurried forward to provide provisions. Now the barge offered no comfort or protection from the elements but a piece of rush matting to pull over himself. Mosquitoes swarmed about them, drawn to the blood from the pustules he scratched dementedly. He made no effort to sit up in the boat, dreading seeing the scenery he had passed before in such style. Now the river was winding him in like a fish on a hook to Murshidabad.

The monsoon had arrived at last in all its fury. Each day the rain beat down while the Chief Magistrate and the three young writers huddled beneath the inadequate matting. So great was the force of the rain that when each shower subsided the barge was awash with water and the boatman demanded they bail it out. Between showers, Holwell lay and stared up at the angry grey arc of the heavens. A strong wind pushed thick clouds across the sky, constantly forming and reforming them into fantastic shapes. The Chief Magistrate felt he watched the changing form of a vindictive god whose fierce breath blew him towards his destiny. About him the river, whipped by the elements, pitched the boat about, its tides running beneath like lightning. At times he grew frightened, for between the river and the sky, he seemed pressed in by wrathful spirits determined to annihilate him.

Once, the sun came out and the Chief Magistrate looked up to see a broad rainbow arching above him. Never before had he seen so clear and vivid a sight. His breath caught at the beauty of the shimmering arc spanning the river. For a moment it seemed like a powerful omen sent from above to fortify him. Then he remembered that to the Hindus a rainbow was said to emanate from a serpent that lived beneath the earth. Through a hole in the ground it blew its searing breath, which immediately formed a rainbow. The Chief Magistrate's surge of simple joy quickly dissipated.

Each night the barge was tied up and the boatmen lit a fire and cooked their dinner before they slept. The Fort William men were given a handful of rice, and water. Holwell slept fitfully, racked by fever and the painful boils still erupting all over his body. The piece of matting did not adequately protect him from the rain and he woke each night cold and sodden. Yet once, he had opened his eyes to a clear starry sky and had lain for hours staring at the heavens, thinking over his life. He had looked at the moon with a new sense of awe. He saw at last that through its descent into darkness it had found the secret of renewal. Then, as he watched, the sky was suddenly filled with innumerable meteors descending towards him like the vivid streaks of fireworks. He sat up in excitement, but when he looked again the phenomenon was gone. In all his years in India he had never seen such a sight. And although he could see nothing but the still, luminous sky, he was suddenly sure God wished to tell him something that he must struggle to decipher.

They stopped on their journey at Chandernagore and were allowed to meet the French residents there. They could not leave the boat, but on the bank of the river a tent was erected where the

French were allowed to offer the prisoners food, fresh clothing and a few hours of companionship. Some strength returned to the Chief Magistrate after these refreshments, and he found the energy to explain to the Frenchmen what had happened at Fort William. When he came to speak of his incarceration in the Black Hole he found his mouth ran dry. Something hot seemed to burst in his head and the words dried on his tongue.

'And then what did they do to you?' The Frenchmen sat before him, untouched by battle, immaculate in their formal coats of decorative design. Their eyes were enquiring but cool, filled with sympathy and incomprehension. Their lives, thought the Chief Magistrate, had not been brutally tossed aside by an arbitrary ruler. After his departure they would calmly return to their wine and cards. The Chief Magistrate began his story of the Black Hole, struggling with his anger and anxious to make a dramatic impression on the impassive Frenchmen. The imprisonment of thirty men, however hot and thirsty, with enough air to keep them alive and space to crouch down, however cramped, would not constitute atrocity. The Chief Magistrate knew that it would at once be pointed out that those who had died in the Black Hole were already sick or wounded and fast approaching the end of life as the door of the cell closed on them. Some stretching of the truth was needed to adequately convey the horror and humiliation of that night. The Chief Magistrate's rage flared up anew each time he thought of it. In his mind now everything seemed confused; a multitude of images from the last few days crowded his memory and unravelled before him as he spoke.

'Two hundred helpless women and children were taken with us at swordpoint. We were thrust into a warehouse too small for such numbers and left there to endure a night beyond all imagination. We could not move. Water was denied us and there was no air to breathe. The cries of the children were pitiful. Through the bars the guards looked on and laughed, enjoying our discomfort. Countless numbers expired in the night. In the morning, even though so many had already died so cruelly, the devils set the building on fire. By some miracle we escaped as the fire crashed about us. Out of two hundred, we and a few more are all that are left. The others were freed. Only I and these three unfortunate men are to face the further revenge of Siraj Uddaulah.' The Chief Magistrate had the satisfaction of seeing the Frenchmen stir in unease at his description. Outside the tent, rain began to fall again, thrashing upon the canvas.

'Give me pen and paper. I will write it down. Let it be recorded, for if I do not return from Murshidabad, then who will adequately state what has happened?' the Chief Magistrate announced.

A quill and paper were quickly brought and Holwell leaned forward over the table, his anger suddenly channelled as he moved his pen across the page. His mind was now in a feverish state and he could not stop scratching the boils on his body. Already blood trickled down his legs and stained the clean shirt he wore. He wrote for some minutes, absorbed in his task, unaware of the men before him, reliving the humiliation of the last few days with every word he wrote. For good measure he now made the victims in the warehouse three hundred, and he diminished the size of the building until the crowd were forced to sit upon a carpet of those trampled to death beneath them. He remembered again the privateer captured by the French whose crew had been forced to drink their own urine to assuage their thirst, and added the detail to his own account. At last the Chief Magistrate put down his pen and sprinkled the parchment with sand.

'If I do not return, see that the world and Leadenhall know of the evil of Siraj Uddaulah,' the Chief Magistrate urged the Frenchmen.

Eventually they reached Murshidabad, drawing slowly into that iniquitous city. Against his inclination, the Chief Magistrate felt forced to take note of his arrival. He sat up in the barge to view the place that he had faced with such certainty before. Now his boat passed the bank unheralded. His filthy face drew no more than curious glances as they neared the landing stage. The palace of Siraj Uddaulah slid past, its great walls austere and almost windowless, meeting the river's edge. The Chief Magistrate could not view it without a wave of fear. They did not draw up at the quay near the palace where he was used to arriving, but pulled on to the wharf that served the common people. Here, the Chief Magistrate and the writers were told to disembark.

Once more, Holwell and the three men were paraded through the town, fetters clanking as they shuffled along. The people of Murshidabad jostled to catch a glimpse of them. The Chief Magistrate kept his head down, as was now his policy in such situations, and hardened himself to the scorn. So great was his resolve to show no emotion that he did not flinch when a rotten guava and then some eggs were thrown at him. He was determined that, whatever his fate at the hands of the heathens, he would meet it with dignity. For the men trudging behind he was an example of fortitude and helped them to find resolution. At last they came again within sight of the river and trudged along its bank. Soon they turned back into the town and stopped before a disused stable. They were thrust inside and thrown down upon a bed of straw.

At first the Chief Magistrate felt a sense of relief. After the slimy wet boards of the boat, the straw was dry, and the roof above them would give protection from the rain. It did not take long for the Chief Magistrate to realise his mistake. The straw was filthy and crawling with vermin. And although the cell had a roof, it lacked a door and was open to the road. The populace of Murshidabad had ample opportunity to view the Hatmen for as long as they desired. And this they did, pushing and shoving, gawking and giggling. A stream of red betel-nut spittle soon landed on the Chief Magistrate. At this insult he struggled to his feet to remonstrate with the crowd. A guard pushed in and threw him back on the straw. Later, he realised that the guard was actively announcing that the Hatmen were there for viewing, as if they were circus freaks. He knew then that this stall had been especially chosen for the public access it gave to them.

At times that night he slept, but longed now for the openness of the barge with the arc of the heavens above. Soon, sick and feverish, he lost track of time, unable to tell if days or hours had passed. He felt himself falling to a timeless place beyond sleep where he was no longer conscious of the world. From this place he rose, delirious, to eat a handful of rice whenever the guard remembered to feed him. He knew in this place he faced death. The familiar smell of the river came to him, and in the night he could hear once more the hollow honking of frogs and the soft lapping of water. A new fear entered his dreams. The black goddess, that bone-wreathed mistress of the place of skulls, appeared near enough to breathe upon him. He shivered at the visions that now engulfed him. Sleeping or waking, he felt the goddess's rage. He whimpered, turning on the straw, but could no longer deny her. Her slimy attendants, the frogs, croaked from the river through the night, taking force and form in the Chief Magistrate's mind as if to wreak further terror.

He saw then the lonely transience of his life, puffed up with ambition and emptiness. He saw a vision of ruin and rubble, like the town he had left, overgrown with weeds in the pitiless heat as he himself was overgrown with expectation. He knew that if he could acknowledge the reality of this vision, the goddess would at once be as merciful as she was now merciless. But as he could not do this, could not renounce himself, there was no release from his fear.

Other visions forced themselves up, as if some indigestible substance had been stirred and now spewed out of him. His wife and dead child and then the girl, Sati, swam before him. Her amber eyes had pleaded with him on that long-ago day, even though she had been mute in his grasp. He had not cared as he had forced himself on her, ripping her body apart, cracking her life in two as he sought his revenge on her mother. The pain he had inflicted on her came to him now as his own.

As this vision died, another memory rose. He saw fields of lavender-coloured pampas grass and the white splash of egret storks. Coconut palms and mango trees stood about a pond and the mud huts of a village he had come to in a tour of duty as Chief Zamindar.

Dogs slept in the shade of trees. Blue water hyacinths clustered on the pond beside a group of women washing clothes. A girl swept the ground before a hut; gourds dried on top of roofs in the neat and orderly village. On the walls of the huts and every other available surface, pats of cow dung were drying. Fresh pats stood out in a darker brown and all carried the pattern of fingers. The Chief Magistrate found the village distasteful, for like all villages, it seemed to be built on a foundation of dung. The smell of excrement was in the air and formed the walls of huts. It was used for fuel, poultices and religious fires and was plastered thickly on the trunk of the tree behind him. Nearby, a mound of fresh dung was kneaded like dough by three women. Their hands sank deep into the stuff, coating their arms to the elbow. They gossiped as they worked, feeling no revulsion in their task, shaping dung biscuits between their fingers just as Holwell's cook fashioned the rolls he ate for breakfast. *People of dung* was how he saw them, lost to all effort of civilisation. A wave of strong feeling passed through him. He refused the food the villagers brought to him, eating only what his own servants prepared. At times, after such a tour of duty, the Chief Magistrate returned to his wedding-cake house with a strange energy pulsing through him. It was almost as if he absorbed from these illiterate villages the very throb of their submerged life. He felt himself grow large amongst them, his authority strengthening, his ambition swelling.

That day, beneath the tree, his coolies set up the chair and table from which the Chief Magistrate would dispense his justice. The men of the village squatted in a circle about him, their expressions unreadable, their dark eyes without emotion. The village was troublesome, never paying rent for the farms leased from Fort William without intervention. The Chief Magistrate had brought with him three *gomastah,* the men whom he sent abroad to buy goods in the villages. He had been warned about the village and felt he should be prepared. The *gomastah* were rough men, as they had to be when dealing with an irksome people; they had the power to seal leases and mete out punishments as they saw fit. The populace was afraid of them.

The Chief Magistrate called the first plaintive and immediately an argument began. The village was adamant they could not afford the rents for their land. The harvest had been bad and cholera plagued the village. Normally, the Chief Magistrate would have listened with some sympathy and tried to find a compromise, but the attitude of the villagers annoyed him. One man in particular appeared the ringleader, encouraging the others to speak out, stepping forward in a bold manner to make demands on behalf of the village. The *gomastah* were enraged, for it appeared this man was the chief offender, never paying his rents on time, always full of excuses, fearing no one. He came right up to the Chief Magistrate's table and spoke without restraint or even humility, as if he was an equal. Such insolence filled the Chief Magistrate with fury. He demanded past ledgers be opened and the sum of the villager's debt investigated. The man had then become unruly and lunged at the Chief Magistrate with a knife. Others in the crowd rose up to join him. At last the man had been restrained by the *gomastah*, and his hands tied behind his back.

Although the danger was averted, the knife had come so near Holwell's heart that his waistcoat had been slashed. When order was finally restored, one of the *gomastah* lay dead, stabbed in the manner the Chief Magistrate had avoided. At the moment the villager had sprung towards him, Holwell, out of the corner of his eye, had seen the dead *gomastah* fall, but could not identify the murderer. Now the remaining *gomastah* urged the Chief Magistrate to dispense a quick judgement that would erase once and for all further thoughts of rebellion in this and other villages. At Holwell's agreement a rope was found and hung from the mango tree behind his makeshift table.

There was much struggling by the bound man and much shouting from the villagers. All this was ignored by Holwell. It could not be determined who had killed the dead *gomastah*, but everyone knew it was not the man being pushed to the rope. The Chief Magistrate gave no weight to the fact that the man was innocent. He knew his anger exceeded his sense of right, but an example was needed immediately. When he saw that his fate was unavoidable, the bound man fell silent, as if bending to his destiny. As the rope was placed about his neck, his eyes settled on the Chief Magistrate, not in appeal but in defiance. Amongst the circle of villagers now all protest had ceased; only the sobbing of women was heard. A girl with a baby at her breast and two children clinging to her sari had stumbled forward and collapsed at the Chief Magistrate's feet, pleading for the man's redemption. The Chief Magistrate had taken no notice. Above the hysterical woman's head and the cries of her children, he had given the nod that tightened the rope about the villager's neck.

The jerking body soon quietened at the end of the rope. Yet at the moment when life had been taken on his order the Chief Magistrate had looked away. He fixed his eyes beyond the man and saw the flash of a kingfisher diving towards water. When he eventually returned his gaze to the tree, the man hung lifeless from the bough. Holwell had at once ordered his table packed up and retired to his tent a short distance away. There he had called for a glass of Madeira. His blood ran quickly in his veins in a not unpleasant manner. He interpreted this feeling as the satisfaction that came from completing a repellent but necessary task. Afterwards he gave the incident no further thought. The slashed waistcoat had been burnt.

Now, in his prison in Murshidabad, this incident came before him, as if it had been lurking in a prison of its own, waiting for release. He saw the face of the doomed man again, and heard the pleas of his wife and children in a way he had not experienced at the time. It was as if through the years the incident had distilled within him to a substance so potent it would destroy him. A great ache that he could not locate filled the whole of his body.

He no longer knew if it was day or night, who came or went. Fever racked him. At one point he was aware that they were taken from the stable and transported on a cart to another prison. Here it was enclosed and dark, and an iron-bound door swung shut on them.

The door was opened periodically and food of some kind was pushed inside. Guards appeared from time to time to inspect the Chief Magistrate and the three writers, prodding them with a stick or a foot to determine the degree of life within them. Once they came with lanterns and he saw the lights as if at a great distance, swinging above him as they turned him over. He was unprepared for the stab of pain that suddenly tore through his body. He thought his end had come. In his fevered mind it seemed they split him open, ripping out his entrails. He heard the young writers cry out with a pain equal to his own. Soon the door was shut again. And still he lived.

His fever roared and his spirit seemed to float free. A great pain filled him, rising to new intensity whenever he moved. He could no longer smell the river and thought at first the wretched black goddess was gone, leaving him to his fate. But then he saw her, rising out of his body, as if she were a creature of his own depths and held the key to his fate. There was nowhere to run to in the darkness. He was forced to stare at her open-eyed. Then other repugnant visions began to show themselves; pot-bellied devils with spindly legs and long fat noses, toads, lizards and rats of fantastic size scampered about him. Even when he stared into empty darkness, this too began to stir and throw forth weird forms. But always, above all these visions, the dark goddess reigned supreme. He knew she had led him into a hell that was no more than the embodiment of himself.

So great was his terror that he was forced to acknowledge all that was shown him. At last he cowered before the very wretchedness of himself. In the darkness the goddess appeared to weave about him, sinuous as a spiral of smoke. At last he relinquished himself to her.

Then, at that moment of surrender, he saw the goddess change, her repulsive skin whitening, her features diminishing, her sagging breasts tightening, her long tongue disappearing. She shimmered in her nakedness, filling him then with a degree of desire he had never known before. A light came from her, encasing him in sudden warmth. He saw then that both the light and the darkness of this goddess flowed within himself in one mighty stream. He had to make his peace with both these parts to possess at last his own wholeness. The visions left him then, and soon he slept a dreamless, undisturbed sleep.

It was impossible to gauge how long he was kept in the cell. Eventually the door was opened and he was pulled roughly to his feet. He could not stand at first, and a dull ache throbbed through him as if he recovered from a wound. He shuffled forward, bowed and filthy, the three young writers behind him. Daylight suddenly sizzled about them. He saw he walked through courtyards planted with jasmine, where the sun played on fountains and filled the air with myriad rainbows. He suddenly caught sight of his own hands and was shocked. They appeared like the claws of a bird, thickly encrusted with a layer of filth. The perfume of blossom filled the air. Marble flagstones were hot beneath his bare feet; flowers and bright birds filled his vision. He saw he was once more in the palace of Siraj Uddaulah and neared the Hall of Audience.

The nawab sat as before on his gold throne. Arches inlaid with precious stones led one by one to his dais. The Chief Magistrate stumbled towards him, his fetters knocking the marble floor, his knees barely able to hold him up. The nobles drew back in silence. The Chief Magistrate remembered, as if at a great distance, how he and Drake had walked this short distance, a band playing proudly before them. At last he was pushed to prostrate himself at Siraj Uddaulah's feet. To one side of the dais on which the nawab sat stood the treacherous Rai Durlabh. His eyes ran coldly over Holwell before he looked away.

Siraj Uddaulah bent forward and stared for some time at the Chief Magistrate, frowning. He expressed surprise at finding the Chief Magistrate still in Murshidabad, as if he had forgotten his order to send Holwell up river. A string of large pearls hung about his neck, above a chain of diamonds. A ruby still sparkled like frozen blood on his turban, emeralds large as quail's eggs covered his hands. The sun blazed on these jewels, surrounding the monarch with light. Once more Holwell was questioned about the treasure, and he could make

345

even less of a spirited appeal for innocence than before. He lay without answering until he was pulled to his knees and a knife was held against his throat. He was beyond caring and could only shake his head. At last the questioning petered out and he heard Siraj Uddaulah speaking with Rai Durlabh. The nawab suggested that the Chief Magistrate was past his usefulness and should be allowed to go free. He had lost interest in him. Soon the Chief Magistrate and the three writers were marched from the nawab's presence, and thrust beyond the palace gate.

After a while they picked themselves up, reviving slightly at their luck. Holwell knew his bearings about the palace and soon led the three writers the few hundred yards to the nearest sanctuary, the Dutch settlement in Murshidabad. There they were received with consternation. The Dutch spared no effort to restore them to health. Food, clothes, medicine and baths were ordered for them unstintingly. Slowly the first ravages of the trauma lessened, but nothing could alleviate the shock that faced the Chief Magistrate on his first day at the Dutch settlement.

Once they had eaten, baths of medicinal herbs were prepared, to ease away the thick crust of grime on their bodies. The Chief Magistrate gratefully shed the stinking items of clothing he had worn through the last weeks. Although his limbs were still sore with boils, the dirt fell away in the hot water. At last he stepped from his bath and entered his bedroom to take stock of himself in a mirror. He saw then that what he had thought to be pustules around that most private part of himself was instead the slashed wound from a knife. He stared down at himself in disbelief, remembering the pain in his delirium that had seemed to tear open his body. He knew then with a sickening horror that the Moors had branded him with the mark of their race. He remembered now that circumcision was a practice sometimes inflicted on captured infidels. The Chief Magistrate turned in distress before the mirror and examined himself once more. In his hand his organ now appeared a freakish stump, like the wrecked limb of an amputee. He let out a howl of despair. Wherever he went, whatever he did, this mark would be upon him forever.

He found that the three young writers, Court, Burdet and Walcot, had also been circumcised along with him. Anger gave him strength, and when the Dutch began to question him about the events of the last few weeks, the Chief Magistrate did not hesitate to once more write down his account of things, as he had done for the French. The trauma between the time of meeting the French and arriving at the Dutch settlement had caused him to forget what exactly he had written down at Chandernagore, but this did not deter him.

Once more the Chief Magistrate put pen to parchment and his anger flowed anew, greater now for his treatment in Murshidabad. He forgot about warehouses, fires, women and children. He saw himself back in the Black Hole. His mind was now full of the men who had died so bravely defending Fort William in the fight against Siraj Uddaulah. Coales, Valicourt, Dalrymple, Jebb, Page, Ballard . . . He saw their faces pass before him, young men struck down in their prime. He began to write the names down, for they might just as well have died in the Black Hole, sacrificed as they had been to the wrath of Siraj Uddaulah.

One hundred and sixty men were locked into a cell eighteen feet long and fourteen feet wide with only two small windows, wrote the Chief Magistrate. *Only twenty came out in the morning.* He wrote of sitting on a carpet of bodies and of a thirst so great he was forced to drink his own urine from the heel of a shoe in order to survive. He wrote of the terrible deaths he had witnessed and the efforts he had made to avert them. At last he laid down his pen. In his mind the Black Hole, the filthy stable and the dark prison in the nawab's palace had each become interchangeable. He knew that he would be caught forever within these dark chambers of his mind.

CHAPTER THIRTY-FOUR

From the women's quarters of Omichand's house, Jaya and Govindram looked out at the garden as they sat on a wide veranda. Mohini dozed beside them, propped up against silk bolsters. Outside, Sati rocked on a swing beneath a mango tree, eyes half closed. With his women gone, Omichand had opened his house to the Devi Ashram until new wives and concubines were chosen.

'The Goddess has left Sati only because her work is done,' Govindram remarked. The air from the garden was fresh after a night of rain.

'She has rid Calcutta of the Hatmen and brought us safely through the siege,' Jaya agreed. The smells of damp undergrowth rose pleasantly. All about was a sense of renewal.

On the flattened expanse of Black Town, new huts were already being constructed. Those houses of White Town that were still habitable were now occupied by Black Town families. They wandered the many rooms in wonder and hung laundry from the balconies where their bare-bottomed children played. Families unable to find room in the houses were established in stables or the servants' quarter, or had erected rough shelters in gardens. The Goddess had arranged this too, thought Jaya. She had flooded White Town with Black Town people, returning to them what was rightfully theirs. It was her revenge on the Hatmen. Jaya suddenly felt full of power.

Even the Kali temple, stolen by the Hatmen and filled with their weapons and gunpowder for years, had now been returned to the Goddess. The Hatmen and the remains of their inflammable deposits had been thrown out on to the road willy-nilly. The temple had been cleaned and swept and ceremonies had been held to exorcise it. Then, the Goddess had been carried back to Her abode. Her statue rode on the shoulders of jubilant men; all night drums had been beaten in revelry. From the veranda of Omichand's house, Jaya could see the tall padoga-shaped towers of the temple rising proudly once more to the sky. The nawab had renamed Calcutta Alinagore, as if a new era had begun, and to seal her sense of a new beginning, Jaya had seen Hatman Holwell led away in chains. Her hatred for the magistrate welled up anew, unimpeded by fear now. She could never forget the terrible day Sati had been sacrificed to the man's lust. The pain she had felt for the child would never go away. She remembered the way he had stolen her jewels. All these things the Goddess had seen, as Jaya had known she must. Now the Chief Magistrate was reaping the harvest of his deeds. Jaya sighed with satisfaction.

She watched Sati rock gently on the wide swing a short distance away. Behind the coconut palms beyond the swing a young man stood, half hidden, staring at Sati. Jaya kept her eyes on him in case he should misbehave. A peacock appeared and raised its great tail, filling the garden with colour. Jaya turned back to Govindram.

'The Goddess also returned my diamonds to me. This is something I can never forget.' The miracle had not ceased to amaze her. She continually searched for a reason to explain why the gems had not only been taken also so dramatically returned.

'I feel there is something the Goddess is wanting me to do but I cannot yet understand what it is,' Jaya told her cousin with a perplexed frown. Behind her Mohini gave a loud snore and turned on the bolsters.

'Why are you never content? You have your diamonds safe again.

349

Give them to Sati as you were wanting to do before,' Govindram replied, preparing to leave the women's quarters, where he knew he had already spent too much time. Omichand would be waiting for him.

'Maybe Sati will never marry,' Jaya whispered, voicing the fear at last.

'Why should she not?' Govindram enquired, although his thoughts were in tandem with his cousin's. The effort of renewing his search for a husband for Sati already weighed heavily on him.

'Because she has become the Goddess's creature. The Goddess belongs to no man, Her *shakti* is too great. She is like a warrior. And She will keep Sati for herself.' As she spoke, things seemed to clear in Jaya's mind, revealing the shape of the future.

'Perhaps the Goddess has no more use for her and has left her free to marry,' Govindram suggested, seeing the seriousness of his cousin's expression. As Govindram finished speaking, the loud roar of a tiger came from the nearby jungle.

'It is the Goddess. She speaks to us,' Jaya gasped, clasping her hands together. As she spoke, a thought flashed through her mind. It came to her so spontaneously and remained in such a convincing manner that she knew at once that this too was the work of the Goddess.

'I will sell my diamonds to Omichand,' Jaya announced. Govindram turned to her in alarm. Omichand was back in business again, working now for Siraj Uddaulah, his vast resources and wily mind at the nawab's convenience, his funding once more oiling the wheels of state.

'And with the money we shall set up a proper ashram. This will be better than marriage for Sati. She will be known far and wide. People will come from all over Bengal for her *darshan*. This is what the Goddess wanted me to understand.' Once more the tiger roared, and Jaya began to smile. Behind her Mohini stirred, sat up and rubbed her eyes.

'So much noise you are making. I cannot sleep,' she complained with a yawn.

'While you are sleeping the world has been remade,' Jaya retorted.

Govindram looked at his cousin with new respect, for he saw the sense of her decision. 'Your idea is a good one.'

The smile spread across Jaya's face. 'Then I shall do it in the morning. Please speak to Omichand.'

'What are you talking about?' Mohini yawned again.

At that moment Jaya saw the strange man behind the coconut palms step out from his hiding place and walk towards Sati. The old woman rose hurriedly to her feet.

The further Emily Drake walked into the garden, the closer it seemed to press about her. The place was overgrown, untended since Omichand's arrest. The scent of jasmine was in the air and the branches of shrubs sprang forward to brush her arms. The smell of damp leaves and soil rose from the earth. Her childhood home had had the same look of neglect about it. The memory of that other garden returned to claim her. She had played there with the servant's children and listened to Parvati's tales of fantastical gods who seemed always more absorbing than the bearded man her mother worshipped. Parvati told of gods afire with power or large with benevolence, all facets of a single being. In the schoolroom, prayers were learned and hymns were sung but nothing took Emily out of herself like the tales Parvati told her. Unbeknown to her mother, the servant's children taught her other prayers and pulled her into their rituals. Within these strange rites she found an inspiration never conveyed to her at home.

She remembered one of the children's rituals. It took place in the cold winter months, in the early mornings before the sun had risen or the first birds had begun to sing. Secretly she had left her bed and run into the dark, silent garden to join the servant's children. They made a small crude figure of mud without proper arms or legs. The mud doll was positioned in a secret place and a small moat was dug about it. They called the figure Jamburi, and offerings of water, flowers and grass were laid before it. Suddenly the old words of that rite came back to Emily.

'*I bring thee water before the crow has drunk of it; I bring thee flowers before the bee has sucked them.*' The words fell about her in the overgrown garden of Omichand's house as she remembered the story of Jamburi. She had no feet or hands, nor even a mouth, yet Jamburi could accomplish anything because she had a will. This was what the children learned from that crude mud figure in the darkness before the sun. Each day the rites became more intense. Each day the story of Jamburi was retold like a bridge across which the limbless creature gave her essence to the children. Without hands Jamburi could neither give nor receive. She had no feet to walk upon and her eyes could barely see. Her experience of life was not as others knew it. Left with no guide but intuition, Jamburi had to find her way to that place of transformation deep within herself. Emily remembered with surprise that Jamburi had been no more than a clod of earth. Yet she had returned to her bed each morning as the sun came up, filled with a sense of wonder. Something had been communicated to her that could not be conveyed in words. A new reality entered her by which she was herself transformed. Her mother and Jane knew nothing of her early morning sorties. The secret of Jamburi was something she held to herself.

Now, in Omichand's house, the peacock came before her again, pecking the ground, placing his feet deliberately, arching his neck. Once more as she watched he fanned out his tail. The magical diadems of colour burst before her, shimmering as he moved. It was as if in this garden, filled with the scented fragments of childhood, she recovered her memory. She saw that Jamburi did not dwell in a world apart, but was dissolved deep within herself. The journey Jamburi had spoken of was no different from her own. The intuition that guided was the source of her own renewal.

All her early memories had been of wholeness, and she knew now she must make the passage back to that same beginning. She stared down at the bright checks of the dirty *lungi* draped about her and touched the turban on her head. She was content to rest in this genderless state, beyond colour or creed, belonging to no one but herself. It was then, as the peacock swayed, moving forwards then backwards, his feathers brushing the ground like a skirt, that she saw the spirit girl, Sati, sitting on a swing as if waiting for her to appear.

Sati looked up and saw the Governor's wife dressed in the clothes of a man. Sooner or later she had known she would come, although she did not know how she knew this. Durga had disappeared but it no longer distressed her. The crack by which Durga had entered her soul now appeared to have fused. She tried not to recall the long night in that cell in Fort William, for its terror remained with her still. And yet, in that dark descent, some alchemy was done; her memories had made her whole. Neither past nor present could touch her now. She looked up into the face of the Governor's wife and knew that perhaps this was the thread that joined them.

Almost immediately Jaya rushed up. Sweat stood out on her brow and collected between her great breasts. She took hold of Emily Drake, wrestling her to the ground.

'*Badmash* boy. How dare you come into this garden. What are you doing here?' Jaya screamed. The peacock looked up in alarm, closed its tail and fled.

Sati jumped off the swing and tried to pull her grandmother away. 'It is the Governor's wife,' she shouted.

Govindram hurried up, but stood helpless before his cousin's energy until Sati repeated her statement. He reached forward to pull Jaya back but she shook her head, making no sense of Sati's words. Emily's turban had now fallen off to reveal the sheared remains of her hair. Jaya stepped back in shock, recognising the Governor's wife at last.

'How are we supposed to know who she is? All Hatmen ladies look the same, I cannot tell one from the other. And why is she dressed like a Black Town man?' Jaya demanded angrily.

'I only . . .' Emily began in a fluster.

'She will rest here a while,' Sati announced.

And suddenly then Emily Drake saw that indeed this was what she would do. She would rest in this androgynous state for as long as she needed. The rich smell of damp undergrowth rose up about her, filling her with wholeness. The future would take care of itself. Like the spider that sits in his web, she knew now she was both the centre and the source of her world, its lightness and its dark. The future would emerge when ready, just as the moon returned from darkness to flood the sky with life. And whatever that future might be, she would no longer live a confiscated life but one that would be her own. She looked up at the circle of people about her and rose awkwardly to her feet.

The old woman who had grappled with her and held her down now nodded in invitation towards Omichand's house. Emily Drake followed gladly. Govindram walked beside her, undecided suddenly of his role. He was unsure of how to speak to the Governor's wife, who was so strangely dressed and had been so strangely manifested in their midst that he did not know what to make of it all. He had no doubt there was a reason for her presence, which would soon be revealed to them all. Already, as they walked to the house, he could hear Jaya explaining to Sati her plan for establishing a proper ashram. It was a good idea, thought Govindram. The Goddess would be pleased. On the breeze he smelled the river, still full of the rancid Salt Lakes, and knew that as all rivers find rebirth in the ocean, a new beginning awaited them all.

EPILOGUE

Fulta, January 1757

Rain had fallen through the dawn, abating as the sun increased. Now fog obscured the riverbank. The ship was anchored at Fulta until first light; no pilot took a vessel down the Hoogly at night. The early morning mist moved about the Chief Magistrate as he stood upon the deck. It lifted above the water lapping, opaque with mud, around the boat. Holwell stared down at the river and was reminded of a mutton curry that had left him ill for days. The tide was out and revealed a thin beach below the bank. Gossiping villagers squatted there attending to their morning rituals. A wind blew the reek of the river to him, the vapour weighting his coat as if it were blotting paper. The Chief Magistrate pulled down his hat and turned up his collar, but the ripe, clammy odour seeped to his bones.

Beyond the defecating villagers he could see the thatched huts in which now lived the survivors of Fort William. Others still resided in pitiful conditions aboard the *Dodaldy,* anchored in midstream. Holwell's own ship, the *Diligence,* had been lost. On the way down river it had struck a sandbank and been plundered by a raja who lived in a nearby fort. All Holwell's plate and jewels were gone. On his arrival at Fulta, he had found a ragged, dejected but fully functioning White Town community established in an order identical to that previously held in Calcutta. Drake, Manningham,

Frankland, Mackett and everyone else on the Council was there. Only Bellamy was sadly missing. Drake had once more set himself up as Governor, but it seemed his wife was gone. Some said madness had consumed her and that she had jumped from the *Dodaldy* and drowned. The Governor appeared to have quickly recovered from this sudden bereavement, showing no signs of grief. The sight of Drake, slimmer and even more careless about his person but still strutting about giving orders, was more than Holwell could bear.

In Fulta too he had found Demonteguy and Rita. The Frenchman had displayed further violence towards the Chief Magistrate and would not believe the diamonds were lost. For once Holwell told him the truth. On the journey from Murshidabad to Fulta the Chief Magistrate had stopped briefly in Calcutta. He had found it a painful experience. The remains of his home had been occupied by Black Town residents and bedecked with laundry. He had had no difficulty in entering the fort, for it consisted only of its outer walls. Across the parade ground he found the stairs to the waterhouses intact and descended with a racing heart. On the journey down river from Murshidabad he had imagined this moment again and again, like a reward that waited at the end of his sufferings. He visualised the magnificent gems spilling into his hands and knew that whatever was lost in money and pride he would soon regain through old Jaya's jewels. His mouth had been dry with expectation as he prised the loose brick from the wall. At first he could not believe his eyes when he saw the empty hiding place. He had sat back on his heels in disbelief, the future crashing about him.

The telling of this story to Demonteguy had not elicted sympathy but only raised further wrath in the man. The Chief Magistrate was not intimidated. He had lost his last fear of the Frenchman on hearing that Dumbleton, the Notary, had died of a fever soon after reaching Fulta. Within days of Holwell's arrival, the Frenchman took a ship to Malacca, where he had heard there was money to be made, leaving his wife to fend for herself. She had at once thrown herself on the Chief Magistrate, who, after his treatment in Murshidabad, was loath to resume their relationship for fear of her derision. Instead he found a boat that would carry her back to Calcutta, to her daughter and mother.

The Chief Magistrate then found a place for himself on the first ship sailing back to England. Once home he intended to inform Leadenhall in person of the events that had occurred in Calcutta. He enquired from Drake about the Young Begum's treasure and found a share had been kept for him. It was considerably smaller than he had anticipated, but he was helpless to protest. Others from the settlement besides the Fort William Council now knew of the treasure and had demanded a share in the spoils. Since the taking of the treasure was the cause of their present suffering, these people could not be denied. The mood in the community was not only menacing but there was nowhere to hide such treasure in Fulta. There had been no option, Drake explained, but to divide the riches amongst all the survivors. The Chief Magistrate had fumed at this further cruel twist of fate during his short but uncomfortable stay in Fulta. The mud hut in which he was forced to live was infested with insects which descended from the thatch each night to crawl unheedingly on him. Nightmares still plagued him, food was scarce and the sight of the ragged community depressed him more than he could say. Images of a world far away, that he had once desired only to leave now obsessed him.

From the deck of the ship that would take him to England, the Chief Magistrate looked back in the direction of Calcutta, but only a wall of mist was seen. As always, the river lay in his mind as a mercurial road, leading to Murshidabad. *Murshidabad.* Feared and fabled, city of domes and minarets, of kings and alabaster, of depravity and shit; he knew it now too well. By day the city soaked in sun, by night the ground discharged its heat. He remembered its fire against his cheek on that bed of straw in the stable. He turned his head now to stare down river. Somewhere lay the ocean. Its rolling back would carry him home, like a packhorse returning a wounded soldier. Then, from that parched place deep within his soul, he would vent his anger.

The settler made history; Chief Magistrate Holwell knew this now with certainty. Legend was his to cut and fashion, tucked or bias-bound, knotted about iron stays. Within its manufactured shape identity strutted and strayed. And what if egos did engorge, like the flayed skin of a goat filled with water? The native learned only to stay in his place, and by doing so served his purpose; defining light by darkness, knowledge by ignorance. The Chief Magistrate pushed from his mind the sudden vision of a water skin, the stubs of goat legs thrusting skywards, riding high upon a swarthy shoulder.

History was a storybook within which time embroidered unpredictably, ignoring truth, condoning lies. Such a capricious winnowing of fact was the basis of all stories. The Chief Magistrate looked again towards the shrouded land. Behind the mist, India, like a tenacious female, had worked to dispossess him. He would not be denied. What she refused to yield he would force from her now.

Fog still hid the shore. But Holwell saw suddenly that this did not matter. Calcutta would rest in his imagination beyond a far horizon. And, like the story he would tell, the further the truth receded within the mists of time, the stronger it would eventually emerge from those same mists, moulded to his will. The dead had no tongue with which to speak. Their story was always told by the living. Time was his tool. As the sun rose higher his shadow grew away from him on the deck as if taking a life of its own.

Now at last the boat began to move. The leadsman was taking soundings, heaving the lead from the paddle-box. His voice sang out into the morning.

'By the mark six. A quarter less three.' The treacherous, shifting sands that could catch a ship slid safely past below them. And slowly, then, India too slipped away, unseen, still shrouding herself to spite him. For a moment he caught the smell of the river as the water stirred about him, as if the black goddess reached out a last time. But already the scent of the ocean reached him.

He made his way down then into his cabin and took up his quill, as he knew he would, at this strange moment in time. As the heathens believed a soul took rebirth, so too, he now saw, experience might enter the crucible of the alchemist. In this ending was his beginning.

He knew what he must say. Already, on that journey down river from Murshidabad, he had copied out a rough draft. But this would alter yet again, and yet again, until it pleased his pen. He pressed the quill upon the paper, shaping those first words.

From on board the *Syren-Sloop*. The 28th of February 1757.

A Genuine Narrative by John Zephaniah Holwell Esq. of the Deplorable Deaths of the English Gentlemen and Others who were suffocated in the Black Hole in Fort William, at Calcutta, in the Kingdom of Bengal in the Night succeeding the 20th Day of June 1756.

To the Reader,

The following narrative will appear, upon perusal, to be a simple detail of a most melancholy event, delivered in the genuine language of sincere concern. It was written on board the vessel in which the author returned from the East-Indies, when he had leisure to reflect, and was at liberty to throw upon paper what was too strongly impressed upon his memory ever to wear out . . .

AUTHOR'S NOTE

John Zephaniah Holwell returned to England on the *Syren-Sloop* in 1757. On his arrival he soon published his story of the Black Hole, in which he claimed that one hundred and forty-six people went into the small prison at Fort William and only twenty-three survived. It created a stir. He did not remain in England for long. He soon recovered from his ordeal at the hands of Siraj Uddaulah and returned to Calcutta in 1758.

At the time of Holwell's departure from India in ill health, Robert Clive defeated Siraj Uddaulah at the battle of Plassey, on the 5th of February 1757. Both Rai Durlabh and Mir Jaffir took part in the attack. Siraj Uddaulah fled the battleground but was soon found and murdered. As a result, Calcutta returned again into British hands. With Clive's consent Mir Jaffir was installed as the new nawab.

On his return to Calcutta, Holwell once more took up his duties on the Fort William Council. From January to July of 1759 he briefly held the post of Governor. During his short time in office he erected an obelisk in The Park to the victims of the Black Hole. Holwell finally returned to England in 1760, supposedly after a quarrel with Robert Clive. He settled first in Walton-on-Thames before moving to Pinner, where he died in 1798 aged 87.

Roger Drake stayed on in India and had a part in the Battle of

Plassey. His share of the loot from the battle was 133,000 rupees. He retired in 1759, after being demoted in favour of a rotation government. He died in 1765 aged 43.

Calcutta was soon entirely rebuilt. Clive's military dominance and his alliance with the Murshidabad court established the British in the position of king-makers, able to place on the throne of Bengal compliant nawabs of their own choosing. The era of Empire had begun.

Although some of the happenings and characters in this book are based upon real events that took place in Fort William and Calcutta in 1756, their interpretation is purely imaginative. Some characters have kept their real names from that time but their personalities again are of my own making.

Meira Chand

ACKNOWLEDGEMENTS

I would like to thank Professor Edwin Thumboo and The Centre for the Arts, National University of Singapore, for giving me the space in which to work during part of the writing of this book.